A Time To Wander

By

Chera Thompson and NF Johnson

Publisher's Note:
This is a work of fiction. All names, characters, places, and events are the work of the author's imagination.
Any resemblance to real persons, places, or events is coincidental.

Solstice Publishing - www.solsticepublishing.com

Chera's Dedication:

To my mom for reading me the stories from *Journeys through Bookland*. And to my dad for singing me the songs from the *American Songbook.*

NF's Dedication:

To my mom for showing me the open road. And to my dad for giving me the compass for my map.

Part I: Starts and Fits

Chapter One
Hello It's Me - January 2010

Lena

It pops up while I sit reading my emails and Facebook messages, drinking my morning cup of coffee.

> *January15, 2010*
> *Subject: Kent State Roomies Reunion*
> *Is this the Lena Borelli who wears paisley bandanas and blockades buildings? Who likes hitchhiking through Chicago at midnight and thinks cats are smarter than dogs? If so, I just wanted to say hi and hope things have been well in your life. This is Kris—what's it been, about forty years? The last I heard, you were living in France. I ended up in Minnesota. Married, with four grown kids and too many animals to count. I'm in a good place—just a little fatter and a lot less hair. I hope the same is for you. But not the fatter and less hair part. –Kris*
> *PS Attached is the invitation to the Roomies Reunion. All the old gang should be there. Interested?*

It's him!

My coffee splashes over the keyboard as I lean in to stare at the picture. The rich brown hair which fell to his shoulders has been replaced by short strands of gray. But his eyes…the same still-water blue looking straight through me. Like they did all those yesternights ago. Making every nerve in my body tingle with anticipation. And through the years that followed, his memory still teased a warm smile from me when certain songs played on the radio.

My fingers fly over the keyboard:

Reply: re: Kent State Roomie Reunion
Is this the Kristofer Anderson who rescues damsels in distress, harasses Chicago cops, and uses dogs as chick bait? If so, I just want to say—Kris!!! You don't know how many times I've wondered about you. I'm fine, live in Brooklyn, and work as a freelance travel writer. Married, empty nesters, with one brilliant cat. Shhh about the hitchhiking! No one has a clue. – Lena
PS Absolutely to the reunion!

The cursor hovers over the SEND button. I swivel my chair away from the screen and gaze out the window. Slowly I get up from the desk and head toward the attic. Sitting in a cobwebbed corner is my grandmother's old steamer trunk she gave me when I left for college. I open the lid and catch the faint scent of patchouli. I rummage through sealing wax, sandalwood incense sticks, and tarot cards. There, lying at the bottom... my college journal. I slide my hand over the time-worn cover and open it up, my heart pounding. *Should I be doing this?*

A photo sticks out from between the pages. A long-haired Kris with wire-rimmed glasses, patched jeans and an army jacket stands holding a cardboard sign with the word "Chicago" scrawled in black magic marker. Next to him, a smiling girl flashes the peace sign. Silver hoop earrings peek out from under her long frizzy hair and even in the faded photo, there's a shine in her eyes.

I remember that girl.

And that chance meeting in the middle of all the chaos.

Chapter Two
Kent State Unrest - Friday, May 1, 1970

Kris

It's quarter-a-beer night and the last of my change crosses the polished mahogany to John the bartender. I barely have a buzz, but what could I expect from 3.2 piss water? Old enough to kill people in Vietnam but not old enough to drink real beer. What a load of crap. Larry, a townie regular a few years older than me, opens the front door, silhouetted by flashing red lights.

"It's getting crazy out there. Hey, John, get me the usual." Larry squeezes up to the bar. "People are getting all worked up over that Cambodia shit."

The neon Pabst Blue Ribbon clock on the wall says ten-thirty. I pivot my barstool and survey the packed house. Larry's right. Inside and out, the word on everyone's lips is Cambodia since Nixon announced we invaded it yesterday. Lying prick.

Mara, the waitress, forces her way up to the service station next to me. "Hi, Kris. Think there'll be trouble tonight?"

Her eyes are thick with black mascara. Her dark hair is tied back with a leather clip. My eyes drift down over her tie-dyed halter top and stop at her hiked-up jean skirt.

"I don't know," I say. "There were a lot of pissed-off people on campus today."

Mara nods. "Uh-huh. Hey, John, I need a low PBR draft, two Strohs, and a Rolling Rock."

John, a pre-med student, stops washing bar glasses and dries his hands as if he's prepping for surgery, then pulls chilled bottles of brew from the cooler. He hands them over to Mara as he says, "We invade Cambodia, the NBA playoffs are on, but the big news is it's Friday night and Kris Anderson is all alone."

I light a cigarette, look at him and shrug. "What can I say? Both meaningful relationships went home for the weekend."

"Maybe you should shop around," Mara says.

John waves his bar rag in the air. *"Viva la sexual revolucion, mi compadre."*

Mara grins. "If you need a friend, I'm off at one." She picks up her tray of beer bottles and walks away.

John looks at me and shakes his head. "You haven't found your groove since Sophie, have you?"

"Nope." I look down into my beer. The night I told Sophie something was missing, she cried. I'm not sure who I felt worse for, her or me.

John dumps the ashtray. "If it makes you feel any better, there are a couple of guys who are happy you screwed up that relationship."

"Hey, asshole," I say. "I thought your job was to cheer me up."

"Tip better and I'll think about it."

The front door busts open. A cop marches up to John. "You've got five minutes to shut it down. All bars are closed in Kent by order of the mayor. If you don't close it down, you're goin' to jail."

"Yessir. Can I offer you a Coke?"

"You got five minutes, smartass." The cop turns and leaves.

John unplugs the jukebox and the music skids to a stop. "Hey, everyone, The Man just closed us down. Everyone has to leave."

I stub out my smoke and drain my beer. "Later, dude." I slide off the stool and jostle my way to the door. I'm funneled into a street full of crazy. Bodies darting in all directions. Whirling red and blue lights flash against the white incandescent marquees and neon store fronts. Sirens wail. Yelling. The crash and crack of things being destroyed.

A woman bounces off me. "Hey! Get out of my—"

A beer bottle explodes against the wall inches from us.

"Fuck!" I step back and shake glass from my hair, then look over at her. "You okay?" Her face is familiar.

"Idiots are throwing shit and the cops are going nuts. I have to get out of here," she says.

"C'mon, this way." I point toward the alley that'll lead to the tracks. Once we're there, we'll be out of the crowds and we can go our separate ways.

I look back and see her touch a cut on her forehead. I steer us to the warehouse next door and stop under a light. "Look up," I say, squinting at the cut.

She tilts her head back. "Is it bad?"

"Not too bad, but you better put something on it when you get home." I pull off my bandana and hand it to her. "Here, this will help." I dig into my pocket for an elastic hair-wiz and pull my long hair back into a ponytail as she ties the bandana pirate-style around her head. We quick time it up the alley. Her black hair flows in a mass of tangled curls down her back.

I glance over. "That looks better on you than me. Gypsy."

"Ha. Thanks... I think," she says, walking around a trash can lid.

"You live on campus?"

She nods. "Terrace."

"Really? I live in Dunbar. Why haven't I seen you?"

"You have." She grins. "Shakespeare."

Aha. The class I slept through and would've flunked if Eve hadn't bailed me out with her notes and papers. I smile back at her. "I thought you looked familiar."

"Lena Borelli."

"Kris Anderson."

We weave our way through trash cans as sirens echo off buildings across the Cuyahoga River. I glance back at her. "We're gonna keep the buildings between us and the nuts, then loop past the riot to get back to campus."

We make it to the railroad tracks and run along the ties. Warehouses and bars are all that stand between us and the chaos, which is growing louder.

"I was in a riot at Ohio State," I say between breaths as we run. "Things can get unpredictable. Protestors, drunks, townies, cops... everyone goes looney tunes."

"It started out peaceful," she says. "It's this God-awful war." She touches her forehead. "And now I have a souvenir."

I grin. "You can show it off years from now and tell people you got it when you crashed into your white knight."

We can hear the chants of protesters. "One, two, three, four. We don't want your fucking war," mixed with shouts of "Pigs off the street."

"Okay, Lena, let's keep moving. Cut up here to Water Street," I say, taking the lead. "It should get us past the worst of it."

A tear gas canister streaks overhead, flying between the warehouses, and lands behind us.

The gas forces us forward onto Water Street. Another canister hits the curb across from us, spinning as it releases a noxious stream of gas. Lena latches on to my elbow as she pulls the neck of her sweater over her nose.

"That won't help," I yell. "It's the eyes."

A firecracker detonates in a trash can to our left. We jump off the pavement into the grass, scared shitless. And there's my friend Cheet, half owner of my dog, Reggie, standing five feet away with his Zippo still lit, laughing his ass off.

"What the hell, Cheet! You trying to get us shot?"

Cheet keeps laughing. He's got to be speeding.

"Hey, you didn't bring Reg down here, did you?" I yell, scanning the area. This is no place for a dog.

"Nope, he's chewing on a bone at the pad. Oh shit, surf's up!" He backpedals as protestors and police surge toward us. A wiry looking guy throws a rock at a car. A cop grabs him and throws him on the hood of a late model Ford parked at the curb in front of us. The billy club beating begins—five quick thumps and the man crumples.

Four police cruisers come to screeching stops. We cross Water Street, looking for the safety of an alley. Three guys are already there and, with a grunting heave, they throw rocks over our heads, aiming at the cop cars. The police dodge behind their cruisers. A cop's arm comes out over the hood of the car. My heart stops. His pistol is aiming at us.

We tuck against the side of the building for cover. The stone throwers run into and over each other, and end up in an intertwined heap. Looking like some kind of six-legged, six-armed tangled creature, they skooch across the pavement as if in a bizarre crab race. But the cop doesn't fire. Thank God.

Cheet appears in the street. He rushes out behind a deputy and taps the back of his helmet. Dodges the furious swing of the night stick and sprints off into the dark swinging his arms over his head like he's running with the bulls at Pamplona.

"Your friend is an idiot," Lena says.

"He's okay. It's just because his brother, Ben, was killed in Nam. They grew up down the street from me."

Her voice drops. "My friend Craig got killed last year. My brother's in the next lottery."

We look at each other. She turns her face upward and shouts, "Go to hell, Nixon!"

We're stuck in an arena of piercing sirens, shattering glass, and the dull bass thuds of something heavy rammed against metal. Yelling and screaming, more bottles breaking. Cheet and a bunch of others are circled by the fuzz and dragged off to the paddy wagons. I think about running over for exactly half a second, then stop. Cheet's on his own for this one.

I grab Lena's arm. "We're gonna have to use backyards to loop back to Terrace. Stay low and quiet. We don't need any townies shooting us in the back."

We make a break for it across Water Street. Through alleys filled with eye-watering smoke and dodging scrums of cops and protesters, we weave our way gradually out of the violence to a neighborhood. We walk in silence, catching our breath as we move through yards of suburban dreams: swing sets, patio furniture, and barbecue grills.

"You okay?" I say, putting an arm around her shoulders.

"Better than your friend," she says, glancing over with wide, scared eyes. "What's going to happen to him? I watched the Democratic convention in Chicago. Not pretty."

I stop and step back. She looks pale and shaky, like she's ready to puke. "He'll be okay. This isn't Cheet's first rodeo."

"Really?"

"Yeah, really. He'll be fine. His parents will bail him out first thing in the morning."

"Okay. But this is awful. Somebody's gonna get hurt bad or killed."

"You gotta get your mind off it." I grab her hands. "Think of your favorite place."

"Huh?"

"Play along with me. Take a deep breath."

Lena inhales and tilts her head up. A porch light spills over her olive complexion. Italian? Greek? Maybe Spanish.

"What do you see?"

"Cobblestones, balconies, and cafes."

"Where are you?" We sidestep a swing set.

"In the south of France."

"Why France?"

She opens her eyes. "Because I've spent years memorizing French verbs and I want to travel. See the world. Find out the meaning of life."

"But then you'd have to translate everything... to get it."

"Get what?"

"The meaning of life!"

She bites her lower lip. I can feel her thoughts shuffle.

"Hey," I say, "in every corner of the world, day in and day out, life moves along... just in different colors."

"See!" She shakes her forefinger. "That's what the Impressionists thought... and they were French!"

A light flicks on in the house next to us and a guy sticks his head out the window. "Get the hell out of my yard, you dirty hippies! They should shoot all of you."

I flash him the peace sign. But I really want to give him the finger. Stepping out of his yard, I say to Lena, "Well, I'm still trying to understand what's right in front of me... in English."

We make our way toward campus. Cops and protesters block the main gate. I nudge Lena.

"Cheet's place is a couple blocks up. We can stay there."

She hesitates. Her voice is soft. "Okay."

"Hope you don't mind dogs. Reg is kind of big."

"Never had one. Only cats."

"We got him from the shelter—an Airedale with papers. Thought we'd make some money breeding him. But haven't found any female Airedales yet."

"So, you got him to make money?"

"He's great protection too. No one wants to mess with him," I say.

"You need protection?"

"Well, all the girls on campus think he's a big lovable teddy bear. Reg reels everyone in."

Silence. Shit. Tear gas went straight to my brain. I try to backpedal. "He's just a good dog. He's my buddy, you know?"

We reach Cheet's house and I get the key from under the doormat and unlock the door.

Reggie lunges out, tail wagging, and makes a beeline to the yard.

I point to the porch steps. "Take a seat, I'll get us something to relax."

God only knows how long Reg was inside. Nothin' turns chicks off more than dog poop on the bedroom floor.

Chapter Three
Gimme Shelter

Lena

Kris shuffles out of the house with a baggie and a pipe and sits on the porch step next to me. Reggie sprawls out between us. He's huge! And smellier than the cats I grew up with. I try to find something nice to say about this shaggy bear lying next to me.

I twist a lock of his frizzy curl around my finger. "You've got my hair, poor fellow. But you wear it well."

Kris looks amused. "So where you from, Lena?"

"Outside Los Angeles."

"LA? What're you doing here?"

"Divorce. Mom lives in Ohio. Dad lives in LA. I go back and forth."

He nods. "I'm from Minnesota, but I live in Columbus with my dad and stepmom. Mom died when I was small. But I go back to Minnesota whenever I can. Never stopped calling it home."

I watch him light a bowl of weed. The scent is comforting. He tokes and hands me the pipe over Reggie's head.

"It's a... proven... riot remedy," he says as he exhales. "Calms the spirit."

I inhale slowly, hoping the drug will erase the slideshow running through my mind. People dragged through the street, faces filled with anger, smeared with blood. Bottles crashing and windows breaking. The pop of rubber bullets. A small cry escapes my lips and I lower my head into my hands.

"Hey." Kris moves Reggie over to his other side and puts his arm around me.

My fingers clench. "I hate this war. Hate what it's doing... to us. To them. I hate Nixon. I hate... hate—that I hate."

Kris pulls me close. I turn sideways and bury my face in his chest. His embrace muffles the shouts, the screams, the sirens. All the things I wanted before tonight and all the reasons for wanting them are fractured. I can't even remember what they were.

A cool breeze blows over us. Kris pats my back, pulls me to my feet and leads me inside. He points to a door down the hall.

"There's the bathroom. You should wash that cut. Need help?"

"No, I got it."

I close the door, but I can hear Kris talking to Reggie like they're catching up on the day's news. My hair is a snarled mess. I sigh and take off the bloody bandana before splashing water on my face. I wash the cut with a sliver of soap stuck to the dirty sink. At least my bangs will hide the cut. My face clean, I look at the bandana, then shove it in my purse. I'll wash it at the dorm before I give it back. I take a deep breath, put on a brave face, then open the door.

I walk into the living room where Kris is sitting on a shabby couch with a faded barnyard pattern on it. A tattered afghan blanket that somebody's grandma made is thrown over the back.

"Does anyone else live here besides Cheet?"

"Nope. The landlord lives in the apartment upstairs, but he's cool."

A poster of Jimi Hendrix hangs on the wall behind the couch. A rabbit-eared TV balances on a lop-sided end table, next to a battered Lazy Boy.

"I'm moving off campus next fall," I say, trying to envision the drab room with feminine décor. "Sharing a house with seven other women."

"Hope it has eight bathrooms."

I roll my eyes as he smirks. "If you want, you can stay in Cheet's room. I'll sleep down here." He pats the lumpy cushion beside him.

"What if Cheet gets out?"

"Fat chance. But even if he did, he can crash on the recliner."

I nod. "Okay."

Kris stands and waves for me to follow as he heads down the hall.

He pushes open the door to a small room. Faint light from a street lamp shines through the window. A couple of concrete blocks next to the bed serve as a nightstand. An empty gallon wine bottle with a candle in it sits on one of the blocks. Kris lights the wick. I stare at the rainbows of wax that have dripped down its long neck and over its smooth, round body. A stained glass swan.

I set my purse in the corner of the room and sit on the bed. Water rolls under me. "Really? A waterbed?"

Kris plops down and the waves rock us together. As if on cue, we lay back together, close but not touching, relaxing in a harbor of gentle rolls. Kris skims his hand up and down my arm.

"Feeling better?"

I feel myself warming to his touch. Then my rulebook opens—I don't know him. I don't do this.

I gaze through the open window. The leaves of a tree brush against the screen. Moths flutter in and out of the shadows. It seems impossible, but we're worlds away from the insanity.

"If this was your last night on earth," Kris murmurs, "what would you want to say about your life?"

I look at the candle flame flickering next to us. "That I made a difference."

"But did anything make a difference in you?"

I shrug. "I need to go out into the world to find that out. What about you?"

"I don't know. But I don't think it's anything I have to look for. I think it's something that happens on its own."

He leans up on his elbow and we stare into each other's eyes. Then he pulls me close. I hold him, feeling safe in his warmth. My heart starts pounding. He slides my top over my shoulders and drops it to the floor. His fingers skim under the belt of my jeans. I know this is the point of no return. His eyes melt me. His lips string a necklace of kisses around my neck. I unbuckle his belt, slipping it through the loops. We tug and pull, ebb and flow with the waterbed. The sheets are cool against my body.

Should I? What will happen if I do?

I wrap my arms around his neck. His kiss fills me with light.

I close my rulebook.

We lock together on the verge. Of falling into. Each other. Down deep, untouched by the outside world. I don't need answers. I need... this moment.

Chapter Four
Morning After

Kris

My eyes open as Reggie slathers my face. He looks at me, his brown eyes saying, "Where the hell's my breakfast?" I squint at the clock. Eight o'clock already?

"Reg, it's too early, buddy."

Light shines like kryptonite through the window. The shower is running in the bathroom. I sit up and run my fingers through my hair. What a night. Smiling, I swing my legs over the edge of the bed and throw on yesterday's clothes.

I trudge downstairs to the kitchen with Reg on my heels.

"Any opinions on this one, buddy?" He gives me a small "Woof" as I open a cupboard. A jar of instant Folgers and a bag of dog chow share a shelf with a half empty box of Cap'n Crunch. I open the fridge. It smells funky from old bologna, with its edges curled up, and something unidentifiable in the vegetable bin. A couple of bottles of Rolling Rock are lying on their sides.

I grab a pot from the cupboard, slosh water around in it and put it on the stove to boil. Then I fill Reggie's bowl, wondering if Cheet's parents will make him sweat it out before posting bail. I drum my fingers on the table. What's next?

Lena walks into the kitchen, her hair hanging in wet ringlets. Never thought curly was as sexy as straight, but...

"Morning," she says.

"Want some coffee?"

She shakes her head. "No, thanks. Got to get back to the dorm and change for work."

"My job's not 'til later, but I'll walk you back to campus."

Reggie wiggles up to her, wagging and sniffing. She pets him, but doesn't do the baby talk like other girls. I open the back door and let Reg into the fenced yard.

"Where do you work?" she asks.

"Psych lab."

"What do you do there?"

"Clean up, feed the animals, and try to work on my comparative psych project with two baby monkeys."

"No way!"

"Yeah, Patty and Penny are my two main babes."

I recognize the look Lena is giving me. Everybody likes monkeys.

"You want to see them sometime?"

"Sure."

"Okay," I say. "So, where do you work?"

"I'm in the work-study program at the library. Vonnegut and Hemingway are my main babes."

I smile. She's quick. I gulp down the last of the coffee and lead the way into the light-filled day. I give her a sideways glance as we walk down the street. I should've asked if she's on the pill. She's got to be, who isn't?

"How's that cut?" I ask, squinting at her forehead.

She lifts her bangs, revealing a tiny red line. "Not too bad, thank God."

We walk through downtown, avoiding the trash and broken glass. Shop owners are busy cleaning up. A few scowl at us.

Lena whispers as we pass them. "Are they blaming us for that drunken riot? This doesn't help the cause. I know some of them are as much against the war as we are."

I pick up a spent tear gas canister and lay it on top of an overflowing trash bin. "You can't blame them.

There's no way to separate the protesters from the assholes."

"My parents think outside agitators come onto campus to get everyone riled up," Lena says.

"I don't think we need help with that."

"I know. But I don't want anyone getting hurt. I just want to know the truth, you know? Some vets back from Vietnam study at the library. They know what's going on. I've tagged along with them to some of the rallies. They're the ones I believe."

We wind our way through campus. Standing at the bottom of the hill that leads to Dunbar, I scan the windows of Terrace. I've had to climb in or out of some of those windows after visiting hours more than a few times.

"Thanks for the rescue," Lena says.

"Anything for a damsel in distress."

Lena laughs. There's a pause, the awkward moment where good old Romeo from our Shakespeare class would kiss her hand. I clear my throat, then say, "You busy tomorrow?"

"I work 'til five. Then I have a study group at seven." She wrinkles her nose. "Exams, you know?"

"Sure. Well, good luck with that." I turn to walk up the hill toward my dorm.

She calls out, "How about Monday? There's a noon demonstration. I'm going. You?"

I stop and scratch my beard. Mondays I usually hang out with Eve, but… "Um, how about after?"

"About one o'clock then? At The Hub?"

"Make it one-thirty."

"Okay. See you."

I watch her walk away. There's something different about her.

I walk to my dorm and up the stairs to my second-floor room, turn the knob a couple of times and fumble loudly with my keys. That usually gives my roommate and whoever he has in there time to get decent. I finally push the door open, expecting to see naked bodies. There's nothing but a pile of 'ludes on the dresser and sheets hanging off the top bunk. Remnants of my roommate 'Lude Dick, the traveling train wreck. He lives up to his nickname by scarfing down quaaludes, sopors, or downers with beer 'til he's slobbering all over himself and flopping on the floor like a fish. Knowing Dick, he either got lucky, got arrested, or both last night. I hope he stays away all day. I want to live off campus next fall, but with my shitty grades and tuition-paying parents, I don't see that happening.

I pull the shade down and set my clock radio for two. A little over four hours to crash. The lava lamp oozes in the corner. I turn the FM on low and stretch out in bed. The two girls I'm seeing—Gwen and Eve—come back Sunday night. I'm not hiding anything—they know about each other. But it gets dicey. Got to be on top of my game to keep everything cool.

My thoughts roll back to Lena. Guess I should've gotten her phone number. The usual warning sounds in my head: *'Attention! You're involved with enough women!'* I picture Eve's gymnast body, Gwen's 'scientific experiments.' But Lena's different.

I roll over and close my eyes.

Maybe different wouldn't be so bad.

Chapter Five
Aftermath

Lena

I walk into my dorm room. Ginny is standing in front of the dresser mirror, putting on makeup, her golden-brown hair rolled up in electric curlers. Riot or no, Ginny's always prepared.

"Thank God!" she says. "I almost called the campus police. Where have you been?"

I give her a backhand wave. "I got caught in that mess downtown." I rifle through my dresser, pulling out jeans and a short-sleeved top. "Massive chaos."

"I know," she says. "I stayed at Mike's house until things calmed down and came home around 3:00 a.m. I freaked out when you weren't here. What happened?"

"I ran into this guy Kris from my Shakespeare class. We stuck together. It was like being in a war zone. People throwing rocks, setting things on fire. His friend got arrested, and look"—lifting up my bangs— "I got cut."

Ginny stares at the gash. "I've got some cover-up for that." She pulls a small suitcase—her makeup bag— from under the bed.

"Later. I'm running late," I say, grabbing a bag of M&M's from my bottom desk drawer. "See ya."

I'm surrounded by the scent of freshly mowed lawn as I walk to the library. The feeling in the air is calm… but waiting. Like hitting the space key on a typewriter.

My thoughts clench. I slept with a guy I hardly know. Me, Miss Love Before Sex. Not that I want a long-term commitment. But at least love!

I keep walking, remembering the look on Kris's face as he pulled me through the mob. Strong jaw. Determined eyes. I picture his tall, lanky frame as he guided us away from the fray. Feel his steady arms around me on the porch. The scent of peppermint on his skin. His touch. The rolling of the waterbed… Wait, wait! What's his major? Monkeys? I shake my head in disbelief. I slept with a guy and I don't even know his major.

Ginny would handle this with no problem. 'It's not about being easy, it's about experiencing the moment. Being a free spirit.'

So, am I a 'free spirit' now? I want to be, but intimacy always connects to my heart. What happened last night was intimate, but… where's my heart? In the light of day, I feel like what happened last night was just sex.

I open the door to the library. It's packed with students studying for midterms. I check in and walk over to the cart filled with returned books. At least I'm not on desk duty today. No way can I fake a smile and small talk. I'll just bury myself in re-shelving books while I obsess about last night.

For instance, obsession number one—are there any consequences? Well, I'm not on the pill. Why? Because I'm not in love. Not in a relationship. My only experience was limited to my high school steady. He took care of those things. So why didn't Kris? Why didn't I ask him to? What's happened to me? I shudder. A one-night stand. That's what it was.

So, what happens now if he doesn't show up at The Hub? Or, even worse, what happens if he does show? We can't have a typical first date when we've already had sex. Favorite band? Sport? Food? Nope. It's all backward. He'll expect to go back to my room. Probably thinks I'm easy. One little riot is all it takes to get me into bed.

He asked what I was doing today only because he knows he doesn't have to wait to get what he wants. It can't be because he likes me—he doesn't even know me. But, there is the other side.

It wasn't a typical night.

I can still smell the tear gas. Feel the crowd closing in. Pushing. Shoving. Yelling. 'One, two, three, four. We don't want your fucking war.' It was chaos.

And in the middle of that madness, I can still hear Kris asking me, "But what was it, in the world, that made a difference in you?"

I put down the book I'm re-shelving and bite my lip, thinking it over. Last night *was* different. And now... so am I.

Chapter Six
Working Man - Saturday, May 2, 1970

Kris

Nine o'clock, the last cage is hosed down, every critter is fed, and I'm out of here. I smell like cat pee and monkey chow. It might be a turn-on for Gwen, my research junkie, but I can't stand myself. I've got to hit the shower before I run into anyone.

Downtown's out tonight, thanks to the mayor's eight o'clock curfew. But there's still plenty of time to party at the dorm dances. They should be big considering they're the only place to get alcohol. And who knows? Maybe I'll run into Lena.

Lab locked down, I jump-skip down the back stairwell of Kent Hall and catch the smell of burning wood and tar. Then the sirens. Jesus Christ! Is the building on fire? How in the hell am I gonna get all the cages outside?

I run down the last few steps and slam through the door. Flames twist like angry snakes in the night sky, the ROTC building is engulfed. The flashing of red and white bounces off the silhouettes of figures crisscrossing the darkness in front of me.

A couple of campus cops are watching the fire. Then they're looking at me. Shit.

"You. Halt!"

I stop. "Yes, sir."

"What's your business here?"

"Uh, home. Just got off work."

One of them looks me over and lifts his baton. "Home, huh? Is that the truth?"

"Yes, sir."

He turns to the other cop. "I don't care what the Chief says, someone needs to teach these commies a lesson."

The night explodes with a machine gun-like eruption. The cops duck, and I spontaneously duck with them.

"God damn it!" one of the cops growls. "The ROTC ammo. Get the hell out of my sight. If I see your face again, you'll be kissing my friend Billy." He slaps his night stick into the palm of his hand.

Ammo? Serious shit. And burning down the ROTC building? A siren whines, then another and another. A line of Jeeps roars down the street, screeching to a halt. Holy shit, National Guard. Shouts, screams, and chants of "ROT-CEE off campus!" reverberate through the air. People dart around me in all directions as I edge away from the chaos.

A familiar face emerges from the crowd, "Gwen!" I say, over the cacophony of misplaced sounds of destruction. "I thought you were in Buffalo."

"Came back early when I heard the revolution started." She walks into my arms. "Where are you going?"

"Back to my place. I just got off work."

"Forget it—come with us."

"Nah, I got enough action last night. Cheet got hauled off to jail."

"You're kidding!"

"He's home. His parents bailed him out, again."

"Then come on!"

"Nah, burning buildings isn't my thing."

Gwen tosses her long blonde curls over her shoulder. "It's the only way to get the Man's attention."

"I know. But I'm more into the peace and love thing."

She leans in and kisses me, then whispers, "Sometimes you gotta fight for peace and love." Her green eyes blaze as she grins and backs away, joining her friends.

"Hey, watch yourself, the cops aren't playing around." I turn to leave, then have an afterthought. "Gwen," I yell. "Strongbow is playing the curfew party at Tri-Towers. Meet you there later?"

"Sure, if I'm not in jail! Cheet won't mind if I drop his name to get a bottom bunk, will he?" She flashes the peace sign.

I watch as she and her friends walk in and out of helicopter spotlights and into the smoke and gas-covered Commons. A pop, pop, pop of teargas canisters, and small human figures scatter in bursts as the ROTC building burns. I walk home with a thought rattling around my brain. *Does the science of how to kill belong on the same campus as the science of understanding why we shouldn't?*

***

The curfew-induced dorm party went into the wee hours of Sunday, which is why I'm dragging ass as I head downstairs carrying an armload of textbooks and a bag of stale Cheetos. Missed breakfast and lunch. Partying with Gwen isn't for lightweights. We've been hanging together since Easter. Since Sophie. Gwen has everything sexy and smart. Still it's the same old thing: I can't commit. But she's fine with it.

I stack my textbooks on the table in the lobby. Exams snuck up on me. Gotta get it together.

Fifteen minutes in, I'm feeling like I'm getting somewhere when the lobby door blasts open.

"Hey, man."

It's 'Lude Dick, with a rumpled grocery bag in his hand. He rushes up to my table and waves at the outside.

"Did the revolution start or what? What's with all the guards at the door? Almost shit my pants thinking—is the whole campus getting busted?"

I roll my eyes at him. "What rock have you been under? Those guards have been here all night."

Dick smiles. "I just got back from Youngstown." He pushes the brown bag at me.

"Hey, man, not here!" I push it back at him and gather up my books. "What's wrong with you?"

Back in our room, Dick says, "Saved us forty bucks, too, my friend, with my superior palate and suave bargaining skills. They were trying to pass this off as Jamaican. But they couldn't slide that by me. First toke, I knew: Mexican."

"I thought this wasn't goin' down 'til tomorrow," I say, opening the bag and dumping the brick on my desk. "And what about Cousin Frankie—wasn't he with you? I thought he was dope master general."

"Well, Cousin Frankie, spotted it first, but I knew right off." Dick taps his head. "I knew."

Cousin Frankie's name wasn't Frankie and he was nobody's cousin that I knew of. His real family was old-school Youngstown—the kind of people you don't screw with. Somehow Dick hooked up with him and roped me into lending a hand moving a truckload of furniture from Youngstown to Kent. Nothin' says family like lugging dressers, a sofa bed, and slate-top pool table up two floors for nothing. So, Dick and I now get the Cousin Frankie family discount.

Dick drops some crumpled bills on my desk. I count it and look up. "Forty bucks? There's only thirty-nine here."

"Ahh, on the way back I got the munchies for a Big Mac and fries."

"You took that into McDonald's?" I point to the now empty grocery bag. "Every cop in town eats there."

"It's my good luck that they're all here."

I shake my head. "Let's break this kilo down. And we've got to figure out where to store it in case they search the dorms for communists or something. The cops are crawling all over campus."

"That ain't gonna happen. This is a free country. We got rights."

"Yeah, sure."

I open the closet and pull out the scale I borrowed from the lab. "Spread the newspaper and I'll get the baggies."

Dick unfurls a copy of the *Kent Stater* and smooths it out across the floor. "Five-finger bags?"

"Yep. One O-Z each."

"Some dudes are selling five-finger bags for twenty."

"It's bad karma when it's all about the money," I say. "Give me a hand. This shit is packed tight. And we stay at fifteen."

Dick fills each bag with a real handful and puts it on the scale. I top it off with a bud or two and lick the baggie to seal it closed. The work goes quick. It takes my mind away from studying—like I need another excuse. I seal another bag, set it down on top of the growing pile and smile. This ought to supplement a couple of concerts coming up.

Dick crashes on the bunk. I head downstairs and out the lobby door with my bag of unsellable pot debris. It's eight o'clock and a crowd is gathering near the Victory Bell again. Someone on a bullhorn is reading the Riot Act or something. I watch until they start the march to front campus. I don't want to get busted holding a bunch of worthless stems. I make a discreet exit to the woods just beyond my dorm.

Chapter Seven
Tin Soldiers - Monday, May 4, 1970

Lena

*J*ournal:

God it's scary around here. Men in uniforms with rifles stand outside my dorm and patrol the campus. Scary looking Jeeps scuttle like cockroaches while helicopters fly overhead. The air is thick with fear and frustration. I can't BELIEVE they burned down the ROTC! But I admire it! I don't have the guts for that. My parents called and practically ordered me to come home. No way. I need these credits. I promised them I'd stay away from the riots, but I didn't promise not to go to the demonstrations. They don't know the difference. And there is a difference. It's important that we band together to stop this war.

Yesterday started as a normal Sunday. We thought maybe the Guard would leave, but as soon as it got dark, the riots and tear gas started. I think more people are protesting the Guard on campus than our army in Cambodia. Can't wait for the noon demonstration. It's got to be powerful AND peaceful. Not a riot. We need to behave so the Guard will leave. Everyone's so uptight with them on campus.

And I'm uptight about my lunch date with Kris. Is it too late to go back to falling in love before falling in bed? Hmmm. The problem is...

Passion.

And there's another problem.

His eyes. Not dark blue, but not light. Denim. Blue jean eyes.

Just before noon, I head toward The Commons. The profs have been pretty cool about not marking us absent when we go to the rallies. We're not absent. We study the demise of ancient civilizations, then watch the slaughter of our generation every night on the six o'clock news. Going to those rallies makes us great students—witnesses to the history unfolding around us.

I close my eyes. I'm not radical, I only want to stand up for what's right. I want our country to be what's right in the world. Attacking a country that didn't attack us doesn't seem right. So what if they want to be communist? Majority rules! That's what our system is based on, right?

I breathe in. Only a few more weeks until summer break, then I'll be home, lying in the California sun for three months. This craziness should all be over by the time I come back in the fall. But for now, there are still classes, exams and a guy to meet.

I round the corner as the Victory Bell rings in the noon rally. Hundreds of students are in The Commons. Some wave black flags, some are heading to class. Most are milling around. Almost normal, except for the hundreds of soldiers in riot gear stationed by the burned-out ROTC building. I plop down on the grassy slope of Taylor Hill and inhale the sweet scent of spring. A Jeep appears, circling the area. Students throw rocks at it.

"Pigs off campus!"

"One, two, three, four, we don't want your fucking war!"

More rocks are thrown. Some Guards throw them back.

A voice bellows over a bullhorn, "Disperse! Disperse!"

I stand, trying to decide whether to stay or go. The decision is made for me as a canister of tear gas shoots into the air. Then another. Plume after plume of the thick white smoke arcs over us. Tears stream as I pull my T-shirt over my nose and run back in the direction of my dorm. Oh my God! This is for real! That thought stops me in my tracks. *Take a stand.* For my brother and Kris who could both be sent to war. For all the guys coming back in body bags night after night. And for all those coming home with screwed up heads and broken bodies. My generation.

I look up to see the Guard split into two groups. They march up the left and right sides of Taylor Hill, using their bayonets to drive students up the hill between them. The noise of the crowd rumbles like a wave heading toward shore. Shouts and screams and curses. I weave across the side of the hill through the people standing on the perimeter. Popping sounds, like a long string of loud firecrackers, echo. People look at one another in disbelief. Some surge toward the sound and others back away. Then people are streaming down all sides of the hill, running toward The Commons.

"They're shooting!"

"Run!"

"Get down!"

"Real bullets!"

"Blanks!"

"They're killing us!"

Chaos unfolds around me in slow motion. Frozen, I watch students scatter. Someone yells, "Strike! Strike!"

I sit down on the ground with hundreds, maybe thousands of people. Another voice on a bullhorn is begging us to leave. It's a faculty member, pleading with us to go. Saying that if we don't, there will be more bloodshed. His voice twists into a strangled scream. Fear and anger blanket the hill. I watch the others for direction. Ambulance sirens head toward us. I feel myself start to shake. I can't breathe. Slowly, one by one, very slowly, we stand.

I stumble toward my dorm surrounded by the wail of sirens. People are saying at least four students, maybe more were killed. Gunned down, *on their own college campus!* Dozens wounded. My eyes burn with tears.

Word spreads that we have to hurry and pack up and get out. Campus is shut down.

Not just shut down, shot down.

Someone announces they're sending buses to take students to Cleveland, Akron, and Columbus. All the phone lines are tied up. Fleeting thoughts of Kris and exams are buried in the chaos. Four dead kids. My age! How can I come back to a campus where they shoot students?

Like robots, Ginny and I load up her Pinto. Silent with sadness, we follow the stream of traffic out of Kent. I have this feeling that I left something behind. I look in the side view mirror back at the abandoned campus. The bright May sun has dimmed.

It isn't something I left. It's something I lost.

Chapter Eight
The Party - October 1970

Kris

First party of fall quarter at Dick and Mike's house. I give my dorm room the once-over. My stepmom always said, "Make your bed. You never know who might come into your room." But I don't think she had in mind what I have in mind. Though there's been no one exciting lately. Maybe tonight's the night.

I'd used the lame excuse of "it's me, not you" to cut loose from Eve and Gwen over summer break. We'd exhausted all of our common denominators. Not that there were that many to begin with. I haven't run into either of them since classes started. Or Lena. She was on my mind more than I care to admit over the summer. Never made it to The Hub to meet her. All hell broke loose that day and they only gave us like an hour to pack up and get out.

A couple of weeks ago, I stopped by the library where she said she worked. One of the librarians told me Lena wasn't working there anymore. And she didn't remember her last name either, which didn't help.

Hitting the sidewalk, I breathe in the night as I head toward the party. I guess it's nice being solo for a change. When it comes to girls, sometimes it's better when I just wing it.

I arrive at the old Victorian smack in the middle of town and walk up the creaky steps. The house is one hundred years old and, as Mike the artist says, a vision of excessiveness. Newly painted in its original colors, lime green and plum purple, not one room in the place is the same size or shape. Windows butt in and out, rooms angle in every direction, and embossed tin with cool patterns covers the ceilings. The place is great for lying back, smoking joints, dropping acid, doing 'shrooms, and getting laid. There are six guys living here and I wish I was one of them. It doesn't matter though. I crash here whenever I want, like everyone else. It beats stumbling the half mile back to my dorm room with some girl.

The place is shoulder-to-shoulder jam-packed. I immediately recognize the hot chick who sat next to me in astronomy last year. Pam always wore Danskins, which made it tough to keep my eyes off her and on the galaxy. I glance her way, she walks over, and before you know it, we're talking. Within seconds I'm groping for cosmic ties. I'm the consummate professional when it comes to 'openness,' which in my case means revealing my feelings on life and love. My rule is 'keep it positive with a hint of vulnerability'—no talk about genuine hurt or embarrassment. Sometimes it leads to a trip to their bed, but that's their choice. I'm just along for the ride. Before we get too deep, Pam excuses herself to go back to her date who has returned with their beer. Smiling, she slips me a piece of paper with her phone number before she turns to go.

Bobbing in the sea of bodies, I glimpse my old roommate, 'Lude Dick. His eyelids at half mast, he's already on his way to becoming a slobbering puddle of Jell-O. An annoying image of babysitting his ass at a couple of parties last year flashes through my mind. I turn my back on him and scan the room, disengaging from any responsibility for Dick and the poor, unfortunate dark-haired girl he's got himself poured over. I bet she's having the time of her life. There's no dignified way of getting rid of him. The more you struggle, the deeper you sink. But he's her responsibility now—I already paid my dues.

Mike pushes through the crowd and hands me his bright yellow bong.

"What's the big grin for?" he asks. "See something you like?"

I take a hit, hold it, then blow out. "Nah. Just wondering how long it's gonna take for that girl to punch 'Lude. We still have the rule—if he doesn't remember the name…"

Mike looks over at 'Lude and laughs. "You mean 'no name, fair game'? Oh yeah. I used the rule last month. But it doesn't matter, he can't even make it through a night remembering their name." He points over my shoulder. "Hey, check out the dining room."

It's a trippy scene, overflowing with pretty Alices and flipped out Mad Hatters. The girls these parties attract ride the edge of creative crazy. Dancers, artists, theater majors. All kinds of possibilities. I walk into the dining room, feeling like I'm climbing the first hill of a roller coaster. This is going to be a hell of ride. I watch a dude with a Fu Manchu in sunglasses announce that he will only receive words that are slid sideways across the table to him from the left. Then he nods, gathers his imaginary words in his hands and stuffs them into his mouth. His female companion is in an intimate conversation with each of the spider plant babies that droop down from a pot in the window. Another guy sits at the head of the table, asking what the color red smells like. The girl in a skimpy tie-dyed dress sitting next to him is eyeballing me. She stands, walks over, dips her hands in the punch bowl, and says, "Would you care for some of my Grandma's old fashion nuclear elixir?"

I smile. "Thanks, but I'm good."

I feel around my pocket for my drug of choice—sopors. I only need a couple to get my creative juices flowing. I don't want to be wrecked before the party is even started, like 'Lude Dick. I look back into the other room, wondering if he's still tormenting that girl. Then she turns and I see her face for the first time. Damn! It's Lena.

I'm moving before I'm thinking. I got this damsel-in-distress thing down pat. Maybe she'll give up a little gratitude later on tonight.

Chapter Nine
Free Spirit

Lena

I'm pressed against the wall like a flower in a scrapbook. Everyone's spaced out on speed or tripping. Halfway through my third beer, I fake-toke the reefer being passed around. Haven't seen Ginny in over an hour. She pushed me down this rabbit hole of floating heads and jabberwocky mouths and then disappeared. Perfect.

"First party of the year at Mike's house," she had said, poking her head through my side of the attic curtain divider. "C'mon, it'll be fun. You can wear my sexy red sweater you're always wanting to borrow. The one with the cut-outs down the arm."

I agreed, only because I was beginning to feel like a loser, curled up with a book on a Friday night—and because Ginny hadn't gotten a call back from her latest Mr. One-Night Wonderful.

Now I've got this doper slumped next to me. He's passing out. And his beer can is tipping. Shit—it's gonna spill on Ginny's sweater. "Hey, watch it!" I grab his hand and tilt the can upward.

He opens his eyes a slit. "You wan' summa my beer?"

"No, thanks."

His eyes open wider. "You're real pretty. I like you."

Oh, great. Just what I need. I ignore him and look in another direction.

"I've always liked you. Ever since we met."

"We haven't met."

"But I still like you."

I shake my head and turn away, looking for an exit through the immoveable crowd. He grabs my arm.

"You wanna see my penguin?"

"Whaaat? No." I push his hand off my arm. "I'm allergic to feathers."

His gaze lowers to my chest. "I just wanna be friends."

Oh, for God's sakes. He's staring at my chest. *In that way.* With his ears showing through his stringy hair and with his pointed goatee, he looks like the eighth dwarf. Except he's six feet tall. It's time for me to lose Stoney the dwarf. My eyes search the room for Ginny. "I've got to go find my friend."

"I'll help," he says.

Ignoring him, I twist through the bodies and catch sight of Ginny, cuddling up with cute puppy-dog-eyes on the couch. And surprise, she signals me not to wait for her. I knew this would happen. She gets what she wants and I end up with Stoney. Where's my jacket?

I zigzag through the room with Stoney one step behind, the tips of his guppy fingers nibbling at my waist—pawing my back. "Hey, watch the hands!" I say, scowling.

"But you feel sooo soft. He grabs my hand. "Touch my shirt, it feels good, too." Before I can pull my hand back, he kisses it.

Yanking my hand away, I push through dim rooms of lava lamps and black lights, bumping against shapes entwined in the shadows. Coats and jackets are piled on the floor along the walls or thrown over the backs of chairs and couches. I rip through the coats like a wino tearing into a trash can for a half-empty bottle of Mad Dog. Damn, where did I put it? In my frenzy, I bump into Ginny's friend Mike. He's carrying a bong, offering it to people like it's a bottle of champagne.

"Hey Lena, what's happenin'?"

"Mike! Thank God. This guy won't leave me alone. Can you get rid of him?"

"Just point him out and he's as good as gone."

"Here he comes!" I say, watching Stoney stumble closer. "Just throw him out, please."

Mike shakes his head. "Sorry, I can't. It's his party, too. 'Lude Dick lives here."

"Lewd Dick?" I groan in disgust and push past Mike into the next room. Lewd Dick follows, reaching for me. I'm going to kill Ginny!

A huge round of laughter erupts. I look toward the kitchen and oh my God... there's Kris. He's surrounded by girls, fluttering around him like fireflies. I turn so he can't see my face. I've got to get my coat and get out of here. Fast. But Lewd Dick has a hand clamped on my shoulder.

"Leave me alone," I growl, dragging his dead weight as I search for my jacket. Where the hell is it?

"A damsel in distress again?"

I turn to see Kris wearing an amused expression.

He puts his arm over Dick's shoulder. "C'mon, Dick, it's time to say farewell." He pulls Dick toward the stairway.

Dick waves at me. "Thew wanna slee with me?"

"Sure she does," says Kris. "But you gotta get in bed first. And then she'll be right up." Kris winks at me as he pushes Dick up the stairs.

Dick flails his arms toward me. "Wassher name again?"

"Juliet," Kris says. "Her name is Juliet." He looks back at me and grins. "Parting is such sweet sorrow." He hauls Dick up the stairs.

My face grows hot as I hear people laughing and hooting. Humiliating! I put my head down and head into the next room to hide. A crowd of people hover around a long table loaded with food. A big glass punchbowl sits in the middle and a guy offers me a cup of punch. I accept and beam my Mona Lisa smile toward Kris, who's coming down the stairs. He walks up to me and taps my hand that's holding the cup. "It's electric."

I hurriedly put the cup down, splashing its contents on the table. I'm paranoid about tripping. He laughs, then holds a make-believe joint between his fingers, lifts it to his lips, and blows out invisible smoke. "Go for a walk?"

He can go light up with any of those girls that were fluttering around him. The ones with the flowing hair and perfect bangs. But he's asking me.

I nod.

A girl wearing a skin-tight top and slinky skirt walks by. The tip of her cigarette glows as she sucks in. She tilts her head back and exhales, her blonde hair waterfalling down her back. She smolders a look at Kris, and mouths the word "later" as she strolls past. Barefoot. I look down at my boots. Well, it looked like rain. I smile at Kris and lead him into the living room where I search through piles of coats and jackets. Finally, I find mine. I slip into it as I follow Kris outside. We turn down a lamp-lit street. I keep pace beside him.

"Sorry about Dick," he says. "He's a sucker for true love."

"I shouldn't have led him on," I deadpan.

Kris laughs. "Did he try that penguin line on you? As stupid as that line is, it works about half the time."

"It was hard to resist."

Kris smiles. "So, how you been, Lena?"

"Fine. And you?" Stay cool. No big deal that we slept together the second we met.

"I tried looking you up but couldn't remember your last name. And that Monday we were supposed to meet, well..."

"God, I know." I tighten, remembering the horrifying result of trying to change the world. "My parents almost didn't let me come back."

"Yeah, lots of people transferred. Like it's going to be different anywhere else."

I shrug. "But they couldn't refuse the financial aid package. It's practically a free ride since the shootings. I just had to promise to stay away from demonstrations. Might be easier to do now that I moved off campus."

"I remembered that. But you're not at the library anymore."

He looked for me. "No, I'm waitressing at The Hub now. Didn't you move too?"

"Yeah, but just down the hall in Dunbar—to a single. My folks made me sign up to work a few hours behind the desk. They aren't amused by my grades and think the responsibility will make me take life more seriously."

"So, no more monkey business?"

Kris laughs. "Sure there is. I'm still taking care of Patty and Penny. Couldn't leave my girls, could I?"

"How's Cheet?"

"He's good, but he had to move. Reg bit the landlord. They live in a house out on Route 59."

"No! Not sweet and cuddly Reg! Are you sure it wasn't Cheet?"

"Ya never know." Kris pulls out a joint, lights up, and hands it to me.

We walk the side streets, smoking. The pot softens my awkward edges. The night becomes a mist. A group of girls pass. One of them calls out, "Hey Kris, where's Reggie?"

"In the library, boning up for anatomy class," he says. The girls laugh and move on.

"I miss my old job," I say. "Can't get much reading done at The Hub."

"The library puts me to sleep."

I smile. "It inspires me being surrounded by all that knowledge."

"I'm more a hands-on type," he says.

I look down, feeling my face flush. *I doubt it not.*

"I meant I'm in the lab more than the library."

"Eh, I don't do labs," I say. "I barely survived botany last year. Those poor plants were glad to see me leave."

We walk to Main Street and Kris stops in front of the Robin Hood, a brick and mortar tavern. I always cringe when I pass it, remembering my first public puke standing in line in front of the women's restroom. Six shots of tequila all over the floor. It was quite the freshman orientation.

"You thirsty?" he asks.

"A little."

"Great. You can buy me a beer."

"Such a gentleman."

"I had the pot. You get the beer. Fair's fair, right?"

I look at him with narrowed eyes. "We shared a joint. We'll share a beer."

He nods. "Okay. And I'll share something with you that I've never shared with anyone. But then you have to share something with me."

Hmmm. He can share whatever he wants, but there's no way I'm going to share my puke story.

He pulls open the heavy wooden door and I pull the collar of my coat a little tighter around my face. I peer through the crowd at the bar, hoping the bartender who cleaned me up back then isn't working tonight. Kris leads me to a dark booth against the wall. He bows slightly, waves me in, then slides into the bench across from me. Old posters are varnished into the wood paneling on the walls. The glow from electric candles in wall sconces casts a soft radiance over the posters and Kris's face. His eyes shine behind his wire-rims.

"My favorite booth. She found me during freshmen orientation," he says pointing to a movie poster hanging between us. It's of a dancing, dark-haired woman from the 1930's. Her partner is old-fashioned, suave. "Lena, let me introduce you to someone special. Claudette, this is Lena. Lena, Claudette."

"What's a nice girl like you doing with a guy like Kris?" I say, playing along. Her smile replies "Ditto."

Kris takes a pack of Kools out of his shirt pocket and offers one. I don't usually smoke, but what the hell? He leans over and flicks his Zippo like we're in an old-time movie. Sigh. I puff away on my Kool without inhaling, buzzing with the night's pot and beer.

Kris glances up at the poster. "Claudette takes me for who I am. No questions asked. And she'll never leave me."

I lean over and blow smoke into his face. "Because she's stuck on a wall."

"We can connect with anyone, anywhere across space and time," he says. "Like parallel lives."

A barmaid sets a mug of beer on the table. "Here's your usual."

Kris asks, "Can I get two straws?"

She laughs and walks away.

Kris offers the mug to me. I feel his knee press against mine as I drink. He has a dreamy look in his eyes. *No. Look away.*

He blows a perfect smoke ring. "Now it's your turn."

"To do what?" I say, putting the mug down.

"I shared something. Now you."

"Well, I do have *one* phobia."

He looks me over. "Spiders? Snakes?"

I shake my head. "Tornadoes. We don't have them in California, but you do here."

"So, *The Wizard of Oz* scarred you for life, too."

"Freaks me out. But I'm only here for one more year, then I'm transferring back to California. No more tornado worries."

His eyes widen. "You're leaving because of tornadoes?"

"Because I'm going to France."

"Ah, yes, France. But France isn't in California."

"My road to France is."

"Can I hitch there with you?"

"I don't think so."

"Why not?"

I roll my eyes, take a deep breath. My head is spinning. I look at my watch, it's almost one thirty. "I have to leave."

Kris touches my hand. "Let's end the night with one last beer."

I shake my head. "I never stay to the end."

"Meaning?"

"Meaning… meaning… the end…"

"Justifies the means?" He gives my hand a squeeze.

It feels nice. Warm. No! Not falling for that again. But I don't pull away.

"Sometimes the means *is* the end," I say.

He smiles and drains the beer mug. Standing, he holds out his hand. "C'mon, I'll walk you home. It's the very least I can do, for half a beer."

"Actually, it's the very most you can do."

He laughs. Not the phony "I'll laugh at anything to get into your pants" laugh. A genuine, "I think you're funny" laugh. We slide out of the booth. He takes my hand, then looks into my eyes. *Kiss me.*

"Do you have munchies at your place? I'm starving."

I sigh. "Maybe." The communal fridge, shared by eight girls, is usually a wasteland on the weekends.

We make our way to my house, his arm around my shoulders. It feels so good. Natural. But where am I heading? Should I try to turn back the pages in my rule book? Or should I try to be like all the other girls? The ones who are barefoot and give Kris knowing smiles at parties.

We get to my house. He reaches up and picks a heart-shaped leaf off the tree.

"I used to collect these cottonwood leaves when I was a kid."

He holds it over my head. Back lit by the porchlight, it glows golden. We both stare at it. It becomes more and more translucent. "An angel feather," he whispers. "Mind-blowing brilliance."

His voice pours through me like moonlight. He wraps an arm around my waist. I instinctively slip my arms around him and we stand face to face. I feel like he's looking inside of me.

"Everything is connected," he whispers, holding up the leaf. He presses his cheek against mine. "Like the roots of this tree and the branches spreading into the sky. They will never forget the wonder of this single... luminous... leaf."

His lips lightly brush against mine. Soft. Sweet. *Kiss me, Romeo, I'm waiting.* An image of that barefoot girl smiling at him intrudes on my thoughts. All those girls at the party flittering around him. I pull back. He hands me the leaf and I carefully slide it into my pocket. He cradles my hand.

I open the front door and lead Kris through the living room. A late-night movie is flickering on the TV and my housemate Trish and her boyfriend Eric are asleep on the couch. I turn off the TV and walk past the dining room converted into a bedroom, complete with bunk beds and dressers. In the kitchen, a half-eaten pizza is miraculously still in the fridge. I grab the pizza box along with two cans of Rolling Rock and lead the way upstairs. On the second floor landing, I open the door to the attic and we climb the narrow staircase to the room Ginny and I share. A small bathroom divides the room in half and we each have a curtain for privacy. Ginny's curtain is open. Lucky break, she's not here.

I slide my curtain back and step into my space. Moonglow filters through the front window, under the half-drawn wicker shade and over my single bed wedged into the corner under the eaves. I never had an attic in California. It's so cozy. I turn on a small study lamp on my desk, angling the light away from us.

I take a step toward Kris, then stop. Almost forgot. I go to my dresser and pull open the top drawer, take out the bandana and hand it to him. "I washed it in the hottest water, but the blood stain still wouldn't come out," I say.

"That's okay, makes it real."

I catch my breath. It *was* real.

He starts to wrap it around his head, then stops and sniffs it. "Um, what's that smell?"

"Oh, that's my patchouli oil. Like it?"

"I guess you gotta get used to it."

"Yeah, like tobacco."

"Do I smell like smoke?" Kris pats the pack of cigarettes in his shirt pocket.

"A little. You smell kind of pepperminty, too."

He laughs. "Good old Dr. Bronner's Peppermint Soap. You can use it eighteen different ways."

"Like?"

"Toothpaste, deodorant, cleans out your sinuses, and on the other end it can…"

"Okay, okay, I get it," I say, laughing.

He hands me back the bandana. "Here, keep it for a souvenir. You never know when you might need it." He reaches over and touches my hair, sweeping back my bangs. "No scar?"

"Nope," I say. "Like it never happened."

Kris pulls me close "Seems like it happened in a different life."

We sit on the blue shag rug and lean against the bed, with the pizza and beer between us. Kris lights up a joint. I light a stick of jasmine incense. He flips through my crate of albums and puts *Days of Future Past* on the stereo. Moody Blues. Perfect.

Through a hazy high we talk from all angles. Life and death, love and hate, commitments, no commitments. I never met a guy so willing to open up. They usually hide behind impassive shrugs or macho clichés. But now, stretched out next to me, someone is listening and responding.

He tilts his head, strokes his beard and the blue of his eyes deepen. "You ever feel anchorless?"

My eyebrows crease.

"The kind of anchor I'm talking about is inside you. Everything that is you is tied to it," he says.

"I don't want to be tied to anything. I like to free float."

"I like free-floating women."

"I mean free like… like a free spirit in the universe," I say. "Sharing peace and love. A friend to all."

He pushes the pizza box away and pulls me down onto the shaggy rug.

"Well, free spirit," he murmurs into my ear. "Can friends be lovers?"

Friends?

Chapter Ten
Board Stiff

Kris

Where the hell am I? A streetlight floods through the window straight into my eyes. Shit. Hot, sweaty, itchy, groggy... Wait, wait—Lena's on the floor with me. And I'm stiff as a board in more ways than one. I rub my eyes. According to Psych 202, my condition is nothing more than a physiological response to REM. That's bull. It's just an uncomfortable reminder of some frustrations that were never taken care of last night.

Lena's still asleep, rolled up in her quilt. Wind rattles the window panes—it's getting ready to storm. Time to head back to my dorm. I've gotta get some sleep in my own bed. I struggle to my feet, careful that I don't knock over the half empty beer bottles. I grab my army jacket and button it up for the long walk home. Then I lean over Lena, pull back her tangled hair and whisper in her ear, "Catch you later." She rolls over and sighs, deep in sleep.

I jog toward campus with autumn drizzle blowing in my face. Wide awake, freezing my ass off, sprinting home at the crack of empty-handed dawn. What's with her? It's not like we haven't done it before. Her transferring back to California should've nailed it. Women get off on that "we may never see each other again" shit.

Everything was lined up perfectly. One, I saved her from 'Lude Dick. Two, she said she wants to be some kind of cosmic friend or whatever. Three, should've been naked, rounding the bases and sliding into home. But all I got was a lot of muffled "huh-uhs" and a "maybe."

The rain is coming down harder, stinging my face. Struggling against the wind, I open the glass door to my all-male dorm, cold to the core. My waterlogged shoes leave puddles behind me. I walk to my room, smelling sour tennis shoes, old musty suitcase, stale smoke, and industrial cleanser. My home of higher education.

I grab my towel and my bottle of Dr. Bronner's all-in-one soap and head for the showers. As I'm about to enter the shower room, Rosie pops out wrapped in a towel. She's a cute Puerto Rican whose boyfriend, Miles, lives two doors down from me. Some mornings I hear them giggling as they sponge down together in the stall next to me. She hugs me with one arm and gives me a peck on the cheek. "Just strolling in, Kris? Make some girl happy?"

I shrug. Oddly, I don't feel like sharing. Rosie smiles and shakes her head. "Noooo?" She pats me on the backside. "Some people live vicariously through you—don't let us down." Then she laughs and trots her bare butt back to Miles' room.

It's the weekend, so I steel myself for the horrors of the bathroom as I open the door. I don't know how Rosie can stand using this place, even in a dire emergency. Someone's ralphed all over toilet number one, toilet two has overflowed, and three and four—well it's a guy's dorm. Worse yet, nothing gets cleaned in here 'til Monday.

Thank God, no one puked in the shower stalls like last week. I turn on the water and let it run hot for several minutes in case someone peed in the shower. Satisfied the shower is reasonably clean, I step in and let the warm water wash away the literal poop parade on the other side of my shower curtain. Then I smell it. Patchouli! The steam is picking up Lena's patchouli oil. I roll my eyes. Damn— what was with her? I know she wanted it as bad as I did.

I soap up and feel the water pouring down my back. Oh, hell, I'm not gonna get bent over it. She's not my type, anyway.

Chapter Eleven
Downtown

Lena

*J*ournal:

> *Can friends be lovers? Lovers can be friends, but...
> friends are friends—right? Damn Kris. His stupid question
> let the air out of my free spirit AND crumpled it. Why can't
> I be free and easy? I just want to live in the moment.
> Loosen up and have fun. Can free spirits be free but not
> easy?*

It's already afternoon and all my efforts at studying
have failed. French verbs stay unconjugated in my
notebook, papers lay unwritten on my desk. I sit on the bed
reading the same paragraph over and over in my Lit book. I
hear Ginny's footsteps on the stairs and slap the book shut.
She peeks through my curtain.

"Hi. I'm baaack. The party was a blast, wasn't it?
Aren't you glad I forced you to come? Mike said you left
with Kris so I made sure I stayed at Tim's. He's really
sweet. He has a—hey, what's wrong?"

She walks into my room and sits next to me. I fall
backward on pillows propped against the wall and stare at
the ceiling.

"Can friends be lovers?"

Ginny shrugs. "Sure, why not?"

"Kris spent the night."

"And..."

"And nothing."

"What?" Her brow wrinkles. "Why not? I mean you
told me you already—"

"Because he didn't want a friend or a lover. Just a one-night stand."

"He told you that?"

"No, but I heard this girl at the party tell him she'd see him later."

"But he stayed with you."

"Yeah, but I kept thinking of her waiting for him. Couldn't, you know, get past it. Then he left before I got up."

"No! That asshole."

"I pretended to be asleep."

"You did the right thing." She pats my hand. "When I told Tim I didn't want to come back here last night because it might be occupied, he made a crack about Kris sneaking in and out of the women's dorms. He told me he's got more X's than a Xerox salesman. I thought he was just trying to be funny, but..." Ginny puts her hand on my shoulder. "Don't worry. Plenty of other fish in the sea." She gets up, pulls her fingers through her long, thick hair, and yawns. "I have to take a nap. Handing out free makeup samples at work for six hours tonight, then meeting Tim."

I watch her walk toward her curtain. "Well, I've got to get out of here and clear my mind," I say. "You need anything downtown?"

"Can you pick up some nail polish remover? The cheap kind." She waves bye and closes the curtain, humming to herself.

My gaze drifts to the poster that's tacked on the slanted ceiling over my bed. Lovers walking hand in hand on a beach. I sigh, pull my poncho over my head, grab my macramé shoulder bag, and trudge downstairs.

The sun is out and the air is fresh. I step over puddles from the early morning storm. As I approach Main Street, I can't help glaring at the stately Robin Hood. I can picture Claudette's 'I tried to warn you' eyes from the poster over our booth last night. I'll never hear from Kris—

he didn't even ask for my phone number... again. Maybe he'd call if we did it last night. I picture the girl at the party. Maybe not.

On the way home, I traipse past all the bars, headshops, record stores, and pizza and sub restaurants that line the street. Bars outnumber the other businesses by far. Some are refreshed Victorians. They pose like elegant ladies, but they're betrayed every weekend by the trash that gathers around their stoops like anklets. Some are hole-in-the-wall dives trying to pass as cool. They certainly don't smell cool. They smell like stale beer and vomit.

I push open the dark green door to Cucumber Castle, my favorite head shop. The Dead is playing on the stereo. Black lights shine on fluorescent psychedelic posters. Optical art illusions of insects that seem to be breathing, line the walls. The shelves overflow with pipes, bongs, beaded jewelry and tie-dyed clothing. It all makes me feel at home and comfortable, which I really need right now.

I pick out some sandalwood incense sticks and a vial of patchouli oil. Its woodsy fragrance makes me feel earthy and exotic. Like the blend of Kris's warm tobacco and zingy peppermint. On his skin. His hair. Peppermint mixing with patchouli. On my sheets. My quilt. My breath quickens. Oh, for God's sake. *Stop it!*

I walk up to the counter and recognize the clerk from my French class last year.

"Hey, *bonjour*," he says.

"*Bonjour*, Rod, *ça va?*"

"*Très bien. Et tu?*"

"*Comme ci, comme ça.*" But so-so doesn't even begin to describe how I feel.

"Hey, you hear about that new French restaurant out on Route 43?" Rod asks, handing me my incense and oil.

"No. You been?"

"Not yet. Maybe we can get some people from our class together and check it out."

"Bonne idée!"

I turn to go and stop short. Oh, for God's sake. Kris and his dog are walking across the street toward the store.

"What's your phone number?" Rod asks.

I mumble it as my gaze flicks from Rod to Kris. Rod asks me to repeat it. Oh, God, now Kris and Reg are standing right outside the door talking to some girl. I say my number again. It's barely out of my mouth before Rod says, "Slower this time."

Doesn't he understand English? Look at the way that girl and Kris are smiling. Now they're laughing. *"Reg reels everyone in."*

Do I stay inside or go out and accidently on purpose bump into them? *No way.* I retreat to the other side of the counter behind a rack of belts hanging near the window to watch Kris and his hippie Barbie. Man, this is just plain lurking. But I can't help it, dammit. Look at him. Lover boy. I'm glad we didn't do it again. Glad!

I rake my fingers through the belts. I'm not spying, *I am shopping.* Besides, I was here first. I reach for a belt and knock some off the rack. They clatter to the floor and Rod looks at me with raised brows. I mouth an "Oops" in his direction as I pick up the belts and wiggle them back on the hooks.

Chapter Twelve
Headshop

Kris

Reggie's stubby Airedale tail rises to attention when I spot a sexy blonde in front of Cucumber Castle. He reads me so well. Through caramel colored fuzz, his wet black nose and bright brown eyes shine and he has the overall appearance of a caffeinated teddy bear. The girls can't resist his cute and cuddly look. But sometimes Reg doesn't have a friendly disposition toward strangers. So, when I hear his low growl, I playfully pull his stumpy tail or scratch his ears to loosen him up. In some cases, I don't mind people thinking 'My, what big teeth you have.' Like when I'm carrying a little extra cash or pot. But this isn't one of those times.

And sure enough, when she turns, the blonde does a double take on Reggie. Following script, she lets out a high pitched "Where did you get that puppy, he is soooo cute! Can I please pet him? Pleeease?"

I lean down and beg through my smile, "C'mon, Reg, let her gush over you just a little… for me?" I scratch his ears keeping him preoccupied so he doesn't rip off her arm. Grabbing his choker, I can feel his growl vibrate through my arm. He's absolutely not interested in the blonde other than as a chew toy.

Dammit, Reggie, work with me here, buddy.

"Sorry, he's in a bad mood," I tell my potential playmate. "But I'm not."

She turns her attention and bats her blue eyes at me. Reg lets out a small snarl.

She takes a quick step back. "I don't think he likes me. But I've got to catch up with my friends anyway." She waves and walks off. Damn, she must have had some really bad karma for Reg to act that way. Most of the time he'll settle in and endure baby talk for a ten minute head scratch.

I'm temporarily blinded as I walk into the dimly lit Cucumber Castle. The smell of all the headshop incense is overwhelming, in a good way. Why can't someone mix up all the incenses to make that smell? Someday, I'll make my fame and fortune cooking up that incense, and I'll name it "Headshop." My eyes adjust and I see her between the racks.

"Lena? That you?"

I walk over. There's no low rumble from Reggie— he remembers her. Trying not to sound eager, I ask, "How are you?"

She gives me an "Imagine seeing you here" smile. We manage an awkward hug and kiss on the cheek. I can't tell if she's pissed that I left her in the middle of the night, but I'm guessing she is. She plays with some belts and beads on the rack, looking everywhere but at me.

"So, what are you up to today?" I ask.

She tells me about the English paper she has to finish by Monday. I tell her about the research I'm supposed to be doing. After that, the lull is deafening.

"Well, see ya," she says, heading toward the door.

"Uh, yeah, see ya around." I scramble for a recovery line. "Hey, you want to grab a couple beers at the Robin Hood tonight? I think I owe you."

She turns around slowly. "Sorry, can't... I'm ... busy... writing that paper."

"How 'bout if I stop by for a few minutes?"

"Well... ok... maybe... for a few minutes. But no beer. And I'm not smoking."

"No problem."

I pick up a bottle of Kama Sutra oil. "Hey, do you have any oil at your place?"

She glances at the bottle in my hand. *"No, I don't."*

"Okay, I'll bring my own." I can barely keep a straight face as she jerks the door open and hurries out.

Chapter Thirteen
Study Break

Lena

*J*ournal:

Two years ago today, my life changed forever. The night Jamie and I celebrated her new driver's license by driving up the coast to watch the sun set. It didn't register that it was Dad's UPS truck in the Beach Café parking lot until he opened the restaurant door. His arm was around the waist of some woman, her fluffy blonde hair against his shoulder as they walked toward his truck. "They're probably just friends," my best friend said, trying to soften the blow. I can still hear him pulling into our driveway as I was getting ready for school. See him sitting at the table with Mom, having breakfast, reading the paper like it was a normal day.

It's 11:00 p.m. and my roommates are gone. Out enjoying life while I'm lying on the couch watching *Somebody Up There Likes Me* with Paul Newman. The boxing scenes turn my stomach, but they're distracting me from thoughts that have been slapping me around since ten o'clock, the absolute outer edge of study break time. I'm caught cold. Sucker punched.

The doorbell rings. I drag myself off the couch. Who forgot their key, again? I open the door and there's Kris, smiling and holding a grocery bag.

"Hi," he says, "Hungry?"

Who the hell does he think he is? *I'm not just a late-night stand. Hurry. Slam the door. Now. Before it's too—*

"Sure," I mumble. He walks in and heads for the kitchen. *Back in the ring, again.*

He spills brownie mix, eggs, and a bag of grass across the kitchen table. His eyes sparkle as he hands me a bottle of Mazola cooking oil. "I got the oil," he says, grinning. Okay, he got me.

Whipping up his herbal brownies, he jabbers away like it's noon instead of midnight. I try to act nonchalant, like I always have dates that make me lick brownie batter in the middle of the night. But I don't, and it's fun. And that irks me.

Thirty minutes later, the brownies are done. He reaches into his magic bag and pulls out an album.

"Ever hear Todd Rundgren?"

"I don't think so."

"He's got a whole different sound. Wait 'til you hear it."

We glide upstairs. One thing leads to another and once again we're rolling around the shag rug tangling with my yes, no, maybe, and *what ifs*. Damn. The feeling is right. The guy is right. So, what's wrong? I'm not sure.

I yield to the chocolaty candle glow moment with one hell of a kisser. And that little thing he does—Oh! He's got all the right moves. Round and round we swirl, dizzily on the edge. Then we plummet over. Freefalling.

I wake up cocooned in Kris's arms. The stereo needle crackles, caught in the final groove of the record. I reach over and turn it off. Morning light sifts through the window and onto the pages of my internal rule book lying scattered on the floor with our clothes. Friend, lover, free spirit. What's being in love got to do with anything? I can live in the moment like everyone else. And stay true to myself.

I feel a tickle on my toes. Blue, the house's newly adopted kitten, has a foot fetish. I push him off but he creeps back under the quilt.

Kris wiggles awake. He nudges Blue off the bed.

"Sorry," I say as Blue purrs and jumps between us, curling up. "You don't like cats?"

"They aren't that bright."

"Smarter than dogs."

"Oh, c'mon," Kris says. "Look, if I tell Reg to stop doing something, he stops. If I tell him to sit, he sits."

I roll my eyes. "Oh, right, obedience is a real measure of intelligence."

"Cats do whatever the hell they want."

"I rest my case," I say, stroking Blue's black and white fur. Yin and Yang wrapped into one. Right on cue, Blue gives me an annoyed look and jumps down. I try to grab him, but he scampers away.

"I rest mine," Kris says.

I poke his side. He snickers and turns away.

"Ticklish?" I go after him with gusto. He grabs my arms and pins them to my side.

"I happen to know something about cats," he says. "Back in high school I got into a little legal trouble, stealing street signs. And my dad sentenced me to work in the Ohio State psyche lab with cats. They proved cat brains are smaller than dog brains."

"What did you do at the lab? Not experiments, I hope." I wriggle out of his grip.

"Nope. I cleaned the cages and held the kittens. Kept them from going wild."

No wonder he's such a good cuddler, I think, snuggling against his chest. "What a cake job."

"It would've been, but I'm allergic to cats. I wheezed my way through the job."

"Why didn't you tell me? Now I feel bad letting Blue get under the quilt."

"One isn't bad. Being in a room with a bunch of them is the problem. But there were some fringe benefits. I got to name them."

"How cool! How many were there?"

"Eighty."

"Oh wow, I'd name them after all my favorite book characters, like Oliver or Macbeth or Lady Chatterley. Or—hey, I got it: Steppenwolf!"

"Uh-huh."

"So, what did you name them?"

"Suzanne… Michelle… Darlene… Cassandra."

"So, are these girls you knew, or what?" I lean up on my elbow with an indignant look.

Kris smiles and gathers me back in his arms.

"What kind of exotic summer job did *you* have?" he asks.

"Worked at an amusement park."

"Running the rides?"

"No, I was a greeter. Got my picture taken with the kiddies. Dressed as Alice in Wonderland."

"You? Alice is a blonde!"

"You have a thing for blondes, don't you?" I poke him in the side.

"Yeah, and brunettes and redheads too."

I pull the pillow out from under his head and press it over his face. "C'mon, say it. Say it. Blondes are more fun."

A muffled sound comes out from under the pillow. I lift it up and climb on top of him. I shake my head back and forth, sweeping my hair over his face. "Are… they… really… more fun?"

He twists a handful of my curls around his fingers, then tugs. "It's all advertising hype."

I pull back and roll off of him. "Not in California. There, it's all about long, straight, and blonde. Not dark and frizzy."

Kris holds his hands up like a movie director framing a scene, eyeballing me. "Your curls make one of those fancy frames that all those old famous pictures have."

"But those frames are gold!" I laugh. No guy has ever said anything nice about my hair. I feel myself easing into a warm safe place.

Kris rolls his eyes. "So, why are you going back to California if it's all about blondes?"

I exaggerate a sigh, but my heart feels a pinch. "I told you why."

"Oh, right. The ticket to France."

"Some part inside of me needs to go."

Kris pulls me close. "Which part?"

I lay my head on his shoulder. "I don't know. That's what I need to find out."

Chapter Fourteen
Walking Reggie

Kris

We're just a few weeks into seeing each other and Lena and I are doing the "I like you a lot, but I don't want to seem desperate" tango. It's quite a dance.

One step forward—I like spending the night with you.

Two steps back—But it doesn't mean we're committed.

This should be fine with me. I'm the guy who's gone crazy with wild ones who've turned me inside out. But this is different. It feels like Lena is turning me outside in.

She has no filters. She shares hurts and humiliations, struggles and dreams. I'm practiced at the art of listening to women. Their stories usually pour through me like a sieve. But Lena's stories get stuck inside me. I know her. Feel her. Like, I know she's upset over her parents' divorce and it makes her feel like she's split in half. We have a stream of consciousness between us. No thought or topic is untouched. We break ourselves down into little parts and then we fit our parts together like a jigsaw puzzle.

I've never had anyone listen to me so hard. Except Reg. And right now he's letting me know it's time for a midnight walk.

I glance at Lena. She's asleep, she's never up this late. As usual Reggie and I are left to our own devices, or should I say vices? I get up as quietly as I can and go downstairs to bring Reg up from the basement, along with a couple lids from my stash. It's hidden between the floor joists, but I keep the scales and baggies at my place. The money is a different story. It's spread out in several places. You can never be too careful.

Lids in hand, we head toward the front door for some door-to-door deliveries. I sell a few ounces a week to close friends, but I don't mess with people I don't know. Too easy to get taken down. And the last thing I need to do is draw attention to my connection, Cousin Frankie. All I need is a few extra bucks and an ounce every now and then for myself. I'm not sure if Lena's cool with me dealing, but she doesn't ask and I don't explain.

I put the old rope leash around Reggie's neck and he starts jumping around as we head out the side door toward our well-worn path across town. I know every one of Reg's favorite trees, building corners, and fire hydrants by heart. Even when I'm alone, habit makes me pause at them. How does an eighty pound dog carry that much pee? I bet he could put out the Empire State Building if it was on fire.

We're barely out of the yard when Reggie muscles up to full attention. His favorite pastime, like mine, is coming our way. A female. Sunshine, the Golden Retriever from two doors down, probably out for last call. She comes wagging down the sidewalk to greet her fuzzy tough guy. They do the butt sniffing shuffle, 'til Reggie tries to get lucky. Sunshine stops that as quickly as it starts. Probably a good thing—that would be a weird mix. Golden and Airedale, a loveable dog with a nasty streak. Dani, Sunshine's owner, pokes her head out the door. Some nights Dani joins us on our walks. But tonight, I've got some business to take care of, so I'm glad when she lets out a whistle that has Sunshine tearing for home.

Off again, toward downtown, Lena weighs on my thoughts.

"I wish she'd get on the pill, Reg. What's she waiting for?"

I'd do it if they had one for guys. Rubbers blow the spontaneity, not to mention I feel like a high school kid buying them at the drug store. I'm not sure what I'd do if she got pregnant. Abortions cost money and New York is a long way away. When the hell will Ohio legalize it?

"There's enough unwanted kids and pups in the world, right Reg?"

Reggie looks up at me, and then snaps his head toward two pretty girls jaywalking across Main Street. As they get close, they start baby-talking to Reggie. It's a great fringe benefit, horning in on the chicks Reggie draws in. Harmless fun, but I get the feeling that Lena doesn't see it that way.

The shorter girl rubs Reggie's head. The taller one seems more interested in me. She invites me to their vague impromptu party. I play it cool and extricate myself from their friendly, "Are you sure?" hugs.

As we watch them walk away, Reg strains at his leash to follow. "Sorry, not tonight Reg," I say, holding tight.

I make a few stops and wind up at Bill's house. He's a late nighter too. I let him try my stash. He rolls a tight one then dumps the leftovers from my stash into his bag. Cheap bastard.

By the time Bill and I finish the jay, it's pushing one a.m. Reg and I head back to Lena's with a good buzz. We walk past Sophie's house. A familiar heaviness comes over me. I loved the sound of her voice. Her smile, like her personality, was always on—radiant and unique. Her long auburn hair smelled of summer. And when she walked into a room, people couldn't help but be drawn to her. She was oblivious to it all. But that was Sophie's charm, her unassuming nature.

She was way out of my league, the fact that she chose me was a big rush. Everyone, including me, thought she was 'The One.' The problem is I think they're all 'The One,' even though I've had the same thought a hundred times before. Then the nagging doubts creep inside my head until I weigh her every move, every word. Eventually I begin to think she's not the person I imagined she was. Then the relationship unravels and the latest beautiful girl floats away.

I sigh. "Nothin' lasts forever. Better to leave than be left. Right, Reggie?" He cocks his head and I reach down to pet it.

Deep inside, I desperately wanted to touch and be touched by Sophie.

"Do you think there's something wrong with me, Reg? Why can't I connect?" I say, remembering the day I ended it with her, and how she asked, "Why?"

I answered with, "I'm just not feeling it anymore." Not wanting to sound like a complete schmuck, I hurriedly added, "And that's not fair to you."

She left in tears.

I look down at Reg, shaking my head.

"I wonder if this is how it's always gonna be? Caring too much and feeling too little."

Reggie pulls me around the corner and up the hill to the white house on Willow Street. He's ready for home. And so am I.

Chapter Fifteen
Beginnings

Lena

Journal: Falling, falling, plummeting...Into each other... Into ourselves. I'm cartwheeling in the moment with Kris. His silky blue eyes, his gentle brown hair. The taste of his words, the scent of his thoughts. Classes are irrelevant. The dust of ancient history dissolves in his ocean gaze. Sonnets pulse with every breath. I diagram the sentences of his touch.

Kris reads my words while they're still inside me. He listens to them rubbing against my soul. His steady hands massage the quirks that push me toward dark edges, edges that fill the pages of my journal... in the time before Kris. Now my words smile back at me. Happily. Finally. California slumbers under the bed, like a hibernating bear.

"Listen to this, Lena," Kris says softly. "Prather really has it down. He thinks my thoughts. It blows me away."

I nestle into his favorite poems until he closes the book. We find each other under the quilt, scattering unread textbooks and half-written papers. Candlesticks flicker light through the room. Incense twirls in tendrils around us. Todd Rundgren sings the songs I now know by heart. Kris's eyes soak me in. I tread in their still water. They say 'I love you.' My eyes say it back. His mouth whispers the words. But mine can't. Not yet. Because everything is almost perfect...

Almost.

It's after midnight. The empty place in bed pulls me from my dreams. Kris isn't here. Because it's at this precise hour that Reggie always needs a walk. There's more to this than meets my wary eye—the eye that wants to give him 'the look' our quasi-open relationship says I have no right to give.

He always invites me to go, but he also knows when I go to sleep. So, Mr. Night Owl gets no credit for asking. But I'm reasonable. Dogs need a walk, Kris needs a smoke. There's no doubt in my mind that a smoke and a walk is all that's going on. No doubt at all.

But around 1:00 a.m., my insecurity starts talking. *Where is he? And why? Who's he with? What are they doing?*

Jealousy has the answer. She's a familiar friend. She whispers in my ear, "Open your eyes, you idiot." She points out worldly temptresses I'm too naive to notice. The woman next door, with the hair wisping, not frizzing, around her neck. The waitress at the café wearing tights and a mini-skirt, not patched jeans and a sweatshirt. And all the other girls from his past. Jealousy lines them up for my scrutiny. Smaller nose and straighter teeth. Check. Poutier lips and bigger boobs. Check.

"He loves me," I say aloud.

Jealousy smiles, her green eyes flashing as she keeps me company while I watch minutes turn into hours. When I finally hear his footsteps on the landing, my stomach turns with the doorknob. When I feel his arms slide around me, I pull away.

"Where have you been? Who were you with? What did you do? WHY DO YOU DO IT?" The more he tells me, the more I don't want to hear. I want him to stop. I want him to go. I want him to stay. I want him to make me believe, understand, accept. But Jealousy pounds the gavel and cross-examines him. She tells me what to say and what not to do. Kris recognizes her and calls her out. She chews up his words and spits them back at him. He can't understand her, tries to reassure her. But she hisses at his alibis and indicts innocent bystanders. Then Kris gathers me up, kissing me a hundred different ways. She fights it at first, then weakens and fades away until all is right with the world again.

But she knows where to find me.

Chapter Sixteen
Dirty Laundry 101

Kris

Love is a word I've never shied away from. And I've used it in many ways.

I love you right now, I love what we're doing, I love you today, tonight, this week, this month.

I'm a master at throwing it around. And I always got it back. 'Til now.

Lena won't say it. It's a word that she seems to attach to a carved-in-granite commitment. To her, our relationship is casual. "No commitments!"

So, I change my tack. I dump my 'I love you.' It doesn't matter to her, why should it matter to me? If this happened in a past relationship, I'd be looking for the exit ramp. But for some reason I let things play out. In the meantime, my jeans are beyond gross and I'm down to my last pair of inside-out underwear. Lena's working a double shift, so I grab Reg and we head to the laundromat.

The weatherman said a high in the 50's today so my present fashion statement is low-top Converse tennis shoes, no socks, and green and gold high school gym shorts perfectly matched with my white button-down dress shirt. I enter the front door and survey the situation. Halloween has nothing on this crowd. And there are at least three other people who dressed worse than me.

These washing machines are made to survive a nuclear holocaust and I pack my washer to beyond capacity. Whether I wore it once or fifteen times, it all goes in. The way I see it, each load costs me two happy hour beers.

Suds and Duds is a great place to meet women because we're all prisoners in this sweat box. There are thirty washing machines and fifteen giant dryers. The usual pack of predators is here today with their hands full of quarters, ready to pounce. I once made the mistake of leaving during a spin cycle to get a pack of smokes. In the time it took to walk across the street and back, my wet clothes were spread out on the tops of four washing machines. And someone had the balls to rip off my Grateful Dead T-shirt and my favorite navy surplus bellbottoms, the pair with the mushroom patch that Sophie sewed on. That'll never happen again.

I sit on top of the washer crammed with two weeks of my sweat and filth. Reggie watches warily as the agitator wobbles back and forth. I'm trying to focus on my textbook when a pair of curvy legs in cut-offs walks in front of me. I'd recognize that five-foot gymnast body anywhere. I look into Eve's face, her emerald eyes, dimpled cheeks, and perfect teeth. She smiles as she puts her basket down and pets Reggie.

"Hi, Kris. How've you been? I never see you anymore."

I jump off the washer and hug her. "Great. Everything's cool."

She scans the room and frowns. "No free washers. This'll cut into my workout time. I'm desperate. I've got a time slot at the gym."

"My wash cycle just started." My voice rises as an unbalanced washer two machines away begins to thump out a bass beat. "I can take some things, well, a bunch of things out, and we can share."

Eve wrinkles her nose. "Huh?"

I lean in closer. "We can share!"

Eve shakes her blonde ponytail and shouts, "I know what's in there. But maybe…" She points to her half-filled basket. "Well… maybe if we just mix… personals?"

I stop my washer and unload five pairs of grimy jeans and several shirts into my basket, leaving my 'personals.' I watch her carefully put her things in, remembering her penchant for silk and satin.

I hop back onto the machine and she leans against a dryer.

"So," she says. "Seeing anyone?"

I laugh. Eve never wastes any time getting to the point. "I just started seeing someone, but not sure where it's going."

"Do I know her?"

"Maybe. Lena Borelli? She was in our Shakespeare class last year."

She scrunches her brows. "Hmm. Wavy dark hair?"

"Yep."

"Oh, I think I remember her."

"What about you?" I ask. "Seeing anyone?" Stupid question. When we were seeing each other Eve always had one guy or another knocking on her door. Never bothered me, because I was also seeing Gwen. Seemed to work for both of us.

"Nobody too special." She steps forward and puts her hands on my knees. "Umm, speaking of Shakespeare, remember how I got you through that class?" She bats her big green eyes.

I laugh, remembering her creative tutoring methods. "Strip Shakespeare" was the most effective classical conditioning experiment I ever participated in. Certain lines are locked in my memory and not for Shakespearean reasons.

"Math class is kicking my butt," she says. "But I know you aced it. How 'bout you repay the favor? And you can name the price."

"Yeah, no problem. When?"

"Tonight? I have homework due tomorrow."

I do some quick calculations. Lena's working 'til ten. "Seven okay?"

"Sure. Dunbar?"

"Yeah, I'll be in my room," I say.

"Can you keep my laundry too? I really need to get to the gym. Regional meets coming up. I'll get it from you tonight."

"Sure thing."

***

I drop Reggie off at Cheet's and I head back to my dorm. Killing time 'til Eve comes over, I take Hugh Prather's book *Notes to Myself* off my desk. It's like reading my journal, if I kept one. I see all the things I let slide by, and I have this unsettling feeling that maybe I don't really know myself as well as I think. But I know one thing: I'm tired of rushing into relationships, only to be plotting my way out at the same time. Disconnecting. I still don't know where I stand with Lena. She says one thing, then acts completely different. Makes it hard to respond to her. I'm not sure what she needs. Or is it my needs I'm worried about?

It's seven o'clock when there's the knock on the door. It's got to be Eve. I'm glad the summer break-up didn't screw up the... friendship. I move the basket of 'personals' out of the way and open the door. Eve's wearing a light coat and is clutching a book to her chest. She's wearing the same smile I've seen her put on for the judges when she nails the perfect landing off the balance beam. Her hair falls off her shoulders as she puts her book on my bed. When she takes off her jacket, I realize I had washed *all* of her 'personals.' Eve's very thin and gauzy shirt scores an '11' from this judge. And she's wearing my favorite perfume, too.

We make ourselves comfortable on my bed. Eve slips off her shoes, puts my pillows against the wall and leans back. She opens her math book and snuggles close. "I miss hanging out like this," she says.

"Me, too," slips out.

Eve turns and breathes into my ear, "I don't understand polynomials at all. Can we start at the very beginning?"

I focus on the page. "Well, they're simple to break down. Do you know the formula?"

"I'm not sure," she says, sliding her hand under the book onto my thigh. "Maybe we should take a break first."

I turn and before I can say a word, we're kissing. She presses into me. Her breasts feel just as I remember, firm and soft. Her book falls to the floor. We pull off our clothes. Heavy breathing. Skin on skin. Like nothing's changed since our last time together.

And then the question.

Eve asks between breaths. "What about... Lena?"

A knife turns in my stomach. Eve never asked about Gwen last year. She knows the rules. But, somehow, this feels different. I pull back and exhale.

Everything comes to an awkward halt.

Chapter Seventeen
Friends and Lovers

Lena

*J*ournal:

    Kris and I are lovers. Lovers. The word follows me to school, sits with me in class, and waits for me after work. It wriggles around while I read, write, clear tables. Lovers. It tickles and whispers and shouts, trying its best to drown out the chorus of Kris's exes who've had their "I love you" cancelled.

"Maybe that's my main attraction," I say, sitting on Ginny's bed, petting Blue stretched out beside me.

"What?" Ginny asks, smearing free makeup samples she got from her job on my face.

"That I come with a time limit," I say. "That I'm going back to California."

"Do you ever talk about the future?" asks Ginny.

"He says he loves me, but we both know I'm leaving."

"So, what does that mean?"

"I don't know." I pick up the hand mirror from my lap and peer into it. "This is too light. I look like a ghost."

"We'll put blush over it. Why don't you just stay? See where this thing with Kris goes?" She brings out black eyeliner and dips the brush in a small bowl of water. "Close your eyes."

"Careful with that. Black makes me look hard," I say, then close my eyes. "Anyway, I can't stay—I might never get this chance again."

"I'll add some pink. Pink shadow is good for brown eyes."

"Pink? All the way up to my eyebrows?" I sigh. "It's hard, this love thing."

Ginny's steady hand lines my eyes. "Love is weird. You ruin it if you over-analyze it." She sweeps frosted pink across my lips. I press them together, tasting the lipstick, then look into my hand mirror.

"Kris doesn't analyze anything. He lives in the moment," I say. "This tastes good. What is it?"

"Cotton Candy. Well, just enjoy the moment, then. Live for today, like the song says."

"I'm trying. I really want to," I whine. "Everyone else is."

"I know Kris is," Ginny murmurs.

I lower the mirror and eye her. "What do you mean?"

She shrugs. "Well... I didn't want to make a big deal about it, but I saw him and Reggie with the girl a few doors down. The one with that big dog."

"Oh, Dani. They're friends. They do the dog walk thing."

Ginny's large green eyes are steady on mine. "They were at the park. Flying kites." Ginny registers the look on my face and adds, "With the dogs."

Acid gurgles in my gut. I take a breath, hold it for three seconds, and exhale. "We're not into that 'opposite sexes can't be friends' crap. Male or female, it doesn't make a difference." I raise the mirror again. *Shouldn't make a difference.*

"Right on. Look up." She rubs rose-colored cream on my cheeks. "That's what being liberated is all about."

"Just because you're in a relationship, does it mean you're not allowed to have friends?" I say.

"Of course not, as long as he comes home to you every night."

"Yeah, he comes home to me—and Reggie." I make a face. "I think he tells Reggie things he doesn't tell me."

Ginny laughs. "I guess I'm your Reggie then."

Hmm. I don't confide deep dark things to Ginny. That goes in my journal. But I do talk to her about Kris. She likes him, but she has a definite checklist of relationship do's and don'ts, and he falls short. She says the trick is to find someone who loves you more than you love them. Then you'll always be treated special and have no reason to feel jealous. I was in a relationship like that, and she's right, there's no jealousy. But there's no passion either. Just some guilt. No, the trick is to be reasonable. If he has friends, so can I. But is it possible to be reasonable and passionate? Guess I'll have to find out.

"By the way," I say, "this guy who was in my French class last year wants to get together at that new French restaurant next Saturday."

"Who's that?"

"His name's Rod. He works at Cucumber Castle."

"Kris going too?"

"No. He doesn't, well, you know, speak French. He'd feel out of place."

Ginny gives me a look. "You haven't told him."

"Not yet, but I will," I say. "There's nothing wrong with going out with a friend. Keeps things from getting boring."

"Who's bored?" asks Ginny.

"Nobody… yet." I picture Kris flying a kite. "Anyway, we both agreed in the beginning—no commitments."

"Then no problem." Ginny steps back and throws her arms in the air. "*Voila!* A sexy new you."

I stare at my face in the mirror, thinking about dinner with Rod. Thinking Kris is not going to go for it.

Ginny reads my mind. "Maybe Rod will like sneaking around with you."

"Stop it," my sexy pink lips say. "He's just a friend."

***

Kris takes one look at me and laughs. "I see Ginny got to you again."

My cotton candy smile droops. I feel like a clown. Not sexy. Kris sits beside me.

"Why do you let her put that junk on you? You're prettier without it."

I take a deep breath. Please don't compliment me now. "Because." I can't do it. "Because I needed a distraction. I'm flunking anthropology."

"Maybe I can help." Kris begins to massage my shoulders. "Pink is my new favorite color," he mumbles into my neck.

I'm going down in flames. Pulling back, I moan, "I'm serious. We're in the physical unit and it's all math. I want to study the story of man, not his molecules."

I've never been a fan of equations where 'A' plus 'B' equals 'C'. I'm more like my philosophy professor, who argues, "'A' plus 'B' doesn't always equal 'C'." I glance at Kris. Like passion plus intimacy doesn't always equal commitment. And love minus commitment doesn't always equal zero.

Kris's strong hands drain the tension from my neck. I've got to stop stalling—I need to tell him about Rod. He doesn't have double standards. If he can have friends of the opposite sex, so can I. What's the difference between eating at a French restaurant and flying a kite?

I blurt it out. The friend, the dinner.

Kris shrugs it off as no big deal.

But I notice a look in his eyes. I stare at him for a moment, trying my best to decipher the meaning. If only I knew what he thinks 'C' will equal.

"I'll miss ya," he says and gives me half a hug.

Chapter Eighteen
The Date

Kris

I started out unattached and liked it that way. Alone, but not lonely. Come and go as I please. These days it's different. There's a lot less go and a lot more stay. Reggie and I are practically living with Lena, but she still hasn't returned an 'I love you.'

I'm in a holding pattern, ready to land, but held at bay by her constant reminders of our "casual" relationship. And her latest announcement doesn't help matters. Did someone narc on me about my study-break with Eve? What's to rat about? *Almost* doing it doesn't count. *C'est la* fucking *vie*. I'll play her game.

The rest of the week I play it down. Saturday night, I hang around, getting high with her roommates while she gets ready. It's weird, but I can't think of anything else to do. I give her a stupid peck on the lips as she leaves for her stupid date.

"Know what, Reg? She's not the only one with a chummy classmate." That cute chick in astronomy, Pam, has asked me more than once to come over and check out her telescope. I can get into a little Milky Way. Now where the hell did I put that phone number?

I drop Reg off at Cheet's place and head back to my dorm. I rustle through my desk drawer and find the piece of paper Pam slipped me at Mike's party. Conveniently, she lives in the dorm across the street and isn't busy. She asks if she could bring her telescope over to my place because we'd have a better shot of seeing Venus from that angle. Any angle to get a chance at Venus works for me.

I clear out a space at the window for the telescope and light up the lava lamp. Next thing I know, it's early Sunday morning and my arm is asleep because my stargazing partner is using it as a pillow. So what? Ms. No Commitment has made it perfectly clear that nothing's defined. An assortment of questions ran rampant in my brain throughout the night and are starting up again. Why am I doing this? What's Lena doing now?

This is bullshit! I shouldn't be second guessing myself. Ever. My date is everything I could want and she isn't hesitant at all. But I know it's my first step back to nothing. Damn it. I don't need Lena. Why do I stay? I should've hit the road, a long time ago—like I always do.

At 8:00 a.m. my phone rings. Only one person I know wakes up this early on a Sunday.

"Aren't you going to get that?" says a sleepy voice next to my ear.

"They'll call back."

By noon it's rung four more times. One o'clock brings a pounding on the door. Pam rolls over and gives me a fishy expression. After the knocking stops and the footsteps recede, I admit that I might have been kind of involved with another person recently, but I thought the relationship was on the rocks. I tense up for the worst.

Pam says, "I've been through that. Things can get touchy." She leaves, telling me she had a good time and if things don't work out…

But I can only think of Lena. The phone rings again. I grab my jacket. We've got to do this thing—whatever it is—face to face.

I climb the stairs to the attic with slow, heavy steps. I don't feel guilty, only uneasy. I don't want to end it, but something's got to give. My gaze rises over the attic floor. Lena's sitting on the corner of her bed with Blue on her lap. Her journal's next to her. I can only imagine what she wrote.

"So?" I say, standing at the foot of the bed.

She closes the journal and leans over to slide it onto the desk. Blue jumps down and slinks away. "So, what?"

"Did you have your French fun?"

Now I get the full glare. "No. Did you have yours?"

"This was your idea, not mine." I sit down on the end of the bed.

"My idea was there's nothing wrong with going out with a friend."

"C'mon, that was a date."

"I just wanted to have dinner with a guy, a friend, from my French class at a French restaurant."

"And?"

"And the whole time I kept thinking I'd rather be listening to albums in the attic... with you." Her voice rises. "I wanted to see if I could go out and not feel my gut wrench wondering if you're doing the same thing." She picks up a pillow and throws it at me. "And the answer is no—I can't."

"Then what the hell do you want?" I throw the pillow down.

"I thought *you* wanted an open relationship," she says.

"But you want *me* to only want *you*."

She purses her lips, I go on. "Look you're the one that keeps saying 'no commitments, no commitments.' Either you want one or you don't."

"What about the 'friends and lovers' thing?"

"Huh?"

"You said, 'Can't friends be lovers?' our first night up here."

"What?" I throw my hands up into the air. "We've been together night and day since then. I thought we were way beyond that."

She's staring out the window. I've got to dig deeper. "You're fooling yourself, Lena."

She turns. Her face drawn, eyes tense. "I can't trust my feelings. They change from one minute to the next. Yours do too. I know your history."

We sit in silence.

She fidgets and twists. "I tried not to let this happen." Her voice is ragged. "I let you break all my rules."

I sigh and slide over to her. "Well, whether we wanted it to happen or not, it has."

She half smiles. "So, are we friends or lovers?"

I put my arm around her. "What do you think?"

Her voice softens. "I just don't want us to get hurt."

"By what?"

"By what could happen tomorrow."

"Tomorrow?" I put my hands on either side of her face and stare into red watery eyes. "We need to take care of us today."

Chapter Nineteen
The Pill

Lena

*J*ournal:

Now that I'm in a relationship that I wasn't looking for. Now that I'm totally wrapped up in the moment of being in love when I never thought you could wrap love up in a moment. Now that I'm getting into sex and love along with everyone else in my generation... It's time to stop worrying about the Catholic Church and what my parents think, and start worrying about getting pregnant. It's time to go on The Pill.

"What will the exam be like? What kinds of questions will they ask us? Will they want to know everything we do and who we do it with?" Ginny's voice is uneasy as we sit on the attic steps reading a Planned Parenthood flyer.

"I heard the Pill has some funky side effects," I say. "And I'm sure I'd have them. My body overreacts to everything." One No-Doz tablet keeps me wired for two days. A couple of hits on the bong knock me flat. If I ever took acid, I'd probably end up on the cover of *Life* magazine balancing on a fire escape.

"Planned Parenthood has regular doctors and nurses. It's got to be safe, or they wouldn't give it to you," Ginny says.

"Yeah, you're right, they wouldn't."

"What are you doing now?" Ginny asks.

I hesitate. How much of this is considered intimate information? Would Kris tell his best friend Mike what we do? "We uh, you know, he... we're careful."

"Risky."

I give her a half-hearted shrug. "I know. But Kris hates using rubbers."

"It's a pain, but it beats the alternative. I keep one in my purse. Just in case."

"God, what would I do if I got pregnant? I can't imagine having a baby, let alone taking care of one."

Ginny nods and lowers her voice. "A girl I worked with last summer went to New York for an abortion. She was only gone a few days. She said there was nothing to it."

"Nothing except a few hundred bucks. Where would I get that? Couldn't very well ask my parents."

"There's always a med student," says Ginny. "I hear they do it cheap."

I shudder. "I don't think I could go through with it. Even if I had a real doctor."

"Why? You're not against it, are you?"

"No, but... I don't know." I hug my knees. "I get uptight when I can't change my mind about stuff. Some people make a choice, deal with the consequences, and move on. But I'm not one of them. I can't let go of things easily."

"Well, I'd never get one, either," Ginny says.

I look at her with surprise. I can't picture Ginny with a baby.

"But I don't judge anyone who does. Like they say, 'her body, her choice.'" Ginny locks her gaze on me. "What do you think Kris would say if you got pregnant?"

I tilt my head. We've never talked about it. A question lodges in my mind. Why not? We talk about everything else. Maybe he thinks it's a no-brainer. "He'd probably say, 'Get an abortion.'"

"Maybe he'd ask you to marry him," Ginny says. "It wouldn't be much of a change—you're together night and day as it is."

"That's different. There's no kid."

Images spin through my mind of couples wheeling their strollers around married-student housing on campus. No way are we ready for that. My best move would be to go to some home for unwed mothers and put the baby up for adoption. I'm going to California anyway, so Kris would never know. But then I'd spend the rest of my life wondering what happened to our child.

"I'm making the call," Ginny says, interrupting my thoughts. "Should've done it months ago. Better safe than sorry." She gets up and walks toward the phone, taking the flyer with her. "We'll go together."

I let out a long exhale. "Okay."

As Ginny picks up the phone, I feel tension and worry drain from my body, replaced by a sort of exultation. I feel free! Is this the way guys feel? I'll ask Kris. I want him to know that it's more than having the freedom to love in the moment. That for me, going on the Pill, symbolizes a real commitment. Committing myself—to the person I love.

Chapter Twenty
Touchy Situation

Kris

Leaving Lena's, I make the usual ten-minute pit stop at my dorm for a shower and a change of clothes before class. I'm gathering my Dr. Bronner's, towels, and some reasonably clean duds when there's a knock on my door. I'm already late for my class, but there's no getting around it—I've got to go through my door to get to the showers. Reaching for the knob, I dial up the shortest responses and actions for every scenario: you can borrow the album, I'm out of pot, my class notes are for shit...

I crack the door wide enough to stick my head out and my date, Pam the astronomer, is leaning on my door jamb.

"Can I come in?" she asks.

I open the door with a towel wrapped around my waist.

"Hi. How are ya? Did you forget something?" The last question slips out a little harsh.

"Uh, I'm okay, I guess. I just need to talk with you."

"I'm late for class like always, you know."

"I won't stay long. I don't, uh..." Tears start to brim.

My plan to steer this to a quick end crashes. "What's wrong? Are you okay?" I hug her, wondering what the problem is. We haven't exchanged more than a smile in class since that one date.

"I got some bad news from the Health Center."

Fuck! I loosen my hold as I face her. She said she was on the Pill.

"Uhh, what is it?"

She clasps her hands. "This is so hard for me."

I take a deep breath. "What's the matter, Pam?"

"They said I have gonorrhea."

My stomach drops.

"The symptoms say I got it a few weeks ago, but I didn't know. I'm so embarrassed."

She bites her bottom lip. "I don't sleep around, honest. You're only the second person I've been with in the last year. I'm not a bad person, I'm really not."

I sink down to the edge of my bed, and in the remains of my hug, I pull Pam with me. I struggle to put my thoughts together. How is this going to play out?

"I'm not a bad person. Really, I'm not."

"You're not," is all I can say to her.

This is something that happens to other people, not me. Unlike Bullhorn Bob down the hall I heard accusing some poor girl of giving him 'the clap'. I won't trash the messenger. I need all the good karma I can get. But I know everything's about to change.

She whispers, "Sorry." And that ends the conversation. I give Pam a faint smile, thank her for stopping by—God knows, some girls wouldn't have—and watch her walk out.

Damn. Just when things are going good.

Class has become irrelevant. I wander around campus, then go over to Cheet's and let Reg out of the fenced-in yard where he hangs out when we're in class. We sit on the porch.

"How the hell am I gonna tell her, Reg?" I stare into his trusting eyes. "Um, Lena, I've got to tell you something. It's embarrassing, but you've got to know." My mind is a nonstop flurry of scenes and consequences. Not one of them ends with Lena reassuring me that I'm a good person.

I drag my feet up the attic stairs. Parting the curtain, I walk over to where Lena's shuffling through some notes at her desk. "Hey, babe."

She puts the papers aside and gets up from her desk to put her arms around my waist. I brush my lips against her cheek, hold her hands, and look directly in her eyes.

"Um, Lena, I've got to tell you something. It's kind of embarrassing."

"Uh… huh." Lena's smile shrinks, and she slips on her guarded tone. "What is it?"

I feel the heat spread over my face and into my ears. "Well, uhhhh, ummm…" I hesitate, studying the shag carpet.

"C'mon, spit it out. Is it something to do with you and me?" Her voice tightens, like she's bracing for a strike.

"No. Not you and me. Well, kind of."

Here I go, stumbling into another awkward moment of truth. Get your shit together before Lena turns this into a game of 'Twenty Questions.' Taking a deep breath, I refocus on her. "I caught one of those diseases that takes two shots to cure."

"Two shots of what? Tequila?" Lena's small laugh trails off, as she registers my non- response. "What are you talking about?"

"The Clap."

"The Clap?" She stares at me like a fish on a hook.

Jeez, do I have to spell it out? "VEE-DEE."

"What? VD? You have VD?" She drops my hands.

My eyes dart between her face and the carpet. "I just found out. I had to tell you. Because…"

"Oh, God. Because now I have it, too." Her fingers fly to her mouth. "Oh, God."

"I'm sorry, I really am."

"VD! Jesus! What do I do? What do I do?" She does a half turn toward the desk and puts her hand on her forehead, her eyes stare up into empty space. "Don't you go blind? I won't be able to have kids."

"That's an old wives' tale." I put my hand on her shoulder. "A couple shots of penicillin cures it. Nothin' to it. We can go to the Health Center."

She jerks her shoulder away. Her eyes zero in on mine. "How long have you had it?"

"About a week. But I didn't know."

She pauses to calculate the time. "So… your date?"

"Yeah."

She puts her hands on her hips. "How did you find out? Did she call you?"

"She wouldn't do that. She came over and told me in person."

"But she would go around giving people a disease!"

"She didn't know. Someone gave it to her. It could happen to anyone."

"You mean anyone who has a one-night stand," she throws back.

"That's exactly what I mean." I nod my head in the direction of Ginny's side of the attic.

Lena angles her body so I can't read her face.

"The date thing was your idea, not mine," I say.

She lifts her hands into the air and grabs both sides of her head. "A date! A date! Dinner with a friend. Not screwing a stranger!"

"Those are your rules, not mine." I keep my gaze steady. "And she's not a stranger, she's a friend."

"Friend?" The incredulous pitch. "With a friend like that…"

"What's the big deal about friends?" I snap. "She didn't have a problem with it, so why should you?" I know I just napalmed the situation. I grab her arm, but she twists away. "Look, last week, we didn't know where we were going. I thought we were together, but you're the one who wanted it open. Well, this is what open looks like, no rules, no regrets."

Lena slams the desk with a clenched fist, knocking over a cup of pens that clatter across the desk. She turns to me, eyes flashing. "No regrets? You don't regret that you gave me a disease?"

"That's not what we're talking about and you know it."

"Well, let me tell you what my regrets are. I regret every time I bump into your past walking around campus. And now I regret that I'm attached to one of them through some nasty disease. Oh, God, and all their 'dates' too!" She starts laughing through wild-eyed tears. "It's all in the one big fucking family."

"Stop it." I grasp her shoulders. "I have a past, but it's not the sleazy one you make it out to be. Truth is I'm pretty damn picky." I let go of her shoulders and take a step back. "If you can't deal with my past, then let's get it out now and be done with it, because there's nothing either one of us can do about it."

"Get out! Go back to your other women." She punches out the words. "Screw them! That's all you want anyway."

I turn to go.

"You were just using me."

I slowly do an about-face. "Using you? What the hell are you talking about? I've never used you or anyone else. I'm here because I wanted to be here. And you wanted me here, too. Or at least I thought you did."

"You're so full of it, Mr. Congeniality. I'm not stupid. Once around the block is a dog walk. Two hours roaming around town is cruising for something or someone. And it's not me."

Shit, it's not what she thinks, but I can't bring up my pot deliveries now. I shake my head. "I always come back to you."

"For what? Your 2:00 a.m. fuck?" Her brows pinch. "I am not a slut!" She takes a roundhouse swing at me. I block it mid-air, stopping what could've been a damn good sucker punch. We stand motionless. Lena seems stunned until she yanks her arm free and backs off.

"Get away from me. Get out of my life," she says, then drops face down on the bed crying. Big shaky sobs.

This should be where I make my exit. Chalk another one up and move on. But... after several moments of indecision, I walk over and crouch next to her. Her body is trembling. She waves me away.

"Lena, I'm not perfect. If I could do it over again, it'd be different. But I can't. If you want me to leave, I will. But if I leave I'll never..."

She doesn't respond. Well, that's my answer. I stand up and pull the curtain open. I walk down the steps. So this is it.

"Wait." I hear her voice from the attic landing. "Don't go."

I stop but don't turn around. "You sure?" I turn to look up the stairs at her. "I'm just doing my best. I don't need it shoved back in my face."

"Come back. Please."

Against everything I ever thought I was and all that I think I am or ever will be, I walk back up the stairs to her. Lena lowers her gaze, presses her body into mine and turns her face up to me. Her brown eyes are wet and swollen. She holds my hand.

"I know the date was my idea and I know we don't have the same rules. But when I wake up at night and you're not here, all these thoughts run through my mind. Twisted, crazy, thoughts. It makes me hate myself. And now this." She sits on the bed and puts her head in her hands.

I sit next to her and put my arm around her. "Lena, I've always been a night owl, that's who I am. Just like you're an early bird. Do you want me to grill you about what you do every morning 'til I get up?"

"No." A small laugh. "But six in the morning is different than two in the morning. And you know it."

"Okay, who do you sit next to in your classes? What do you talk about? Who are the cooks and waiters you work with at The Hub?"

"Okay, okay, I get it." A sigh. "I just feel like I'm nothing special to you."

I stroke her hair. "That's not true. We've got something real. The rest is all superficial crap. You know I love you."

I feel her nod against my shoulder. This was my make it or break it moment. I've backed away for lesser hassles, without a second thought. But this time I didn't. Is that what makes it real? It feels like a new start and I have the sudden thought that I should talk to Cousin Frankie about cutting back the late-night deliveries. I kiss Lena on top of the head and whisper, "Do you want to go to Student Health together?"

She hesitates and then pulls away slightly. "I know you are trying to be… That might be a little too weird. I mean what if we run into…?"

I finish her question in my mind. '...all the others?' I give her a squeeze. "Okay, okay." I'll come up with something to make her feel special. Something that will be just ours.

Chapter Twenty-One
House Party

Lena

It's been raining for days. A funk has set in despite the unusually warm fall weather. We need some good vibes before the midterm moratorium on fun, so our house ignores the no-party clause in our lease and gets ready to throw a big one. We all pitch in for pizza, Kris makes his herbal brownies, and some of our older friends buy us the beer, liquor, and Boones Farm wine.

Kris asks if I want to do some 'shrooms. He likes getting high on them, but I tell him I hate mushrooms. Kris laughs at my yecchy face and says, not to worry, they're nothing like regular mushrooms. The magic ones, he says, are a whole lot chewier and taste more like shit. All I have to do, he says, is psych myself into thinking I'm chewing on a mildewy old shoe. He's so helpful.

I've always wanted to trip, I tell him, but I'm scared. And it's not like I can change my mind after I take it—unless I chuck it back up. But I'm also scared of choking on puke. Kris laughs and says they aren't that strong, and all that's going to happen is I'll feel like smiling a whole lot. That's a good thing. But I'm still not happy with the whole eating a mushroom that tastes like an old shoe thing. Grinning, Kris pulls out a Milky Way bar. Now that's helpful.

We munch down 'shroom ala chocolate bar. It tastes like crapola. Kris says it'll take an hour for me not to notice that aftertaste. We brush our teeth with his Dr. Bronner's peppermint cure-all toothpaste and make-out like crazy because new adventures always turn me on, even with mushroom breath. I'm already smiling when we go downstairs to the party.

The stereo is cranking Led Zeppelin and all the rooms are aglow with candles, black lights, lava lamps, and the burning cherries of joints and pipes. People are cozily crammed together on the living room couches, and sitting on floor pillows in the den, and lounging on the beds in the dining room. The kitchen sink is filled with beer and wine bottles. The counters overflow with quarts of this and pints of that. There are tons of people I don't recognize. Everyone is eating and drinking and smoking and talking... and smiling. I feel my smile stretching to the corners of the room, but that's me, not the 'shrooms. I always smile at people if they smile at me. It's really hard not to. Kris and I wander around. I don't think the 'shrooms are affecting me at all, so we take another one and down it with Strawberry Hill. It doesn't taste as crappy as the first one, but we still have moldy mushroom breath.

The rain lets up around midnight. The moon shows its face, beaming like a spotlight. We all run outside to do a reverse rain dance, slip-sliding in the gloppy muddy yard. I twirl around and around until I lose my balance and drop under a cottonwood. Looking up, I see its leaves falling, rotating, intertwining like pieces of glass in a kaleidoscope.

I grab onto the trunk. The leaves are spinning into pentagons and hexagons and diamonds dappled with patterns of moonlight. "Do leaves dance?" I ask Kris who's sitting beside me.

"Only the mambo."

I laugh so hard my jaw cracks. I'm snorting, grunting, gurgling. Can't stop. Kris is hooting. I lean back against the tree gasping for air. The clouds separate into layers of shadows that form gray and white doilies, the kind that cover my grandmother's tables. They drop over the earth like a lacey dome. There's a rumble and the sky shakes. The falling leaves turn into heart-winged seagulls floating to the ground. I look around and the pile of leaves we're sitting on begins to breathe. Slowly heaving up and down, back and forth, in and out. Cool. We're all breathing together.

I tell Kris and he says it's 'shroom talk and tackles me, pinning me into the moving pile of muddy seagulls. They fill the spaces where the air used to be and plaster my face and hair. He's drawing a peace sign in mud on my face, the center line down my nose. I close my eyes. When I open them, the gulls are dive-bombing us. I've got to escape. I grab Kris's hand—it transforms into a rooster's claw. I scream and push it away. Kris is trying to pull me up, but I scramble away in the mud. I feel him tugging my waist. Slowly I look. It's just his hand, not a rooster claw.

Everyone is peeling off their clothes and smearing mud over their bodies. Kris and I make squiggles on each other's face and neck. We streak it down our arms and legs, smiling so hard I think our mouths might break. Then the sky opens up and rain pours out, washing our artwork into the earth.

Some of my roomies are handing out towels and blankets. We wrap ourselves, squeeze into a corner of the parlor and flop into a couple of beanbag chairs. The paneling across from us is alive. Moving like dark brown waves in the ocean. So that's why the gulls are here. The knots in the wood crunch together, then stretch and flatten out, making faces with eyes where the mouth should be and the mouth is upside down, but they're smiling and I'm smiling and it's all so happy.

A loud shriek in the next room pierces through me.

I turn to Kris. "Is that real?"

Kris nods and jumps up. More screaming and yelling comes from the front porch. Like helium escaping from a balloon, I feel my high crashing through the parlor floor.

As the ruckus moves from the street toward the house, people start scattering. Some run out the back door, some go upstairs. I stand frozen in place. In slow motion, I make my way toward the stairs thinking Kris will follow. But when I glance back from the landing, an enormous hulk of a guy is bursting through the front door. He rips a wooden spindle from the banister and swings it around. Lamps crash against the wall. The floor length window in the hall shatters, spraying shards of glass.

"Where's the motherfucker?" he yells, whacking the telephone off the end table. The room breaks apart as I watch from above. Where's Kris?

Two more massive bodies storm in, charging through the house like horses through a gate, their mouths frothing and their eyes blazing. They push through the doors to the first-floor bedroom, bathroom, kitchen, and into the parlor where some party goers are huddled in corners.

"We're gonna find you, asshole!"

My housemate, Lyla, puts out her arms, screaming at them to stop. The biggest one with curly brown hair and long sideburns picks her up and hurls her onto the couch. More breaking, yelling, and screaming. I crouch on the landing, peering around the corner. Any minute they'll be stampeding up the stairs. I know I should hightail it up to the attic and lock the door. But first… my eyes dart around the living room and find the phone. The receiver's off the hook, but the cord runs to an outlet near the staircase. Then I spot Kris. He's standing in front of the basement door— where he put Reggie to keep him from crotch sniffing and peeing on our partygoers. His shirt is ripped. He sees me. "Run!" he yells.

Two of the giant rampaging jocks, they've got to be jocks, eyeball Kris and grin. One pushes Kris out of the way while the other grabs the basement door knob, twists and pulls.

Eighty pounds of pissed off Airedale flies out of the basement and tears into the jock's leg. His screams pierce the air, converging with frenzied barks and growls. He pries himself out of Reggie's grip and runs for the front door. Reggie turns his attention to the guy who's swinging the banister spindle at him. Lips curled, gigantic teeth bared, Reggie lets out a snarl, leaps, and locks his jaws around the spindle in the guy's hand. The guy lets Reggie have it and runs for his life, leaving the third jock trapped somewhere in the back of the house.

Kris grabs the fur on the back of Reggie's neck as he snarls and looks for someone else that wants to play. "Get the hell out!" Kris yells. "I can't hold him back much longer."

The last guy edges out of the broom closet in the kitchen. He inches his way along the wall, his gaze pinned on the furious, barking, fang-filled face of Reggie, and disappears out the side door. Reggie is really letting it rip, his bark deep and frenetic.

Most of the party guests have evaporated. My housemates pace around in various states of shock and confusion. We assess the damage and try to come up with theories for why those thugs busted into our party. Flashing lights pull up in front of the house. Kris lures Reggie into the basement with some treats and we go to talk with the police.

Half an hour later, Kris and I head up to the attic but we're too wound up to sleep. We lie in bed, going over the events. The police think that the guys got the wrong house. We massage the shape of the night out of our unsettled selves as we relive the whole party again and again until dawn.

Reggie lies on the floor beside us, chewing on his reward bone. I'm thankful for his heroic deed, but a part of me is still apprehensive.

"Do you think Reggie would go after just anybody?" I ask.

"No. He was just protecting his home and family."

"So, I'm part of his family now?"

Kris waits a moment, looking at the ceiling, then says, "Yep." He grabs my hand and squeezes it, then turns to look at me. "But keep your hands off his bone," he says with a smile.

I shake my head, smile back, then give him a kiss.

"That's a deal," I whisper.

Chapter Twenty-Two
The Letter

Lena

*J*ournal:

It's here! It's here! It's here! The letter I've been waiting for my whole life has finally arrived. I've read it so many times I know it by heart:

Dear Ms. Borelli,

Thank you for your interest in the study-abroad program. We have reviewed your qualifications and are pleased to inform you that your name is number eight on the waiting list. You will be informed of any changes to your status during Spring quarter 1971.

California State Board of Regents

My stomach is fizzing like champagne. My head is swimming in the Seine. My mouth waters for chocolate croissants. I made it to the waiting list! But I shouldn't get my hopes up—would the seven people ahead of me really reject a program they had applied for? Then again, a lot of things could happen between now and next September. I have a chance and that's all that counts. I can't wait to share my news with Kris. Wait. How will he take it? Maybe I shouldn't tell him yet. Waiting would be the smart thing, my head tells me. But my heart is louder.

I need to be honest with him.

I sit on the bed with Blue, listening to his steady purr, nervously stroking his fur. Waiting. Listening, until I hear Kris's footsteps on the stairs. He sits beside me and I hand him the letter. He reads it slowly, then puts his arm around me.

"That's great, Lena."

My words fly around the room. I'm talking, not even sure what I'm saying. Something about how it doesn't change things between us. How I'll probably never get off the waiting list. Half-truths and half-wishes scatter in all directions. He listens, starts to respond, then stops and just holds me—holds onto the here and now. Holds onto us.

Chapter Twenty-Three
I Know She'll Do It

Kris

Happy hour. Mike and I are at The Loft, throwing back twenty-cent drafts. A television announcer talks about today's body count in Vietnam with pictures of the bodies to go along. I concentrate on my beer.

"Hey, man, what are you doing for winter break?" I ask Mike.

"Making the scene with my folks in Pittsburgh. How 'bout you?"

"I've gotta come up with something special to do with Lena. Something original she'll remember forever, and that doesn't cost a lot of bread."

"Go south, dude. Fort Lauderdale." Mike's brown eyes light up.

"Hell, I can't afford that. And there's nothin' original about Fort Lauderdale."

"A million babes on the beach is plenty original for me," Mike says. "If I had a few bucks, it'd be bye-bye Iron Town, hello Bikini Beach."

I gulp my beer, swallow and sigh. "I need original, but I'm coming up with nothin'."

"Maybe you're trying too hard," Mike says. "Maybe it's all been done before."

I laugh. "Maybe."

Mike waves the waitress over and we order a couple of burgers and more beer.

"I'm ready to bag the whole idea and just tell Lena my folks are making me work over the break."

Mike slaps the table. "I got it! Any of her roommates staying at the house?"

"Nah, everyone's goin' somewhere."

"There you go!"

"What?"

"You'll have the whole place to yourselves. You can 'do it' anytime. Anywhere." Mike leans back against the booth with a self-satisfied smile.

I shake my head. "No wonder you don't have a girlfriend. Give me something I can work with."

The waitress returns with our burgers and beer.

Mike digs in, talking between chews. "Why don't you just take her to Columbus and introduce her to your folks? That's worked for me a couple of times."

"Me too, not original."

"Well, what's she into?"

"Music, books."

"Hmmm. Well, man, it's your break too. What trips you out?"

"Uh, the usual. Getting high, getting loose, getting laid." My mind latches on to Mike's beach idea. Maybe he has something there. Actually, it's sounding better and better. But not just any beach—a special beach.

"I got it," I say.

"Got what?"

"A beach. But not Fort Lauderdale. Green Lake."

"Never heard of it. Where is it?"

"Minnesota."

"Minnesota? And you call me an idiot?"

"It'll be great. My Aunt Ella lives up there. She's a flat-out trip. More hip than my dad and stepmom. And the family cabin on Green Lake isn't far. It might be frozen, but there's a beach under that snow."

"How in the hell are you gonna get there? You don't have a car," Mike says.

"We'll hitch."

"Hitchhike? In the snow? How far is it?"

"Eight hundred miles. No big deal. It'll be like eight Kent to Columbus trips. I do it all the time. A breeze, man."

"More like sixteen, if you're coming back. That's going to take a long time. And it's gonna be frigid, dude."

I reach for my mug. "I'm sure we'll find some way to make use of the time and fun ways to keep warm."

"If Lena goes for it," Mike says.

"Are you kidding? How can she resist? It's got all her favorite things—meeting new people, travel, and a whole lotta lovin' me."

"And it won't cost you a dime." Mike lifts his glass for a toast.

We clink our glasses together.

"You better jump on it, brother," Mike says, wiping beer foam off his mouth. "Winter break's next week. And what are you gonna do with Reg?"

"Cheet takes him to Columbus over breaks. His folks have a huge yard."

"You're a genius, Kris."

"You got that right," I say, grinning. "This is gonna be great."

I know she'll do it.

Chapter Twenty-Four
Leaving

Lena

I pull back the blue and brown paisley curtain to Ginny's room. "Ginny, Ginny, guess what? Kris invited me to go with him to Minnesota on winter break."

Ginny looks up from her desk. "Far out! What's in Minnesota?"

"His Aunt Ella. But we're starting out from Columbus so I get to meet his dad and stepmom too."

"Way to go!" Ginny gives me the thumbs up. "About time."

"And we're hitchhiking."

"Whaaaat?" She turns in her chair to face me. "Say again?"

"Hitchhiking."

"You're crazy."

"A lot of girls hitch," I say, holding my thumb out.

"Around campus. That's different and you know it."

"On the highway, too."

"Yeah. And they get dumped on the side of the road with their throats slashed."

I cross my arms. "You're as paranoid as my parents."

"You told your parents?" Ginny's mouth drops open.

I make a sour face. "No, and no one's going to tell them, either."

"It's one thing for Kris to stick his thumb out, but asking you to do it too!" Ginny pushes back from her desk. "I'm going to give him hell."

I grab her by the wrist. "Don't you dare. I want to go." I relax my grip on Ginny's arm, tilt my head, and half smile. "And," my voice sweetens, "it'll be so romantic. Just me and Kris on the lonesome road, under the setting sun. Who knows what could happen?"

"That's my point," she huffs, and breaks my hold.

"Don't worry. I'll be safe. Kris will protect me."

"C'mon, Lena, Kris is no he-man. What if something happens?"

I visualize Kris with his slim build and wire rims. What would he do if something really serious happens? No! I'm not going to let Ginny's paranoia—

"He was on the wrestling team in high school," I say defensively.

Ginny sighs and shakes her head. "Lena—

"He's done it a million times." I step back toward the curtain. "He's got it all together. Says we'll be on his aunt's doorstep in one ride. Besides, it's the Interstate for heaven's sake. If anything happens, we can go to a pay phone and call for help."

Ginny's worry lines soften. "I guess. Well, make sure you leave me your mom's phone number."

"No way! She panics over the smallest thing. And you know I'm not talking to my dad. I'll give you my grandparents' number. They can reach my dad. Wherever he is." I walk over to Ginny, put my hands on her shoulders, and stare into her big green eyes.

"Hey, I missed out on Woodstock. I'm not missing out on this."

I give her a hug and traipse over to my side of the attic. I know she's being a good friend. But she needs to stop raining on my parade. I'd be excited for her if she was doing something this adventurous.

Journal:

Who picks up hitchhikers? Are they abnormal or lonely or just being nice? And are you supposed to make small talk, or be quiet and stare out the window? Should we both sit in the back, or should one of us go up front? What if we don't like the looks of someone? Do we have to take every ride?

And what if someone hassles us? I'm no beauty queen, but I get my share of cat calls and come-ons. Especially from truck drivers and construction workers. Will Kris be able to deal with that? And does it even occur to him he might have to? Oh, well. What am I worrying about? Kris has it together. More important—what will Kris's parents think of me? What kind of girl hitchhikes? Not exactly a great first impression. And what if my parents find out? Should I really do it?

The scented candle on my desk flickers in the cold draft coming through the window. I stare out, watching the snow flurries in the lamplight. I'm swirling on the brink. Of adventure… or disaster?

I put on a favorite album. Joni will help me sort it out. An unidentifiable urge stirs inside me. The seasons are going round and round. I don't want to look back from where I came and feel any regret for things I could've done, but didn't. It's now or never. And yes—I want to be with him. And yes—I'll lie to my parents. And yes! I'll do it!

Chapter Twenty-Five
On Our Way

Lena

Where the heck is he? I pace, waiting for Kris to pick me up. My things are ready to go. Did I forget anything? Let's see, long johns for the road, good bells and a mini skirt for someplace special, flannel pajamas for Minnesota nights— even though I know Kris will keep me cozy warm—and an extra sweater. I'm wearing my jean bells and boots. I scan the room I share with my nine-year-old sister, Jackie. Barbie dolls and stuffed animals. It's all her stuff, because I'm not home much. But when I do come home on holidays, she sticks to me like glue, tagging after me and my friends, pestering me with a million questions. Now she's hovering over my bags giving me her "I know something you don't know" smile.

"What?" I snap.

"Nothing." She starts inching away, with her hands behind her back.

I move closer to her. "What do you have?"

She waves a small disk in my face. "Can I have one? Huh? Please?"

Oh my God, my birth control pills! "Give me that!" I pounce on her and bend her backwards, prying the dispenser out of her clenched fist. I shove it into the depths of my bag and zip it shut.

"MOM!" Jackie yells. "Lena has some candy and she won't share."

"I'm saving it for the trip," I yell back. And saving myself from having a baby. "I'll bring you back some better candy from Minnesota." I watch her sulk off, her blonde ponytail swinging. I hope they invent pills for guys by the time, she gets to be my age. It's such a pain to remember them. Kris says he'd take them if they had them. And he has a great memory.

My mom pokes her head in the room. "Is everything okay?"

I wave her off. "Yeah, fine."

She smiles and leaves.

I feel a pinch of guilt. I don't lie to my mom… much. Just your normal white lies. But, I have to admit this trip is a bit on the dingy side of white. She's meeting Kris for the first time today. With his long hair and beard, who knows what she'll think? The last guy I dated was a clean-cut jock. I've mentioned Kris to her, but she's so damned conservative. The fact is, I never go into any details about my life at school. Not the parties, who I'm dating, or that I'm involved in war protests. She'd die if I showed up on the eleven o'clock news blockading buildings or sitting in the middle of traffic protesting the war. And she'd have heart failure if she knew Kris and I were sleeping together. I told her Kris and I met last spring. That is absolutely true. I just didn't say we slept together the first night we met. I also told her we're driving up to Minneapolis. We just aren't the ones doing the driving. If she knew about the hitchhiking, I'd be grounded for life. I'm just trying to make it easier on everyone involved.

I stop pacing and look out the window. *Where the hell is he?* I want to get this thing over with and leave. My heart leaps as I see his dad's red Chevy station wagon appear. I'm at the front door in seconds. He barely gets the first knock in before I fling it open, yank him in by the front of his army jacket, and hiss, "No mention of hitchhiking. Don't even think the word."

He gives me his sweet and innocent smile and whispers, "Who, me?"

I introduce him to my brother, Tony, who's stretched out on the couch, watching football on TV. They talk about Ohio State and the Big Ten. My mom comes out from the kitchen and Kris offers his hand. I see her eyes checking out his long hair and beard while Jackie dances around him.

"We should go now," I say. "We don't want to hit traffic or bad weather." Because it's the middle of a cold but sunny Saturday afternoon, I hope Kris takes the cue to put a lid on the chit-chat. I go to the bedroom and bring out my orange overnight bag.

"Whoa," Kris says shielding his eyes. "We might have to trade that for one of my backpacks when we hit Columbus."

"Why? Too small?"

"We'll talk about it later."

"Have a sandwich before you go," Mom says. "I made tuna for lunch."

"Yech, I hate tuna." Jackie makes a face.

"Sounds good," Kris says.

I purse my lips as Mom sets five plates on the kitchen table. This is her engraved invitation to step into the interrogation room. I hold my breath as we all sit down. I know Kris won't lie. I just hope he'll figure out a way to answer her questions without giving away the truth.

"What route are you taking?" Tony asks, helping himself to a sandwich.

"Hoping to take 70 to Indianapolis, 65 to Chicago, and 90-94 to Minneapolis," Kris rattles off.

"What do you mean hoping?" says Mom.

I kick Kris's leg under the table.

"Might be some construction," he says, reaching down to pinch my calf.

"Roadwork?" Mom looks puzzled. "There's snow on the ground here. You'd think it'd be worse the further north you go."

"I never know my route for sure," Kris mumbles, his mouth full of tuna.

Kick, kick. What the hell is he doing? He could blow the whole thing. I hope his shins are bleeding. I can't take much more of this.

I widen my eyes at Kris. "We have to go or we'll never get there. Mom, I'll tell you all about it when we get back."

"I hate to leave so soon, Lena," Kris says. "These sandwiches are delicious and I'm just getting to know your mom." I see him wince as my shoe connects with his shinbone again. "But I guess we better go before the roads get icy," he says, pushing away from the table to rub his leg.

"I wanna go, I wanna go," whines Jackie.

I give my mom a hug and a kiss, and we're off.

"You're going to love Minnesota," says Kris as we walk to his car. He throws his arm around my shoulders and squeezes. "I can't wait to show you around. Hopefully my shins will have healed by then," he says with a grin. "We're gonna have the best time."

A few hours later we pull up to his house in Columbus. Kris sets my bag next to a knap sack and back pack on the living room floor. Then he unzips my orange bag.

"Hey, what are you doing?" I ask.

"I'm re-organizing. We don't need this bag."

"Oh yes we do. It's got all my stuff."

"It'll all fit into my two packs." Kris says.

"But it's my personal stuff."

"But it's so orange. Like Tang."

"What? I hate that drink!" I snatch the bag. "It goes where I go."

"Well, that means three bags instead of two. We'll have to share the load."

I walk out of the living room to the kitchen where his stepmom Barbara is cooking dinner and his two younger sisters are setting the table. She takes me to the family room in the basement and shows me how to pull out the hide-a-bed couch. She gives me a thin smile and I detect a flicker of disapproval in her eyes. If her gaze could talk, I know what it would say.

What kind of girl hitchhikes?

And the answer.

The kind that's sleeping with my stepson.

It's a look of disdain that I know very well. I see it on my mom's face when she drives by 'hippie' girls standing on the road hanging onto their "freaky" long-haired boyfriends. The girls who don't wear makeup or bras, letting everything hang out. She would remark, "Where are their mothers? How could they let them walk out the front door looking like that?" Now she too is an unknowing member of the Clueless Mom's club. At least I wear camisoles instead of going braless.

Kris and I make it through the family dinner without me having to kick him once. Afterward we go to a neighborhood hangout and I tell him how I feel. He says it's all in my head.

"Barbara doesn't care. She's probably thinking, 'What has Kris gotten this poor girl into?'"

I'm not convinced. "What about your dad?"

"My dad? Lots of his students hitchhike, including girls. He even picks them up on his way to campus."

I keep forgetting that Kris's parents aren't old school Italians, and they live and work around college kids. I could've misread Barbara's look. But still.

"Well," I say, "they might be okay with you hitching, but I'm sure they'd feel differently if your sisters were doing it."

"No way."

"And sleeping with their boyfriends?"

"Okay, there might be a little denial, looking the other way," Kris says. "Parents don't want to think about it, unless you put it in their face."

"That's what I'm saying," I persist. "Our bed is tucked away in an attic. It's out of their sight. They don't think about what we do there. It's not like the bed in the basement. Not," I hurriedly inject over Kris's grin, "that anything's going to happen on the bed in the basement. It's just—oh shit. You know what I mean." I give an exasperated sigh. "And I'll have to go through it all over again with your aunt in Minnesota."

Kris laughs. "Aunt Ella? She's probably doing exactly what we're doing and maybe more."

I spend a restless night on the hide-a-bed. The next morning Kris says, "My dad offered to buy us bus tickets."

"Really?" I feel a surge of relief.

"Yeah, Barbara's on his case about you."

"I knew it!"

"I told him, 'Thanks, but no thanks.' I said you're psyched about the trip. And that we can be there faster than the bus."

"Uh-huh." I focus on stirring cereal in my bowl. I ask casually, "But wouldn't it be easier just to take the bus with the cold weather and all?"

"What's the fun in that? The bus stops at every little town between here and Minneapolis. We'll use up half our break getting there and the other half getting back. A pain in the ass."

"I think I'm getting hitching jitters."

Kris reaches across the table to grab my hand. "I'll be right next to you. We'll be fine."

I'm so uptight, I can't even make small talk with Kris's dad as he drives us to Kris's "sure ride" drop-off point on the Interstate. I stare at the back of his head, his dark hair grazing the collar of his gray blazer. I try to imagine Kris in his thirties being a professor. Kris told me that he and his dad were close. That after his mom died, his dad tried to spend all his free time with him and his sisters. But with his working and doing research, he had to ask

Kris's Grandma and Aunt Ella to step in and help. Neither of them could quite fill the mom part. His stepmom, Barbara, came close, though.

"Do you have enough money?" His dad interrupts my thoughts. "In case you get stuck."

"We're not going to get stuck," Kris says. "We've got around a hundred. That's enough to buy us two hundred McDonald hamburgers up, and two hundred back. Plus, Aunt Ella will be cooking up her Swedish specials."

His dad pulls over at the Interstate on-ramp. He reaches into his wallet and hands some cash to Kris. "Never hurts to be prepared."

I'm relieved. A hundred dollars between the two of us doesn't sound like much.

Kris pushes his father's money away. "No, thanks, we're covered."

Are you kidding? We get out and I watch the last sure thing I know drive away.

Two guys are thumbing on the opposite ramp, holding a sign saying Florida. Something inside me likes having company even if they are on the other side of the road going the opposite direction. Kris puts down our packs. He grabs my arm, gives me a smooch on the mouth, and pushes out my thumb.

"You're a natural," he says, swiping his hair from his face as a semi blows by us.

I feel a rush. I'm doing it! Really doing it! A shiver runs through me. Ah, the feeling's back. I'm not sure if its anticipation or the cold wind. I set my bag down and give Kris my "I'm back on track" smile. He stares at me with a blank expression.

"What?" I ask.

"You look kind of tubular stuffed into that maxi coat."

As best I can, I give myself the once-over. Long underwear—at least I found some blue and pink flowered ones, instead of the usual boring beige—turtleneck sweater, jeans, and knee-boots. All wrapped up in my navy blue maxi-coat. My neck snuggles under an extra-long, white knit scarf and my hair frizzes out from under a matching ski hat with a pom-pom on top. No part of me is uncovered except my face. I pull out some lip gloss to try and add a little pizzazz. But, by the look on Kris's face, I might as well be putting lipstick on a sausage.

"You're the one who told me to wear layers," I say.

"Yeah, the mummy look is the new thing for every cool thumber chick."

"Well, your fuzzy red mittens don't exactly scream Jack Kerouac!"

"What? You don't like a man with red hot hands?" He reaches down, packs a snowball, and tosses it. I feel the cold splatter through my scarf against my neck.

"Kris, stop! I don't want to get snow all over our first ride." I shake my shoulders trying to brush it off, but it only falls deeper down my shirt.

Kris comes close and tugs on the scarf. I twirl around slowly, unwinding the long, knitted strand as he winds the other end around his neck.

Unwinding me.

I drop my arms to my sides and we stand embraced by a scarf.

"Can you feel them?" Kris says.

"What?" I lean back and look up at him. His eyes dance in the sun and snow.

"All my 'I love you's' trying to get through all your layers."

I smile and bathe in the warmth of his words.

He pulls a line from Romeo and Juliet. "She speaks yet she says nothing. What of that?"

I bend down, scoop up a handful of snow. "And what of this?" I squeal as I stuff it down his army jacket. "What of this?"

Part II: Each Ride

Chapter Twenty-Six
Rule Number One

Kris

Tang at her feet and knapsack on her shoulder, I step back and watch Lena thumb for the first time. She's got a big 'I'm ready for you to pick me up' grin on her face. She's a trip. But after a bunch of cars pass us, her mouth stretches into a tense speed-freak smile. I put down our cardboard sign with "Chicago" written in black marker and walk over to her.

"C'mon, babe, relax." I give her a quick peck and a tight squeeze. "One thing about thumbing, you gotta take it easy and let the rides come to you. Always look for the good, but be aware of the bad. That goes for people and surroundings."

Lena lowers her thumb. "Bad? You never said anything about bad. What bad?"

Shit, I should've left well enough alone. "Ignore that. I've gotten mostly good rides," I say, raising her thumb back up.

"How many were bad?" she says, putting her hand behind her back.

I sigh and shake my head. "None of them were bad. Just a few run-of-the-mill weirdos you can come across anywhere." She doesn't look convinced, so I continue, "Most people are really cool. Some have driven hours out of their way for me. The trick is to make a connection right away. Get into a groove with the driver. Someday I'll write a 'Rules of the Road' book and rake in a ton of bread."

"Enough to buy a car?"

"Why buy one when you can get rides for free?"

"That's pretty bogus."

I backtrack. "Listen, for the first couple of rides, let me do the talking. Rule number one, get the driver to talk about himself. Everyone likes talking about themselves."

Lena gives me a thumbs up, so I keep talking.

"All you have to do is ask three questions. Where are you from? What do you do for a living? And what are you into? Believe me, they'll spill their guts right into your lap."

"Yech." I get a thumbs down.

I move in close and wrap my arms around her waist. "But don't forget the golden rule, the driver is always right. Never, never argue with the driver." I give her our cardboard sign. The letters are crooked and uneven and the last 'O' had to be squeezed inside the 'G'.

"People will think we're drunk when they see this," Lena says, holding the sign in front of her.

I pinch her butt through her ten layers of clothes and tell her I love her, hoping to loosen her up. She slaps my hand away and gets to work, flashing her smile and waving our Chicago sign at passing cars. Fifteen minutes later, a big Buick pulls off the freeway. I'm psyched. Lena's about to receive her hitching baptism. I'm also more than a little relieved that her first ride isn't in the back of a pick-up truck filled with farm animals.

I open the front door. The driver is an average older guy with short graying hair. A bit paunchy in his dark gray suit. Maybe late forties or early fifties. He has straight brows, and his eyes are small and serious. His face is vaguely familiar.

"How far you goin'?" I ask.

"Dayton area, hop in," the driver says, pointing to the back seat. The front seat is piled with magazines, papers, and brief cases, so, I open the back door and slide in first with the packs. Just a precaution. Don't want anyone taking off with Lena or the gear. The car has that 'just off the lot' smell. We spread out in the spacious rear seat. Pulling onto the freeway, the driver half turns and says, "Cub's the name."

"I'm Kris," I say, pointing to myself. "And this is my girlfriend Lena. We're headed up to Minnesota." The name Cub conjures up an image from local TV news. Pow! It hits me. Name, face, and where he's headed. Holy shit! A Republican congressman. What's he doing picking up two hippie hitchhikers? I clear my throat and smile. "I've seen you on TV. Politics, huh?"

"Yep. Finished a session and goin' home." He looks into the rearview mirror. "What I'm wondering, is why you two are heading north instead of south, like everyone else."

"Going to see family," I say. "I want to show Lena where I'm from."

"Your folks know what you're doing?"

Lena's eyes shoot me the question, 'Do I have to confess to a complete stranger that I lied to my parents?' I take the lead and say, "Yeah, they know where we're going. Matter of fact, my dad dropped us off." Jeeze, this guy's got balls. But I guess that's a politician for you.

The congressman gives a long sigh and changes his tone. "Well, things sure have changed since I was a student. Back then it was drinking beer, drive-ins, and backseats. Now it's free love and smoking dope. Do you two live in those two big OSU dorms—what do the newspapers call them, Sodom and Gomorrah?"

"We go to Kent," I say without thinking. I bite my lip. The can of worms is officially open.

"Well, now, do you?" Cub says in a flat voice. "That was a terrible situation at Kent with those shootings. Never should've happened."

"I agree," Lena says. "Damn guard. Idiot governor."

I give her a warning look. Cub squints at us in the rearview mirror. "You radicals? Or outside agitators?" His mouth purses into a tight line.

"Neither. Just students on winter break," I say.

"Those students shouldn't have rioted," he says. "That doesn't belong on a campus."

Lena's gripping the armrest and giving the back of his head a steely glare. Nudging Lena's knee I tap my lips with my finger. She ignores me and leans forward.

"Killing doesn't belong on campus, either."

I move our bags to my lap. Shit, I hate being dumped between exit ramps in the middle of nowhere.

Cub stammers, and then says, "The kids started it, throwing rocks. The Guard had a right to defend themselves."

"With bullets?"

"Well, like I said, all that rioting and marching doesn't belong on campus. That's a place for learning."

I can see Lena's jaw muscles flex as she grits her teeth, then says, "Believe me, we are learning. Learning that Americans can die when they protest peacefully for what they think is wrong—even when they're on college campuses."

Cub's voice rises. "There are other ways to get your point across."

"How? Write your congressman? With all due respect, they don't care. Their sons go into the National Guard or get medicals." Lena crosses her arms.

Cub glances in the rearview mirror, his face red. "Student deferments are expiring. In fact, a lot of my big contributors are having their sons drafted and sent off to 'Nam. Both sides of the aisles are losing their boys. It was stupid to get involved in the first place, but it's like riding the tiger, young lady. We can't get off or we'll be eaten alive."

"We're already being eaten alive," says Lena. "And Nixon is lying about it. How can you stand behind him?"

Cub starts shaking his head. "You don't understand. In politics, things change. If you want to keep the job and make a difference, you have to vote the way your constituents do."

"But we can't vote until we're twenty-one," says Lena. "Our generation will be wiped out while you think you're making a difference."

I lean back against the car's fresh upholstery. Any moment now, Cub's gonna hit the brakes and say, "Get the hell out of my car and find a ride with a Democrat." It's time to take control of this tête-à-tête and swing it back to a topic that will get us to Dayton.

"Hey, Cub, you ever been to Fort Lauderdale? My friend Mike says the beach is warm and sunny with a hundred percent chance of bikinis. Ha, ha."

Cub steadies his voice to monotone. I glance at the rearview mirror and see a vein standing out on his forehead. "Our word is at stake. Other countries will never trust us if we walk away from Vietnam. We've got to rid the world of communists. They're out to bury democracies. There's no graceful way out."

Lena shakes her head. "Being graceful isn't more important than saving lives."

"So, what's the answer?" I say as we pass a sign, *Dayton I-675—10 miles*. We just need ten more minutes. "What do we do?"

"Wait for the right peace treaty. It's coming soon."

"Not soon enough." Lena says, and looks out her window.

Cub speeds up and pulls into the right lane. "You know what? I'm taking a short cut home," he says. "I'll drop you off here."

He swerves the car down the exit ramp and pulls over. The sign reads *Springfield - Yellow Springs*. Damn.

Lena jumps out like her pants are on fire. I slide out and stick my head in the door to thank Cub. He eyes me and says, "Son, you better put a lid on your feisty girlfriend or you'll be walking to Minnesota." He grins, good ol' boy style. "I think we can both agree that she should be in a bikini on a beach somewhere, rather than shooting her mouth off."

With both packs, I step back next to Lena and shut the car door. We watch him drive right back onto the freeway. Shortcut my ass.

"Where's he going?" Lena says. "He's getting back on the freeway."

"No shit. We just got dumped." I kick a chunk of snow into the road. "Thanks to you."

"What do you mean? He's a jerk. Why didn't you back me up?"

"First off, you violated the golden rule," I say, with an edge in my voice. "Don't disagree with the driver. He's just a ride."

"He wasn't just a ride! He's a congressman who votes, for God's sake. He's got the power to help stop the war."

"Oh, c'mon. Lena, get real."

"Well, you could've said something," she snaps. "You're the one who could go if you lose your deferment. I thought you hated the war."

"I do." I hear my voice tighten. Cars are zooming by. This isn't the time or the place. But I know she won't let up until she gets some kind of explanation.

"We both have friends who are over there right now," she says. "Who knows if they'll come back? How could you just sit and listen to his crap and not put him in his place?"

"Lena, you think the two of us could get him to see the light? Not a chance in hell. All these congressmen have businesses in their districts that make a living off the war. Money talks. Second, we're twenty. We can't vote for another year and—"

"So you can kill and get killed but you can't—"

"Let me finish. Hating the war doesn't change whether I go or not. If I get drafted, I get drafted. I've been over all the options. Sneak into Canada, and never see my home and family again? Or prison? No way."

Lena raises her voice. "Aren't you a pacifist? Be a conscientious objector!"

"Being a pacifist doesn't automatically make me a conscientious objector. I think violence is justified sometimes. As a last resort."

"Like when?"

"Like World War Two or someone hurting you. Or me."

"That's different."

"No, it's not. Violence is violence. Some so-called conscientious objectors throw rocks and bottles. I'm not one of them." I put the Chicago sign under my arm and shake out a cigarette from my coat pocket. "It's the principle of the thing," I murmur as I light up.

Lena rolls her eyes. "What principle? Dying for a country that assassinates its leaders every other month and tells us we're fighting for their people's freedoms? It's a crock and you know it." She turns away and stomps on a pile of gray slush that splatters both of us.

"Damn it," she says, wiping her coat. "I'm sorry."

I shake the slush off my pants, "I'm just saying, I couldn't live with myself if I lied my way out of going and then someone else went in my place."

"Doesn't it scare you?"

I exhale long and hard. "Yeah, it scares the hell out of me. But it's not the going. It's the killing."

"But don't you see? That's why you have to say something when you have the chance, so you and no one else has to kill, kill, kill!"

"Lena, I've been in as many protests as you, and you know it. The whole idea of this trip is to get away from that heavy shit. I just want to have fun." I put a hand on her shoulder. "I'm not selling out. I'm just keeping my mouth shut. Sometimes that's the price of the ride. Okay?"

Lena's eyes soften, and then start to water. "Okay." She gives me a weak smile. "I hear you."

I toss my butt on the ground and tap it out with my boot. I grab Lena's hand and start walking her back toward the freeway. "I know how you feel, but today, a ride's a ride," I say as we step over dirty chunks of ice and snow. "Now let's go get another one."

Lena nods, then squeezes my hand. "All the way to Minnesota."

Chapter Twenty-Seven
School Bus

Lena

A couple of short, smile–and–keep-my-mouth-shut rides later, Kris and I find ourselves on the western edge of Richmond, Indiana. A giant billboard juts out of the grayish field behind us, announcing we've arrived in Camper Country. The crisp December wind nips our faces, chapping our lips, but the sun is warm on our backs. I breathe in the thick scent of mud and slush, trying to keep my thirst for adventure alive, but I'm still not sure about this hitchhiking thing.

Kris's cheeks are as red as his mittens. His eyes are an unclouded sky. He smiles and stands casually, with one leg bent, cradling the sign in his arms, like he's waiting for a friend to pick us up. His nonchalance spreads over me, and as much as it sometimes frustrates me, I find myself depending on it. And that irks me too.

I stick out my gloved thumb and gaze across the field at a massive stockyard of brand new school buses.

"This exit has potential," Kris says, pointing his mittened hand at the lot.

"Why?" I'm puzzled. "School busses don't pick up hitchhikers."

"They might need to deliver a bus to a school district in Chicago or, better yet, Minneapolis."

"Dream on," I say, but I have to admit that I should pay more attention to the potential of things. Especially out here on the road.

I don't think we've gotten very far, but Kris says everything's cool. According to him, we're moving along at a decent pace, but haven't hit that 'big ride' yet. I can't tell if he really thinks that, or if he's just saying it because he laid it on so thick about how easy it would be.

A bus pulls out of the stockyard and heads in our direction.

"Hey," Kris nods. "Here comes our big yellow taxi now."

"Ha! You're crazy. No school bus is gonna pick up hitchhikers."

"Keep the faith, babe."

The bus rolls up to us and squeals to a stop. The doors flap open and the driver yells out, "Need a ride?"

Unreal. A school bus picking up hitchhikers. What kind of a driver does this? I mean, we could be Bonnie and Clyde.

I nudge Kris's back as he picks up his pack, and whisper, "This might be illegal."

Kris whispers back, "Don't be so uptight. This might be our 'big ride,'" as he steps toward the open door.

Kris lugs the backpacks into the empty bus and wrestles them onto seats a couple rows behind the driver. The Grateful Dead plays on a portable cassette player on the floor next to the driver's seat. Kris puts his arm around me. We stand there, smiling, listening to *High Time* come out of the tinny speakers. I giggle. The driver appears to be in his thirties, chubby, with dark hair straggling out from his baseball cap.

"How far you goin'?" Kris asks.

"About ten miles. You guys are lucky I was out this way getting the Big Banana a tune-up. That's what the kids and I call her."

I sense Kris's body deflate. The Big Banana's not going to be our 'big ride.' Kris gives me an apologetic look and we slide into the front seats catty-corner from the driver with Tang between us. The smell of crayons and peanut butter and jelly sandwiches hangs in the air.

"I'll drop you off at the exit before the school. A lot of thumbers use that exit. I have to make a quick phone call at the pay phone down the road before I pick up the kids."

"Not a problem, we appreciate the ride. Are you from Richmond?" Kris asks, starting his "getting to know you" routine.

"No, Portland. Oregon. Name's Ken."

"This is Lena and I'm Kris. How'd you end up in Richmond?"

"My wife's family lives here."

"That had to be a trip for you, going from the west coast to the middle of farmland."

"No kidding," Ken laughs. "We're Deadheads. We met on a commune in Oregon."

"Cool," Lena and I say in unison.

Ken smiles. "It was. We spent our first couple years following the band around the country. Having fun, letting life take us where it wanted. Kinda like you."

Kris and I look at each other and laugh.

"The next thing I knew we were pregnant. My wife wanted to be around her roots so we ended up here. Got married in a field of sunflowers. Marcy's an artist. Loves that Van Gogh stuff."

"I love him too," I say.

"She teaches art to kindergartners. I don't have a diploma so I got this job. It's okay, but not forever. We've got plans. We want to get ourselves a little farm. Live off the land, like we did on the commune. I'll build a studio for Marcy. Been saving for it."

We pull off the Interstate and into a gas station with a pay phone in the lot. Ken turns off the ignition, sets the emergency brake, and turns in his seat.

"Marcy hasn't been feeling herself lately. She took some tests and the results should be in. Won't take a minute to check. I'll be right back."

We watch Ken walk out to the phone booth.

"Seems like they had a cool life," I say. "Living on a commune."

"Yeah. Wish I could do that."

"What's stopping you?"

"I want my degree." Kris pounds his fist into his hand. "I don't want to be driving a school bus when I'm in my thirties."

"Yeah, but he's still got a dream."

"A farm's not the same as living on a commune."

"What do you mean?"

"It's not as free," Kris says.

"You mean free love?" I laugh. "He's married."

"That's what I'm saying. It's not the same. But I guess that's where it's at when you're thirty."

I feel a pinch of panic. Will I still be dreaming about France when I'm thirty? Or will I be substituting France for something else? Like... like... I've been dreaming about France for so long, I can't come up with a substitute.

We look out the window. I watch Ken cradle the receiver against his ear, his lips moving slowly. Then his shoulders sag. He hangs up the phone and slumps into the corner of the booth. His arms droop to his side as he walks back to the bus, face drawn, eyes down.

"Not the news we were hoping for," he says quietly.

Do we ask why or wait for him to tell us? I keep an eye on Kris for a cue.

"Man, I'm sorry," Kris says.

"Me, too," I add. I want to say more, but what? Without knowing him or her, would it sound trite? Or nosy? I'm surprised at the sadness welling in my chest for a total stranger.

Ken starts the bus and leaves the music off. He keeps his eyes straight ahead and only breaks the quiet with heavy sighs. We're riding the same bus, but the journey is different now. Kris intertwines his fingers with mine, his touch trying to erase the sadness in the silence.

The bus jolts to the right, then swerves erratically back to the left. Ken is wiping his eyes with the back of one hand and grasping the wheel with the other. His thick shoulders are shaking as he downshifts, trying to regain control. Kris jumps up and puts his hand on Ken's back.

"Hey, man, if you want me to take over for a while, I can."

Ken pulls the bus over to the side. He drops into the seat across from me. Head down, silently heaving, he mumbles the name of an exit. Kris turns the ignition and grabs the gear shift. We lurch forward as the gears grind into place. Careening back onto the highway, the thought of Kris getting us all killed disappears as Ken begins to sob.

What can I do? What can I say? I dig into my purse for a tissue. I squeeze his hand as I give it to him. *Something, anything. Maybe...* I reach into the inside zippered pocket in my bag where I stashed some snacks for the road. My fingers close around my one and only Hershey bar. Nothing calms my nerves like a sweet chunk of chocolate. I break it into squares and hand one to Ken. He gives me a watery smile and pops it into his mouth. He settles back against the seat, eyes closed, mouth in mindless motion, chewing the chocolate.

Hesitantly, I ask, "What about picking up the kids at school?"

He opens his eyes and wipes his nose with his sleeve. "I'll be okay."

I stare out the window, struggling to ignore the wrecking ball swinging inside me. Small clapboard houses dot the road. Houses that hear the everyday sounds of life, laughter, and congratulations. Words of love and sympathy. But everything can change with one phone call. Kris chugs to the side of the road at our exit and pulls the bus to a stop.

"Thanks, man," Ken says, moving past Kris to the driver's seat. "Sometimes—" his voice catches as he watches us gather our packs "—life hands you a big box of rain."

My heart feels like it could break for this poor guy that I didn't even know a half hour ago. As I walk past, I put my hand on his shoulder. "But the sun always shines again."

He stares at me with tears in his eyes, then holds up his hand in a trembling peace sign.

We get off the bus and stand back as Ken situates himself back in the driver's seat. Kris pats my shoulder. "That was nice of you to say that," he says in my ear.

"For all the good it did," I whisper back.

But then Kris nudges me as the door to the bus closes. And there we both stand, shoulder to shoulder, smiling at the tinny sound of the Grateful Dead slicing into the cold air as the bus pulls onto the road.

Chapter Twenty-Eight
Lost Rides

Kris

I stuff my hands into my coat pockets and hunch my shoulders against the cold. I need a breather before our next ride. The school bus left me with this need to hold and be held. I conjure up my two baby monkeys in the psych lab, desperately clutching their surrogate terrycloth mother. Comical on my good days, it guts me on my bad.

"Have you ever had anyone close die on you?" I ask Lena.

She breathes in, then says, "Craig. Vietnam. But I didn't find out until a week or so after he was gone. I didn't watch him go, obviously. We were just friends, but he felt like family." She pauses. "You… your mom?"

"I was four years old."

"How long was she sick?"

"About a year, I think. But at that age it was hard for me to tell. There were small changes one day to the next. Nothing seemed different. There were days I had to play quietly outside. I got shipped off to my grandparents or Aunt Ella a few times."

"How did you say goodbye to her?"

"I didn't. How do you say goodbye to the sun and the moon? They're supposed to always be there for you. It was like this giant, invisible wall that I had no idea how to climb over or get around."

"That must have been so hard," Lena says, putting her arm through mine and pulling close.

I trudge forward, glad to feel her touch. "I remember the first day of kindergarten when we had to stand up and say something about our family. I wasn't sad or upset, just embarrassed about not having a mom. My sisters were too young to understand, and in a way, they were lucky. I knew it wasn't normal not to have a mom."

I pull off a mitten and reach into my coat pocket for a cigarette and damn, the pack's empty. I ball the empty pack in my fist. Lena opens my fingers. The empty pack drops to the ground. She picks it up, puts it in her pocket, then interlocks our fingers.

"You must've been lost," she says. "I know I'd be, no matter how old I was."

I look past Lena at a drainage ditch cutting through the field behind us. Broken sheets of ice bob and dip in the culvert on their way toward the large cement pipe at the end of the off ramp. My mom left like that, drifting farther and farther out of sight 'til she was gone and I was left behind.

I turn to Lena. "Every day afterward I asked my dad what happened. He'd put me on his lap and try to explain that she wasn't coming back."

"It must've been hell on him," Lena says.

I grunt in agreement, even though I'd never really given much thought to how it was for him. When we moved to Ohio, there was Barbara. After a while, she became mom.

Lena interrupts my thoughts, saying, "I can't imagine dying inch by inch."

"I'd spend my inches making things right with the world, say my sorry's, then soak in every last minute."

"I'd travel," Lena says. "Unless I was too sick. Then I'd read my favorite books and watch my favorite movies and spend time with my favorite friends."

"And favorite boyfriend?"

"Especially him."

I hug her around the waist, drawing her in. Pushing aside her mass of curls, I whisper softly in her ear, "I'm really glad you're here."

"I'm really glad you're here, too, and not in Vietnam."

"I hope that doesn't happen either, believe me."

"I can't help thinking about that stupid Congressman."

"Aw, Lena, don't take it so personal."

"It is personal. It's you. It's me. There's nothing more personal than that. I don't want anything to happen to you, or to us."

"Nothing's gonna happen. I'm here, aren't I?"

"That's what bus driver Ken and his wife thought, too."

She's right. We're not invincible. Life doesn't go on forever. One day everyone's lined up nice and neat, and the next there's an empty space where someone once stood before the war, the car accident, or the drug overdose. It makes me think—how would I want to go out?

I know how.

I grab Lena's hand and lift her arm up over her head, giving her an old-fashioned rock and roll swirl. She giggles as I dip her backwards, no small feat with all the stuff she's got on. I'm struggling to keep my balance on the snow, not crash both of us to the ground, when a rust bucket swerves toward the gravel shoulder a short distance ahead of us, skidding to a stop on the edge of the drainage ditch.

The car could pass for my stepmom's white 1960 Valiant. We call it the Swissmobile, because it looks like a piece of Swiss cheese with rusty brown around the holes. You need a tetanus shot to ride in it.

I heft up my back pack and run toward the waiting junk heap with Lena shuffling about twenty feet behind me. I open the front passenger door and the neck of an empty liquor bottle pokes out from under the bench seat. Clothes and trash are strewn all over the interior. And the smell. It's like a trash dump soaked in alcohol.

The driver is slouched forward, face resting on arms folded across the top of the steering wheel. He has a greasy, unkempt look and a smile I can't nail down. Not sinister, but not sincere.

"Hop in," he says.

I signal behind my back for Lena to hold up. I'm familiar with drivers that have a good buzz goin' on when they pick you up. Usually I'll offer to take over the driving. But we're not that desperate... yet.

"How far you going?" I ask, deciding no matter what he says, it's either not far enough, a bad exit, or the wrong direction.

The driver slurs, "Three exits, I'm thinking. I can take you or your girlfriend. Not both."

Yeah, right. This guy is working the 'ladies first' angle. A real sweetheart of a gentleman. I smile and shrug. "Thanks a lot, but we're a package deal."

I close the door and jump back. The drunk jerks his car out on the freeway right in front of a honking car, swerves, and careens down the road in a cloud of burning oil. Lena's looking at me with wide eyes.

"Easy come, easy go," I say. "We didn't need that ride anyway."

She stomps her feet in a mock temper tantrum. "Are we there yet?"

I step behind her and grab her waist with both hands. "We're here," I say, pressing down hard through her layers of clothes into her right hip. Damn, I wish it was summer! I wiggle my fingers halfway up to the middle of her back. "This is Chicago." I finger-walk to her left shoulder. "Over here, Wisconsin." My fingers dig under her scarf and tickle the back of her neck, "Here's

Minneapolis." I gently tug on her ear lobe. "And the moon over Green Lake." Laughing, she shakes me off.

We put our thumbs out and keep walking.

Chapter Twenty-Nine
Stewed

Kris

Even though our rides have included an hour's worth of salesman blather and a tour of historical Indianapolis, we've made good progress. Chicago is only one hundred and eighty miles away. We're working the highway, thumbs out, when a van displaying a golden-winged Pegasus on its side swoops by, then slams on its brakes. It backs up, not on the shoulder but on the Interstate. Cringing, I grab Lena's hand and pull her off the berm into the grass as I watch a semi barreling down on the van. The semi blasts its horn as the van swerves onto the shoulder, barely escaping a catastrophic end. Great, it's a van of bozos. But then I look closer. Holy shit—it's a truckload of women and they're waving us in.

Lena jumps in first and beats me to the far back where there's room to stretch out on the floor. I shove the backpacks next to her and make myself comfortable in the backseat next to a cute redhead.

"Are you going on vacation?" I ask, nodding toward the luggage in back that Lena's now rearranging.

"Not exactly, we're stewardesses," the driver says, glancing back. Her dark eyes flash under her straight black bangs. "Headed to Chicago to work a flight. We're a little strung out from an all-night music jam in Indiana."

Red looks back at Lena. "Hey, be careful with those bags. I've got some expensive French perfume in one."

They're still flying high from last night's concert, singing along with the radio. I ask them the usual questions, they introduce themselves, and brag about meeting members of some underground rock band on a flight they worked. The band invited them to their album debut party in central Indiana last night, the hometown of the lead singer. Sheila, the driver, pops in a cassette of the group and cranks the volume, killing any chance of Lena joining in the conversation from the way back.

"Want some reefer? It's Columbian." Kitty in the front passenger seat tosses her long blonde hair over her shoulder before lighting up a joint. Kitty hands it to Sheila, who takes a deep hit and passes it to me. I pass the joint to Lena, who's now in a makeshift bed between the suitcases. A few tokes and she'll be out.

After a half-hour of toking and trying to relay my stories about the Congressman and Kent, the stews begin to rehash their weekend long orgy. I glance back at Lena, crashed out, then give my full attention to the stews describing acid-laced, whipped cream 'threesies,' and who-did-what-to-who. Their stories and my stories fly around the van like a spinning top and I can't tell if I'm comin' or goin'. They move on from rock and roll to telling stories of rocking and rolling in the airplane bathroom. The sky's the limit with these chicks. Too bad I'm not with one of my hitchhiking buddies, Jim. He's gonna flip out when I tell him about this ride.

Mindy, next to me, starts to wrap her red corkscrew curls around her finger. "Why are we moving so slow? I'm going to be late," she whines.

Sheila points at two tractor-trailers driving side by side in front of us. "Nothin' I can do. These two semis won't move."

"Well, I can't afford to be written up again. They'll put me on crappy puddle jumpers," says Mindy.

"I'll pass as soon as one of them gives me a chance," Sheila says.

"We're still gonna be cutting it close," Mindy says with a pout.

Kitty turns to face Mindy. "Why don't you start getting ready now? Screw the shower. That'll cut thirty minutes off. Just throw on some talcum powder."

Mindy looks at me and grins. "Do you mind?"

I exhale a big cloud of smoke, say, "Uhh, no," and pass the joint back to the front.

Mindy pulls out a hot pink makeup case from under the seat and hands it to me. "You can be my valet."

I glance back at Lena's peacefully sleeping body and murmur, "Sure."

Mindy wiggles out of her jeans, showing her bikini underwear, and then whips off her skimpy T-shirt. Wow! There's nothin' under that shirt but what God gave her. And by the looks of it, God was generous.

"Here, hold this up so I can have some privacy," she says. She hands me her tiny T-shirt.

"Okay," I say, glancing back at Lena, who's still sleeping. I balance the makeup case in my lap and keep the T-shirt up while she fumbles through bottles and jars. Mindy peeks around the T-shirt and pats my nose with her powder puff. I do my best to keep my gaze off her. *Pull your shit together, your girlfriend is right behind you.* I'm holding the T-shirt so tight my knuckles are white.

"Hang on," Sheila yells from the front. "We're passing these trucks."

The van swerves to the left and almost throws me into Mindy's lap. She catches me and giggles. I force my gaze out the window and see a sign for West Lafayette. I look back over my shoulder. Lena hasn't budged.

"Sweetie, can you hand me my blouse?" Mindy purrs from behind the T-shirt curtain. "It's in the suitcase under your girlfriend's head. Right on top."

I re-enter the real world and hand Mindy her T-shirt. I reach back slowly, and oh so carefully slide the bag out from underneath Lena's head.

Brown eyes open. She gives me a groggy smile. I tell myself to be cool, act natural. I'm not doing anything wrong. I've helped Lena get dressed lots of times. She'll understand. It's all for the ride, man.

I yank a white blouse from the bag and shove it into Mindy's face. Then I hang over the back seat to obscure Lena's view. "Sorry I woke you up. You can go back to sleep, we have a long ways to go yet."

Lena pulls herself up on her elbows. Her eyes grow wide, and then narrow as she takes in Mindy in nothing but her bikini underwear, twisting her hair up onto top of her head. With both of her long, smooth arms extended over her head, Mindy flashes me a smile. "Oh, and can you get my bra, too, please?"

Flames shoot from Lena's eyes. I plunge my hand into the suitcase and grab the first thing that feels like a bra and throw it into Mindy's lap. I'm in deep. I swivel away from Lena. "Hey, who's got the joint?"

Kitty looks back from the passenger seat, the joint hanging from her mouth. She turns it around, offering to shotgun me. Tempting, but I'm not *that* stupid. I reach over, snatch the doobie out of her mouth, and hold it out to Lena. Anything to draw the attention away from Mindy who's putting her boobs into her bra. I give Lena a reassuring "I-see-nothing, no-big-deal" smile, but Lena crushes it with 'the look' and ignores the joint. I take a deep toke, searching for an explanation, but can't find a thing. I reach my arm over the seat to take Lena's hand. A little lovey-dovey never hurt.

"What the hell are you doing?" Lena hisses at me, slapping my hand away.

"I'm trying to hold your hand."

"I mean with her." She points an accusing finger at Mindy.

"Who, her?" I look at Mindy, who's now in uniform from the waist up. Her bare legs are crossed. She sees me looking and flashes a conniving grin. I set the makeup case up like a wall between us. "Uh, nothin'."

Lena leans forward and yells over my head, "Pull over and drop me off. RIGHT NOW."

Sheila and Kitty are bouncing in the front seats, singing at the top of their lungs to the radio. *"She's a HOOOONKY Tonk... Honky Tonk Woman."*

"What?" Sheila yells back, giggling.

"Nothing! Don't stop," I shout over the radio. "Keep going."

Lena's eyes spark like firecrackers. I know it's a lost cause, but I've got to try to reason with her.

"Please wait 'til the next exit. It's safer."

Lena hisses through gritted teeth. "You can wait. I'm getting out here. Pull over!" She starts to claw her way through the suitcases for the sliding door. I reach out and grab her.

Yanking her back, I say, "Quit acting crazy. She's just getting dressed. For work. That's all."

Sheila looks back over her shoulder and yells, "Knock it off! Do you want to get us all killed?" She pushes down on the accelerator.

I eye Lena. "C'mon. Pull it together. Just relax."

Lena crosses her arms, glaring. Two songs later, Sheila swerves to the bottom of an exit ramp.

"Here's your stop, Prudence and the Prince. It's been a real pleasure."

Lena flings the door open and Mindy helps us unload by kicking Tang out into the road slush.

"If you ever make it to Chicago," she calls to me, "be sure to look me up." She jerks the sliding door closed and they roar away, drowning out my thank you. I snatch my backpack by one of the leather straps. It immediately breaks and my pipe falls out. I pick it out of road slop and zipper it into the front pocket of Tang. I cross the road to the gravel where Lena's standing and drop her bag in front of her. She's still glaring.

I shake my head. "Jesus, Lena! That ride could've taken us to Chicago."

Lena sets her jaw, looking like she could kill. "How dare you!"

I exhale and recite the 'Rules of the Road'. "Rule Number Two—never quit a ride unless it's going to kill you."

"How about killing our relationship? Huh? Where's that rule?"

"That's under 'Thou shall not freak out over nothing,'" I say, kicking the gravel between us.

"If I'd known hitching was just another way for you to party and get naked with girls, I would've stayed home!" she yells, slinging her bag at me.

It bounces off the guardrail and rolls onto the ramp just as a car drives by and clips it. The driver swerves, but Tang cartwheels into the air.

"Idiot!" the driver screams out his window as he speeds away.

I sprint into the road and grab the bag. I open the zipper pocket to see if my pipe is in one piece. The familiar stink of patchouli oil hits me. I fish out my pipe. The bowl is cracked and completely doused in patchouli. Damn.

I lift the broken pipe and wave it in the air. "Happy?" I slam Tang down next to Lena and hurl the pipe into the field behind us. "If you want to go home, we can turn around right now."

Lena sits silent against the guardrail, her back to the road, eyes fixed on the treeless field spreading to the horizon. I perch on top of the cold metal about six feet away from her. We sit in knife-cutting tension for ten minutes before I realize one of us has to make the first move or this trip is headed back to Ohio.

"It's not my fault who picks us up," I say. "Just what was I supposed to do?"

"You could've told her to get off your lap and go to hell," she spits out. "She was topless!"

"I barely noticed. I was looking the other way."

"Liar."

"She probably does it all the time."

"No kidding! She's a stewardess for God's sake. *'Coffee, Tea or Me?'*"

"You didn't need to flip out over it. You could've at least waited 'til after we got halfway through Chicago. We could've fought about it then."

Lena shakes her head. "You don't get it. You never get it. What if they were pilots instead of stews?"

"Huh?"

"What if I helped a sexy pilot put on his pants?"

I ramble on, hoping I can outmaneuver her logic. "The point is, it's all about the ride. I'm done arguing. We're going to Minnesota. You can do what you want when we get there."

I pick my frozen ass off the metal guardrail and stick out my thumb, trying to keep the picture of Lena and pilots out of my head. I wouldn't lose my shit over it. I'd keep my mouth shut and work it out later. At least that's what I'm trying to convince myself of as I dig a fresh pack of smokes out of my back pack and light up. The truth is, we have bigger fish to fry than arguing about naked stewardesses or imaginary pilots. It's late afternoon and we haven't eaten anything but Ritz crackers and peanut butter since breakfast. The sunlight is fading and the temperature's dropping. My guess is after a couple hours of this, Lena will jump into a car full of completely naked stewardesses.

Chapter Thirty
Adonis

Lena

He'll never change.

I snatch up the Chicago sign and hold it in front of my face to avoid looking at him. Why did he have to go and ruin everything? And now he's acting like I'm the one with the problem. Infuriating.

I blink fast to hold back tears. Beyond the highway there's nothing but fields of dirt. I should just walk away. Disappear into the horizon. Would he care? He probably wouldn't even notice I'm gone. I squint into the distance. There's got to be a farmhouse around here. Or a barn. Someplace safe and warm where I can get my head together and figure a way out of this nightmare. I'll call Ginny to come get me. Or she can Western Union money for a bus ticket. I scan the blankness surrounding me. I don't even know where we are. Uneasiness filters through me like cold water. I could go back to Kent. Stand on the other side of the highway and jump into the first car that stops. But what if all those terrible things my parents warned me about are real? Damn. I just don't have the guts to do it alone. Kris said we could turn around. If we do, I can ditch him as soon as we get back to Kent. For good. Ginny's "I told you so's" ring in my ear. I'll never hear the end of it. And I'll never trust my own judgment again. I've got to at least make it to Minnesota. Once I'm there, I'll just play sick to his Aunt Ella and get on the first bus back to Ohio. My head clears. My breath evens out. I feel like a quitter, but at least it's a plan.

A ruby red VW Bug slows to a stop and the driver leans out the window. Whoa! A blond Adonis. He points to our sign.

"I can take you most of the way to Chicago."

My knight in fading twilight. Thank you, karma!

"Shotgun," I say, pushing past Kris as the driver pops the hood. I open the passenger door and pull the front seat forward. Kris stuffs our two packs in the small space under the hood and then squeezes into the backseat with Tang. He can curl up and go to sleep while I make friends with Mr. Gorgeous.

I try to smooth my windblown hair, cursing the trucks under my breath. The driver smiles at me. Dimples! He's beachboy cute, but no baby face. Smile lines around soft brown eyes. Maybe late twenties. He's wearing a white long-sleeve shirt and khaki pants. So clean and fresh and… damn! I probably smell like exhaust fumes. Oh well.

I get in the front and close the door. "Hi. Thanks for stopping. I'm Lena." I flip my thumb over my shoulder. "And that's Kris."

"Glad to meet you. I'm Rob."

Kris leans forward. "Where you headed?"

"Just outside Chicago." Rob glances in the rearview mirror and pushes the gearshift knob forward. We chug onto the highway. "How long you guys been on the road?"

"Too long," I say. I feel a thump against my seatback. I ignore it and sweep my gaze over the hands on the steering wheel. No ring. My mind runs through Kris's goofy rules. *Get them to talk about themselves.*

"Where are you from?" I ask.

"Originally? Indy."

"So, how's Indy? Nice place?"

"Down home people. Too conservative for me, though," Rob says. "I was visiting my folks. I live in Chicago."

"Chicago? That's cool! What do you do there?"

"Dentist."

Bingo. Ginny would be circling dreamboat on her checklist. The car is starting to heat up. It's time to strip out of this snow suit and get comfortable. Real comfortable. I need to strike up a meaningful conversation and I want to look good doing it. I know I can come up with something deeper than rock bands and orgies. I struggle to gracefully remove my coat. No small feat with the layers of clothing I'm wearing. Kris reaches over the seat to help.

"Thank you, but I can manage," I say, waggling one arm free. I glance back at him. "If you want to help, get a blouse from my bag. I'm getting a little warm." I hear Kris slump in his seat. Ha. I can imagine his frown.

Rob reaches toward a small dial on the dashboard. "I can try to lower the heat. But you know Bugs. It's all or nuthin'."

"No, I'm okay—now," I say, smiling at him. "So, you're a dentist. That must be... interesting."

He smiles back as he points to his mouth. "It's a holey experience."

"You picked us up just so you could use that line," I tease.

"For the millionth time, I bet," Kris's mumbles.

"Zillionth," Rob says. "So, where you guys from?"

"Ohio," Kris says, poking his nose in the space between us.

"*He's* from Ohio. *I'm* from L.A." I raise my voice. "And I'm transferring back there next fall. I can't wait."

I hurl the words out, wanting them to fall on Kris and give him a taste of our last ride. But they hang in the air, like someone else said them.

Rob raises his eyebrows. "Oh yeah? I went to dental school in San Francisco."

"Oh wow—San Fran?" I feel a rush. "The drive up Highway 1 is so amazing, my release from L.A.'s freeway hell."

"Went surfing every chance I got. Ocean Beach."

"Bitchen."

Rob grins. "I haven't heard that word since I left California."

Bet Kris never heard it. Kris can undress all the stews he wants. I'm bonding with a surfer! A dentist!

"You must've froze your ass off," Kris says from the back.

I whip my head around, to scowl at him. Now who's breaking the "Be nice to the driver" rule?

"Definitely wetsuit water," Rob says, seemingly oblivious to Kris's remark. "But I miss it."

"I grew up on a lake in Minnesota. I miss it every day," Kris says.

I roll my eyes. "How can you compare a lake in Minnesota to the Pacific?"

"Did more surfing than studying... or anything, for that matter," Rob says, ignoring the rift between me and Kris.

"But being so close to Berkeley too, all the action... did you go to any sit-ins?" I ask.

"No." Rob's voice turns apologetic. "I didn't get involved in any of the protests. I was afraid if I got arrested it would ruin my career."

"We go to Kent State," I say. "We can't avoid getting involved."

"Really? Did you see the shootings?"

"No, but we were on the edge of it," Kris says, leaning forward again. "We were supposed to meet right about the time it happened."

My heart quickens. "I couldn't see what was happening, but I heard the gunshots and the screams. I didn't know what to do. Couldn't tell which way to go. Then they shut down campus."

The warm air wafting up from the heater vents suddenly feels stifling. I shift in my seat, trying to get comfortable.

Kris reaches over and gently grips my shoulders. His fingers trace the back of my neck and begin to massage my shoulders. I stare out the window and feel the tension fade into the barren snow-covered fields.

"It's hard to talk about," Kris says. "There's still protests, student strikes, and sit-ins every other day it seems. Even the townies are showing up."

"Yeah, the more the body count goes up, the more people realize it needs to end," Rob says. "I think just about everyone I know has lost someone."

I nod. "We blockaded buildings with the Vietnam Vets," I say. "They were there. They're saying we shouldn't be involved. It's a civil war."

"Yeah," Kris says, still massaging my neck. "And the side we chose has a coup every other day with a new dictator assassinating the old one. And the side we're fighting against has a constitution based on ours. The whole thing is upside down."

Rob turns the radio down. "I've always regretted not standing up. I should've been out there protesting."

I stare out the window, watching the landscape speed by. "Well it's understandable. You were in dental school." My thoughts swirl. *Is that a good enough reason?*

"Only because my dad's a dentist and one of his old fraternity buddies pulled some strings to get me in." Rob shrugs. "I wasn't really into it, but I had no other plan. And there was no way I was going to 'Nam. When I graduated one of my dad's friends got me a medical exemption." He shakes his head. "Dad will be cleaning that guy's teeth for free forever."

My mind flashes to Craig. He was no dentist's son. And where did good health get him? Six feet under. But how can I blame Rob for not wanting to die? And what about our first ride with the Congressman? I accused good ol' Cub and his buddies of doing the same thing for their sons, and now I'm letting it slide for Rob? Shit, no one should be going to this war. I should be ecstatic Rob got out of it, grateful that some people are lucky enough to have connections. I shift uncomfortably in my seat.

"So, you got a job after you graduated?" I ask, wanting to exit the riots and war. Get back on the road to normal life.

"Dad got me an interview with a big dental group in the Bay Area. All they could talk about were their pads on the beach, Porsches, and country clubs. They offered me a job."

"Wow, right out of school! How lucky!"

Rob glances at me, his jaw tight. "It really turned me off. Just because I didn't go to protests doesn't mean I want to sell out to the establishment."

"Oh, right, right."

I look down, feeling the vibe between us quiver. *What's wrong with me?* I sound like a materialistic pig. But why else do you become a dentist? It's not like you're saving lives or finding a cure for something. You do it for the money, right?

"So, what do you want to do?" I ask. I feel Kris tapping the back seat with his toe. Why? Am I being too nosy?

"I thought I'd work at a free clinic or something," Rob says. "But my dad said only losers did that kind of thing. He said I owed it to him, and his frat brother who pulled the strings to get me admitted, to make something of myself." Rob sighs and glances at me. "When I turned down the position, my dad about lost it."

"But couldn't you have done it and just donated the extra bread to a clinic?" says Kris.

I hate to admit it, but Kris does come up with some good ideas every now and then.

Rob shakes his head. "I would've had to put up with all those plastic people. I couldn't do it. At least not then."

We sit in silence for a while. Walking away from a career after all those years in school. Who does that? Usually someone who totally drops out of society or forms some kind of cult. Obviously Rob hasn't done that. He wanted to do something worthy. It sounds like he's still messed up over it.

"But now you're a dentist in Chicago. How'd that happen?" I ask.

"Well, for a while I worked construction. Dad kept threatening that he'd get his friend to void my exemption, but Mom got on his case and they pretty much left me alone. Then one night I was getting stoned with my friend, Davy, who got exempted for flat feet. We got it into our heads that we wanted to hitchhike around the world."

"Far out!" I feel a rush.

He flashes his dimples.

"I dream about going to France," I say. "If I could hitchhike there, I would."

"Ha, right," Kris says. "This is only our first day hitching and you've wanted to bail out at least seven times."

I whip around in my seat. "No, only once. And you know why."

"Actually, it would've been easier having a chick with us," Rob says. "More rides and not as lonely."

"That's what you'd think," Kris says.

I turn away from Kris and slam my back against my seat. Wrath tightens my throat so I can't even choke out a comeback. I breathe in deep and stare a thousand miles down the road. I just want to get to Chicago and call Ginny. I don't care how many times I hear "I told you so." I can't wait to get as far away from Kris as possible.

"Anyway," Rob continues, "we started making plans. We decided that we'd travel for a year and work odd jobs along the way. Davy's a bartender and I had my construction experience."

"I bet that plan blew everyone's minds," I say. Mature, gorgeous, *and* adventurous.

Rob snorts and glances at me. "My dad freaked out. Called me an ingrate. Said I was irresponsible because I still had school loans to pay off. My mom thought I was being brainwashed by some California cult."

"I think it takes guts to do what you want and not what's expected," I say. "Did you make it all the way around the world?"

He rakes his fingers through his blond waves. An anxious look transforms his face.

"We hitched down the California coast through Mexico, all the way to Costa Rica. The most serene setting in the world. The people are so open and friendly. The surfing was outta sight. For the first time in my life, I got up at dawn to surf. What a religious experience, watching the sun rise over the waves. We decided to settle in for a while."

"What'd you live on?" Kris asks.

"It didn't take much. The hostel was only a few bucks a day. Pot was super cheap. Davy got a job in a café. I did some construction work around the village."

"Sounds like paradise," I say.

Rob turns toward me and our eyes meet. "It was."

I envision long sunsets on a warm beach. Interesting conversations over fruity drinks. Then another thought strikes. "Do you speak Spanish?"

"Davy did. I tried to pick it up, but after a few months I felt time ticking away. I got restless. Needed to keep going, stick to our plan."

He pauses.

I wait.

He takes a deep breath, then continues.

"Davy wanted to stay. He'd met a girl. Liked the whole scene down there. He wasn't ready to leave. I should've gone on alone, but I didn't have the balls." He pauses again, takes another deep breath, then sighs. "So I laid a guilt trip on him. About how I gave up a shot at a big time career. How he could come back here when we were done. He finally agreed. We got as far as Panama."

"And?" I prompt.

Rob clears his throat. "And one morning, while I was surfing, the police raided the place where we were staying and found our stash of weed."

"Ohhh, bummer," Kris says.

Rob's eyes squint into the rearview mirror. "They busted Davy. Hauled him out of bed and threw him in jail."

My mind flashes through all the stories I've heard of foreign prisons. Torture, filth, hard labor. Behind bars until death or bribery. I feel his dream warping into a nightmare. Becoming all the *what ifs* everyone warns you about.

"Did they get you too?" I ask.

"They tried, but couldn't pin anything on me. I was lucky."

"What happened to Davy?"

Rob clenches the steering wheel. "He's still there."

He presses down on the gas pedal and the car surges. My heart races as the Bug's motor strains past eighty. I'm trapped in a small hurtling object. Trying not to freak out, I look back at Kris, who's now sitting forward. Our eyes meet. His steady blue gaze calms me. Like always.

"Can you get the State Department involved?" Kris asks.

"His parents are trying everything," Rob says, his voice catching. "Got lawyers both here and in Panama. But there's not much you can do when you're caught with dope down there."

"So, what did you do?" I'm hoping for a happy ending. Trying to stay cool, but anxious for Rob to let up on the gas pedal.

"I hung around for a while, but there was no way of knowing when his case would go to trial. After a few weeks, he told me to go on ahead. He'd catch up with me when he got out. I felt so guilty leaving him, but there was nothing more I could do. So I left."

I bite my lower lip. What would Kris have done if it was us? What would I have done?

"Did you go back home?" I squeak out.

"I made it up to Canada. But everyone thought I was a draft dodger. So I came home after a few months."

I hang on tight to the armrest as we veer into one lane and then another, passing cars right and left.

"I felt like such a loser," he says, his voice bouncing with the car. "So, I gave in and joined a dental practice in Chicago."

The speedometer drops to seventy-five, seventy, sixty-five. My Wild Mouse carnival ride levels out. I suck in as much air as my lungs can handle without being obvious and let it all out. "Well, you can't give up," I say.

"I won't." Rob's voice hardens. "I've been sending Davy money to help with the legal cost. And I'm paying bribes to keep him healthy." He gives me a weak smile. "That's what keeps me going."

"Well, that's a good thing." I settle for the not-so-happy but hopeful ending.

"You're lucky you have a job that lets you do that," Kris says. "You know, help out."

"Yeah," Rob says, his tone pensive. "But as soon as he's free, so am I." He turns to me, his brown eyes crystallizing. "I just can't see being a dentist forever."

I lean back, staring out at the passing farmland. I've already changed my major three times. What could I do forever? An idea jumps into my head.

"There's rotten teeth in Costa Rica, too, right?"

"For sure," Rob laughs. "But there's no money. And money's the ticket. At least until I can get Davy out of that hellhole."

Money. He had turned it down to be free, now it's helping to buy freedom for Davy. Does money make you free or tie you down?

"We're here," Rob says, pulling off the road at his exit. I open the door and we get out. Rob pops the hood. I lean back inside to say goodbye to Rob.

Rob touches my shoulder. "Wait." He opens the glove compartment, fishes out a coin the size of a half dollar and hands it to me. I stare at it under the car's interior light. Etched into the silver is a shining sun over the sea and mountains. A peaceful feeling washes over me.

Rob looks into my eyes with a smile that I now know isn't so carefree.

"It's enough to buy you two beers," he says, "but only in Costa Rica."

I put a hand on his and look directly into his eyes. "Thank you, Rob. I hope you find your dream soon."

His voice is soft. "Thanks. And don't lose yours."

He watches us pick up our packs and waves goodbye. As he drives away, I realize dreams never really disappear. They just lie inside you until something nudges them. I watch Kris shuffling ahead of me with the pack on his back. I imagine a briefcase in his hand. Substitute a suit for the army jacket. An office for the road. I finger the smooth, cool silver coin in my pocket, my heart thumping. I run up to him. His look shifts from surprise to curious as I press the coin into his hand, locking our fingers together. Costa Rica isn't on our route, but being young and free is. Being in love is. This is our map.

Kris studies the coin under the highway lamp. He looks into my eyes.

"Lena?"

"Yes?"

"I want you to know that no matter how pissed you get, or I get, or whatever else happens, I'll never leave you stranded in Panama."

A small laugh escapes me. "Not even for a sexy stewardess?"

Kris's eyes dance. "No." He flips the coin back to me. "And not for all the beer in Costa Rica."

Chapter Thirty-One
First Citation

Kris

Lena puts her backpack on the ground, sticks out her thumb and smiles at me. Our world is in balance again.

I hear a siren in the distance. Maybe there's an accident ahead. Hopefully no one's hurt, but slow traffic might mean more chances for a ride. I settle in next to Lena and look down the highway. A cop car is speeding in our direction, lights flashing. It's got to be heading toward the accident or whatever happened down the road. Lena and I watch it scream our way. As it gets closer, I can see the officer. It looks like he's staring straight at us. He starts to slow down. Dammit, he's pulling over.

Lena looks at me. "We're not doing anything wrong, are we?"

I shrug, watching the cop car come to a stop in front of us. "Not that I know of."

The cop gets out of his car and walks toward us. He's a big dude and he's not smiling.

He stops in front of us with a hand on his holster and scans us head to toe, then says, "Can I see your IDs?"

I hand over my license. Lena rummages through Tang, finds her wallet and hands over her license, giving the cop a huge, sunny California smile. The cop stares at her driver's license, and then stares at Lena.

"Where are you going?"

"Minnesota," she says.

"Where in Minnesota?"

"Hope to make Minneapolis by late tonight," I say, smiling.

"Why are you going to Minneapolis?" the cop asks.

"To visit my boyfriend's aunt," Lena squeaks out.

What's up with this guy?

The cop eyes us. Neither of us breathes. He taps our licenses. "Both of you wait right here." We watch him walk back to his patrol car, get in, and talk into his radio microphone.

"Is he taking us to jail?" Lena asks. Her eyes shift to the cars slowing down to gawk at us. "Everyone is looking at us like we're criminals."

"Just be cool," I say, as I smile and wave at a car of rubbernecks. "These people should take a picture. It would last longer."

"What's taking him so long?" Lena says, squinting at the cop in his car.

"He's probably calling our names in to the FBI to make sure we aren't anti-American radicals or wanted by the narcs."

"Whaat? The FBI?"

"Didn't you tell me you joined up with some of the Vietnam Vets protesting the war?"

"Yeah, but all I did was blockade buildings." She wrings her hands.

"Well, let's hope these guys don't have pictures of you in their federal data base."

"No one told me it was a federal offense. And I only did it a couple of times."

"We'll probably both go down for it. They'll usually handcuff you together and throw you in solitary," I say, trying hard to keep a straight face.

Either Lena doesn't get my joke or doesn't care.

She grabs my arm. "What can they do to me?"

"I don't know. Maybe they'll give you a ticket for soliciting."

"Soliciting? No way! Look at the way I'm dressed." She sweeps her arm across her coat.

"Soliciting rides, you nutcase. Lighten up." I grin and poke her in the side.

"Stop it!" Lena's voice goes up a notch. "Will it go on our permanent record? I've never even gotten a parking ticket."

"Oh, yeah, we'll both be branded as known convicts."

"Stop joking. My parents are going to kill me, Kris! Why didn't you tell me this could happen? You said everything was cool. You've done it a million times."

"And a million times it *was* cool."

"So, you really don't know what they'll do?"

I shake my head and laugh. "Take it easy. At worst, we'll probably have to mail in some tiny fine."

She gives me a hard push. "This isn't funny."

"Just let me do the talking."

"Yeah, right. You're the one who got us into this," Lena huffs.

The cop gets out of the car and walks over. "What's going on between you two?"

I put my arm around Lena. "Nothing sir. I was teasing her a little."

"You think this is funny?" he says.

"No sir, not at all."

The cop stares us down, his jaw clenched. "I should do your parents a favor and send you back home to work off the fine." He hands us each a pink slip of paper. "But I'm letting you off with a written warning this time. It's against the law to hitchhike or walk on the roadway. So, get off this interstate."

"Oh, thank you, sir. We really appreciate it," says Lena.

I breathe a sigh of relief and thank him, then say, "If we're not allowed to hitch or walk, how do we get off the interstate?"

The cop stares bullets at me. Does he think I'm being a smart-ass? Thank God Lena butts in, getting his attention off me as she says, "Please give us your advice, officer. This isn't as fun as I was told it would be." Then she turns and glowers at me. I've changed my mind—I'd rather have the cop staring me down.

The cop softens his stare as he looks at Lena. "You, young lady, should reconsider your choice of boyfriends," he says, glancing at me in disgust. "But for the time being, both of you come with me. I'll take you down to the next exit. The rides should be easier there. Just stay off the interstate. You don't want to spend time in the Cook County Jail."

We thank him and climb into the back of his patrol car. While the cop is talking on his radio, Lena leans over and whispers, "Why is he doing this?"

"Maybe he wants us out of his territory," I whisper back.

Whatever the reason, I'm pumped to be moving closer to Minnesota.

After a short drive to the next exit, we get out, he rolls down his window and leans out to give us the evil eye. "Remember. Stay off the interstate. The cops around here will throw you in the hole just as soon as look at you."

I smile, thank him and wave goodbye as I look at the citation. Damn. For all my miles of thumbing, I've never been written up once. Ticks me off. I crumple it up and jam it in my pocket as I look around. He didn't do us any favors dropping us here. I've been dumped at this spot before. Even with the Holiday Inn sitting right in front of us, this is the 'Calumet Expressway Black Hole of Hitching' exit. Getting a ride out of here isn't gonna be easy.

Lena and I stand with outstretched thumbs as cars pass. I'm starting to feel the reject vibe. We spend an hour playing I SPY but as the temperature drops, we're stuck on words like popsicle, ice cube, and frozen. It begins to sleet, so we switch to a game of "I'm as warm as…" an hour later we're no warmer and our conversation is getting prickly. By hour three we're reduced to arguing about which are smarter, dogs or cats. All I can think is that Reg would be giving me a lot more warmth than what I'm getting from Lena.

"We've got to do something," Lena says, hopping up and down, rubbing her hands together.

"Like what?" I ask, knowing there's nothing we can do. "We've just got to hang in there for a while. Somebody will stop."

"Why isn't anyone picking us up?"

"How should I know?"

"You're the expert, the one who's done this a million times. And by the way, what's your 'Rules of the Road' on freezing to death?"

"There aren't any," I say.

"Because?"

"Because a ride always comes."

"Maybe you should rewrite your rules and make them reality instead of fairy tales."

"You want reality? Maybe you should start showing some leg. Maybe that'll get us a ride."

"Oh, really? So *that's* why you asked me to come. Male chauvinist pig! You're all alike! You want me to show some leg? I'll show you some leg."

She pulls up her coat, kicks me in the shin, then grabs her stupid suitcase and marches off toward the road.

I'm laughing out loud and rubbing my leg as I watch her waddle off. "Where the hell do you think you're going?" I yell. "Minnesota's five hundred miles—in the opposite direction."

"I'm going anywhere you're not," she yells back. "Oink, oink."

I take a deep drag off the last of my smoke, throw the butt on the ground, and go after her. This is getting old.

I catch up with her and grab her arm. "Lena, don't act crazy. We can't walk around the Southside of Chicago this late. There are gangs around here. We'll end up in the morgue."

"We're going to end up there anyway—frozen solid."

I wave at the Holiday Inn next to the ramp.

"Look, we can get something to eat at that hotel coffee shop." I've been hoarding our cash for emergencies, and this qualifies. It'll give us a chance to warm up and think over our next move.

"Fine," she says. "As soon as we get there I'm going to call Ginny and tell her she was right. This was a stupid, idiotic idea."

"Do whatever you want," I say, then add, "You're a liberated woman."

"Go to hell, Kris," she says. Her voice breaks. "I trusted you."

Being told to "go to hell" is nothing new, but the trust thing hits me like a punch to the gut. It brings back a memory of my dad's speech when he dropped me off the first day at Kent. How he said that being on my own meant being responsible for the decisions I make and for how they affect others. I guess this is one of those times that he was talking about.

Should we splurge on a room? It'll blow all our cash, but we won't need it—we'll catch the big ride tomorrow. A room will give us a chance to get cleaned up, get our heads straight and get in a soft bed together. There's nothing wrong with any of those outcomes. But, as we head down the ramp toward the hotel, a *No Vacancy* sign blinks in the darkness.

I glance at Lena, who's shivering and holding her gloved hands under her armpits.

I put my arm around her as we walk toward a black Cadillac idling at the lobby entrance. A big man in a long, camel-colored coat gets out of the car, opens the back door, and escorts a couple of sexy chicks into the hotel. Bet they won't have any trouble getting a room.

The coffee shop is practically empty. A row of lemon-yellow vinyl booths line the walls. Tables with fake-wood laminate occupy the middle of the room. We slide into a booth and read menus printed on the paper placemats. After eating nothing but cheese crackers and cookies, the soup-of-the-day and hot chocolate will be a feast. The waitress takes our order and Lena sinks into her seat, eyes closed. I light up a smoke and try to figure out what to do next. I've got to be calm and reassuring, but I'm stumped. What if no one picks us up? Could we survive a night out in sub-freezing weather? I haven't brought it up yet, but I didn't even bring a sleeping bag. I just didn't think I'd need it. Based on past experience, I'd be nice and cozy at Aunt Ella's or at least sacking out in the backseat of someone's warm car right now if I was hitching alone. But I know I'm gonna pay for it big time if I don't get us a ride out of this hellhole soon.

"Okay, Kris," Lena says between sips of chicken noodle soup. "How much longer are we gonna do this?"

She sounds almost reasonable. Like Grandma says, 'There's nothing like chicken soup to cure what ails you.' "It's still kind of early, just past nine," I say, knowing she loves my optimism. "Something will turn up."

"With our luck, that something is going to be a blizzard," she says. "Oh, but I forgot, your 'Rules of the Road' should save us from that."

"Jesus, Lena, give me a break." Her hammering me with my "Rules of the Road" pisses me off. If I was with Jim, we wouldn't be wasting our time in a coffee shop. We'd stay out on the highway 'til something turned up. It always does. But Lena's not Jim. She's coming unglued.

I stand and take out my wallet. "Warm up and relax. I'm gonna check in with the front desk. Maybe they've got a room."

She rolls her eyes. "Didn't you see the 'No Vacancy' sign?"

I turn my back on her, murmuring, "Maybe there's a cancellation," and head toward the front desk. I'm grasping at straws. As I walk, my mind is buzzing. I should've planned this trip out a little more, but how could I know we would get stuck? Anyway, things will work out—they always do. Don't they? I glance back at Lena and smile. I exhale, counting my cash as I approach the front desk.

I nod at the night manager and start talking, knowing there's only one certainty in my life at this moment. If I don't get us a room or find a ride, one of two things is going to happen.

Lena's either gonna kill me, or she's gonna drive me insane.

Chapter Thirty-Two
Big Man

Kris

The night manager looks like a career woman, navy blue suit with the motel logo embroidered on her coat, no-nonsense eyes and a set jaw. But hey, deep down inside, she's still a woman—I can work my magic. I explain our situation, giving an Oscar-worthy performance as I deliver our tale of woe. She shakes her head and says in a clipped tone, "Booked solid. You know, because of the bad weather. You should've called ahead."

Boy, don't I know it. I can hear the pinging of ice hitting the windows. I look back at Lena. She's still eating her soup. I decide to take a little detour before I have to tell her I struck out. Outside I stand hunched under the awning, smoking a cigarette. Different thoughts of survival pass through my brain but they extinguish as quickly as the butt that I flick onto the sleet-covered parking lot. I walk back inside. Time to face the music.

"We should have asked a couple hours ago," Lena says after I give her the news. "Like when it first started sleeting. Maybe we could've gotten one then." She throws her arms up in frustration. "Why does it always take you so long to do anything about anything?"

"Because if you weren't with me, I wouldn't do anything about anything. I'd just go with the flow. Because that's what I do. Because things always work out." I sigh. "Lena, you have to get off my case."

I shove all the complimentary crackers I can get my hands on into my pockets, stand and wave at her to stay put. "You stay here. I'll get us a ride. Just keep an eye on me—I'll wave for you when someone stops."

I slide out of the booth. She doesn't look up from her cup of hot chocolate. As a last minute thought, I grab Tang, her fluorescent orange bag. She looks up, but says nothing. I head out the door, back to the overpass. In the sleety darkness, I put Tang in front of me like a beacon. Someone's got to notice it in their headlights.

I can just make out Lena's silhouette through the window of the coffee shop. Leaning on the table, her head in her hands. The more I stare, the more our situation gets to me. How the hell can things go so wrong? It's been twelve hours, two fights, a warning ticket, countless broken road rules, and now we're stuck in the frozen rain at the Black Hole exit. I shouldn't have asked her to come. But she hasn't called Ginny, so she hasn't given up yet. I light my last cigarette. After about half an hour, Lena trudges out of the coffee shop.

"Your turn to warm up," she mumbles from behind her thick wool scarf.

I may be imagining it, but I think I hear an apologetic tone.

We take turns standing in the freezing rain with our thumbs out. The colder and later it gets, the longer we stay inside getting wired on coffee and hot chocolate. Cold, wet, tired and hungry. It doesn't get any better than this.

Around midnight, the coffee shop begins to close. Spending the night under the overpass is about to become reality. Lena slumps further into the booth, her hands gripping the coffee cup, like a life preserver. Knowing I'm not gonna get a word out of her, I walk up to the cashier. Maybe we can borrow some blankets from the motel. I fill her in on our dilemma, ask about the possibility of blankets, and move on to general bullshitting with her. A few minutes later, I walk back toward Lena, feeling a little better.

"Hey," I say, sliding into the booth. "Geneva's not going to charge us for the coffee and hot chocolate refills."

Lena gives me a weak smile. It's a start.

"And guess what? She loves Airedales. She used to have one as a kid. I told her all about Reggie." I keep my tone upbeat. I'm buying time to think of a gentle way to say it's time for us to bed down under the overpass. I nod and drum the table. "She says she'll try to sneak us some blankets."

"You keep the blankets," Lena says. "I'm not moving. I'll sleep here under the table. Let her call the cops. At least the jail will be heated."

I reach across the table and grab her hand. "Lena, I'm just as bummed out as you, but we're going to have to make the best of this." Her big brown icy glare and the way she pulls her hand away tells me she's more than bummed.

My attention is drawn toward the door. The big man in the camel-haired overcoat comes in and walks toward Geneva, who grins and starts chatting him up. She nods her head in our direction a couple of times.

Geneva is turning out the lights. I stand in front of Lena with my hands on my backpack. I keep my voice calm and reassuring. "They're closing down. We've got to keep it together. We have two choices. Keep thumbing or camp out under the overpass." Out of the corner of my eye, I see Big Man walking toward us.

"Excuse me," he says. "My friend Geneva tells me you're in a fix. I might be able to assist you. If you're interested."

Interested? Hell yeah, I'm interested. "We sure are," I say.

He points outside, toward the highway. "There's another motel down the road and let's just say I sort of have a controlling interest in it. I can probably arrange a room."

"Sounds good," I say casually. Can't be too over-anxious, there might be a catch. With his cigar and slicked back hair, this guy looks like he's straight out of a mafia movie.

"Okay," he says, nodding. "I'll give them a call. I can give you a ride."

Thank God. My luck showed up at the eleventh hour. A warm bed is the perfect way to end this disastrous night. What could it cost, twenty bucks?

"We're ready," I say, beaming at Lena. But I get 'the look' from across the table. I turn to Big Man. "Do you mind giving us a minute?"

"Not at all. I'll say good night to Geneva, and you can tell me what you decide."

I wait for him to get out of earshot, and then sit down across from Lena. "Now what?" I ask.

"I don't like the looks of that guy."

"What? You're nuts."

"I don't want to go with a complete stranger to a roadside motel in the middle of the night."

Lena looks scared. And it's not the "I'm scared of freezing to death" look she had earlier. I can tell she's more than skittish.

"Lena, we've been doing this all day long. Your thumb was out as far as mine begging for rides from total strangers on the freeway. This guy is offering us a ride to another motel. It's the same thing." I'm standing my ground on this.

"Kris, you saw him out front. Girls were getting out of his car and they weren't selling Girl Scout cookies."

"You're crazy. He's not going to do anything. Plus, you have me to protect you."

"No one has any idea where we are. He could bump you off and I'd be forced to be one of his girls. Like all those runaways everyone reads about."

"I can't believe you." I roll my eyes. She's gone off the deep end.

Her gaze slides over to him, then back to me. "I'm serious, Kris. He gives me the creeps."

"Well, sleeping in below zero gives me the creeps," I say, searching for a way to make this work. "Look, he knows Geneva. He's a businessman. And you don't look anything like those girls, and I mean that in a good way." I grab my pack and push Lena's bag toward her. "Just follow my lead." I signal thumbs up at Big Man. He walks over to the front desk to make the call.

I coax Lena along as we trail behind him to his Cadillac. The sleet has turned to snow. I get into the front seat and Lena sits in back behind Big Man. She stares out the side window like she's being led to the gallows. He pulls onto a service road that curves away from the main drag.

"Where you from?" he asks.

"Ohio. Lena's a California girl."

"Really? I lived in California for a few years. It was nice, but I ended up back home in Chicago. How long you two been on the road?"

"Since eight o'clock this morning. We were hoping to be in Minneapolis by now. But rides have been short and far between. And this crappy weather doesn't help. We really appreciate the ride to your motel. You pick up a lot of hitchhikers?"

"Sometimes—it depends. When I saw you two in the coffee shop, you kind of reminded me of my own kids."

"Oh, do they hitchhike?" a relieved voice pipes up from the back seat.

Big Man doesn't answer. You can cut the silence with a knife. Great.

"Well," I say, "if they do hitch, tell them never to get out at the Calumet Exit. It's the black hole for catching rides."

"Actually, I can't tell them anything. I don't know where they are."

I start flipping through my mental Rolodex for small talk in awkward situations.

"Did they disappear hitchhiking?" Lena asks.

"Oh, no. Nothing like that. Divorce. The judge said I was a bad influence. Their mom disappeared with them years ago."

Based on his answer, I don't want to ask him what he does for a living. I'm curious, but there's a good chance the answer might be something Lena doesn't want to hear. Before I can figure out what to say, he rambles on.

"I often wonder what they're doing. I'm hoping college, making something of themselves."

"That's too bad you haven't seen them," Lena says. "Maybe they're looking for you."

"When I saw you two, I kind of imagined them. Hopefully they're adventurous and seeing the world like you."

"There's no way you can get in touch with them?" Lena asks.

"No. But a day doesn't go by that I don't think of them."

Finally, we pull up to a two story L-shaped building, darkened except for the flashing vacancy sign. We stop under the awning at the lobby entrance.

"Well, here we are," Big Man says, keeping the motor running.

We start getting out of the car and he reaches out and pats my shoulder.

"Look, I don't get many chances to help out kids like you." He pulls a big wad of bills from his pocket and hands it to me. "Here, take this for your trip."

"This is way too much," I say, handing the money back to him. I get what he's trying to do, but this much money makes me uncomfortable.

"Well, there's a room waiting for you. Take this in case you get stuck tomorrow night." He gives me back a twenty dollar bill.

I thank him and stuff it in my pocket. I shake his hand, realizing that taking the money is kind of a twofold act of kindness, doing as much for him as for us. I look back at Lena. She opens the door, and then pauses. She puts her hand on his shoulder and gives it a squeeze before she slides out. We stand on the curb and watch him drive away.

A little bell tinkles when I push the motel lobby door open. I'm hit by a warm wash of sweet and dirty smells. A swirl of haze trails behind us as we walk through layers of smoke to the front desk at the far end of the room. The carpet is a tie-dye of stains and cigarette burns. It's sticky under my boots. A girl about our age sits on a shabby vinyl couch, with a cig perched in the "V" of her fingers while staring at a small black and white TV that's bolted to a table. Through strands of mousy brown hair, her dark eyes look at us indifferently. Her makeup is laid on thick. She takes a drag and shifts her gaze back to the television.

There's no one at the front desk and no bell to ring for help. Lena heads down the hallway to the restroom while I wait for someone to check us in. I look back over my shoulder at the girl on the couch. Even though she's wearing all that makeup, she has a peculiar look in the black and white glow of the TV. It's as if the flicker of light in her face that normally gives depth to dimension is missing. She zeroes in on my awkward attempt not to stare. In the dim light, I see her rough edge, a veneer that won't wash away. I want to say hello, be cool, do something normal, but I just turn back to the desk.

"Can I help you?" The clerk walks in from a back office door, bringing the pungent smell of booze with him. Maybe he has an extra bottle I can buy. It's been a long day.

I wonder what name Big Man gave. I don't even know his name. "The guy in the Cadillac said…"

"Yeah, yeah. I know." The clerk swings the registry book across the chipped Formica counter. Is he smirking? Maybe it's just a tic.

This signing in business strikes me funny, like something out of an old Western. I consider signing in as Black Bart. What does it matter? But then it hits me like a freight train. I'm gonna have to sign in both of us, like we're married. My ears feel a rush of heat. I fidget with the pen.

The clerk grins. "Forget your name?"

I know my face looks like a stoplight, but I ignore him and do what I need to do.

He squints at the signature. "Mr. and Mrs. Anderson?" He snorts. "Like the fairy tales?"

Lena walks up and stands behind me. I inhale the fresh scent of soap. I grab the room key off the desk and take Lena's hand. "Exactly."

The girl on the couch says, "Don't mind him. He thinks he's so funny."

We walk away from the front desk. I wink at the girl watching television and she winks back at us. Lena looks at me like I'm crazy but doesn't say a word.

I think she's starting to get the hang of life on the road.

Chapter Thirty-Three
No-tell

Lena

The room decor is part Disney Cinderella, part Jane Fonda Barbarella. There's a fluffy pink bedspread with frilly red pillows. The scratched and cigarette-burned furniture is spray-painted white and gold. The garishness makes me uneasy. I pace, opening drawers, reorganizing my bag, feeling awkward. I've never spent the night in a motel with anyone but my parents. Kris turns on the TV, kicks off his boots, and flops back against the big fluffy pillows. He looks totally at home. I'm wondering how he can be so comfortable in these surroundings when the snow-covered overpass enters my mind. A night in a makeshift bordello beats a night under that concrete freezer any day.

I walk over to the window and pull back a corner of the faded beige curtain, looking out over a parking lot of semis. The motel's blinking neon sign strobes a red glare on my face and an emptiness comes over me. I can't ignore the frustrations of this day, but I don't want to take them to bed either. Maybe there's a place I can keep them until tomorrow. I hear the shower running. Kris beat me to it. I don't want to wait. I've got to scrub this day, these feelings, away. *Now.*

I tap on the bathroom door, then push it open and enter the steam-filled room. I strip off my clothes and pull back the shower curtain. Kris moves over as I step under the showerhead and turn my back to him. I lift my face to the spray of warm water. I'm desperate not to feel desperate. I wash myself, squeezing the washcloth, and the day's grime and frustrations down the drain. Then I just stop, standing with my hands at my sides, letting the hot water rain down on my face. Warm soapy water runs over my neck and shoulders. Kris takes the washcloth from my hand and slowly, softly, washes away all the things that came between us today. He lightly kisses my ear, my neck, and I turn to face him. Through the steam, we join in a shared desire to forget this day and transform this night. His hands slide down my soapy back, gripping my butt and lifting me onto his waist. I wrap my legs around him and we slide against one another until he's inside me. With my arms around his neck, I hold on tight as the hot water rolls over us, his hands slipping and sliding over my thighs as we push and pull and find our rhythm. The water eventually turns lukewarm, but we're making our own heat as Kris carries me to the bed. I fall back with him on top of me and every bad thing about the day falls away. We create our own map, following our passion in every which way imaginable.

Afterward we relax, exhausted, but happy. The motel is stingy with its gas on this cold Chicago night. They must be counting on body heat to warm the rooms. I reach out from under the blankets for Kris's backpack and take out the road map and one of his flannel shirts. I slip the shirt on and sink into its warm embrace. Our day rumbles through my head. I turn on the table lamp and spread the map on the bed. Carefully, I circle our hitching stops and draw symbols of our rides. A peace sign on the US flag, a sad faced Deadhead bear sitting on top of a school bus, a bra with a pair of wings, a sun rising over a mountain that's the shape of a molar, a get-out-of-jail-free card, and a large ruffled pillow sham with dollar signs all over it. A trickle of pride runs through me. I just hitchhiked four hundred miles!

"I wasn't that bad today, was I?" I say, looking at Kris, but he's already crashed out. His face is peaceful, almost vulnerable, peeking out from beneath the pink fluff.

Did I gripe too much when things got heavy? I know it wasn't his fault we couldn't get a ride, but his laid back attitude gets on my nerves, along with how he helped that blonde Barbie get dressed. Still, I need to get over it. Tomorrow, I'll try not to be so uptight. This is supposed to be an adventure. If I wanted a walk in the park, I could've stayed in Cleveland.

I turn off the TV and turn out the light. Pushing aside the mounds of pink frill, I snuggle up to Kris. His steady breathing is a soothing balm and I sink against his warm body. My mind, however, is still churning over the day's rides. I know that I won't rest until I put my thoughts into words. I turn on the bedside lamp and dig my journal out of my bag. In the dim light, I write:

> *The Cadillac waits, shivering.*
> *Headlights, speckled with snow*
> *Light the way to gilded mirrors*
> *On flocked bedroom walls.*
> *Simple words bounce then sink*
> *Under ghosts of loss and regret.*
> *Money clip flashes*
> *Words of thanks crystallize*
> *Then swirl with the flakes and smoke*
> *To our feet.*
> *An elevator door opens.*
> *The ice machine clinks*
> *Hot water dances over us*
> *As I remember*
> *Why we came.*

Chapter Thirty-Four
Breakfast of Champions

Kris

The droning sound coming from the bathroom serves as my daily alarm clock, even on the road. Lena's up and drying her hair. I can't understand why she doesn't just let it go natural. As soon as we're outside, it'll be like that blow dryer never existed.

I roll out of bed and throw on yesterday's clothes. I glance at the clock, almost eight. We're six hours and possibly a couple of rides away from Minnesota and I'm psyched. I spotted a drugstore down the street last night. I'll restock the snacks while Lena's getting dressed.

The drugstore is old. A marble soda fountain counter has been converted to a display case for gum and candy. Scarves and hats hang on its chrome soda dispensers. The ceiling is high and the off-white paint is cracked, but the store has everything it should. When I was a kid, it was comic books and Bazooka bubble gum. Now it's a few packs of Kools and a jumbo bag of Hershey's Kisses for Lena. That's money well spent. In times of trouble, chocolate's supposed to be the best cure. The final addition to today's trip is a movie theatre-sized box of Good & Plenty.

Back at the motel, I stuff all our snacks into our packs. Lena sits on the bed, smiling. I blurt out what's been on my mind all night. "You know, I signed us in as Mr. and Mrs. last night. I think in some states that makes us legal."

"Legal what?" Lena's eyes widen. "No! Really? I don't believe it."

"Well, just in case, let's keep it our little secret."

We leave the key in the ashtray and head toward the buffet. For a divey motel, I can't believe they serve a breakfast. We heap bacon, doughnuts, eggs and fried potatoes to the teetering point on our plates. I'm sure the Big Man wouldn't mind us snagging a couple pastries and stuffing them into the knapsack. Hopefully, our next meal is in Aunt Ella's kitchen.

Our window table sits on the sunny side of the room. We soak up the sun and scarf down our breakfast. Another top ten rule: When a free meal is offered, take it. I stare out the window, trying to get my thoughts together. I want Lena to understand how I thumb. It's hard for someone to get it when they're used to jumping into the family car and going. I wait 'til she takes a big bite of her jelly doughnut. I don't want any interruptions.

"Lena, I need to tell you something. Last spring in my Asian Culture class, I realized that hitchhiking is a Zen thing. It's letting the world come to you. Swimming with the current. Time becomes irrelevant. It might sound like a bunch of hooey, but hitching like that is what works for me."

She's quiet, listening, or maybe her mouth's too full for a comeback. Anyway, she likes that mystical stuff, so I go on.

"We don't get rides on a set schedule. They come when they come. Some might be hours apart or come in bunches. Some are short and some are long. It's all about letting go and being in sync with the universe. Like last night. Things always have a way of working out."

She reaches across the table for my hand and we interlock our fingers.

"I don't think it's hooey," she says, her brown eyes looking steadily into mine. "Maybe I jinxed us last night. Remind me to stay positive."

Getting up from the table, our stomachs stuffed and pockets full of napkin-wrapped pastries, I watch Lena load on her layers. I pull a plastic flower from the vase on the table and hold it out. "For my road rose."

Lena takes the flower and puts it in her hair. "You just now reminded me of the 'Jester' on my tarot cards. A knapsack in one hand, a rose in the other."

"What does it mean?" I ask.

"New beginnings, new adventures, and…"

"And?"

"Unlimited possibilities."

"Well, those tarot cards must be pretty good," I say. "That's just where we're headed."

Lena returns the flower to the vase. "I think so, too."

The motel's aging limo gives us a lift to the nearest roadway entrance ramp. The girl from the lobby is sitting in the front seat. I say, "Hi" and she gives me a weak smile. The limo pulls into a trailer park and stops. The girl gets out without a word and walks down the road crammed with trailers.

It's just Lena and me now, and I feel like a rich kid having Jeeves drop us off at our exclusive hitchhiking spot. When we get to the ramp, Lena and I try to open our own doors, but the limo driver gets out with that whole coat-and-hat thing goin' on and unloads our packs from the trunk. We thank him and give him a dollar tip.

After he drives away, I survey our surroundings. Lena isn't going to like it, but in my most 'matter of fact, I know what I'm doing' voice, I say, "There's not enough traffic here. We're gonna have to stand farther down the ramp."

"No way." She shakes her head. "That cop meant what he said. You heard him. They'll take us in the next time."

"But now it's daylight, people can see us. It's the only way we'll get a ride."

"Kris, the cops can see us too. I don't want to go back on that highway. Can't we try it from here for a while?" She plants herself at the top of the ramp and sticks out her thumb. So much for going with the flow. During the next half hour, a few cars pass, gunning it to get onto the highway. There aren't any other roads around and I don't want to end up back at that motel. I finish a smoke and grind the butt into the asphalt.

"C'mon." I pick up the backpack and start walking down the ramp. "We gotta get closer to the roadway. It'll more than double our chances to get rides."

"You're really pushing your Zen luck," she huffs. "We could go with the flow right into jail."

Forty-five minutes later, a Chevy station wagon stops about a hundred yards in front of us. I grab the big backpack and run toward it. I glance back over my shoulder to give Lena an "I told you so" look and see her running with Tang in one hand and the knapsack bouncing around her back. The buckle's busted, so the flap never quite closes all the way. Good & Plenty are popping out of the knapsack, leaving a pink and white trail down the berm. Lena must've had her fingers in the box already. At least we still have that jumbo bag of Hershey Kisses.

The radio's blasting AM Top 40 and two cute teenage girls wearing gobs of makeup and pale pink lipstick are giggling nervously in the front seat. The driver has dark curly hair like Lena's. Her friend's brown hair is pulled back in a ponytail. Through wads of chewing gum, they hit us with questions as we drive off.

"What's it like in college? Do you live together? What kinds of parties do you have? Do people do other stuff besides drink beer?" Chomp. Snap. Giggle. They're fishing for something.

"No parties," Lena deadpans. "We just study all the time."

I'm laughing on the inside. At least she still has her sense of humor. I give her hip a pinch, but I know she can't feel it through the layers.

"Hey, do you guys have any pot?" The curly haired driver blurts out. So that's it. Teenyboppers looking to score some weed.

"Nope," I say. "By the way, how far are you going?"

"A couple exits. We're headed back to the burbs. This side of town is too scary."

Fantastic. My Zen bites the dust.

About fifteen minutes later, the car slows to a crawl on the exit ramp. Under the overpass, the driver pulls off to the side and slams on the brakes. Both girls jump out. Lena and I watch as they spray paint SWASHY DOG in three-foot-tall black letters. Swashy? Never heard of it. Laughing and high on excitement, they throw the spray cans in the back. One hits the side of Lena's boot and leaves a dark smear.

Lena grabs the door handle. "We're getting out here."

I'm right behind her. We don't need this schoolgirl bullshit. We pull our packs out of the car, shut the door and they zoom off as we walk up the overpass ramp to the highway.

***

A couple of short rides later, we're only fifteen miles closer to Minnesota. Then a salesman picks us up on his way to O'Hare. We're slowly working our way out of Cook County. He lets us out in the middle of miles and miles of intertwining ramps. Cars coming and going in every direction in and out of the airport.

"You need to go that way." The salesman points over his shoulder to an overpass on the right, before pulling away.

I look out over the highway. With the jets roaring overhead, I can barely hear myself think.

"We're gonna have to make a run for it," I shout.

I can see Lena's adrenaline kicking in. She grips Tang's handle and takes a deep breath.

I give the signal and we tear across the lane. We make our way to the first ramp, no problem. But on the mad dash across the middle of the second ramp, the whole bag of Hershey Kisses comes flying out of Lena's knap sack.

We watch a pickup truck run over the bag. There's a pop and shiny silver kisses shoot out all over the ramp. A herd of passing cars finishes the job, squashing every kiss into the pavement.

"Dammit," I say, trying to catch my breath. "I could just cry."

"Cry me a river of chocolate silver tears," Lena sniffs.

She's being funny, but this is no time to wax poetic. I scan the highway. "We're on the wrong ramp." I feel my stomach drop. "This goes toward Milwaukee."

A whirring noise builds overhead. A helicopter is circling us. Now what?

The familiar sound of a police siren breaks through the roar of traffic. A patrol car appears and pulls next to us. The cop gets out, displaying black shades and a tightlipped expression. He holds out his hand and says, "IDs."

We dig them out and hand them over.

He closes our IDs in his fist and raises his chin. "Show me your hands."

What? Why? We stand palms up while he inspects them.

Finished with our hands, he walks over to the bags and unzips Tang. Lena gives me a panicky look. I shake my head.

The cop rifles through Tang and looks at us. "What's that stink?"

I poke Lena.

"Patchouli," she blurts.

His eyes narrow. "Some kind of drug?"

"No, no, perfume."

He turns to the big pack and dumps everything out. "Where's the cans?"

"Huh?"

"The cans, the spray paint cans. Where'd you throw them?"

Damn, those teenyboppers. I shake my head. "We don't have any cans."

"Two kids fitting your description were seen spray painting graffiti under an overpass. You want to tell me why you'd do that?"

I try to keep my voice steady. "It wasn't us, officer. We're just trying to get to my aunt's house." I give a slight nudge to Lena's foot.

She looks down at the spray paint streak across her boot, then crosses her feet to hide it.

"Your aunt, huh? The judge should like that story." He opens the rear door of his patrol car and nods at us. "Get in. We're going for a ride."

Lena's mouth drops open as her eyes dart to mine. We slide into the back of his car. He gets in the front seat. He twists around to glare at us through the metal grate separating the front and back seat.

"You're already in the system. You were warned yesterday. I'm gonna give you some time to, what do you hippie-types call it? Meditate on what you're doing? It's real peaceful in Cook County jail."

Lena clenches my arm.

The helicopter drones overhead. Another cop roars up on a motorcycle. Our cop gets out of his car, walks past our packs still on the side of the road, to talk to him. This is bullshit. Don't they have anything better to do? Like murders? Or drug busts? For God sakes, it's Chicago.

"I can't do this anymore," Lena says, her voice cracking.

I put my arm around her shoulders and feel her shaking. She's losing it. "We'll be okay,"

She pulls back and stares at me. "Okay? This is serious! It can affect our whole future." She shakes my arm off and slides to the other end of the seat. "I'm done with your phony Zen road trip. I have my own rulebook. I'm going to kiss up and beg forgiveness." Through clenched teeth she says, "Going on this trip is the worst decision I've ever made."

As I'm trying to process just how much Lena hates me, a call comes in on the patrol car's radio announcing a code that makes both cops stop what they're doing. They look at each other, run back to the car with alarm written on their faces and exchange information in rapid fire dialogue. The motorcycle cop guns his bike and roars off. Our tormentor jumps in the front seat. He scribbles something on a pad, pushes two warning citations at us and shouts, "If I see you on my highway again, you're both going to jail." We scramble out, grab our bags and watch as he screeches off. The helicopter tilts sideways and buzzes after him.

"Woo-hoo! Saved by the real bad guys," I say in a joking tone, but my forehead is damp with sweat.

"I'm going home," Lena says low and cold. "I'll find a payphone and call Ginny." I trail her down the ramp to a coffee shop. We unload our packs at the booth. The waitress sets down two cups of coffee and points the way to the restrooms and payphone. Lena digs in her purse for quarters. I roll two across the table. She stares at me, her eyes drained of emotion as she picks them up, then turns and walks away. Ten minutes later, she's back.

"Ginny's in Florida with her cousin," she spits out, sliding into the booth. Her face is stripped of color and her hair is tangled beyond Medusa.

"Lena, nothing's happened to us. I mean nothing really bad."

"You want to wait until it does?" She pounds her fist on the table. "Put me on a bus back home."

"I can't. I don't have the money."

"I don't want to end up in jail with a record. Can't you call Ella to come get us? Blame it on your wimpy girlfriend."

'Your wimpy ex-girlfriend' is what she really means. I make a play, hoping I can somehow fix this. "There's no way I can ask her to drive all the way to Chicago. We've got to hang in a little longer. When we get there, you can do what you want. But let's just finish this out, okay?"

She looks at me but doesn't utter a word. No curses. No names. No mocking of my 'Rules of the Road'. Taking a breath, she exhales as a look of resignation takes hold. It's an infinitesimal victory, but I'll take it. At least now I have a chance to redeem myself.

Chapter Thirty-Five
Circus Ride

Kris

So much for the dream vacation. But I'm not throwing in the towel yet. I think I can still save this hitchhiking disaster and maybe our relationship. I pull out an old thumbing trick—staring down rides. The eye-to-eye guilt factor has a way of stopping some cars. My plan works. Here come two guys pointing and gesturing as they pull over down the ramp. I walk up to the white early sixties Corvair. The passenger side is crushed in. The car is sputtering and smells of burning oil. I'm not feeling really good about this car. But, the snow is coming down in giant flakes, reminding me not to be picky.

The passenger rolls down his window. "We can give you a ride to Milwaukee," he says. "But we're low on gas. You guys have five bucks?"

They seem disheveled, but harmless. Five bucks to get us out of Illinois would be worth it. I walk back to Lena, nod at the car and say, "They're going all the way to Milwaukee."

"Thank God," she says, picking up her bag.

I add, "Oh, and they need five dollars for gas."

"What? Can they do that?"

"Yeah, they help us, we help them. C'mon."

They push open the rear driver's side door and motion for us to get in. It stinks of rancid grease, cigarette smoke, and moldy laundry. The driver introduces himself as Zeke. He's older than my dad, stubble-faced and has a cheek full of tobacco. His passenger is Biff, who looks like he's in his twenties. Biff sticks his hand over the seat and says, "Ten dollars will get us all the way to Milwaukee."

"You said five."

"I did? Well, it'll probably get us there. Sure you don't have a ten to spare?"

"I'm sure."

They take our money and turn up the country twang on the radio.

Before we can start down the ramp, the Corvair cha-chunks and dies. Zeke rolls down the window, spits and mutters something about a bad starter. Biff, Lena and I get out and push the car so Zeke can pop the clutch. The front passenger door won't open from the outside, so we have to all dive in the only door that works, the driver's side rear door. We push, the car sputters to life, we dive in. Biff crawls over the front seat and we are back on the road, again.

"So, you live in Milwaukee?" I ask.

Zeke shakes his head as he hands a cigarette to Biff and clamps one between his own lips. "We're pretty much from all over, but I was born in Kentucky and him in Ohio. Just up to see some cousins and then we're gonna to spend a couple days in Baraboo at the Circus Museum. We been workin' the carnivals from Texas to Pennsylvania."

The heater's broken so the windows stay rolled up. We're stuck in a dense haze as the boys puff away on their Camels.

Lena chokes out, "I love carnivals. What rides do you work?"

"No rides," says Zeke. "We're the clean-up crew. It's the best job 'cause we get all the money that falls out of them people's pockets. What do you think paid for this car, huh? The Round-Up is the best one for that, right Biff? Biff here's my nephew."

"Guess you meet a lot of different people," I say.

"Yeah," Biff says, as he exhales another cloud of smoke.

"You gotta have lots of stories," I say.

"Oh, we got stories," Zeke says. "'Member that girl, Biff? The one what lost her pants in the House of Whores ride?"

"Hell yeah! Aha, ha-ha."

"How 'bout those people we caught doin' it? Goin' at it like rabbits." He turns back to us and leers.

Lena starts giggling. She rolls up against me trying to hide it. Soon she's coughing and gasping for air. Her hand grabs mine and squeezes. Tears running down her cheeks.

Biff cocks his head at Lena. "Girl, you don't look good."

I feel Lena's head shake against my chest as she grunts out, "It's nothing... really."

Biff ducks down under his seat, then pops back up. He pushes a thermos in Lena's face. He's got what could pass as a concerned expression as he says, "This 'ere'll cure what ails ya."

"No thanks," I say, waving it away. "She'll be okay."

Biff thrusts the thermos at Lena. "Go on. It'll be good for ya."

Lena pushes away from me and grabs the thermos. "Hell, yeah. Anything for the ride."

I watch in shock as Lena takes a long swig. She juts her chin out and passes the thermos back to Biff. She turns and gives me a smug smile. Then her face turns red. She sputters and gags, then doubles over wheezing for air. I pull an old blue gas station wipe from under the seat and hand it to her. She can wipe her mouth or puke in it. She wads it up and throws it back at me.

"Nothin' like some downhome hooch to bring ya around," says Biff, flashing a picket-fence grin. "Imported all the way from Tennessee."

He reaches back under his seat to pull out an unlabeled bottle to top off the thermos. Seeing that, I feel a little relief. It can't be poison if Biff's still walking and talking.

Lena's got her head back against the seat, eyes closed. I hold her hand. It's limp, but she seems okay. She's going to have to scrub those pearly whites awful long and hard before I kiss her on the mouth again. "Hey, babe," I gently pull back her hair and nuzzle her ear. "You in there?"

"I think I just drank antifreeze," she says with a weak smile. I pat her hand, hoping she's able to keep it down.

Twenty minutes later, we pull into a gas station, stalling out at the pump.

"Damn clutch," says Zeke.

The gas station attendant approaches. "Fill'er it up, mister?"

"Not today. I need…" Zeke counts out the change in his hand. "Two dollars and ninety-three cents worth of gas. Then wash the windows and check the oil, brake fluid, and tire pressure. You know the engine in this baby is in the back, right?"

"This ain't the first Corvair I seen."

I'm puzzled. What the hell happened to them needing five dollars to get to Milwaukee?

While the attendant pumps the gas, Zeke fiddles with the clutch pedal. Biff holds a cigarette lighter next to Zeke's head to shine a little light on the problem.

"He's going to set his hair on fire," Lena says in a low voice.

Zeke looks up from under the seat. "Hey, girl, you got one of them do-hickeys in your hair?"

"Huh?" Lena leans up.

"A whatchamacallit?" He points at her hair.

"Or don't you hippie girls wear 'em," Biff says. "Like you don't wear no bras." He snickers.

Lena smiles sweetly at Biff and slurs out, "Some girls need bras and some don't. Just like some guys need jock straps and some don't. Know what I mean?"

A confused look spreads over Biff's face. Lena digs in her bag and holds a bobby pin in the air. "But it seems everybody needs hairpins."

Zeke's eyes light up as he takes it from her. "Yeah, that'll do 'er." He disappears back under the dash.

Biff lights another cigarette and gets out to bug the gas pump attendant. I watch him puffing away on his cigarette as he nudges the poor guy saying, "Nice day, ain't it?"

The attendant's eyes widen. "Yeah, if you don't blow us both up! Can't you read the sign? No smoking."

Biff blows out a cloud of smoke. "The trick is to keep the smoke in one hand and the nozzle in the other. Safety first, you know? Want me to show you?"

"Please step away from the gas pumps, sir."

"I gotta take a piss anyway." He lumbers off toward the men's room.

Lena whispers, "I feel like I'm in a comic strip."

I whisper back, "Yeah, but remember, it's all for the ride."

The gas jockey raps the window. "Everything's good but the oil. You're down a quart. Want me to top that off with our special 10-30 for an extra twenty-one cents?"

Zeke shakes his head. "Naw, we have oil." He looks back at me. "Hey, man, see if you can find that can of oil in the back and toss it up here, will ya?"

I look around and sure enough, there's a can of oil on the floorboard, shoved halfway under the front passenger seat. I hand it over and Zeke passes it out the window to the attendant.

"Don't be spilling any on the engine. I hate that smell."

The attendant rolls his eyes, then disappears around back under the hood. Zeke rests his arm on the back of the bench seat and turns to us.

"I'm betting you two don't think much of this old clunker." He rambles on, "Well, Biff's no rocket scientist, but his little sister Ruth? Now she's the smart one. Smarter than the both of us put together. Their folks has passed on. My sister's dying wish was that Ruth goes to college. Ruth's now living with an aunt in Louisville. We send all our spare money back to her so she can go to one of them private schools. That's why we're driving this hunka junk."

My face flushes. I remember being embarrassed by my family's Swissmobile. My dad didn't care how it looked. He would just say, "It gets me to work and back. I don't need to impress—I'd rather save the money for you kids." A twinge of guilt creeps into my high and mighty attitude.

Biff makes his way back to the car with a cig hanging from the corner of his smile. Lena and I get out to help push start this rambling wreck. The car coughs to life and the three of us dive one by one into the back seat. I grin to myself thinking the only thing we need to make this rolling sideshow complete is a pair of oversized clown shoes.

Back on the road, Zeke and Biff spin tales about their carnie conspiracy theories. Did we know that space aliens run the Catholic Church? That J. Edgar Hoover, the Director of the FBI, likes to wear dresses? And that the Mafia works for the government? I think about getting their expert opinion on the eternal question. Which are smarter dogs or cats? But their answer will probably involve religion, sex, space aliens, and a secret government plot.

Wisconsin welcomes us with the Corvair's left front tire blowing out on the snow-covered freeway. Swerving, honking, and cussing follow. Zeke regains enough control to pull over to the berm. He takes stock of our situation. No spare. Seems that was used two months ago in Arkansas. Zeke and Biff opt to drive three miles to the next exit on the rim. Then an irony comes to me. Ralph Nader's book warning about Corvairs, *Unsafe at Any Speed.* Ha ha. We limp into the gas station and find a pay phone.

Zeke says, "Biff, you think Cappy'll drive down with a spare?"

"He should have an extra. I'm sure not all those cars in his yard are on blocks."

"I'm thinkin' the same." Zeke turns to us. "Hey, you guys gotta dime? I gotta make a collect call, I'll give it back."

I dig around in my pocket for a dime and hand it over.

"Let's take a walk," I say to Lena. Out of earshot of our two friends, I say, "Should we wait for the tire from Milwaukee or try hitching, again?"

"What's the difference? Every ride we get is an ordeal."

"Let's get our bags and split."

We see Zeke walking out of the station and putting my dime in his pocket. He calls out. "Cappy'll be here with a spare in thirty to forty-five minutes. You two want to wait with us?"

"Nah, we're gonna just grab our stuff and head down the road," I say. "Thanks for the ride and stories."

Biff walks up. "One more thing. Stay away from them lava lamps."

"What! Why?"

"Those globs are radioactive. They'll make you as sterile as a mule, buddy. Why do you think all them hippies are having so much sex and no kids? See what I mean, huh?"

"Thanks for the tip, Biff. I'll run out and get Lena and me some lead underwear tomorrow."

We shoulder our bags and trudge over to the side of the road. At least we made it out of Illinois. A convoy of snowplows barrels past, spattering us with road sludge. Lena lets out a yelp as she does a backward kangaroo hop. I can't help laughing.

The good news is she's laughing too. We're closer to our goal and still alive… it's a start.

Chapter Thirty-Six
God and Snakes

Lena

I blow into my gloved hands, watching Kris stub out a cigarette. "You know," I say, "I think Biff really thought he was helping me with that moonshine."

"Yeah, they were a little different."

I nod, lifting my thumb at an approaching car. "Well, I can honestly say I've never met anyone like them."

The car pulls up next to us. The passenger, a woman with big brown eyes and mousy brown hair, rolls the window down. "Where you headed?" She's wearing a white waitress uniform with "Sue" embroidered on the pocket. The driver looks a little like a young Elvis.

"Minneapolis," Kris says.

She squints, shading her face against a cold wind. "We can take you a couple exits."

The car is warm and dry and has a faint scent of motor oil, but nothing like Zeke and Biff's. We do a round of introductions and head off down the highway.

"So, what do people do around here?" I ask. "Farm?"

Sue, glances back at me. "I'm a waitress at the diner in town."

"I'm a waitress, too. It's fun. You meet all sorts of cool people."

Sue laughs. "Not me, sweetheart. Been servin' the same burger and fries to the same people for fifteen years. Same people I've known all my life."

I bite my lip as I try to think of a response. I can't imagine waitressing all my life.

"Marty here works at the gas station."

"So, you're both from around here?" Kris says.

Sue pats Marty on the leg. "Born and raised. High school sweethearts."

"Where you comin' from?" Marty asks. Short dark hair waves over his ears and forehead. His gray work shirt has faded grease stains.

"Ohio," I say.

Kris dives in, giving them an abbreviated version of our trip. They nod politely as he makes light of our adventures with the law and our sleepover at a bordello, but I can tell this isn't a normal everyday conversation for them. Sue whispers something to Marty. He nods, and I can see Sue smile in the rearview mirror. She turns in her seat.

"Hey, our church is having a potluck lunch for a visiting pastor. He's from Ohio. We're on our way to it now. We'd love to have you come as our guests."

"Fantastic," Kris says, nodding and grinning.

I know this has to be one of his road rule things—never turn down free food.

"This pastor comes about four times a year," says Sue. "But I have to warn you, he brings the Holy Spirit with him."

A trickle of excitement rises in me. It's only a couple weeks until Christmas. This will get me in the mood. Maybe they'll have a choir. I love singing Christmas carols. Despite the issues I have with organized religion, I like tradition. And it's always fun experiencing how different denominations celebrate their beliefs.

Marty pulls into the driveway of a simple white clapboard building just off the interstate. The sign out front reads "Church of the Loving God." We leave our stuff in the car and follow Sue and Marty downstairs into a remodeled basement. Roughhewn homemade wooden crosses decorate the dark paneled walls. Worn gray carpeting covers the floor. A few rows of metal folding chairs are set up at one end of the room. An old upright piano stands in one corner. Square boxes covered with towels and blankets are stacked next to it. I can't help but notice there's no Christmas tree. No baby Jesus in a manger. Not even a strand of colored lights. I mention this to Kris.

"The way we do Christmas isn't in the Bible," he whispers back. "Some fundamentalists don't celebrate it."

Marty takes our coats. Kris starts to take his cigarettes out of his coat pocket, but Marty shakes his head. Kris fishes a hair whiz from his jeans and ties his hair into a ponytail.

I look down at my mud-crusted boots. "Guess I better take these off."

Sue nods. "I need to change." She holds up the brown bag she carried from the car.

I follow Sue to the Ladies Room and try to freshen-up as she changes into a long skirt and sweater. I splash water on my face and under my arms, but it's no use. I look and smell road worn. When we emerge into the hallway, I notice Marty has also changed out of his work clothes.

"C'mon," says Marty. "I want you to meet the pastor."

Kris and I put our coats and boots in a pile by the door and follow Marty and Sue across the room. Plain-faced, long-haired women wearing ankle-length dresses and short-haired men in collared shirts, work pants, and worn dress shoes greet us with eager handshakes. We walk past card tables heaped with dishes of fried chicken and hamburgers, vegetable casseroles, Jello squares with chopped-up carrots suspended inside, and white frosted cupcakes. The food aromas transport me. I could be in the dorm cafeteria. But there's no whiff of the only scent I associate with church, incense.

The pastor, a stout man with thinning brown hair, is wearing a powder-blue polyester sport coat and plaid pants.

"Pastor Henry, these here are Lena and Kris," Sue says. "We found them on the highway. They're from Ohio."

I hold in a laugh. 'Found us?' She makes it sound like we're lost. He shakes our hands. So different from the priests in satin robes that seemed untouchable in my church.

"Welcome, dear friends," he says, steepling his hands and leaning back on his heels. "Where 'bouts in Ohio?"

I stare at the pastor's hands. His left forefinger is a stub. A fleshy knob.

"Columbus," Kris says. "We're headed to Minnesota to visit my aunt."

"Praise the lord," says Pastor Henry. "I'm from Marietta, a bit further south. It's God's country down there, let me tell you. Why don't we talk over lunch?" Kris and I nod, and he pats Kris on the shoulder, then walks to the front of the room to stand under a painting of Jesus. A crown of thorns frames Jesus's soft blue eyes and light brown hair. A wooden two-by-four cross hangs on the wall next to the picture. Pastor Henry raises his hands, and everyone goes silent, eyes riveting on him.

"I'm going to ask all my brothers and sisters to bow their heads and pray for our guests. Pray that Jesus protects them on their journey."

"Praise the Lord," the congregation shouts back, staring at us.

I paste a smile on my face and look down, feeling slightly embarrassed.

Pastor Henry folds his hands in prayer and bows his head. "God, we thank you for bringing these two travelers to your house. Keep their souls safe. And may they feast at the table of the Holy Spirit. In Jesus's name, we pray."

The room shakes with a loud, "Amen." I squirm as heat rises to my face. Sue grabs my hand, holding it tight. My face flushes more.

"And may they go where the Good Lord leads them," Pastor Henry booms.

"Hallelujah. Amen."

Pastor Henry says another longer prayer punctuated with "Praise the Lord." Then he motions us over to the buffet table and invites us to take the first helping. Everyone waits as Kris and I nervously spoon the food onto our plates. Then they all line up and dig in.

Sue sits on one side of me. A woman who introduces herself as Wendy sits on the other. She's bird-like, with thin blonde hair parted down the middle. She eyes me, watching me eat, then with a tentative smile asks, "Have you been saved?"

I look at her, a spoonful of Jello halfway to my mouth. "Saved from what?"

"From Satan."

"Yeah, I guess so." I spoon in the Jello and reach for my water, hoping to avert more questions.

"Are you baptized?"

"Yes," I say, between gulps.

"But did you accept Jesus Christ as your personal Lord and Savior?" she persists.

I put down my glass. Sue has turned toward me and is waiting for my answer. I glance at Kris, who's sitting with Marty at the pastor's table. Kris is scarfing down everything while nodding his head. He doesn't even look up from his plate.

"I was a baby," I say. "I couldn't talk."

"Then it doesn't count. You have to do it again," Wendy says, looking at me with a mix of pity and hope.

On my other side, Sue nods and smiles sympathetically. I don't want to argue with them. I don't mind hearing the "good word" but I'm not getting baptized again. At least not here. Should we leave? It's not polite to eat and run. But it's also not polite to talk with your mouth full, so I shovel a spoonful of macaroni and cheese into my mouth.

The meal ends, finally, and the tables are pushed to the side. Wendy walks over to the piano and sits down. She starts playing a lively gospel-style tune. The pastor gets up in front of the congregation.

"I need a smoke," Kris whispers in my ear.

"Wait 'til she's done." I hate when people walk out on musicians in the middle of a song. And the tune Wendy's playing is kind of catchy. The congregation stands, lifting their hands into the air. They begin to sway and move with the music. Words and phrases are shouted out at sporadic intervals.

"Glory praise!"

"Jesus!"

"Savior!"

"Holy Spirit!"

Arms wave side to side. Bodies twirl. Voices hum, sing, shout, and wail. The atmosphere of the room is building into the frenzy of a rock concert.

Suddenly one of the men falls to the floor and writhes around in circles, twitching and shaking.

Everyone stands around him, praising the Lord and the Holy Spirit. I look around. Sue closes her eyes and lifts them to the ceiling. Marty's arm is around Kris's shoulders and they're both rocking back and forth with the music. Then the pastor starts speaking in an urgent monotone voice.

"A hambala asham lacashat. Laybondola."

Sue's eyes open, a look of rapture envelops her. She begins rattling off a string of sounds. "Losotovakayla ashala."

Wow. They're speaking in tongues. I saw this once in a late-night movie. I try to decipher the meaning, but it's like a foreign language. Russian? Polish? Throughout the room, I hear different guttural sounds. I watch Pastor Henry quaking like he's having some kind of seizure. But no one is concerned. They stand around him smiling and swaying, praising the Lord. Goosebumps cover my skin. A big guy falls backward, and a couple of men jump behind him just in time to catch him. They lay him on the floor. He squirms around on the carpet uttering the weird language as a scrawny guy dances around him. Nonsensical words reverberate throughout the room.

I grab Kris's arm and whisper, "Holy Rollers."

"Trippy, isn't it?" he says, rocking back and forth on his heels and toes.

"It's like they're in a voodoo trance," I whisper. "Do they really know what they're saying?"

Kris shrugs. "Who knows? They believe the Holy Ghost is talking through them."

"It's so strange."

"I think it's kind of cool."

A memory of the rituals at High Mass fills my head. The scent of incense, tinkling of the prayer bells, soft repetition of prayers. Then I look around at people having fits on the floor and spouting gibberish, their eyes rolled back in their sockets. I tug on Kris's sleeve, and my voice quakes. "I want to leave."

"Okay." His eyes widen. "Hey, look."

Pastor Henry is bending down behind the piano and pulling the blanket off a box. He lifts up a thick snake. It winds around his arm and juts its flat head into the air. I'm frozen, watching its tongue flicker in and out. The voices rise. Someone begins to pound out a beat on a bongo. The pastor dances around the room, holding the snake above his head.

"Whoa!" Kris says.

Sue sways side to side next to me. "Can you feel it?" she says. She holds out her arms and pantomimes holding the snake. "It's beautiful, like manna from heaven."

I nod, blinking rapidly, as I watch people take five more snakes from the boxes. The serpents coil around the arms and hands of the men. It's creepy, but I can't look away. I can't move. Something inside me is popping like popcorn.

"Better than the dope the hippies take, right?" Marty says standing next to Kris, bobbing up and down with the rhythm of the bongos.

Kris grins. His eyes are gleaming. He's really into it. I put my hand on his arm.

"What kind of snakes are they?" I ask.

Marty says, "The Godly kind."

"I wanna go." I pull on Kris's arm.

There's a yell. Someone's dropped their snake. Pandemonium erupts as people are shouting, jumping, crawling, trying to catch it.

"C'mon," I say, pulling Kris's hand. "Now!"

Marty calls out, "Be not afraid. The Lord is your Savior."

Sue says, "We're protected by the Lord."

I feel something on my foot and look down to see a snake slither over my sock. I scream and kick. The snake's head rises and darts at my leg. I feel instant pain near my ankle. Marty makes a dive for the snake as Kris pulls me to a chair and rolls down my two pairs of socks.

He shakes his head. "Oh, no."

We stare at the two tiny red fang marks. My mouth drops open.

"What'll we do? What'll we do?" My voice is on the edge of hysterical as swelling sets in around the bite.

"Don't move. Doesn't look like he got you deep, but we need to get you to the doctor fast." Kris looks around. The room is a flurry of people putting snakes in boxes and gathering around me. "You got a hospital around here?" he yells out.

"Yes, yes." Sue says.

"Then call an ambulance."

She turns and runs down the hallway.

Pastor Henry stands next to me with his hands in the air. The congregation echoes his chant, "Jesus will save the righteous."

I look at Kris, my heart racing. These people are about to see what real crazy looks like.

Kris pats my leg. "Don't worry, the doctor will give you some anti-venom. You'll be okay." He steps behind me and puts his hands on my shoulders. I lean my head back against him, close my eyes. My heart is pounding. My mouth is dry. Dear God, don't let me die.

The sirens screech to the door and two guys in plaid shirts and jeans rush in, pushing a gurney. They wrap a gauze bandage around my leg from my knee to my foot, leaving the bite marks open and visible. The swelling is still increasing.

"Don't move and keep your ankle lower than your heart," one says.

"And don't panic," says the other.

I sit upright on the gurney as they push me out the front door. How can you not panic after a snake plunges its fangs into your skin? Everything goes blurry. Outside, a long black car with a revolving light on top is parked in the gravel lot. Am I hallucinating?

"A hearse?" I yell as they roll me toward it. "Why are you putting me in a hearse?"

"It doubles as our ambulance, ma'am."

I look at Kris and shriek. "I'm not getting in there! Don't let them put me in that!"

Sue calls out, "It's all we got."

I start shaking. The world is spinning. They slide me inside and Kris climbs in next to me. I grab his hand

and shut my eyes. I don't want to see what the inside of a hearse looks like. It's not natural. I just want this to be over.

When we arrive at the hospital, I wait until I'm out of the hearse before I open my eyes.

The ER doctor draws blood, then comes back to the room.

"Good news. There's no trace of venom. You got what we call a dry nip."

"What's that?" I ask.

"About half the time venomous snakes don't inject their poison. They save it for more important things. Be glad you're not a mouse."

I manage a smile. "So I'm going to live?"

"I'll give you a shot of penicillin and tetanus too. We're going to keep you for an hour or two to be sure."

"Is there a phone around?" Kris asks. "I need to call my aunt."

"In the cafeteria," the doctor says and leaves the room.

I reach out for Kris. He takes my hand.

Kris lowers his voice. "Man, we got lucky."

I take a deep breath and exhale. "Praise the Lord."

Kris smiles and smooths his hand over my forehead. "That's the spirit."

Chapter Thirty-Seven
Gene

Kris

"The doctor said the snake bite was a dry nip," I say into the phone, barely able to believe I'm using the words snake bite and Lena in the same conversation with my aunt. "I'll look for a Western Union or someplace you can wire the money to. Then I'll call you back. Okay... love you, too, Aunt Ella."

I hang up and pull out a dog-eared phone book that's on the payphone shelf. The hospital cafeteria is practically empty, except for a few nurses at one table and a thirty-something black man drinking coffee by himself. He's dressed like some sort of delivery person. I pull out a chair at the table next to his and begin to leaf through the yellow pages to find a bus station. Greyhound should be listed, but it's not.

I see the man peering over his glasses at me.

"You from around here?" I ask.

"Why?"

"Just wondering. I'm trying to find the closest bus station."

The man puts down a clipboard of forms he's been writing on and says, "This hospital has been on my route for the last five years, but I don't believe I've ever seen a bus come through this town. Where you headed?"

"Minneapolis. My girlfriend and I were hitching 'til she got bit by a snake."

He smacks his forehead. "A snake? Pastor Henry must be in town." He reaches out to shake my hand. "My name's Gene Butler. I deliver medical supplies to the hospital." He smiles. "Including anti-venom."

I scrape back my chair, stand, and shake Gene's hand. "Kris Anderson. It's a long story, but right now I have to find a bus to Minneapolis."

"Is your girlfriend stable? I mean, can she leave the hospital?"

"Yeah, if I could find a bus."

Gene waves his hand. "Save your bus money. I'm headed to Minneapolis. I'll have you there in about four hours."

"You mean you'll drive us?"

"That's what I said."

"We can't leave for an hour or so," I say with a sigh.

"That's fine. I have some paperwork to finish up."

"Where do you want to meet us?"

"How about back here?"

I slap the phone book shut. "Meet you here then after she signs out? I have to call my aunt back."

"Take your time. I'll wait."

I help Lena hobble out to Gene's cargo van in the darkening parking lot. Gene moves some boxes to one side. Lena lies down in the back and I stuff my army jacket under her head. She gives me a dreamy smile. The pain medication must be kicking in.

Thirty minutes later, we're back on I-94 and Gene is laughing as I tell our tale of getting a free lunch for a snakebite with a big side of religion.

"You drive this way a lot?" I ask.

"About once a month. I cover all of Wisconsin and Minnesota."

Gene tells me about his job. I look back to check on Lena. With everything she's been through, I'm hoping she sleeps all the way to Aunt Ella's.

"So, you're on the road a lot," I say. "That must be better than sitting behind a desk all day."

"Yeah, the money's good, but it's starting to be a hassle."

"Why?"

"Because of Amy."

"Amy?"

"My daughter. Well, my wife's daughter. It's kind of complicated. Amy's retarded. She's almost ten, she can take care of most of her own needs, but my sister Nancy helps with the big stuff while I'm on the road."

"What about your wife? Does she work?"

Gene leans forward and turns down the radio. "Not anymore. Caroline was young when she married me. She already had Amy and was struggling to make ends meet doing packaging in the warehouse. That's how we met. I'd go in a few times a week to check inventory and eventually I got up the nerve to ask her out. Well, one thing led to another. Amy's father wasn't ever in the picture, so after we got married, I adopted Amy."

"Instant family," I say.

"I'm ten years older than her and already had a steady job delivering pharmaceutical supplies. But us getting married raised some eyebrows with her family. My wife and her family were already on the outs over her having Amy out of wedlock. After we got married, they literally slammed the door shut."

"Why? Sounds like you were her knight in shining armor."

Gene glances in my direction, then back at the road. "Caroline and Amy are white."

"Oh," I say, unsure of how I should respond.

Gene gives me a half-smile. "It was hard on Caroline, her family disowning her like that. One day frustration would build into rage, the next day she'd fall into a deep depression. Sometimes I'd come home and find her still in her nightgown. And then she had her first break."

"Break?"

"You know, nervous breakdown. She ended up in the psych ward."

"Wow, I'm sorry."

Slush spatters the windshield from a semi in front of us. Gene hunches forward, turns on the wipers, and puts on his blinker. He carefully changes lanes before continuing.

"My sister Nancy jumped in to help with Amy, but it was a double-edged sword. It made Caroline feel like she wasn't good enough as a mother and we'd be better off without her. Three years ago, when Amy was seven, Caroline tried to take her own life. She was in the hospital for two months after that, fighting depression."

"That must've been rough."

"You have no idea. For a couple weeks, I just sat on the couch wondering what to do next. That's when my life's purpose came shuffling down the hall in footy pajamas, climbed in my lap, and asked, "Daddy, read me a story?"

"How's your wife doing now?" I ask.

"She has her good days, but lately it seems she's been in the hospital more than she's been out. They're constantly fiddling with her medication. Trying to get the right combination. Now they're talking about electro-shock."

And I think I have problems? I'm at a loss for words. Listening to Gene, I realize how lucky I am.

Gene clears his throat. "Her own family won't lift a finger to help. They tell her she needs to buck up and stop feeling sorry for herself. They don't have a clue about depression."

"It sounds like a tough road for everyone," I say, wondering how I'd handle something so life changing.

Gene wipes his eyes with the back of his hand, then shrugs. "I knew I was taking on a lot from the beginning, but..."

We ride in silence for a bit, nothing but the sound of tires on the road and the heater filling the space between us. Then Gene nods toward Lena, still sleeping in the back.

"You and her in love?"

I stare out the front window. Moonlight soaked snowfields spread out in every direction. I don't know where this conversation is going, but something inside me wants to have it. "I think so. I thought I was in love a few times before." I sigh. "This feels different, but it sure isn't easy."

Gene smiles. "Love doesn't worry about what's down the road." He gives me a knowing look. "It's what Dr. Martin Luther King calls unconditional love. The love is in the giving."

"That sounds right," I say, beginning to feel a heavy peace settle over me like a warm blanket.

"It doesn't just sound right. It is right," says Gene.

I reach back to touch Lena's leg, then settle against the seat. The road lulls me to sleep, his words drifting through my head.

It is right.

Chapter Thirty-Eight
Ella

Lena

The Minneapolis skyline is etched into the midnight sky. I've never been this far north. I shiver with expectation. Gene pulls up to Ella's cream-colored duplex. With hugs and gratitude, we say our goodbyes to Gene and get our bags out of the van. My ankle feels fine and the drugs have worn off. There's no elevator, so we slowly walk up the lighted stairwell to Ella's second-floor apartment. Drifting clouds are painted on the stairwell's sky blue walls. On the second floor landing, I point to a cartoon drawing of a tiny man with a big grin on his face, cartwheeling down through the clouds. Naked.

Kris laughs. "Ella painted it."

If I had to guess, I'd say it looked like St. Peter kicked him out at the pearly gates. But his smile says it was worth it.

Ella opens the door before we knock. "You made it!" With a wide smile, she ushers us inside. We slip through strands of crystal beads hanging from an archway that leads into a softly lit foyer. She turns and hugs us both. She's slim and wears a flowing green and gold caftan. A headband pulls her shoulder-length brown hair, streaked with silver, off her face. Rose tinted granny glasses perch on her nose.

"Come, come. You must be exhausted," she says, leading us into a shag-carpeted room, where a rattan basket swing hangs in the corner. Potted plants and colorful floor pillows shimmer from the light cast by the large aquarium in the corner. She picks up a black Persian cat from the L-shaped denim sofa. "This is Mr. Plum. He's my confidante." She motions for us to sit.

"He's beautiful. Our house has a cat named Blue, and he's super sociable."

"How's that foot?"

I sit, take off my boot, pull up my pant leg, and unwrap the bandage. The swelling is down and the pin prick bite is barely visible.

Ella touches the skin around the bite. "Seems like they did a good job, but we can get a city doctor to take a look at it tomorrow."

"Oh, that's not necessary," I say. "I think I'll live. But I may be steering clear of small town churches for a while."

Ella laughs. "Join the club. Can I get you something to eat or drink?"

"I could use a snack," Kris says. "And a beer."

"I picked up some things from the deli. And there's plenty of beer. How about you, Lena?"

"Just water, thanks."

Ella walks out of the room and down the hallway. My gaze drifts upward. Over the fireplace is a large watercolor of a nude woman leaning over a flower box, smelling a fully bloomed rose. The look on her face is one of pure ecstasy. I whisper to Kris, "Is that Ella?"

"Yep. Been there as long as I can remember. She was a professional model for artists and volunteered for art classes in her younger days. Now she's the curator for the Campus Gallery."

I stare. There's no way I could do something like that. But I find that I admire her, not only for doing it, but for showing it.

Ella returns with a plate of pastrami, cheese, and crackers. I nibble while Kris digs in and gives her the rundown on our rides. He skims over the stewardesses, again, focusing on the carnies and bizarre church service.

"Oh, everyone's got a bit of bizarre in them," Ella smiles. "That's what makes life interesting."

Kris nods. "It was a lot of bizarre for Lena's first time on the road. Probably enough to scare her off hitching ever again."

"Ah, first times," Ella laughs and sets Mr. Plum on the floor. "Some you want to remember, some won't let you forget. Same with last times. It's the in-betweens that get jumbled together."

"I wouldn't have minded, if we hadn't gotten stuck in the middle of nowhere so many times," I say.

"Sometimes getting stuck is just a frame of mind, isn't it?" Ella gathers up the empty plates and glasses. She leads us down a long narrow hallway, with rooms on either side. "The bathroom is down there. Clean towels are in the cupboard next to the tub. Here's the kitchen. I expect you to help yourselves—you're not guests here, you're family." She pushes open the door to our room and says, "Here you are." She walks over to the window and closes the gauzy drapes, casting her shadow over what looks like a plump feather bed. With a wave of her hand, she says, "Sweet dreams." Then disappears down the hall.

Kris and I swap grins as we fall backwards into the creampuff of down comforters. Adulthood tingles through my veins as we spread out on the big brass bed.

"She's sooo cool," I say.

Kris leans on one elbow. "Even cooler than the woman you babysat for, that taught you how to shimmy?"

I picture Mrs. La Roche in her hip hugger jeans, her long black hair falling over her skinny ribbed 'poor boy' top, shaking her ample breasts. I smile. "Even cooler than her."

I sit up and start to take off my clothes. I can smell the day's travels on me. "I've got to take a bath," I say, wrinkling my nose.

"Me, too." Kris rolls off the bed and pulls me to my feet.

"We can't take one together," I say. "What about Ella?"

Kris gives me an 'oh, c'mon' look.

With that settled, we tiptoe down to the bathroom, open the door, and enter a magical forest. Kris runs the water while I marvel at our surroundings. The large claw-footed tub is surrounded on all sides by ceramic vases holding sweet smelling plants and flowers. Lush ferns hang from the ceiling in hemp macramé holders. I pour a capful of lemon sage bubble bath into the tub. A fruity earth scent blossoms in the air. We peel off our clothes and lower ourselves into the steaming water surrounded by a wall-painting of druids and fairies frolicking in an imaginary woodland.

"Look," I say, pointing my soapy finger at magical 'shrooms peeking through the painted flowers. I lean back against Kris, like a butterfly on a flower. I twist around to face him, scooping up bubbles to cover his beard and mustache. His eyes and hands massage every inch of me. Waves of bubbles spill onto the floor and I let myself pour over the edge with them. Gushing, surging, cascading.

The waves calm. Kris takes the hand sprayer and rinses me clean. I pull the rubber stopper and watch my hang-ups swirl down the drain.

Back in our bedroom, we appreciate our world in a most enchanted way.

***

Late morning light filters through the window as I dress in the last of my clean clothes. I poke Kris, ruffle his hair. "Rise and shine." He responds with a groan and rolls over.

I walk to the living room and sit down in the basket swing. Mr. Plum suns himself in the bay window, while strains of acoustic guitar play from the tall stereo speakers painted to look like giant vases. Ella saunters over in jeans and a sky-blue velour top, holding two cups.

"Jasmine tea or Kona coffee?"

"Tea, thanks." I take the cup and inhale the exotic scent. I've never had anything but plain old Lipton. Her hair, gathered in a beaded clip, flows along her shoulders, so different from the short perm my mother wears.

"I like your hair," I say shyly. "I wish my hair was straight."

"Your hair is lovely," she says, then leans over and tugs on my still damp curls. "It has waves like the ocean."

"Thanks, but it's wild."

"Like the changing tide," she says with a smile. Only the moon is in control."

I laugh. "Or humidity."

"Wait." Ella stands and goes into the kitchen. She returns with a teaspoon of oil. "Sunflower oil," she says. "Run it through from your roots to the ends. The curls will calm, but stay naturally free."

She drips it on my palms and I work the odorless oil into my hair. A page in my art history book appears in my mind. Van Gogh's painting of sunflowers. In the south of France.

"What's your sign?" Ella asks, sitting opposite me on the couch.

"Gemini." Kris told me she was into astrology.

"Moonstone is your birthstone."

"I thought it was pearl."

"There's more than one gem for each month. You can choose."

"I've never seen a moonstone."

Her eyes flash. "It's got a soft floating blue glow that changes when you move. It reflects your soul."

"Which is an emotional kaleidoscope most of the time."

She looks up at me as she blows on her coffee. "Do you meditate? All Geminis should meditate."

"I've thought about it. The transcendental meditation gurus come on campus to offer sessions now and then, but I think sixty dollars is a lot to pay for a mantra."

"Just use the sacred sound 'OM,'" she says, then softly chants, "Ommm."

I close my eyes and join in, feeling foolish, but giving it my best. "Ommm."

After a good long chant, Ella whispers, "Now just think it, over and over in your head."

We sit quiet. I have trouble keeping my mind on OM with Mr. Plum sitting on the couch, purring. I wonder if she chanted it when she posed in the nude. After having a free spirit like Ella in his life, what does Kris see in me?

Ella breaks the silence. "If you can do it at least twenty minutes a day, it will center your emotions."

I open my eyes and nod. "I'll try."

Kris walks in and gives the basket swing a slight push.

"Feel my hair," I say, leaning my head into him. "Sunflower oil."

He twirls my newly softened waves in his fingers. "I hope the birds don't peck at your head out on the road."

I bat him off and Ella motions us to the kitchen. We sit around the wooden industrial spool that serves as the table. A jade plant springs from the center. Ella sets down three thick square plates that look like someone dripped paint over them. "Stoneware," she says noticing my quizzical look. Her low, lyrical voice instructs Kris on the art of making a Chinese omelet. Their talk of family mixes with the asparagus, mushrooms, water chestnuts, and bean sprouts. I watch Kris slicing and chopping and mixing.

"You're making a mess," I say.

"Embrace the messiness," Ella says, handing me a radish she sliced to look like a flower. "Something surprising usually comes from it."

"My herbal brownies are messy," Kris says without hesitation, smiling at me. "They bring surprises."

Ella grins and lifts the lid on a cat shaped cookie jar. "Speaking of which…" She pulls out a fat weedy brownie. I laugh out loud. Such a far cry from my mom's cookie jar of Fig Newtons.

After lunch, Ella throws on a knee length coat and wraps a bright fuchsia boa around her neck. She takes us to her stomping grounds, a funky avenue of headshops and artist lofts around the university. She leads us into one of them and introduces us to Shen, a Chinese silversmith with straight black hair pulled into a ponytail that runs down his back. Shen shakes our hands, but his gaze is fixed on Ella. They evidently have a 'thing' going on.

Shen opens a drawer behind the counter and picks out a ring. He buffs it with a soft gray cloth and holds it under a desk lamp on the counter. The three of us lean in. I can make out a band of stars and crescent moons etched in the burnished silver. A small figure in a pointed hat has lightning bolts shooting from his hands. Shen gives it to Ella and she hands it to Kris. He slips it on his right ring finger. It's a perfect fit. Shen waves away Ella's offer to pay. She whispers something, gives him a lingering hug, then turns to Kris and takes his hand.

"If you ever feel your sense of wonder slipping away, just wave your finger in front of you, like Merlin's wand."

Kris waves his hand like he's spreading stars around the room.

It's a beautiful moment, I feel high just being there. I want that sense of wonder, too. And the truth is… I want that ring. I want the glimmering, shimmering moon and stars embracing Kris's finger. Even though I'm embarrassed at my selfish thoughts, I can't deny my feelings. *I want it.*

Walking down the aisles, I pick up this and that trying to push away the envy, but all I see is the glint from Kris's finger. It glows like our magical nights under the moon and the stars. I look up and Kris is smiling at me. I imagine that he senses my thoughts of our hands intertwined on our walks, of his touch on my skin at night. He knows I want that ring to circle my finger like our time together circles my heart. Surely he'll give the ring to me, so we can share the magic. But not in front of Ella. He'll wait. Maybe at the end of our trip, under the last moonlit night, he'll slide it onto my finger. Symbolizing the journey of our love. Not going forward, not going back. Just going around and around forever…

Forever?

I just want our enchantment, our wonder, our magic. Or maybe… maybe I just want Merlin. I laugh inwardly as the thought spreads over me. Maybe I want too much. But if Kris gives me that ring, it would be enough for now.

Chapter Thirty-Nine
Green Lake

Kris

After a late breakfast on Monday, Aunt Ella gives me the keys to the Jeep and cabin. She calls Lena over and pats a brown wicker picnic basket.

"Here's fried chicken for dinner. And for breakfast my Swedish Pancake recipe and ingredients, they'll be just the thing. The Lakeshore Market stays open during the holidays. You can grab something there for Tuesday night's dinner. I left the gas on in the cabin, but you'll need to light the pilot. There's a phone if you need it. Have fun. See you Wednesday."

Flurries fly as we weave our way through the city to Hwy 12. I wonder how different my life would be if I had never left Minneapolis. Then I look at Lena and see the biggest difference it would've made. I'm glad I didn't stay.

"One stop before we leave the city, okay? It's on the way," I say.

"Sure."

Fifteen minutes later we pull into a small gravel parking lot next to the St. Paul Agriculture campus. About thirty corrugated steel barracks in various states of decay stand in rows. "This is where I grew up. The Village."

"I hope they were in better shape when you lived here," Lena says.

"Yeah, but not much. I do remember my dad's leg going through a rotten floor board once."

We get out of the Jeep. "But here's what I wanted to show you." I turn and sweep my arm across the space in front of us. "My jungle."

"You call that a jungle?" Lena laughs. "There's not that many trees and you can see the golf course across the street through it."

"That's because it's winter, you nut. It's a lot scarier when the trees are full of leaves. And keep in mind, I was five. Everything seemed bigger. I was sure it was Eden, from the Bible stories my mom read to me. After she died, I used to collect willow and cottonwood leaves. The cottonwoods look like hearts and the willows look like feathers. I imagined angel wings were made of hearts and feathers." I look up at the sky. "I thought if I had enough of them, I could glue them together, and make my own angel wings to visit her in heaven."

Lena puts her arm around my waist and presses her head against my shoulder. I kiss the top of her head and we walk back to the car. We pass a tangle of grass in the snow. I stoop down and pick up a dried willow leaf and hand it to her. "Here's an angel feather."

Lena smiles. "It's beautiful. I'll put it in my journal with the cottonwood leaf."

We drive about fifty miles and I point toward the right side of the road.

"We're halfway to Green Lake."

Lena stares, as I slow the car at the remains of a dilapidated billboard that used to advertise my family's business, Central Dairy. I grin, remembering me and my sisters yelling "Are we there yet?" from the backseat.

"When I was a kid, we'd be advertising the new Christmas ice cream on that billboard about now. Vanilla with a blue mint flavored church bell in the center."

Lena looks at me. "Mmm. Is the dairy still there?"

"Nope."

After an hour of ice cream stories, I turn onto the old lake road and roll down the window to inhale the fresh scent of the pines. In the summertime, the lake's as clear as a crystal ball. Now it's an expansive sheet of white, with little ice fishing shacks sprinkled across it. Along the shoreline, huge slabs of ice formed by the freeze-and-thaw cycle jut out at odd angles.

I pull down the long driveway to the cabin which sits between the lake and the woods. Gravel and pine needles crunch under the tires. It's an arrival sound I've heard countless times traveling here as a child. We get out of the car and walk through white powder to the front door of the log cabin. Lena swings the wicker basket as she walks, totally at ease. We stomp the snow off our boots on the porch, and as I open the front door, I wonder if I've entered the right place. There's no smell of fresh baked bread or cookies. No aroma of Swedish coffee brewing in the enormous speckled enamel pot that sits on the 1940's stove. Instead, I'm greeted by the cold and musty odor of a long-empty house. But there are familiar sights, including the industrial-size waffle cone dispenser on the wall and the ice cream freezer. It's just the noises and smells of my childhood that are missing, along with my mom and grandparents. I unlatch the cupboard over the fridge and find a bottle of Scandinavian vodka. The sight of it conjures up a sound of clinking glasses and an image of my extended family gathered around the kitchen table, solving the world's problems. I grab the bottle and set it on the counter. Aunt Ella, you didn't let me down.

I get two jelly jars from the cupboard and pour two healthy shots of liquid heat. I slide one Lena's way and hold up mine.

"*Skol.*"

"*Chin chin,*" Lena says, and we clink. She throws her shot back, slams her glass down, and fans her hand in front of her mouth.

"Another?" I ask with a grin. "It's pretty damn cold in here."

Lena nods. "Why not?"

With two shots warming our hearts, I give Lena a tour of the cabin, my childhood, and my Swedish ancestors.

We're in my grandparents' bedroom when Lena walks over to the antique dresser and picks up a framed black and white photo. It's of my mom and her big sister, Aunt Ella. They're standing in the cabin's kitchen wearing aprons, blonde ponytails, and teenager grins. My mom has one arm wrapped around Ella's waist. Ella is waving a wooden spoon at the camera.

"Your mother was beautiful," Lena says, staring at the photo. "Do you remember her at all?"

I look at the photo, and then scan the room, searching for memories. "I remember some," I say. "Her letting me lick the spoon whenever she and Ella baked. Us running around the yard catching lightning bugs. Her reading me all my favorite stories, twice." I shrug. "And being here a lot. When I think of her, it feels a little empty. Not our time together, but more about the memories we never made."

Lena sets the picture back on the dresser. "How often do you get back here?"

My hand fidgets at my side. "Not much. It's not the same since my grandparents died."

"You should try to come more often. I think Ella misses you."

"Yeah, maybe." Seeing Aunt Ella keeps my mom's memory alive for me. It never occurred to me that seeing me might be doing the same thing for Aunt Ella.

We walk to the living room.

"A little music?" I turn on the old AM radio and dial through the static to the only rock station that can reach this far out. Old family photos from different eras fill the mantle. I hold up one of me and my cousins in swim trunks, holding our bamboo fishing poles with stringers full of fish. Freckled faces, crew cuts, and gap-toothed grins.

"I still remember the day this was taken," I say. "We caught sixty-eight Blue Gills in an hour right off the dock."

Lena takes the photo. "I want to hug that little kid." I watch her cradle the frame against her chest. My eyes mist over. How does she know that in this place and this time, it's exactly what I need?

I laugh to cover my shaky voice. "Those summers were great. My cousins and I would run and jump off the dock, paddle around on patched up inner tubes or swing out over the water on an old rope tied to a tree. My grandfather would take the boat out and pull us around the lake on a knee board. I remember one time my dad came out after teaching and him skiing around the lake in a suit and tie while my grandfather drove the boat."

"That's hilarious." Lena puts the picture back on the mantle and nods. "I had fun with my cousins, too, at my grandpa's ranch. He'd pull a wooden pallet behind his tractor with all of us kids onboard. We rode over waves of grass. Grandpa went slow, but sometimes one of us would fall off trying to grab dandelions."

"We used to catch frogs and garter snakes along the lake shore," I say.

"We caught lizards and played hide and seek in the orange grove until it got dark," she says. "Then we'd curl up in Grandma's afghans and tell ghost stories while the grown-ups played cards."

Sharing these memories was warming me up as much as the vodka.

"Let's go," I say, taking her hand. "I'll show you the bunkhouse."

We button up our coats and I get the bunkhouse key from the rack by the door. I pull a flashlight out of the kitchen junk drawer, still crammed with fishing tackle and playing cards. The battery's dead. I flick my lighter. It'll do. I know the way by heart.

We walk down the path to the bunkhouse. I unlock the door and step back into my childhood. Leaning against my old bunk bed, I hug Lena to my side.

"On summer mornings, my grandfather would walk by on his way to the dairy. He'd yell, 'Breakfast time!' All nine of us would run up to the cabin, slamming our way through the wooden screen door. It drove the grown-ups nuts. My uncle used to call us heathen savages. I can still hear my grandma saying, 'Please go back and close the door gently.' Now, whenever I hear a screen door slam, it's summer."

"Did you have any pets here?" Lena asks. "We had goats. My grandfather used to squirt goat's milk into our mouths for breakfast."

"Sounds yummy," I smirk.

Lena makes a face. "It was gross. But my cousins tickled me 'til I did it."

"My grandmother stuck to cooking breakfast," I say. "Scrambled eggs with real cream, toast topped with homemade peach or strawberry jam. Swedish pancakes made into the shapes of our favorite animals. Canadian bacon. I half expected to smell breakfast cooking when we walked into the cabin."

I lift up the lid to an old wooden chest and pull out some sheets and blankets. Even in winter they still have that summer lake smell. We walk out of the bunkhouse toward the cabin. I stop on the path and look up. The sky's a cascade of snow, the big fluffy kind that floats in the air.

"There's a hundred million stars in this sky on a summer night," I say.

Lena tilts her head back to the sky, catching the huge flakes on her tongue. "Are you sure it's not ninety-nine million?'

"I counted a hundred million, a billion times. If you lie down in the canoe and look up, it feels like you're falling through them."

"Maybe they're magical stars. Like the ones on your new ring."

I put the blankets under my arm and slowly turn the ring on my finger.

Lena jumps in front of me and grabs my hands. "Make a wish."

"There aren't any stars out."

"There are stars on your ring. Pick one."

I gaze deep in her eyes, searching for my northern lights. She'll never know that the beauty of her soul shines brightest on a snowy winter night in Minnesota, not in the California sun.

I bring my hand up and look for a star on the ring. "Okay, I've got one," I say.

"Tell me, tell me."

"Not allowed to tell."

"You can always tell your first wish," she says, but her tone is more conniving than convincing.

"You sure?"

"Yes, I'm sure. Absolutely."

"Okay, here goes," I whisper. "I want us to get naked in front of a roaring fire."

Lena laughs and pushes me. "Don't waste wishes on things you know will come true."

We playfully shove each other and make ridiculous wishes on our way back to the cabin.

I've never felt so free with a girl.

Inside, I dramatically point the ring toward the fireplace as Lena shakes out the sheets and blankets and spreads them on the floor around us. "I can feel the power of Merlin. Can you?"

"Is Merlin going to start a fire for us?" Lena says. "We need some heat."

"Oh, I have some heat for you. And a fire, too—if you're good."

"I'll be more than good," she says with a wink. "But start it now. I'm freezing!"

"Get us another shot of vodka and I'll build the fire."

Lena rubs her hands up and down her arms as she walks to the kitchen. I set my Boy Scout skills to work with lots of yellowed newspaper and kindling we keep stuffed in one of the cabinets.

Lena comes back with the vodka, glasses, and the picnic basket. From the weave of her walk, I can tell she has a buzz on. "There's a breeze in the kitchen," she says, with a shiver, setting everything down on the round wood coffee table.

"C'mon over here." I sit down, admiring my blaze. Large flames begin to erupt from the kindling and engulf the tepee of logs.

"Well, this is what I wished for," Lena says, walking close and extending her hands to feel the heat from the flames. She then turns to me with an impish look in her eyes, "Now about that wish of yours…"

I feel a big involuntary grin growing as Lena starts to rhythmically swivel her hips and shoulders to the notes of Born on the Bayou playing on the radio. Her hair swings over her face as she coos, "Do you have anything specific to add to that wish of yours?"

This is a side of Lena I never saw in the attic. But then, of course, there was Ginny behind the curtained wall and no Scandinavian vodka. Lena bends forward, jiggling everything she's got as she dances back toward the fire.

"Whoa, whoa! Be careful," I say holding up my hands. "Watch the fire."

She pauses, places her index finger on her bottom lip and says, "So, what will it be, naughty or nice?"

"Surprise me."

"Well, I think it's getting a kind of hot in here now." She crosses her arms over her stomach, grabs the bottom of her V-neck sweater and shimmies it off in time to the last beats of the song. Now in camisole and jeans, Lena twirls the sweater over her head knocking a couple pictures off the mantle. This causes her to duck and me to laugh. She does a low twist, bending her knees, swooping up the pictures, and piling them on the table.

I compose myself and egg her on, "C'mon, show me what you got, babe!"

The next tune up shifts to the primal beat of *I Want to Take You Higher*. As the beat pulses through the room, Lena pumps her fist in the air and dances her way semi-gracefully out of her jeans and camisole. This time at song's end, she sails them strategically over my head and harmlessly onto the rug behind me. I'm staring up at her breasts and her beautiful skin shimmering in the firelight. As if she planned it, The Beach Boys' *California Girls* fills the cabin. She looks at me, eyes large and intent, dips her head, and slips her fingers under her panty's waist band, running them front to back and front, again, meeting just under her navel. Her body gyrates enticingly for the next three minutes. At the end of the last verse, she stops abruptly, facing me with her legs slightly apart. The panties slide down as slow as honey off a spoon. With a smile, she slips one foot out and then begins to twirl the panties around her other ankle. When she finally tries to flick them off with her toes in my direction, they hang up on her foot. It takes a couple of hops on one leg and a wild kick before the panties land on top of the radio. But I'm still mesmerized by the silhouette of her breasts rising and falling with each deep breath.

She puts her hands on her hips, looks me in the face, and exhales. "Why are your clothes still on?"

"Umm?"

"Do you want this 'California Girl' to keep you warm at night or not?"

The next three seconds consists of my dance of nakedness as my clothes fly in whatever trajectory they're yanked in. With the ball of her foot, Lena presses lightly against my chest and I do an exaggerated backwards flop. I'm flat on my back with her standing over me. Every line and curve of her body seems new. I run my fingers up her legs, pulling her down. She straddles my chest. My hands hold her hips as she leans forward, breasts brushing my chest. She kisses my eyes and begins to slide her hips backward and forward. My every nerve stands on end as Lena envelops me. Wordless thoughts pass with each breath. We trade positions several times as the sheets and blankets are worked into a tangled cloud. Our rise and fall quickens to the heightened pause, and then the cabin stands silent, but for the pop of hot embers as time stops on its edge. We float in the fading light of the fire, and then sink deep into the drift of covers surrounding us.

Lena snuggles against me and blankets me in her warmth. She drifts off. I prop my head on my arm and gaze at her body, illuminated in the fire's soft glow. I smooth her hair that curls and waves in all the right ways. Her long lashes flutter with dreams. I trail my finger from her nose to her mouth. Her soft lips tilt up ever so slightly. I kiss her cheek. If time were to stand still, I wouldn't want it to stop at any other place or feeling than right here and now.

Chapter Forty
Snow Angels

Lena

In the morning Kris cooks up a batch of Aunt Ella's Swedish pancakes on the old gas stove.

"Mmm," I say, licking the lingonberry jam off my fingers. "I'm impressed."

"Soon you'll be as Swedish as Aunt Ella," he says.

When breakfast is done, we walk down to the lake. I stare over the frozen white landscape.

"Wish you could see this place in the summer when everything is green," Kris says. "It's bursting with life. People fishing, boating, skiing... skinny dipping."

I smile, but an involuntary shudder runs through me. I'll be gone by summer. But I'm not gone yet. I tilt my head back for a kiss, thinking only of him and this moment.

We spend the day doing small chores around the cabin and feasting on the fried chicken we never got to last night. Kris tells me more family stories and how connected he feels to this land. In the evening, we strap on snowshoes and go for a hike along the North Shore Drive. Snow-laden pines fill the landscape, standing at attention like guardians of the winter. Quietness sifts through me. As the cloudless night settles, the moon glows softly and the faint trail of the Milky Way blooms across an India ink sky. I wonder what it would have been like to grow up here instead of smoggy LA.

"Nothing like it, huh?" Kris whispers as we wander among the trees. "The Indians call the Milky Way the 'Path of Souls.'"

I inhale and cold spirals through me to my fingertips. I exhale a cloud. "'The Path of Souls'?"

He slides his arm around me. "Their journey through the afterlife."

I lean into the poetry of his thoughts. It's the magnet that draws me to him.

"If you want, we can spend the night outside," he says. "I can make us an *alska* igloo."

I wrinkle my brow. "You mean Alaska igloo, right?"

"Not Alaska. *Alska*. It's Swedish for love. Love igloo. We just have to be careful we don't melt it down." He grins and gives me a squeeze. "On second thought, I can always build us another one."

I toss a handful of snow at him. Surprised, he rushes me. We wrestle to the ground in a bumbling roly-poly tussle, our snowshoes cartwheeling off. Our laughter floats in the air. Everything else is lost in the softness of the snow. We stop our battle and lie back to look up into the endless field of stars.

"Have you ever made a snow angel?" Kris asks.

"No, but I saw it in a movie once."

"Just wave your arms and legs up and down."

I start doing horizontal jumping jacks. It feels silly and fun and I don't want to stop.

Kris gets up and pulls me to my feet. We turn around to admire my angelic outline in the snow.

"Let's make more," I say.

A row of angels soon lines the road, each with their thumb out.

"Fallen angels," I say.

He nods, impressed. "They're thumbing their way to heaven."

I shake the snow off my coat and gloves. "I wish I could feel my thumb."

Kris takes off his mittens. "Here, give me your hands." He interlocks his warm fingers with my frozen ones and pushes our hands deep in his coat pockets. "We'll have to find you a pair of Grandma Anderson's authentic Minnesota mittens. She was an amazing knitter. I bet she could have knitted a house if someone asked her to."

I tilt my head and smile. No wonder everyone loves to be around Kris. The way he talks makes people feel good, whether it's my roommates, his old girlfriends, or the women he meets on his night walks with Reggie. I feel a familiar green burning but push it away. He's mine tonight, not theirs. This night is ours.

"Hey, look." He points up into the branches of a nearby tree.

A soft stream of moonlight peeks through the bare branches, falling over us.

"Someone once told me that being touched by moonlight filtered through a tree is good luck."

He tugs off his mittens and pulls out his pocket knife. He walks over to a pine tree and begins to dig into the frozen bark. I peer over his shoulder to see our initials.

"The bark is pretty hard," he says. Then he jumps up, grabs a branch, and hoists himself into the tree like a monkey. Sitting with his legs hanging on either side of the branch, he begins to pull on his ring finger.

"What are you doing?"

"I'm gonna climb up," Kris points upward and with his other hand pats a tree limb above. "And put the ring in that knot hole, just above this branch. See it?"

"No way!" I stomp one foot. "Why would you do such a thing?"

"You know me. I'm not big on jewelry. I might lose it."

A chorus of 'Give it to me' runs through my head. No, I can't say it. It has to come from him. "You're crazy."

"C'mon," he says swinging his legs back and forth. "This way it will always be there for when either of us needs to make a wish. All we have to do is visualize it." He reaches up with both hands and grabs the branch below the knot hole.

"No, don't do it. You're gonna fall and there goes the rest of our trip. Besides, what would Aunt Ella think?"

"Aunt Ella would understand. You know her motto: 'It's the thought, not the thing.'"

"Sometimes it's both." I tug on his pant leg dangling overhead. "Come down here right now."

He slides the ring back on his finger and swings out of the pine. We burrow against each other. He puts his arm around my shoulders and pulls me in for a kiss. "Do you know how much I love you?" he asks, nuzzling my face.

I look into his eyes. Frosted shades of blue bore through me, taking me to a place I want to be. My heart opens. "As much as I love you?"

His eyes twinkle. "Well, I don't take just anyone on these deluxe hitchhiking trips."

"And I don't stick out my thumb with just anyone either."

We cuddle through twenty layers of thermal underwear, sweaters and coats, feeling the warmth as if nothing were between us. I can feel his voice rumbling through his chest as he talks.

"You know, just before we left, I had this strange talk with Mike. We were shooting the bull at the Hood. The usual: sports, classes, politics. Then out of nowhere, we started talking about love."

"Really?" I half smile.

"I know it sounds weird, two dudes, but at the time he seemed like the perfect person to talk about it with. I was wondering if love grows. And how does it grow? How big will it get? Does it change?"

"And what did you decide?" I know my girlfriends' thoughts on the matter, but I'm curious to know what guys think. It's what attracted me to Kris in the first place. He opens up and lets me inside.

"We decided that love just is. And you," he says, pulling me closer. "I never saw you coming. I wasn't looking. Stopped caring. Then you show up and bam! I'm telling you my life story. You 'get' me, Lena. Like no one else ever has."

He locks his eyes on mine. I feel their warmth and honesty run through me. No music, no candles, no pot. Here, in the still of a northern night, along the shore road, is the Kris I love.

"You get me, too," I say in a husky voice. "I wrote a poem about it."

"Tell me."

I take a deep breath and recall the words I wrote in my journal,

> *"Felt you in my soul,*
> *And in the candle glow,*
> *Heard you in my thoughts,*
> *On our long autumn walks*
> *You've made my timid heart*
> *A vibrant work of art."*

Kris gives a soft whistle. "No one's ever written a poem for me before." He pulls my hand up to his lips and kisses the tips of my gloves. Above, the Pathway of Souls arches over us. Here on earth, his soul embraces mine.

Chapter Forty-One
Holiday in Gary

Lena

*J*ournal:

It's been five days of lakeside walks and fireplace nights. We meet Ella's art gallery friends. They dress in tunics and blazers, beards and beads, and pass around pot cookies and caviar. Whenever I mention California, Ella says stuff like, "How exciting," and "What an adventure." She tells Kris he should consider studying in the comparative psych program at the University of Minnesota next school year. Have his own adventure. He shares stories about his lab monkeys and Reggie. Stuff he's never told me. I feel a little left out. Then it dawns on me that Kris must feel the same way when I talk about California and France. I need to talk to Ella privately about the tug-of-war in my heart. She's open-minded, cool, and we connect on so many levels. But she's Kris's aunt. Can she see my side?

This morning, while Kris sleeps, Ella and I sit in the living room having a cup of herbal tea. It seems the perfect time to talk.

I blurt out, "I don't know what I'm doing, Ella."

"About what?"

"California. France. Kris. It hurts when I think of leaving. But when I think of staying, it feels just as bad. In a different way."

She sips her tea, considering my comment. "Why doesn't he go with you?"

"To France? He's not into it. Or California. You know Kris, he's all about his roots."

"You seem pretty sure about that," she says. "Have you asked him to go?"

"No."

She puts down her cup. "Then I guess the real question is, why not?"

I stare out the kitchen window. Cardinals are sitting like Christmas ornaments on the branches of a snow-covered pine. So beautiful, just being themselves. I turn to Ella.

"I haven't asked him because it has to come from him, not me. I don't want to push him into doing something he doesn't want to do. We'd both end up miserable. He has to want it." I shrug. "And so far, I haven't heard any interest from him."

Ella cocks her head. "Has he asked you to stay?"

"Oh, he'd never do that. He knows how much this program means to me. I'm still on the waiting list. If I don't get in this summer, my name is put on the list for fall."

Ella picks up the teapot and offers to pour me another cup, but I decline. My stomach is in knots.

"Sounds like neither of you want to make the first move," she says, putting down the pot.

"But we love each other."

"And that's a big part of love, giving each other the space to be who you are." Ella smiles. "Twenty is so young. When I think of me at your age..." She nods at the nude over the fireplace. "Well, in my case, it was a time to wander. Along all kinds of roads."

I wring my hands, trying to find a way to explain. "Sometimes when I think of leaving him, I have anxiety, like going up that first hill on a roller coaster. Other times, I can't wait for the thrill of flying down the hill. On my own. There's so much I want to do."

Ella settles back in her chair. "Then you have to do it. Or there will always be a *what if?*"

"But if it's the right thing to do, why does it hurt so bad?" I say, my voice tight. "I don't want to lose him."

She reaches for my hands and holds them in her own. "Lena, nothing's ever lost. Friends... lovers... once you're intimate with someone, a part of them stays with you. Things just evolve."

"But it won't be the same."

"Maybe not, but it's important to be true to yourself. The path you choose is the one you're meant to be on."

***

Our last night arrives. I pack while Kris counts what's left of our travel stash. He ignores Ella's suggestion of taking the Greyhound home. Declines her offer of paying for our bus tickets. I protest, willing to end this trip on a positive, albeit boring, note. Ella suggests we compromise and take the bus around our old nemesis, Chicago. I'm beginning to think that all we do is compromise, and that this trip has been a test of what each of us is willing to give or give up. It's stretched our relationship to the limit.

"Okay, okay," Kris says. "We have enough of our own money to take the bus as far as Gary."

"Gary? Like in Gary Indiana, Gary Indiana, Gary Indiana," I sing out the song from *The Music Man*.

Kris rolls his eyes and goes into the kitchen to phone Greyhound. When he comes back, he has a look of resignation on his face.

"The cheapest route is the longest and gets us in at midnight. But there should be a reasonable motel near the station."

I hear defeat in his voice. I walk over, throw my arms around his waist and squeeze. "Thank you for the bus. But mostly for bringing me here. I'm madly in love with your city. And you."

His face softens. "We haven't left yet," he says. Then he pulls me back to our room—to Ella's feather bed.

***

I watch the beautiful, and now beloved, Minneapolis cityscape spool past my window as Ella gives us a lift to the bus station. With its Victorian neighborhoods and progressive spirit, it reminds me of San Francisco. All you'd have to do is substitute the fog for snow and the bay for the ten thousand lakes. Kris tried to describe it, but I didn't understand until I came here and felt it. I picture Van Gogh's café poster on my bedroom wall and how it helps me imagine myself in France. But I know imagining it won't be enough. I feel a sense of anticipation. I know I have to go to really understand it. Just like Green Lake.

The Greyhound driver throws our packs into the bin under the bus and takes our tickets. Ella hugs us both. She grips my shoulders and says with passion, "Savor each ride, Lena."

I fight back tears, wondering if I'll ever see her again. In one week, she's influenced my life more than anyone I've ever met.

I follow Kris up the steps of the bus and we make our way down the aisle. The bus is filled with people of all ages, sizes, and colors. The only two seats together are near the back, by the bathroom.

"How far to Gary?"

"A long ten hours," Kris mumbles, as he stuffs our coats into the overhead rack.

"Dibs on the window," I say, sliding in.

On our way to the back, I noticed there are definitely more blacks than whites riding the bus. I tense a little, remembering the riots and black power protestors holding their fists high at civil rights demonstrations. I lean over and whisper in Kris's ear, "We're the minority here."

"So?" He adjusts his makeshift pillow and says in a low voice, "When I took Black Cosmology last spring, I was the only white guy in the class."

"Cosmology? What's that?"

"Black history and culture."

"How was it?"

"One of the hardest classes I ever took, in more ways than one," he says. "I had to type a ton of papers and we had a test every other week. But the worst part was when they questioned me about all the racial shit goin' down. I thought going in I wasn't prejudiced. The one thing I learned was, we're all prejudiced in one way or another."

"I don't think I'm prejudiced," I say.

"Well, imagine you're walking down a street in Cleveland and a group of rowdy black teenagers comes walking toward you. Would you cross the street?"

"Yes. But that's not being prejudiced, it's being careful."

"Uh-huh. Would you cross if they were rowdy white teenagers?"

"Probably... depends."

"On what?"

"You know... If they were bikers, jocks, or nerds."

"You prejudge. Prejudice."

I start to protest but Kris holds up his hand. "What if the black kids were wearing suits and ties? Would you cross?"

"Then I... probably not, but—"

"And there it is," Kris says. "It's the same reason some people won't pick us up. They prejudge. They think long-hairs and hitchhikers are all druggies... or panhandlers."

I scowl and slap my hands on my lap. "That's horrible. I'm not like that."

Kris strokes his beard. "Okay, well look around this bus. If you needed help, or even directions, who would you ask, the black or white person?"

I scan the bus and look for a stranger I'd feel comfortable approaching. White. White. Black. "Hey, Gene picked us up and he's black."

"He's been there. When you were asleep, he told me his wife was white."

"Really? So, maybe, being more exposed, makes you more comfortable with things... and people. But I think, I'd still cross the street, black or white. So, maybe it's the circumstances and not the color."

Kris takes a cigarette out of his shirt pocket. "Well, if you're open, you see people as individuals, rather than lumping them in groups. Right?" Lighting his cigarette, he inhales, picks a bit of tobacco off his tongue and turns to me. "Did you ever have any black friends in LA?"

"When I was in junior high, a black family moved into our neighborhood. The three kids kept to themselves. The rumor was their dad had been shot and killed in the riots. Everyone thought they could be part of the Black Panthers or Black Power movement. Sometimes we'd see a police car in their driveway, and boy, did that get the neighbors talking."

"Did you make friends with them?"

"They had a girl my age, Linda. She sat next to me in science class and we got to be friends. After a while, I asked her if it was true her dad was shot in the riots. She said yes, and that he was a cop. I was shocked. I had assumed wrong. The whole neighborhood had gotten it wrong. It taught me a big lesson."

Kris pats my leg. "All we can do is to keep an open mind. Try to learn where people are comin' from and not jump to conclusions."

I lean my head back in my seat and stare out the window as the bus travels through small town America.

Ten foot tall Christmas trees decorate town squares. Santas and angels hang from telephone poles and street lights. There are frosted reindeer in shop windows and wreaths hanging on doors. A sense of security settles into me, knowing that all around America, some traditions live on, even during war and racial strife. We still have hope for peace, love, and justice. I close my eyes and let the hum of the bus's engine rock me to sleep.

When we get off the bus in Gary, it's almost midnight and there's a brittle wind blowing. We walk down the street, past abandoned buildings with broken windows. No white picket fences. No trombones. No Music Man. Kris is swearing under his breath, and looking lost and confused. I start whispering Ella's 'OM.'

I jump as a car pulls up and a man's voice asks, "Need a ride?" I feel my leg muscles tighten getting ready to run before I realize it's a taxi. The driver is black. He looks at us waiting for our answer.

Kris looks at me, then at the driver. "We're okay. We're looking for a motel around here."

"You two really shouldn't be out here on the street at this hour."

"Thanks. But I think it's just down the road," Kris says.

Concern etches the taxi driver's face. "C'mon, hop in. I've got to go in that direction anyway. No charge."

"Okay!" Kris says,

I add, "Thank you."

I climb in back with the packs. Kris gets in front.

"The Holiday Hotel is a few blocks down. Can't see it from here," the driver says. "Close, but still not safe to walk. Especially for you guys."

When we pull in front of the hotel, he says "Merry Christmas," as he drives off.

Inside the hotel, the lobby is clean and well lit, with a traditional Christmas tree in the corner. I can finally breathe easy.

Kris signs the register like he's done it all his life. I look at the few people standing around the lobby. Everyone is black. A man in a pin-striped suit and fedora is staring at me. I look down at the floor. What's he staring at? Does he think I'm someone I'm not?

Kris grabs my hand and we walk to the elevator. The doors open and three women in tight strapless dresses push out. They encircle us for a minute, all high-pitched twitters and sweet smelling perfume, then disappear into the bar adjoining the lobby. We step forward and the elevator door closes like an iron shield. There's no doubt in my mind those women are hookers. No doubt at all… right? And the man in the lobby is a pimp… right? I've seen enough movies to know what they dress like. I freeze, visualizing us, long wild hair, backpacks and mud-crusted jeans. There's no doubt the man in the lobby thinks we're dirty hippies. And probably on drugs. I swallow hard as the elevator door opens.

Inside our room, there's a TV opposite the double bed, and a notepad and pen on the nightstand. Clean towels and a new bar of soap are in the bathroom. I breathe a sigh of relief. Back on solid ground.

Kris strips down to his T-shirt and shorts, and lies back against the pillows. He fiddles with our map, muttering about tomorrow's route. I take out my journal.

Journal:

Hippie types? Hooker types? Is there such a thing as an educated guess? Or is that prejudging? What is prejudice? What made the taxi driver stop? An educated guess that something might happen to us. Is that prejudice? Or is it the circumstances? We had no problem taking a ride with Gene in the middle of white Wisconsin. But I did with the Big Man who was white but looked Mafioso. In all these cases, we were desperate. Desperation is not a choice. But it might lead to opening the door. And that's the objective, right? One thing is for sure: preaching love and peace is easy in your own backyard... but once you step outside, it's complicated.

I put down my journal, turn out the light, and burrow against Kris. He pulls me in tight and it feels the same as it always has. Like I'm right where I should be.

Chapter Forty-Two
Hipster

Lena

It's 8:00 a.m. We're taking a cab from the hotel to the closest freeway ramp. Besides cars, our transportation has included a school bus, limo, delivery truck, Greyhound bus, and now a cab. I can tell Kris thinks he's reached an all-time low using a taxi instead of his thumb. But he took the desk clerk's advice to heart when she said the chances of getting a ride on this side of town were slim to none. Outside, Gary stands bleak and gritty under the morning sun. We're leaving, it's warmer today and our stomachs are full of a Holiday Hotel complimentary breakfast buffet. All things considered, today is starting out pretty good.

The cab pulls over. Kris and I scrape together our loose change. He drives off, shaking his head over our skimpy tip. We take our positions, thumbs out. Within twenty minutes, a dark green GTO slows down and the driver calls out, "Remington?"

"Great!" Kris yells, as he runs to the car and opens the back door.

The driver waves Kris back. "Whoa, leather seats, buddy! Packs go in the trunk." He jumps out wearing a black leather blazer and matching skintight pants. A large gold pendant with the signs of the zodiac swings from his neck. He unlocks the trunk, assesses our roadworn gear, and rearranges several large bags to make room for our packs.

"I got fur coats in here. Gotta protect the merchandise, know what I mean?"

The trunk closes and we get in back, sliding across the black leather seat. I push a full-length fur coat out of the way to make room for us.

The driver points at himself and his attractive blonde passenger. "I'm Nick and this is my old lady, Roxy," he says as he pulls onto the roadway. "You can thank her for making me stop."

I push the fur coat farther down the seat to give myself more room. When I look up, I see Nick watching me in the rearview mirror. "Be careful with that coat," he says, turning his gaze back to the road. "It probably costs more than your mommy and daddy's house."

Roxy turns as we introduce ourselves. "It's Roxanne," she says, before turning to stare out the side window with a fashion model pout. Her blonde hair spills in silky strands all over her thick, cabled fisherman's sweater. A white ski jacket with a fur-trimmed hood drapes over the back of her seat.

"So, where you two from?" Nick smooths his Fu Manchu mustache with his thumb and index-finger. His dark hair is cut in a shag, each layer feathering into the next one.

"Kent State," I say. For some reason, I want to know what side of the fence this guy is on. Sadly, Kent State is the identifier.

Nick nods emphatically. "Were you there for the shootings? I was in Chicago in '68 during the riots. Got my car windshield smashed. New company car, too. Assholes."

"What were you doing in Chicago?" Kris asks.

"I was an alternate convention delegate. My dad's a councilman. He thought the convention would be good for making business contacts. I thought it'd be good for chicks." Nick winks at Kris in the rearview mirror.

"What kind of business?" Kris asks.

"Fur, man. Are you blind? Family business in Milwaukee. We've been making fur coats for five generations. Most of the Hollywood stars wear our coats. Joe Namath, too." He turns and glances back at us. "Hey, you guys party?"

"It's kinda early," I say. There's no way I want to get high with fur man.

"Early? I'm usually just making it home about now." He pulls down the visor and looks in the mirror, patting his hair. "I got some good stuff."

I can see Kris is already smiling, more than ready to get high, so I talk fast. "I'll pass. Can't mix pancakes and pot." I nudge Kris and shake my head, as in, "neither can you."

"Babe, it's Maui gold. You gotta try it. You'll never go back to that Mexican shit. Hey, Roxy, get the stash out."

Roxy reaches under her seat and pulls out a baggie and a gaudy Meerschaum pipe.

"I had to trade a pound of Jamaican and a pair of Chinchilla mittens for that pipe," Nick says. "The guy carved it in my image. It's one-of-a kind, just like me. Huh, Roxy?"

Roxy tamps the Meerschaum bowl full of golden weed. She shakes her hair out of her face and lights up, inhaling deeply. Nick takes a hit and passes the pipe to Kris. Kris examines the pipe, smiles and shrugs, then tries to hand the pipe back.

"Thanks, but—" Kris says.

Nick waves the pipe away. "You're our guests. Take a hit—you can't turn down gold."

Kris looks at me with raised brows. I don't want to smoke, but I don't want to lose this ride more. We both take a sociable hit. I hand it back over the seat to Roxy. She and Nick pass the pipe between them. Nick wasn't bluffing. This stuff is super smooth... and strong. Nick peers at me in the rearview mirror. He smiles and says, "Not the same as O-HIGH-O, is it?"

"I'm from LA."

"La-La land," he snorts. "So, tell me, ever score across the border?"

"No." I give a bored sigh. "Went to Tijuana, once."

"That's not Mexico," he yells. "I'm talking Acapulco, baby, where the real people are. I used to own a house down there next to Mick Jagger's."

Right. If there's one rock star I follow, it's Mick. I hold up my hand to ward off his BS. "Mick lives in St. Vincent. Maybe you're thinking of Frankie Avalon."

Kris nudges me. "Be cool."

"Huh? What'd you guys say?" Nick turns the radio from a blasting ten to eight.

"Cool grass, man," Kris says.

"Well, here, take another hit," Nick hands back the pipe. "You'll be flying into Remington. Right, Roxy?"

"So, what do you do in your fur business?" I ask, trying to change the subject.

Nick taps his chest. "I'm in on all the big deals. Rodeo Drive, Fifth Avenue—all the happenin' places. I soften 'em up and my dad reels them in. He takes care of the contracts—the small details."

I crack the window while Kris takes another obligatory hit. A seed pops and lands on the sacred fur coat. Shit. Kris scrambles to snuff the ember out but it leaves a small singe mark.

"Hey, what's that smell?" Nick sniffs.

"That's just Lena's patchouli oil. Smells like road kill," Kris says.

I give him a pass for trying to divert the conversation off the smell of burnt fur.

"So, it sounds like you have a pretty important job," I say.

"I make the company go, man," says Nick. "Ever been to Hawaii? Not everyone can afford it, but it's my kind of place. Paradise, man. Hey, roll up your window, you're killing the buzz. Anyway, I took Roxy to Hawaii a couple weeks ago in my company jet. It's the only way to travel."

Roxy looks at him and smirks. "I didn't know your family owned Northwest Airlines."

Nick shakes his head. "Not that plane. My uncle's island hopper."

"That's no jet." She looks back at us with a pained expression. "It only has one propeller. Scared me to death!"

Nick takes another hit, coughs, then says, "They grow the gold everywhere. The narcs can't see it in all that tropical vegetation. Small plane is good for finding it."

Ah, so not just into fur, I think, watching Nick scrounge through the console. He holds up a cassette.

"This will blow your socks off. Grand Funk Railroad. I sat in on their recording session a few weeks ago, with Todd. They wanted me to jam with them, but I left my guitar at home."

"Todd?"

"Yeah, Rundgren, heard of him? He's way ahead of his time, producing some far-out shit." He pops the tape in and turns, dark eyes blazing. "This is real rock. None of that sissy folk crap."

The car veers onto the shoulder and he jerks the steering wheel back shouting, "Woo-hoooo! Rock out, man."

I grab onto the door handle, listening to Grand Funk singing they're getting closer to their home. Meaning, the pearly gates. Hopefully we're not heading the same direction.

Nick sings and bops his head to the music while Roxy's vacant blue eyes stare out the passenger window. What's she to him? Or better yet, what's he to her? I'm pretty sure asking her how the hell she ended up with him violates several of Kris's road rules. But I can't help my curious nature.

"So Roxy, what's your thing?" I ask.

"My name's Roxanne."

"I like that name. It always reminds me of the beach, rocks and sand."

The corners of her mouth turn up. She looks back at me. "I'm a student."

"Was a student," Nick says. "I rescued her from that boring crap. Made her a model."

"What'd you study?" asks Kris.

"Fashion design."

"Oh, cool. That's a real art," I say.

"Arty-schmarty. Hot bods is where the money's at, right, Kris?"

Roxanne turns to Nick and narrows her eyes. "Yeah? So, where are all these modeling contracts you were going to get me? It's been six months already. I could've been finishing my degree."

"Hey, I got you those hand and foot photo shoots. There's more where that comes from Roxy baby—"

"It's Roxanne!" She tosses the pipe into the glove compartment. "Why can't you get that right?" She crosses her arms and slouches down in her seat. Kris elbows me and gives me the look that says chill on the questions.

I close my eyes and lean against the door, listening as Nick berates Roxanne, telling her she needs to work more on her posture if she's ever going to make it as more than a foot model. I watch her straighten up and throw her shoulders back. Why does she put up with Fur Boy? She sounds like she once had goals and ideals. She sold out for a fur coat and foot commercials. I glance over at Kris, his head leaning against the door, eyes closed. Will we sell out when we graduate? To what? The American dream? And what is that? I don't know the answers.

Chapter Forty-Three
Puppy Love

Kris

As we wave goodbye to Nick and Roxanne from the side of the road, Lena looks at me and says, "Don't let us ever turn out like them."

I squeeze her hand. "I won't. But just in case, do you like mink or chinchilla?"

Forty-five minutes later, a powder blue cargo van slides onto the ramp and crunches to a stop. The rear doors open and a long-haired guy in a Purdue University T-shirt hollers, "Need a ride?"

We climb in the back doors. The driver yells over the eight-track tape player jammin' out the Rolling Stones, "Where you headed?"

I shout back, "Columbus."

"The best we can do is West Lafayette."

"That's cool." We'll be thirty fun miles closer to home, which means a little less time for road hassles and strange rides.

Two guys and a dark-haired chick make room for us on a worn-out mattress. Lena and I lean against some duffle bags while two gangly Irish Setter puppies leap on us, pressing their cold, wet noses into our faces and necks, and rolling all over us. I try to imagine Reg at that age. Introductions are handed out as I make room for the pups, rubbing their bellies and scratching their ears.

"What're their names?" I ask.

Tanya says, "Paddy and Toke."

"How old are they?"

"Four months," she says. "They have the attention span of a gnat. But they're getting better. At least they're housebroken."

"We've got an Airedale, Reggie," I say.

Lena rolls her eyes. "He's not just ours, he belongs to everybody at Kent State."

I laugh, "Yeah, well. He loves people."

"Especially women," Lena slips in.

"I've heard Airedales can be aggressive," Tanya says.

"He doesn't care much for other male dogs," I say. "But we have rules that keep him out of trouble."

"Rule number one, never take him to peace rallies," Lena says. "It doesn't go over too well, when they ask for a moment of silence and Reggie starts snarling at another dog."

I tilt my head, giving her a warning look. "Reggie's a good boy." I nestle my face into Paddy's soft fur. "I miss him."

"Why isn't he with you?" Tanya says. "Dog lovers would give you a ride."

Lena presses her lips together and shakes her head.

"Yeah, well, sometimes that doesn't work out," I say. I relay the story of the time a chick picked me and Reg up on our way to Kent and she had a female dog in the car. Reg turned the backseat into a hump-fest and we were dropped off a short twenty minutes later.

"Well, there's always that," Tanya says, laughing. "But when I hitch with a dog, I feel like only good people will pick us up. You know, the dog lovers. Sometimes it takes longer, but the bad guys leave us alone. And that's a good trade-off, in my book."

I nod, wishing Lena felt that way. Tanya and I trade more dog stories 'til the West Lafayette exit comes into view. We roll to a stop on the busy county road leading to the college. There are hippy handshakes all around as I reach for my jacket and Tanya slides open the door. A blast of sunlight hits the interior of the van. I'm blinded for a second, but I can feel the puppies making a break for it around my legs.

Tanya shouts "No! Toke! Paddy! Stay!"

"Oh, shit! Grab 'em!" one of the guys yells.

I jump out of the van, dropping my jacket as I try to head off the pups. One crawls under the van and the other one dashes around the front bumper toward the highway. I round the corner of the van as the pup trots into the road. I dive, just catching his rear leg. The high-pitched screech of rubber on cement screams through me. I hear the pup's yip.

My face rolls up from the pavement inches away from the monstrous chrome teeth of a Rambler grill. Tanya runs onto the road and grabs the pup. Traffic is backing up around us. Lena is yelling "Kris, Kris." Her hands claw at my shirt as she tries to pull me up.

"Kris! Are you all right?"

Lena's voice sounds like she's in a tunnel. No sense of my whole life flashing before me. Just the smell of cement. The sound of tires. The shine of chrome. *What if?* I turn cold with the realization… My stomach lurches and I lean over the guard rail. As I straighten, one of the guys throws me an old T-shirt. I wipe my face. Lena takes the clean side of the shirt and gently pats the scrapes on my elbows.

The guys surround Tanya and the pup. The shaken Rambler driver runs up and apologizes. After making sure there's nothing wrong, he drives off.

"Shit, Kris! What were you doing? You could've gotten killed," Lena says. "For a dog!"

Tanya runs up and hands me my jacket. "How could I've let this happen? I've opened those doors a million times!"

"It's not your fault," I say. "I should've grabbed them before they got out."

Lena looks hard at both of us. "It's no one's fault. It could've happened to anybody."

Tanya, with the pup under her arm, pats me on the back. "You're my hero." She turns and runs back to the van.

Lena and I pick up our packs and start walking. I shudder.

"You are so lucky," Lena says, slipping her arm through mine. "We could be headed to the ER now. Or worse."

She's right. I exhale deeply. I know she was worried about me, but she doesn't understand. She thinks Reg is my excuse to take late night walks and talk to women. She doesn't realize that, after her, Reg is my next best friend. I'd be lost without him.

Chapter Forty-Four
John Dear

Lena

A family on their way to grandma's house takes us around Indianapolis and drops us off at the exit ramp to a desolate county road. Stepping out of the car, my gaze follows the flat gray farmland to where it meets the flat gray sky. I scribble the words on my mental postcard: "Wish we weren't here."

Kris looks up at the road sign. "Hey, didn't you tell me that 109 is your lucky number?"

"Yeah." I try to smile. "This must be our lucky road."

We haven't stood for long when a banged-up Chevy Impala pulls over. A stocky man wearing a faded flannel shirt and John Deere cap rolls down his window. "Need a lift?"

He pushes open the passenger door and sweeps a greasy bag of chips off the front bench seat. Looking at me, he pats the seat and waves Kris into the back. I get in and set Tang between us. The man eyes me and grins. My intuition says this guy is trouble, but I'm going to stick with Kris's road rules on this one—be positive, it's all about the ride.

"Thank you so much for stopping," I say.

John Deere wipes his nose with his sleeve and jams the gearshift into first. Scraggly brown hair sticks out from his cap around his ears. A faint scent of alcohol hangs in the air. I edge closer to the comfort of the door, trying to keep my imagination in check. He's probably a farmer, up at the crack of dawn, feeding, planting, and milking. Who wouldn't need a beer or two after a hard-earned day?

Kris leans forward from the back and gives his routine "Pleased to meet you" introduction.

The man nods, then grunts, "Where ya goin'?"

"Columbus," Kris says.

"Or anywhere in that direction," I add.

"Do ya know where you're at?" The driver chews his words with his tobacco.

Kris says, "Not exactly."

"Well, that was a stupid spot to be standing. You ain't gonna get no rides around here." The driver grins.

Is he mocking us or is it just his way of talking? My mind opens up Kris's rulebook. *Make friends. Ask his advice.*

"So, where should we go to get rides?"

"Truck route," he says.

"Sounds good," Kris says.

John Deere jams the gearshift into first, turning down a one-lane road that stretches toward more empty fields. I feel my stomach coil as he drives us farther and farther from the Interstate. He gives me a fleeting glance. His eyes sit small and deep above a bulbous nose. Somehow creepy and farmer don't align. I stare out the front window at endless, dirty snow-covered fields.

"So, uh, what do they plant around here?" I ask, as we pass by a field with brown stubble breaking the crust of snow. "Corn?"

John Deere rolls down the window and spits a brown streak of tobacco. Clears his throat.

"People round here don't take much to hippies," he says, stepping down on the gas pedal.

My chest tightens.

"Uh, we're not hippies," Kris says. "We're students."

"Same bullshit."

He tilts his hat back and gives me a narrowed-eyed glance. "Maybe students are worse. Hiding behind books instead of fighting for our country."

Uh-oh. My stomach squeezes. We should get out. Make him pull over. Will he get angry? Start something? If he hates hippies, why did he pick us up? I stare straight forward. I feel an urgent need to pee.

"Um, I've gotta go to the bathroom. Is there somewhere we can stop?"

John Deere smiles, showing stained teeth. "Wassa matter, little hippie lady? Nervous?" His face goes flat as he pins his gaze on me. "You don't know what nervous is."

My heart thumps against my ribcage. I wiggle in my seat for effect. "Sorry, I really need to go. And um, we're really not hippies."

John Deere's fingers tighten on the steering wheel. "My brother couldn't hide behind no books."

I turn my eyes to the side window and try to keep calm. We pass the mangled carcass of a deer on the berm, its guts splattered over dirty ice. I close my eyes.

"You in back. You hunt?" John Deere asks. His eyes, two dark stones, stare in the review mirror at Kris.

"Sure do. Ducks with my dad back in Minnesota."

"Quack, quack, quack," he smirks. "What kinda gun you use?"

He reaches in front of me and punches open the glove box with his knuckles. "Something like this?" His eyes glint in the rearview mirror. "Now, this here's a real gun. Ready for anything."

I stare at the handle of a black pistol in the glove box. My heart jackhammers.

"We used twelve-gauges," Kris answers in a steady tone.

"How old are you?" John Deere asks.

"Twenty-one," Kris lies.

"A real man," John Deere snorts. "Killing ducks instead of gooks." He swerves the car to the right, then to the left, then right.

I inhale sharply, grabbing the door armrest.

"Whoa. Hey, man, be careful," Kris says, with an edge of panic in his voice. "Watch out for the black ice."

"You telling me how to drive, freak? Ever roll a fucking Jeep? My brother could tell you how that feels—if the gooks hadn't killed him."

I'm trembling. This is it. He's going to reach for the gun and pump bullets into our hippie freak bodies. Or do something else I don't even want to imagine.

"Jeez, I'm sorry," Kris says.

"Me, too, that's horrible," I say, feeling like I'm in a scene from the Twilight Zone.

John Deere considers what we said a moment, then asks, "You God-fearin' folk?"

I can hear Sue and Marty shouting out 'Praise the Lord'. "Oh, yes. We sure are," I say quickly. "In fact, we did some praying with Pastor Henry and the snakes. Maybe you know him? The traveling pastor."

John Deere blinks. Tightens his lips.

"Sure is beautiful around these parts," I say, faking marvel at the treeless moonscape.

"Yes, it is," he says, then reaches over and lays his hand on my thigh. "Especially these parts."

I move closer to the door, but he squeezes my thigh. I shove his hand off of me and turn. He gropes my butt.

"Stop that or I'm going to pee all over the seat," I say in a low steely tone. I look at the gun in the glove box, willing myself to grab it.

"Hey, man, stop the fucking car. Let us out! Now!" Kris's voice booms.

The driver slams on the brakes and yells, "God damn hippie whore." He reaches across me and yanks the door handle open. I drag Tang with me as he pushes me out the door and onto the ground. I'm crawling when the car peels off.

Oh my God. "Kris!"

Through the blast of exhaust, I see the back door burst open. Our packs shoot out followed by Kris tumbling and rolling across the roadway. For a moment he lies motionless. My mind fills with sheer panic. Then he pushes up to his feet and gathers our packs. He hobbles back to where I'm on my knees. He drops our packs in front of me and turns, looking down the road.

"Bastard!" he yells, thrusting his middle finger in the air at the receding speck of John Deere's Impala.

I jump up and grab his arm, pushing it down. "Stop it! He's going to come back and kill us!"

"No, he won't," Kris says.

"You don't know that!" I scream.

"If he wanted to kill us, he would've done it. He just wanted to screw with us, the prick." Kris puts his arms around me. "Us hippy freaks."

The whole ride with John Deere runs through my mind. How he talked to us. How he groped me. I wipe my leg where he touched me, desperate to get any trace of him off me. "When he grabbed me, I wanted to get the gun, but I couldn't move," I say, my voice jags.

Kris hugs me tighter. "Good. If you had, who knows what would've happened? You might have shot him, or he could've grabbed it and shot us."

"But what if it could've saved our lives?" Tears burn my eyes. "I froze. Like I froze during the shooting, like I froze during the house fight. I always freeze."

"Lena, if it was life or death, you would've been able to do it. We're here, we're safe, and that's all that matters. Things worked out the way they should have."

I hang limp in Kris's embrace. He's trying to comfort me, but things don't always work out the way they should. Sometimes you have to make them work out that way. Still, even if I had gotten the gun, could I have pulled the trigger? I inhale deep and look out into the barren fields around us. Ella's voice rings in my ear. *Breathe and stay in the moment.* Calmer, I wipe my eyes as Kris helps me slide the small knapsack over my shoulders.

"Now I really do have to pee." I head off into the field.

When I come back, Kris is staring at the map.

"Now what?" I say.

"We're going back to the freeway."

"What about that busy truck road he told us about?"

Kris shakes his head. "There's no busy truck road. He planned to drop us in the middle of nowhere all along." Kris points on the map. "He only made one turn. I think we're here. About five miles from the freeway. We better get goin' before the light fades."

Kris hoists the big pack onto his back. His mittens, now gray with road slush, hold the straps. His face is drawn, eyes brittle blue. He's limping, but it's a small price to pay for getting away from that maniac in one piece. I pick up Tang and walk behind him.

The sky, dead fish gray, stretches out over us and the snow-patched earth. I try to put the demented driver out of my mind and think of the ocean on a gray day. The cawing of the gulls, the misty sea air.

But he keeps creeping in. And gutless me. I had a split second to make a move and I couldn't do it. *What if* scenarios play out in my head. The relief of what didn't happen wrestles with the terror of what could've happened. I see the gun in the glove box. Cringe at the memory of his hand on my thigh. But in the end, I couldn't do it. And he couldn't do it either. I close my eyes and whisper, "Thank you." Somebody up there likes us.

That much I believe.

Chapter Forty-Five
Boxcar

Kris

The hour and a half hike back to the Interstate is a bitch. I'm cold and achy from the fall out of that asshole's car. The last time I was this pissed was when I let Reggie tear into those jocks at the house party. I should've brought Reg on this trip. He would've put that bastard in his place. That jerk probably would've never picked us up if Reg had been along.

I glance at Lena. Her thumb is out, but her head is down. So far this trip has been a steady diet of near misses with assholes, guns, and jail. But that's okay. Sticking a smiley face on it all, if it doesn't kill us, it'll make our stories better. I twist the ring that Aunt Ella gave me, hoping Merlin will conjure up some good luck. But I know the truth—it's gonna take a lot more than a wish to save whatever dreams of romantic adventure Lena had about this journey.

We're standing on the side of the road next to an empty gas station. We've been here for over an hour and the only thing we've seen has been a lone semi. The roadway is a short walk away, but I know Lena doesn't want to see another cop or have another citation added to her collection. Then again, it's the only way we'll get the cars on the Interstate to see us. The problem is we can't even discuss the possibility because Lena's not talking. Not a word. No comment. No eye roll. Not even a "Why don't you do something?" She stares out over the road, waiting to stick out her thumb for a passing car or truck. As quiet as she's been, I'd even welcome some bitching.

There's no guessing about it, the last ride and the gaps between rides are taking a toll on her. I've always used that lull to process the past ride and look forward to the next. I think Lena views every moment without a ride as a failure. She thinks this is all some kind of test. For Lena though, there isn't a grade—just pass or fail. For her, the space between rides is nothing but an endless wait. And after our last ride, I have to admit, I'm starting to feel her pessimism settle over me.

"Can you call somebody to come get us?" Lena says. Her voice is as weak as the winter sun.

"Maybe."

"Maybe what?"

I shake out a cigarette, light up, and exhale. "Maybe Jim is back from Florida."

"Jim? Your last hitching buddy? Do it. He'll understand. He'll—"

"Only he doesn't have a car."

"Then why did you mention him?"

I hear the exasperation in her voice. "I'm just thinking out loud."

"Instead of thinking out loud, think before you talk."

I take a drag, run through a mental list of all my friends, then shrug. "Everyone I know hitches. Or they've gone somewhere on break."

Lena's face tightens. A hard gust of freezing wind blasts against us and she ducks her face, jamming her hands in her pockets. I finish my cigarette, toss it on the pavement, and stew. I'm adding another line to my 'Rules of the Road'—hitching with chicks is a summer thing. My eyes drift over the stark, windblown countryside. Across the interstate, a long line of standing boxcars grabs my attention. Are they coming or going? Without the locomotive, who knows? But those boxcars will be traveling, even if they don't know where they're bound. Kind of like me.

A year ago, I hooked up with a temp agency for a shitty buck twenty-five an hour. I had no idea what I had gotten myself into—my idea of hard labor was mowing two lawns in one afternoon. My first day I had to unload a boxcar by myself. I needed to move and stack thirty tons of fifty-pound bags of fertilizer, by hand, to pallets on the loading dock. In eight hours. As I unloaded each bag, the only thing that kept me going was thinking about the boxcar. My mind wandered along the rails it had traveled, all the things it had seen. Then I thought about the places I'd been and the places I'd go. On my eighth hour, so tired that my body was ready to collapse, I stuck with it and finished the job. It felt good. No—it felt great. Boxcars became my existential connection to strength and perseverance.

I feel a tug on my jacket. Lena's looking up at me.

"Call your dad." Her voice is thin and cracking like a layer of ice. "Tell him we almost got killed."

I look at her dark eyes—pleading mixed with surrender. I turn away and release a heavy sigh. The soul of hitching is like the boxcar. It's where you find out what you're made of. I think of all the times I hitched alone. How it forced me to face that lost and empty place inside me. I look back at Lena. But I'm not alone. Yeah, hitching helped me face that hole, but now it's Lena who fills that empty place.

I take a deep breath. It's time to make the call. If my dad taught me one thing, it's to give it all you've got, but recognize when something's a lost cause. He'd be proud to know I'm following his advice, but that won't make him any happier while he's driving one hundred and twenty miles to pick us up because my girlfriend's coming undone. He's gonna be pissed.

I look sideways at Lena. Dirty jeans. Frizzy hair. Wet muddy boots. She's come a long way since she first stuck her thumb out more than a week ago. I'll make the call and take whatever crap Dad throws my way. It's the least I can do.

My backpack slides to the ground with a thud. I tramp toward the gas station, hoping I'll find a working payphone. I'll call every friend I have. If none of them can help, I'll save a last dime for my dad. I smile, envisioning the looks on my friends' faces when I play back this trip over a pitcher of brew at the Hood. Memories of our wacky rides and all our adventures run through my head and lightness comes over me. This trip hasn't been perfect, but it's been one hell of a journey. Suddenly I feel like I can fly.

In the wind, Lena's voice is calling me. I look back. A car waits on the berm. This has got to be it. Our big ride.

Chapter Forty-Six
Song Bird

Lena

A blast of warm air welcomes me as I slide into the front seat. Kris puts the packs into the car's trunk and climbs into the back. He tells the driver our destination, then adds, "But we'll go anywhere half a cornfield in that direction." His tone is as light and carefree as it was when we started our journey.

"It's your lucky day," she says. "That's exactly where I'm headed, Columbus."

Her words wrap around me and shout, "It's here, the last ride!" This must be a private limo sent from heaven.

Jane is pencil thin in a black turtleneck and jeans. Her light brown hair is pulled off her oval face into a ponytail that hangs below her shoulders. Gold dangle earrings dance in the car's overhead light. She has model high cheekbones and almond-shaped green eyes. She wants to talk, and Kris leans forward from the back seat, filling her in on the good, bad, and uglies of our trip.

"What an experience," Jane says. "You should write it all down. Something to tell your kids."

I give a wry smile. The emotional entries in my journal would hardly be bedtime stories for kids. *Kids?*

"Maybe I'll appreciate it when I'm old and gray," I say. "But right now, I just want it to be over."

Jane smiles and nods her head. She's twenty-five, she tells us, a grad student by day and a singer by night.

"Ever hear of The Botanist Club?" she asks.

"Sure. I used to hang out there," says Kris. "Great music."

"My brother owns it now. So I've got a steady gig."

"No kidding. What do you play?"

"I do keyboard and vocals with Red Mountain."

"I've heard of them," Kris says.

"What kind of music do you play?" I ask.

"I started with classical piano, but when I discovered Dylan, Dylan discovered me." Her velvety voice is low and calm. "My whole world changed."

Jane and Kris talk about local musicians who are mutual acquaintances. They share a world I have no part in. I wait for my green-eyed monster to appear. Instead I find myself wanting to be as passionate about something as she is. She talks about being on the road, seeing different parts of the country, meeting interesting people. I feel my urge to travel pulsate as she talks. I want to be worldly and together like her, when I'm twenty-five.

Jane turns the radio onto a classical station playing Christmas songs. Kris stretches across the back seat and closes his eyes. We all sink into our own thoughts. It's so nice to end our trip with warm melodies of goodwill. I lean back and close my eyes. I could use a little sleep so I'm bright eyed and cheery when I get to Kris's house and family. I count our rides in my head, starting at the beginning. I try to envision all the drivers that picked us up. Every ride has its own shape and design, like a snowflake. I let myself drift down into those snowflakes and they cover me like a patchwork quilt.

I awaken as Kris nudges me. "We're here."

Jane's car bumps onto the driveway of his house. Christmas lights outline the roof and windows, twinkling through the snow. We pull our packs out of the car one last time and thank Jane. She gives us each a hug.

"Stop by The Botanist the next time you're home," she says, "We'll have a few cold ones on the house."

"We will," Kris says. "I'd like to see what your brother has done to the place."

As she drives away, I pull Kris close. Our eyes meet and I feel his gaze embrace me. We linger on the driveway, letting the solitude of the night surround us.

"I love you a thousand boxcars full," Kris whispers.

"Boxcars?" I pull back.

He nods. "It's just my way of saying you take me where I want to go."

"Well, then, I love you a thousand and one."

We kiss. I stare out over his shoulder at the road. It's like an old friend I've argued with and fussed over. But now that it's time to leave, I'll miss it. It cracked us open and spilled us out. And instead of going down the drain, we found a deeper connection to life. And love. What began as a quest for romantic adventure has given us something more. The soft glow of the porch light beckons us into the warm. And like our love, it is enough.

Part III: Bad Exits

Chapter Forty-Seven
Dormies

Lena

*J*ournal:

Winter quarter is a drag. I have to make up for my 'Kris-influenced' grades from last fall or I could be dropped from the study-abroad program. I also need to start saving for it. Ginny says she's ready for a change of scene and wants to drive with me out to California in June. We got a weekend job in a factory outside Kent for a buck twenty-five an hour. Our job is to put four small wheels, four nuts, and four bolts into plastic bags. We sit on stools and listen to the radio, trying to reach the quota of two hundred bags an hour during our eight-hour shift. It's a mind-numbing bore. Ginny sings, tells jokes and analyzes the guys she's dating. I fidget, going silently crazy.

I tried to get Kris a job at the factory, but he doesn't want to work. He likes his weekends free to roam with Reggie and hang out. I come home to him lounging on the couch, kissing me with brownie breath, talking about the new albums he listened to, or old movies he watched with friends. He wants to do the things we used to do, and I feel guilty that our things are different now. So, I breathe deep and try not to pull the strings that could unravel us.

Valentine's Day is a snowy Sunday. I'm propped up against a pillow, with Elizabeth Barrett Browning in my lap and Blue snuggled at my feet, waiting for the breakfast in bed that Kris insisted on making. He comes up with Reggie bouncing beside him, balancing a tray in each hand. One has two steaming mugs of hot chocolate that he sets down on the end table. The other he puts on my lap and climbs in next to me. I look down at a stack of heart-shaped pancakes.

"Sweets for the sweet." He hands me a bottle of Log Cabin maple syrup.

"How do I love thee? Let me count the ways." I drip out X's and O's on top of the pancakes.

We gobble down our sweet and sticky valentines while I read poems from *Sonnets from the Portuguese*. Somehow, it's not so romantic with a full mouth and Reggie begging and scrounging for fallen crumbs.

"Where'd you get the trays?" I ask, knowing full well they came from the dorm cafeteria.

"Get dressed," Kris says.

"You didn't steal them, did you?"

"I borrowed them. C'mon." He gets up.

"Wait," I say, getting out of bed and pulling out a square package from behind my desk. "Be my valentine?"

He opens the Daily Kent Stater wrapping. "All right! The Cat," he says, looking down at the album cover of *Tea for The Tillerman*. "It reminds me of our trip."

"Me too."

He puts the album on the stereo and we tumble back into bed. Into our own *oh baby, baby* wild world.

In early afternoon, we drop Reg off at Cheet's, and take the trays to Taylor Hill for sledding. We join a crowd of kids who live in the Midway Drive dorms and spend the next two hours sliding down the hill on the trays, wrestling in the wet slop at the bottom. Twilight brings on a huge free-for-all snowball fight. I fight the memory of the last huge gathering on The Commons—bullets flying instead of snowballs.

Soaked and shivering, we return the trays to the cafeteria before going to Kris's dorm for the night. He has to work the desk in the morning, I'll have time to go home and change before my first class. We leave a trail of wet boot prints as we walk down the hall to Kris's room. I check my watch, ten-thirty. Women are supposed to be out of the men's dorm by eleven. Kris tells me to hit the john or I'll have to hold it 'til morning, so the resident assistant doesn't see me.

"I got caught doing some stupid stuff," Kris says. "It's no big deal, but I gotta be careful. You know, I'm on probation."

"What stupid stuff?" My heart thumps, but I want to know.

"Didn't I tell you about the time I helped run the duck races on the third floor?"

"Duck races?"

"It got a bit out of hand."

"I'm sure the RA's loved you."

Kris grins. "My RA was cool 'til I accidentally spilled bong water under his door. It stunk up his meditation rug."

Down the hallway there's an aroma of pot and incense. High-pitched laughter echoes with strains of music.

"I'm so glad I don't live in a dorm anymore," I say as a woman with pillow-mussed hair, wearing nothing but a T-shirt, runs into the men's bathroom. It reminds me of when I shuffled down my dorm hall for a shower. I literally bumped into the cute guy from English Lit as he crept out of some other girl's room, dropping my toiletries. "You're lucky to have a single room," I say, trying to erase my memory of that cute guy helping me pick up my tampons off the floor. "I had a couple of roommate hassles."

"Why didn't you change your room?"

"Well, aside from her nocturnal adventures, I really liked Anne. And all the guys melted over her Southern drawl. I'm surprised you didn't know her."

Kris shakes his head. "Nope."

We hear a squeal coming from another room. I look in as we pass and see the familiar tie-dyed sheets draping over a rollicking bottom bunk.

"I tried smoking a joint before bedtime so that I could fall asleep before the screwing hour, but it didn't always work," I say, remembering spending some nights on the dorm lobby couch. "After about a month, she moved into a sorority house and Lyla the roadkill queen moved in."

"What? Lyla who lives in your house?"

"How many Lylas do you know? She scavenged roadkill to get extra credit for her biology class. You haven't lived until you've reached into the closet for a shirt and pulled out a smashed squirrel in a drycleaner bag."

Kris wrinkles his nose. "How did you stand it?"

"Luckily, it was winter quarter, so they were mostly frozen. If they got ripe, we tried to hide the stench by spraying a bottle of some sexy perfume that Anne left behind. The room smelled like a bordello. Lucky for us she's taking botany and geology this year."

Kris shrugs. "I'm adaptable when it comes to roommates," he says. "'Lude Dick had a different girl there every night. Never bothered me. I learned to work around him. Of course, there was the occasional girl running naked across our room when I popped in unexpectedly."

"Didn't you have a signal to let the other one know when a girl was there?"

"Didn't need one. I was hardly ever there."

"Where were you?" I ask nonchalantly. *Who were you with?*

He keeps his tone even. "Looking for some privacy myself. But there were a few nights I stayed. Had to listen to their moaning and groaning. That was tough to sleep through."

He unlocks his door and turns on his bedside reading lamp. We strip off our soggy clothes and he takes them downstairs to the dorm dryer. I'm under the blankets reading Gibran when he gets back. Turning on the hot plate, he boils water for chamomile tea, and lowers the lamp light. He tunes the FM stereo to WMMS the underground rock station from Cleveland. He stuffs a towel underneath the door, then finds a doobie in his dresser drawer and lights it up. We smoke, tracing the metaphors in Gibran's thoughts until my fingers trace the metaphors of Kris's body.

***

The jarring clang of the fire alarm outside the door jerks me awake. "What's that? Tornado?"

"Tornado? It's winter!" Kris grumbles.

"What is it then?"

"Some idiot screwing around. Go back to sleep."

I lie back down, but stare into the darkness. I hear footsteps outside the door.

"You sure?" I ask.

He throws his arm around me and mumbles, "Happens every quarter. Assholes."

I burrow against him but my foot twitches. I press it against the bottom of his foot to stop it. He hates that and moves away. Doors are slamming. Feet shuffling. Voices. I poke him in the back.

"Kris, can you look?" I poke him again. "Please?"

He rolls over, groping for his glasses. "It's nothing, but I'll do it if it'll make you happy."

What he really means is, "If it'll shut you up." I glance at the clock on the desk. It isn't working. I reach up to the window over the bed and pull back the curtain. Still dark. If I wasn't a girl in a guys' dorm after hours, I'd stick my head out the door and see what was going on myself. But with my luck the RA would see me. Kris would be busted, and it would screw up his probation. God, he's slow. He's pulling on his shorts like he's going to the electric chair. There's a pounding at the door. A bellowing voice.

"Fire! Get Out! Fire!"

Kris stumbles to the door and yanks it open. Beyond him, I see a mob scene of murky shadows racing by. The power must be out—there's nothing but dim emergency lights illuminating the hall.

"C'mon, we gotta go," he says, sitting down on the bed to pull on his pants.

"I don't have any clothes," I hiss. "Remember? They're downstairs in the dryer."

My stomach tumbles like the dorm dryer where Kris left them. Damn midnight passion. Never again. Kris stands and starts rummaging through his dresser. He throws jeans and a flannel shirt at me.

"Put those on. Hurry!"

I'm shaking so bad I can hardly pull them on. I fumble in the dark with the zipper and buttons that are in the wrong places, then look for my shoes. They're nowhere to be found. Kris is digging frantically through his dresser.

"What are you doing?" My voice scales up ten octaves.

"My stash. They use fires as an excuse to go through people's stuff and bust them, just like the riots."

"Are you crazy? We have to go!"

I hear him exhale in relief. "Got it. Let's go," he says.

"Maybe I should go down the back stairs." I say.

"You nuts? No way."

"You're on probation! They'll kick you out if they see me."

"I'll go with you."

"No. They can't see us together." I jump to my feet and head toward the door. "It's okay. I'm not afraid. I'll meet you out front."

We rush into the hall. I turn in the opposite direction of the crowd. The moonlight coming through the window at the end of the hall gives just enough glow that I can see the back stairwell. I know it well from the other times I've had to sneak out.

Shapes move past me in slow motion. I'm trying desperately to keep Kris's pants from falling down, holding them with one hand. His shirt is sliding from one shoulder to the other, so I grip the front of it with my other hand. A voice yells, "Hey, Lena. What are you doing here?" Laughter. Dammit.

I push open the stairway door and step into total darkness. No windows. I grab onto the railing with one hand, clenching Kris's jeans with the other. Trying not to trip on the pants dragging under my bare feet, I make my way down the steps to the second-floor landing. The smell of smoke is getting stronger, but the dark is oddly calming. Much better than getting crushed in a stampede. My heart pounds. Breathing is getting harder. I move slowly down each step. "Haste makes waste" passes through my mind. I shudder. The smoke is getting thicker. "Ashes to ashes..." Stop it! I have to be getting close to the first floor door.

A door bursts open below me. A mass of hulking figures waving flashlights, axes, and gigantic hoses pushes inside. They charge up the stairs, aiming their flashlights toward me.

Shouts of, "Go back, go back," bounce off the walls. "The fire is at this end of the building."

Oh, God. Oh, God. We all hustle up the steps. The firemen shove past me through the second-floor door. One of them points up to the third floor. "Go back up and go down the front stairway." He sees me stumble as I start up the stairs. He hands his axe to another fireman and grabs my arm. I'm trying not to trip, hobbling like a three-legged dog as he helps me up the stairs. Before I know it, we're going downstairs and then he's shoving me outside into the spotlights from the fire trucks parked around the building. I hear hoots and hollers as I run between the trucks. My instinct is to keep running, but the freezing snow on my bare feet knocks some sense into me. I make for the girls' dorm across the road. Someone is running after me, but I don't stop until I'm inside the lobby. I collapse on one of the sofas. Kris runs up and pulls me into his arms.

"I should've stayed with you," he says, holding me tight. "I'm sorry. So sorry."

He nuzzles his face against my neck. Tears burn my eyes. I know he feels guilty. It could've ended so wrong. But... his probation...the war. My body trembles as I search inside. It's not about him. It's about me. And I'd do it again.

Chapter Forty-Eight
Ultimatum

Lena

"You're not bringing Reg, are you?" My tone makes my stance clear.

"Why not? He's a festival dog."

I look at Kris sitting cross-legged on the floor with Reggie's head in his lap. I picture the grassy knoll in South Carolina where the Mud Jam is happening. The big moon, warm air, and cool music. Then I picture us chasing around a mud-caked, half-crazed dog.

"He'd be a pain and you know it."

"Nah, Reg likes good music. Right, Reg?" Kris rubs Reggie's curly head. Reggie tries to nip his fingers.

"Reg doesn't like people," I say.

"Yes, he does. Well, some of them."

"How about the other dogs? What if he gets in a fight?" I try unsuccessfully to keep the whine out of my voice.

"I can handle it. I always do."

"But I can't handle it."

I don't want to spend my first Mud Jam watching dog lovers schmooze Reg and Kris. Then there's keeping him out of fights and looking for a place for him to poop. I take a deep breath and hold it. *Don't get uptight.* Just remove the reason for the conflict, like Ella says. Exhaling, I sit next to Kris, then grab his hand. I look into his eyes.

"Kris, this is supposed to be a time just for us. I don't want to share you with anyone, not even Reg. Can't Cheet watch him?"

Kris pulls his hand away. "Cheet's on the skids with his girlfriend. And he's always wasted. I don't trust him."

"He can watch him for two days. Please?"

Kris tilts his head at Reggie sprawled out beside him, as big as a ten-year-old kid. "Aww, look at him. He'll be good."

I scramble to my feet. "Ok, you take Reg, and I'll go with my friends."

"C'mon!" Kris gives me a "you can't be serious" look.

"No, I mean it. I don't want to spend all my time constantly worrying about him and chasing him around. And I don't want to chase you around, either."

"Lena, you don't know what these festivals are like. No one cares. He'll be fine."

"But I won't be."

Kris's jaw tightens. He stands and pulls back the curtain. "C'mon, Reg. We know when we're not wanted."

I watch in disbelief as he leaves with Reggie. I walk to the window and watch them crossing the street. Did I go too far? Kris doesn't do well with ultimatums. I flash back to 'the date' fiasco. Damn! Where's he going? Is he coming back? Then I visualize us at the Mud Jam festival, in a circle of dancing women petting Reggie and flirting with Kris.

When Ginny gets home, I dump my frustration all over her. "I like dogs, but this dog is hard to love," I say. "You've heard him snarl. And he doesn't listen. We'd be chasing him through the crowd or apologizing when he pees on someone's leg like he did at the last demonstration. And he'll be covered with mud and take up half the tent."

Ginny fake swoons. "Sooo romantic."

"Am I being unreasonable?"

"No way! Kris can take him to all the concerts he wants after you leave."

After I leave. I stiffen. Maybe he's already looking for my replacement. Scouting out women who schmooze dogs at music festivals. I grab Ginny's hand, feeling my brow wrinkle.

"This is so much more than choosing between Reg and me. Why doesn't he see it?"

Chapter Forty-Nine
Mud Jam

Kris

It's all good when the day arrives for our journey to Mud Jam. I sacrifice and decide to drop Reg off at Cheet's rather than ruin what should be a great trip. Maybe Reg will be good company for Cheet while he goes through his latest breakup. Reg and the free baggie of 'shrooms I'm donating to the cause should definitely see him through his heartache.

At the last minute, Ginny has to work, but she offers her Pinto on the condition that Lena drives. I throw my knapsack and Tang in the hatchback with the Boy Scout pup tent and sleeping bag. With us in front and Ned and Mike in the back, we take off toward an old South Carolina farm to hear The Allman Brothers and Friends. Eight hours and four joints later, we hit the big jam. As in traffic. It's a river of people stacked up for miles down the two-lane highway. All the radio stations repeat the constant warning, "If you don't have tickets, don't come! Mud Jam's sold out." I'm psyched. Ginny's extra ticket might be worth a few bucks.

The car is at a standstill for over an hour when we finally figure out that this is as far as we're gonna get. Time to hoof it. We pull off and park nose-down in a ditch. It's twilight, and several campfires flicker and glow across the field. Smoke hangs low in the damp air. It's like one of those ghostly National Geographic night scenes around a waterhole on the Serengeti. Pitch black until a stray headlight illuminates the wandering humans and hulking cars in the heavy mist. Our immediate concern is getting a bag of grass. As it starts to drizzle—they don't call it Mud Jam for nothin'—Ned and I pull up our sweatshirt hoods and get serious, mingling with our fellow Mud Jammers 'til we score a generous five-finger bag of weed.

With the grass situation handled, Lena and I pitch our tent on some high ground next to the car. Ned and Mike spread out their sleeping bags on the damp grass, eyeing the Pinto hatchback for the *what if* factor... as in what if there's a sudden downpour. We pass a joint around and give ourselves a pat on the back for making this whole thing happen. Exhausted, Lena and I crawl into the tent and continue our good time in the sleeping bag until we drift off.

I'm awakened by urgent pokes and excited whispers.

"C'mon, c'mon, time to get up. We'll miss the concert!"

I squint at my watch in the dark, then sigh. "Jeeze, Lena, its five o'clock in the morning. We just went to bed. Nothing's happening for another ten hours." I pull her close. "Let's relax 'til it's light outside."

"Are you sure it's ten hours from now?"

"Maybe more. Close your eyes now and get some sleep."

"Okay. But only until the sun comes up."

"Plus an hour after that."

Eight o'clock rolls around. After thirty minutes of persistent nudging and fake coughing, I drag my ass out of the bag. I'm sweaty, sore, stiff, and still tired. The ground felt a hell of a lot softer when I went to sleep on it, a couple of joints ago. Lena's already halfway dressed and wearing her usual humongous morning smile. She wakes up every day like a champagne cork on New Year's Eve. She scoots off to find a secluded bush. I crawl out of the tent. Stretching, I see that I slept in heaven compared to our pals. It rained during the night. Ned and Mike are curled up in contorted balls in the steamed-up Pinto. I'll need to keep Ms. Bubbly Pants away from them for the first hour or so. I attempt to make myself appear a little less rumpled as a steady stream of other rumply people plod by our small campsite. I start to focus. It's time to kick out the jams.

Ned and Mike emerge from the Pinto like a couple of groundhogs. My stomach grumbles at the sight of the peanut butter sandwiches they're holding. Damn, why didn't we put more thought into our food? Besides the sandwiches, all we have are a few apples, half a loaf of bread to go with the peanut butter, and two canteens of water. I dig the canteens out of the car and give one to Mike and one to Ned. Ned grabs the knapsack with the rest of our meager rations. With him being six-six, he'll be easy to spot if we get separated. We take a last look around to make sure we haven't forgotten anything. Then we're off on our journey to Mud Jam land.

The scene around us is a bedraggled slumber party hypnotically shuffling forward. The miles move by, the dust grows thicker, and the herd becomes tighter, forcing us into a single file line. Music sifts through the air so we know we're getting close—plus the fact that you can get a contact high just by breathing.

Mobile shops on the side of the road are everywhere. VW Bugs and vans are turned into headshops selling pot, hash, 'shrooms, and paraphernalia. Dodge Challengers and Delta 88s hawk the chemicals: sopors, black beauties, and acid. Cadillacs and Lincolns peddle the serious shit—coke and smack. And the dealers dress to match their cars and status. Tie-dyes for the Bugs, jeans and buttoned shirts for the Dodges, and the Super Fly look with a dash of menace for the Caddies. Mixed in with these guys are T-shirt vendors. But no one sells food or water.

"Where are the gates? And who do we give our ticket to?" Lena asks.

"Look down," Mike says.

We're standing on an eight-foot high chain link fence flattened to the ground. So much for our ten-dollar tickets. It's a free concert now.

The music is rolling out over the hills and pouring over people sitting, standing, walking, and dancing. The sight is knock-me-out overwhelming. We're a drop in a vast ocean of humanity. Lena reaches for me. I run my hand over the goose bumps on her arm. A voice from the loud speakers announces that there are over two hundred thousand people. Freaks and hippies coming for music, peace, and love.

We wind our way through the crowd concentrating on every step. Tromping across the middle of peoples' blankets or towels is totally uncool festival etiquette. The going gets grueling. So does the "love one another" smile. Passing the reefer down the line becomes a pain in the ass. Inspiration strikes.

"Hey guys, let's roll a joint for each of us so we can focus on where we're walking."

"Genius!" Ned says.

Ten minutes later, I lift my head to tell Ned something and he's gone, nowhere to be seen. Frantically, I look in every direction for him—he has the pack with the food and one of the canteens. I break the news to Lena and Mike. They seem to take it in stride. The pot is helping their mood. We push on, searching for Ned. Ten minutes later, I turn and there's no Lena in sight and Mike's gone, too. Great. No munchies, no canteens, no Lena, no Ned, no Mike, and no plan. Only two hundred thousand unfamiliar faces. I think about retracing my steps, but what's the use? I take a long hit on my joint. The buzz is really solid. I guess I'll just have to chill and make the best of it. Besides, I'm the one with the weed. For sure they will be hunting for me.

I snake through the crowd, wondering where in the hell everyone went. Lena's probably fuming. The music is playing out the soundtrack to my journey and people are acid-dancing all around. With the rise and fall of each chord, dancers' arms ripple and undulate in unison like hydras caught in a tidal pool. A pretty, red-haired girl in cut-offs and a bandana top, steps out of the crowd and encircles me in her arms. She begins to spin me around.

"Wanna fly with me?" she asks.

"Fly?"

"You know, dance." She twirls around me.

"I'm not that good."

She gets up close to my face. "Only the immortal flames know how to truly dance, the rest of us do the best we can."

She's got a point. I give a quick look around for Lena. Not a bad way to start out being lost. I twirl around the dancer for a while, trying not to look too dorky. Dancing's not my thing. It helps that she's wearing that sexy bandana.

"A little windowpane acid will show you the way," she says.

"No acid for me today, thank you. I lost my friends and have to keep bookin'. Maybe later."

"If you change your mind, you know where to find me," she grins and points to the sky.

"Right, flying."

I plunge forward with the sun beating down as I make my way through the crowd. Getting closer to the promised land near the front of the stage, it becomes evident that these folks are not putting up with any new neighbors moving in or touching their stuff. I feel like a baby bird on a nature show that accidentally wanders from its nest, and all the adult birds squawk and peck the little chick into a fuzzy pinball. I do my best to skirt their blankets. *Where's the love, man?*

I retreat to the left side of the stage, my dignity and sensibilities a little tattered, but wiser. I'm not front-row material. Port-a-potties are lined up over here and people are sitting on top of them for a better view of the stage. Any time someone wants to use the toilets, these Johnnie-squatters have to lift their legs to let them pass into the facilities. I'd rather sit in the back row.

I walk clear of the port-a-potties and the throngs of people 'til I find a tree I can sit and lean against. As I light up, two figures emerge out of the woods. One is a disheveled Ichabod Crane—a tall, scrawny, shirtless guy in vest and jeans, with a face full of scraggy whiskers. Wisps of dirty blond hair poke out from under his worn leather stove pipe hat. Close behind him is a waifish girl with mousy brown hair falling to her waist, attractive in a plain sort of way, and completely naked. They plop down and eyeball my joint as if lunch is being served. My offer to share brings out a smile from Ichabod.

Between hits, Ichabod takes in the passersby, engaging with everyone like they're his subjects.

"Can I have a light?" "Can you give me some water?" "Have an extra sandwich?"

A positive answer gets a resounding "Rock well, my friend." A negative one is slapped down with a sneering, "Jive-ass motherfucker."

Godiva's eyes skip from one passerby to the next with a slight twist of annoyance in her brow. She directs unintelligible mumbles into space. Ichabod pulls some hemp string out of his jeans and passes the strand to Godiva. Her fingers weave the hemp with incredible speed without so much as a glimpse down, as she macramés a bracelet. My gaze shifts between her fingers and other parts of her body. I catch Ichabod smiling at my interest in Godiva and decide it's time for me to boogie. As I'm getting up to go, Ichabod asks for a joint and Godiva hands me the hemp bracelet. I look it over. It's kind of cool—Lena would like it—so the trade is made. As I walk away, I notice that it even has a few green glass beads knotted into the string. I glance back. Godiva gives me a vacant stare as I wonder where the hell she kept her beads.

The clouds darken, and I hear thunder in the distance. Soon, strong winds and raindrops the size of golf balls dump over us. Holy shit, Lena's got to be freaking out. People gather in small groups to fend off the storm with whatever is at hand. Old blankets, plastic bread bags—anything to keep the rain off. Drenched, I keep on truckin', hoping Lena is someplace safe and dry. Maybe she went back to the car, but I doubt it—there's too much of the day left to enjoy.

The concert stops when lightning cracks open the sky, but as the clouds move off, I hear someone on stage playing a Wurlitzer. And like little toads, rain-soaked hippies appear out of the muck at the sound of the music, dancing and sliding naked in the mud. I skirt through the impromptu party and venture out toward the surrounding hills. As I walk, the sun appears, and steam floats through the hills like ghostly vapor. I follow a trail through the woods to the river. People have pitched tents along the banks. Even though it's a mile or so from the concert stage, it's in listening range. Lena loves the water, so maybe…

I stop and scan the riverbank. Then I see it. A red and white checked peasant blouse topped by a ponytail of frizzy dark hair is sitting just ahead, next to a big black dog. I start running as I yell, "Lena!"

She turns and scrambles to her feet.

"Kris!" She throws her arms around me. I give her a long kiss.

"Where have you been?" she says, smiling.

"Searching for you. Who's your friend?"

"Ebony. She belongs to the people in that tent." She points behind us.

I lean down and scratch Ebony's head. "She's almost as big as Reg."

"I know. Isn't she sweet?"

We sit down with Ebony between us, offering up her belly. I try not to let it bug me, but damn, why did she put up such a fight about Reggie? Next festival, no dog dilemma. Then another thought sinks in. Next festival, no Lena.

Lena rubs Ebony's belly like she's scrubbing clothes on a washboard. She shakes her head, saying, "I looked up and you were gone. Poof! Disappeared. I kept calling your name but you never answered. Mike kept saying we'd find you and Ned, but then, poof! Gone. Have you seen them? I smoked way too much pot. Never give me my own joint. I couldn't make out what direction I was going. And I kept dozing off and ending up with my head on someone's lap. People were so nice, but then they were touching. And getting naked. I mean, not that naked isn't nice, but sweaty bodies swarming around me made me claustrophobic. And the speed freaks! Whirling me around and around. I got so confused, I just looked into the sky and headed for the tallest hill. Isn't this beautiful? I think we should move here!"

I grin. "Uh, did you take speed?"

"Just a little. How can you tell? The pill was teeny tiny."

"Lena, I told you not to trust stuff here."

"I know, I know. But I had to stay awake to find you. I was panicking."

"I thought the storm might freak you out."

"Omigod, Kris! It came right when I was going through the woods." She grabs my arm and her eyes darken. "I was running down the path and the wind was howling and the trees were bending and branches were breaking all around me. I kept thinking it was a dark enchanted forest. I was going to dive into this ditch, but then I decided it was too muddy. And there were people dancing in it and rubbing the mud all over each other. Do you know it sucks the poisons right out of you?"

I shake my head, with a bemused smile. It must've been some righteous speed.

"Then everyone got into a mud fight. It was in my hair and nose and I walked right into the river with my clothes on."

"Sounds like you had fun."

"Oh, yeah! But I'm clean now. Some cool people gave me soap and shampoo. One of the guys plays guitar like Cat Stevens. His girlfriend sings like Joni Mitchell, they're really soul mates. They're in that tent over there. C'mon, do you want to meet them?" She jumps up. I grab her hand and pull her down on the grassy mound. She scoots onto my lap, facing me, see-saw style.

"I'll meet them later." I put my arms around her. "Right now, I just want to be with you."

She puts her head on my shoulder. A sense of calm spreads over us. We watch the sunlight fade through the trees over the river. Strums of a guitar hang in the thick air. Tree frogs start singing. A whistle pierces and Ebony takes off in its direction.

I dig into my pocket. "I got you something," I say, slipping the macramé bracelet over her wrist. The beads catch a last glint of sun.

She inhales. "Oh, Kris, it's beautiful!"

"I got it just for you."

"No! Really?" She throws her arms around my neck and plants a whopper on my lips.

Then she leans back and smiles. "I got you something too."

She reaches into her cloth bag and pulls out a red chamber pipe.

"I found it just for you. I felt a little guilty about the one that broke on the road. So here you go, a new pipe. Well, kind of new."

"Cool." I grin and take the pipe. "Found it just for me?"

"Yeah. You better clean it off." She reaches over to wipe mud off the stem.

I slip the pipe into my pocket. "Look." I point to the glow of fireflies filtering through the dusky haze over the river.

Lena peers through the shadows. "I feel like I'm swirling and drifting in the river. Like I'm in it. Like it's in me."

"Are you sure that was speed?" I say, kissing her neck. Lanterns and campfires start up, glowing orange and white. As darkness falls, the trail over the hill fades and disappears.

"How are we going to get back? We don't even have a flashlight." Lena's brows pinch together.

"Let's stay here. Can we borrow a blanket from your friends?"

"Probably. But it's so hot, I don't think we'll need one."

"Let's go for a swim." I jump up, pulling Lena with me.

She yanks my T-shirt over my head. I tug off her shirt. We shimmy out of our jeans and step into the cold water.

"Ooey gooey," Lena calls out.

The river bottom mud squishes up between my toes. Lena turns on her back, floating on top of the water. The moon paints her body in soft white glow. She drifts, peaceful and free. I hang onto her hand to keep her from slipping away. We intertwine and melt into an embrace. The warmth of her body presses against me. Everything that is Lena surrounds me.

"I have another gift for you," she says. She smiles dreamily, "Words I want us to share."

She gazes deep into my eyes and says the words I remember from *The Prophet*.

"Make not a bond of love: Let it be a moving sea between the shores of your souls." [1]

I exhale the still night air. Her eyes are warm—the color of the earth. And I sink into them.

---

[1] Kahlil Gibran, The Prophet, (New York: Alfred A Knopf, 1923.) 11

Chapter Fifty
Losing

Kris

Cheet is sitting on the porch steps waiting for us. I look around for Reggie. Probably under the porch scavenging old tennis balls. Cheet looks like he's been on a monster Quaalude binge. His face is drawn and pale. His eyes are red-rimmed, swollen and saggy.

"Hey," I say.

"Hey, man." Cheet doesn't lift his head as Lena steps around him to the screen door. Then he sniffs, wipes his nose, and glances at me.

"Man, I don't know how to say this, so I'm just gonna tell you. Reggie's dead."

"What?" Lena lets go of the door and it slams shut.

"What?' I echo.

"I'm sorry, man." Cheet doesn't lift his head. "He got away from me. The first night. Got hit by a fucking car."

"C'mon, Cheet, quit shitting me. Where is he?"

"I wish I was. God, I wish I was."

"Fuck, Cheet." I reach out and grab the handrail to the porch and drop to one knee.

"Oh, God, no," Lena says softly.

"How the hell did he get loose?" I say, my voice shaking.

"Well, he got hold of those 'shrooms. Dude, one minute they were on the coffee table, next minute gone. I didn't put it together 'til he flipped out, running around, snarling at my shoes, and tearing through the house. When I tried to put him in the yard, he got past me and ran out into the street, right in front of a fucking car! I tried to catch him. You've got to believe me, man."

"Where is he?" My voice sounds like it's coming from somewhere else.

"Someone called animal control. They took him away. I didn't think you'd want to see him like that."

My head implodes. "You asshole!" My fist glances off Cheet's right cheek and my other hand goes for his neck. Lena screams as we lock together, flailing and wrestling off the porch. My glasses sail into the grass. Everything compresses, and the world slows to mute as "gone forever" rips through me. I let go of Cheet and push him away. My breath jags, "You couldn't even bury him? You know where they take them? To the fucking rendering plant!"

Cheet huffs, "I'm sorry—I couldn't handle it. I just freaked out."

"You're nothin' but a wasted fuck-up!" I shove him down and stand over him.

Lena's voice starts to filter into my head, "Kris. Kris!" She wraps her arms around my waist from behind pulling. I elbow her away and pick up my glasses. She never liked Reg. She's probably happy about this. I turn and leave.

"Kris, wait!" Lena yells.

"He was my dog, too," Cheet calls out.

I flip Cheet off over my shoulder, "Go to hell!"

"Where are you going?" Lena shouts.

"You talked me into leaving him. Just leave me alone."

They can both go to hell. How can they know what he meant to me?

I kick an empty beer can rolling across the sidewalk, then crush it like it's Cheet's neck. I can't stop seeing Reg's curly mane, his deep-set eyes looking at me. Looking for me. Terrified.

Cheet's a lousy screw-up. I turn onto Water Street and stare at the corner where it must've happened. The one soul entrusted to me and he's gone. And what a fucking way to go. My heart feels like it's been ripped out. I hope Cheet takes a shitload of bad acid and runs into a semi. Bastard.

And Lena. Jealous over a damn dog! I tell her over and over I'm not looking for anyone else, but she won't believe me. Never believes me. How the hell did I end up with her? I should've split the first time she pitched a fit about my night walks with Reggie. This never would've happened if she would've... if I would've... *Sorry, Reg.*

I aim for the Hood. No. I need more than a beer. I shift and head toward campus. I have a little hash socked away in my room. That and a few sopors will obliterate this night. Obliterate me.

I lie on my bed and let random moments sift through my head. The night Reg saved the house by chasing off the party crashers. Our late night walks. Our talks of saving the world and a little bit of myself.

The chick-bait thing was just a bullshit bonus. A cover I used instead of admitting that Reg was the one friend that was always there for me. No matter how many flavors of asshole I could be, Reg bounced when I showed up. What could I trade to get him back? Nothing. It's done. If Lena hadn't made me... If I hadn't given Cheet... If Cheet hadn't... If I only...

I go to sleep that night, dreaming that the three of us are plotting Reggie's demise. Our faces and bodies are distorted like a bad trip as we each give him our own poison potion. I wake up soaked in guilt. We're all accomplices.

The morning sun pitches into a brilliant blue sky, but I'm empty. I burrow deep down into it's her fault, his fault, my fault. I turn away from the pipes and pills offered to numb me, the soft shoulders offered to console me. The day passes in shades of gray. I occasionally feel something else struggling inside me, trying to survive. I smother it. Stomp on it. Rage it away. I'm not ready for anything right now, except this pain. This mourning.

This loss of my best friend, who I'll never see again.

Chapter Fifty-One
Lost

Lena

*J*ournal:

> *How could I? Heartless, soulless… it's all my fault!*

I sit on the bed and gaze out the window. The desk light illuminates my reflection on the glass pane. I stare dry-eyed into my face, then bury myself under the quilt, letting the pain spill out. My mind spins out images of matted fur and Reggie's crushed body. Reggie's happy-go-lucky brain freaking out. Reggie's loyal wag following Kris's every footstep. Kris, who would be taking him on his midnight walk right now. A simple midnight walk I poisoned with jealousy. Choking sobs scrape my insides raw. Oh, give me back that midnight walk. Take as long as you want, talk to every girl on the planet! I will welcome you home with open arms. I shout into the pillow, "PLEASE come back!"

I roll over and hug the pillow. How can I ever look at Kris again without seeing the pain I caused? He's right—it is my fault. I'm the reason Reg is gone. And I deserve to suffer.

Ginny tries to console me, but her words and reasons fail to convince me. In a trance, I go to class, go to work, walk past his dorm. I want to knock on his door and ask forgiveness, but I don't dare. I don't deserve to be released from this torment.

On my third day in hell, I gather up my courage and go to his dorm. I lightly knock on his door. Then pound on it. *Please.* No response. I jiggle the doorknob. Locked.

The guy working the dorm desk says Kris didn't show up for work. I go to Mike's house, hoping to find Kris crashed on the couch. Mindless from dope, girls, grief, whatever. Mike shakes his head. He hasn't seen him, but he heard what happened.

Scary thoughts creep into my head about Kris hurting himself. Not intentionally, but accidentally over-doing it. I think of his penchant for sopors and my throat closes. Should I call his parents? The police? I ask Mike. He says to wait awhile. He'll check it out.

On the night of the fourth day, I hear familiar steps coming up the attic stairs. I jump up from my desk chair. I want him—need him. I take a step toward the curtain. But... I'm afraid. What will he say to me? Numb, I walk to the bed and sit down. He pulls back the curtain and stops short of the bed. I look up at him, expecting to see the remnants of Reggie in his eyes. But he's looking over my head, out the attic window. I swallow hard.

"Oh, Kris. I'm so sorry." In a whisper, I add, "It was all my fault."

He sits down next to me, his eyes on the floor. I brace myself, knowing I deserve whatever comes next. But all he says is, "It's everyone's fault. It's no one's fault."

"But if I hadn't—"

He looks at me. "And if I hadn't and if Cheet didn't... c'mon, Lena. We can't change who we are and what we do, any more than we can move the stars."

"But we can try. I know I will. Just come back."

"For what?"

"For..."

"Don't." He holds up his hand. "I've been watching you disappear inch by inch for the last couple of months. We need to stop pretending and get on with it. I dropped out of school this morning."

"What? No! You can't—"

He leans in close. I turn toward his warm, familiar touch. Feel myself crumble against him. *Oh, God*, please make things work out.

"We've both known this was coming," he says in my ear. His lips brush my cheek. "Since the beginning."

And then he's gone.

Chapter Fifty-Two
Home Free

Kris

I lie in bed, staring at my posters from high school. Reggie and Lena haunt my thoughts. Before leaving home, I gave no thought to expectations. After coming back, every day has expectations that aren't being filled. Sleep? I used to love sleep, but now my nights are just a dreary gray. The shapeless pillows don't murmur, don't respond to my touch. At least with anger, hurt, or betrayal, there's a flicker or flame you can wrap yourself around. Rally to "I'll show them!" But this... this has nowhere to go. No up, down, or in-between. And my days are no better. I wander around State campus, like an outcast. My thoughts and feelings slam around in my head with nowhere to go. Without Reg, I've got no one to pour my soul out to.

I time my mornings, making sure I pull my chair up to the kitchen table as my dad pushes his back.

"Find a job yet?" He peers at me over his glasses, then passes me the classified section. He isn't happy with me dropping out. His opinion of my situation can be summed up in the advice he gave me on my first day back home. "Maybe a taste of the real world will teach you more than school did."

I take the classifieds and put them in my lap. "Still looking." I stare into my cereal bowl, so I can't see his "better look harder" stare as he leaves for work. Thank God my stepmom and sisters are giving me space.

I drag myself out on the job hunt every day, with no luck. I'm about to sign up with the temp agency to unload pallets at a warehouse, when I focus in on a job listing in the campus newspaper for a bar-back at The Botanist. Sweet Jane enters my mind.

I make my way over to The Botanist and enter through its dark-oak front door. The door's edges are smooth and beveled by thirsty hands over the decades. The Botanist is way longer than it is wide. Small round tables and Bentwood chairs sit scattered near the stage under the muted light of stained glass lamps. A planked bar extends the whole length of one wall. The smell of cigarette smoke and burnt popcorn mixes with the heavy odor of spilled beer. I spot Sweet Jane at the far end of the bar. She has the same long, straight hair and is wearing a T-shirt with a tie-dyed peace symbol, a long, fringed belt, and tight bell-bottom jeans. She's talking to the bartender. I make a beeline for her.

"Hi, Jane, remember me? Kris. You picked up me and my girlfriend last December somewhere in Indiana. Brought us all the way back to Columbus."

Jane breaks into a big smile. "Kris! I remember you. Your girlfriend's Lisa—no, Lena, right?"

"Yep."

"It's good to see you again."

"I've been meaning to stop by."

She nods at the tall man next to her. "Ray, this is Kris, Kris, this is my brother, Ray."

Ray's large hand engulfs mine in a quick shake. Then it's back to business. "Jane, I'll bring out cases and do the tables. You can catch up stocking the coolers?"

"Need a hand?" I ask.

Ray looks me over and nods. "Sure."

Over the clink of glass beer bottles being stocked, Jane asks, "So, what brings you to The Botanist?"

"Actually, I'm answering your ad. I need a job."

She looks up from stocking the beer. "Is Lena with you?"

"No, she's back in Kent."

"Oh? Are you just looking for a summer job?"

"Nope, moved back for good." I brace for what I know will come next.

"You guys break up?"

Still bent over, my head in the cooler. "Let's just say we're heading down different roads."

"How's that?"

"She's on her way to California and then France." I keep my attention on replacing the empty cases. When I look up, Jane's staring at me. I shrug. "I do miss her, though."

"Well, I'm sure you can keep yourself busy," she says. "Places to go. People to meet."

At the end of the night, shades drawn, doors locked, and bar wiped down, Ray pours us doubles of Jack Daniels with beer chasers.

"Here's to new beginnings," Jane says.

We clink shot glasses. The whiskey goes down smooth.

"Kris here needs a job." Jane gives me a quick wink. "I can vouch for him."

"You ever bartend or bounce?" Ray asks, all business. "And are you twenty-one?"

"I turn twenty-one in two weeks," I say, feeling warmth from the shot spread through my core. "And I used to work the door here, so I have some experience."

Ray glances at Jane. She nods. He takes a deep breath and turns to me. "You'll have to do the door and tables on the weekends at first," he says. "On slow days, after you're twenty-one, I can teach you how to bartend. Money's not great, but it's enough to live on. And the girls and music aren't bad. Still interested?"

"When do I start?"

"Tomorrow night is ladies' night. A good shift to get your feet wet."

Jane laughs. "Hope you like Earth shoes and beads on your women, Kris. You're going to see a lot of that here."

Ray grins. "Don't listen to her. We get all kinds. Hippie to sorority. It's one big party. But your job is to be in control. What happens after hours is your business, but what happens in here is strictly business. Remember that and you'll do okay."

One more shot on Ray to seal the deal and I'm practically skipping back home. This is my thing. I love the hours, plus I'll make enough dough to move out. And the fringe benefits... things are starting to come together.

***

I'm promoted to bartender the night I turn twenty-one. Like patting your head and rubbing your stomach at the same time, talking and making a smooth accurate pour takes practice. These people are two-fisted drinkers. But I give service with a smile, and soon I'm everyone's best friend. I feel like I'm finding my balance. And on some nights I even have one of those fringe benefits waiting at the end of the bar for me. I know these occasional bar flings are as deep as an empty shot glass, but I think I'm finally getting my legs back under me.

Jane and I quickly develop a tight friendship and often spend our free nights getting stoned and philosophizing about life's mysteries. It isn't long before she tells me it's time to move on from Lena. According to her, I need to find myself another real relationship. Yeah, right. I had that and where'd it get me? Right here. I'll pass, thank you. A warm body for the night seems more my speed, right now.

My next move is to take in a stray mutt that's been hanging outside the bar. She doesn't have a collar or tags, and her matted yellow fur is loaded with fleas. But she looks like she needs a friend. I feed her, clean her up and bring her to my newly acquired basement apartment. She makes herself right at home.

Things aren't the way they used to be. But I'm making my way. And with Babe, I finally have someone to talk to again.

Chapter Fifty-Three
Spring Alone

Lena

*J*ournal:

> *Get up, go to class, go to work, come home, study, go to bed. Get up, go to class, go to work, come home, study, go to bed. Get up, go to class, go to work, come home, study, go to bed. Get up...*

A memory of Kris's breath tickles my neck as I lie in bed and stare out the attic window. Thoughts on life and love hang in the air like dust. I wonder if I'll ever love someone that way again.

Ginny has been tiptoeing around me, giving me space. She even skips over break-up songs on her stereo, carefully placing the needle on the next track. The war is dragging on, the clanging Victory Bell sounding a call for protest rallies every Friday afternoon. Classes cancel, and political activists make their rounds inciting action. The campus is a pressure cooker. We can feel the water boiling and hear the rattling of the lid. Demonstrations let off some of the steam, but violence is erupting across the country. Classes, parties, and sports glide by in the background as the music tells us to *sing and scream, dance and march, fight and sit down.* Our music demands that we be the instruments of change.

The anniversary of the May 4th shootings approaches. Inquiries into the shootings have gone nowhere. Like me and the Ohio Congressman, each side points its fingers at the other. At midnight on May 3rd, I join a candlelight vigil. I feel like a drop in a sea of twinkling stars as we walk down Taylor Hill. We pass a twisted metal sculpture reflecting the moonlit bullet hole left from the shootings. My stomach clenches as I remember being on the other side of the hill running in terror from the guard in riot gear, then sitting down in defiance until a professor convinced us to disperse. Not knowing exactly what had happened until later. My heart starts pounding, my breath quickens. People join hands. We stand arm-in-arm around the parking lot where the students fell and died. Someone begins singing *Give Peace a Chance* and everyone joins in, faces glowing in the wavering candlelight. I try to be hopeful for the future. Try to believe in peace and love.

Love. I go back to that terrible-wonderful night when Kris and I met. When hate and chaos catapulted me toward a love I'd never felt before. And now it's gone. He's gone. And I feel empty.

We blow out our candles and solemnly walk our separate paths into the night. At nine tomorrow morning, we'll have a sit-in on Main Street and blockade university buildings. Peacefully bring "business as usual" to a halt. Hopefully, we'll draw attention to all that's not right with the world.

***

In my dreams, I hear the crack of gunshots and bottles breaking. Kris appears wearing his backpack. He grabs my hand and we run through a maze of craziness. Monster cops in space suits are everywhere, trying to stop us. Finally, we see the attic light flickering ahead. We run into a swirling haze. Kris is saying something, but I can't hear what it is. I can't see. I can't breathe. Gasping for breath, I wake up. My face and hair are damp with sweat. I glance at the clock. It's five-thirty. I bury my face in my pillow.

Kris. Come back.

I turn over and stare out the window. Morning is beginning to filter in. Should I call him? What would I say? "Can you come back and just hold me?"

I look at the poster of a Paris street scene on the opposite wall. How many times have I daydreamed of being in that café? Sitting at that table with a latte in my hand, speaking French to intriguing strangers. I feel a smile coming, but it fades fast. Even if I call him and even if he came back, I know he can only hold me for a short time. Until I leave. For California. For France. For my life.

***

There's high energy in the crowd gathered for the sit-in. I look at the hill of front campus in awe. The grassy slope is filled with hundreds of white cardboard headstones. I walk, reading the words scrawled on them. Anti-war slogans, proverbs and the names of friends and family killed in Vietnam. As I reach the main crowd, a group leader assigns me a position. I link arms with others to form a human chain outside the door to an administration building. Hundreds of people sit down along the walkways to the buildings, and in the streets and sidewalks surrounding campus. Police stand along the perimeters, but the mood is peaceful. I look over the sea of denim and helmets and headstones. A few hours later, our duty is done—classes are cancelled. I get a rush, like I'm changing the world peacefully. Like Gandhi or Martin Luther King, Jr.

I walk past an effigy of Nixon swinging by his neck from a tree branch. I'm troubled to find I feel a sense of satisfaction. Gandhi would probably frown on that.

In the crowd, I run into Mike. We make hurried small talk and he mentions Kris is transferring to State and bartending at The Botanist in Columbus. The name rings a bell. Jane's bar! The one she sings at. I try not to dwell on it as I head home, but my thoughts fill with beautiful girls looking over the bar into Kris's deep blue eyes. Eyes that used to look at me. With love. A sense of longing passes through me, even as I tell myself it has no right to do so.

When night falls, I hear the police sirens. Downtown is erupting again, but I want nothing to do with it. Burning trashcans and throwing rocks isn't going to end the war. I light a candle and burn incense. I chant the mantra Ella gave me. Ella! I can almost imagine she's here with me, floating around the attic blowing puffs of inspiration into the air. Sometimes she helps get me through the day. But sometimes there are limits to even Ella's magic.

***

Journal:

I can't believe my lifelong dream has arrived. I cleared the waiting list for the study abroad program. All I have to do is pass the pre-requisite summer course.

I glance around the room. Fading sunlight filters through the attic windows onto half-packed boxes, melted candles, stacks of records and books of poetry. When I leave this place, will some of it come with me? Or will it all just disappear? I hear Ginny moving around on the other side of the curtain. I push my thoughts away as I take posters off the wall, packing the remains of my college life.

When I take a break from cleaning and look around, the bareness startles me. Like the room knows it's getting ready for someone else, another hopeful soul who will dream under its eaves. Like I'm already gone.

I need music to get through this. I search through the crate of albums. Half of them are Kris's. I pull out *Tea for The Tillerman*. The one I gave him for Valentine's Day. The cover illustration shows a sun setting over an old man drinking his tea. A woman blithely dances up a mountain path. Carefree children explore a tree straight out of the enchanted forest. I peer a little closer. A heart is scratched into the tree on the album. What is this? Initials are carved into the cardboard cover. KA + LB. When did Kris do this? I press the album against my chest and feel my heart beating through it.

I look up at the one poster still hanging in my room, a bustling streetscape of Paris. I search for myself in the smear of color and light. A face emerges from the mass of impressionist dots. Flecks of blue. I step back slowly, staring hard at the chaotic brush strokes until the truth emerges. It's people in the scene who matter. *It's the people*, not the place.

I yank back the curtain and run into Ginny's room. "I've got to see Kris. I need your car. Please! It's important."

Ginny slaps her magazine down and looks up. "You're not pregnant, are you?"

"No. But I need to tell him I was wrong about something."

She smiles. "I wondered when this was going to happen." She digs the keys out of her purse and hands them over. "Do you know where he lives?"

"No, but I ran into Mike at the rally. He told me Kris is working at a bar called The Botanist. I'll find it."

Ginny hugs me and I go back to my room. I take out Tang from the attic cubby. In the bottom corner of it, I see something silver. What? I pull out a crumpled Hershey Kiss wrapper. Laughing and crying, I inhale its stale scent. The sweetness is still there, filling my lungs, and my soul. I open my dresser drawer and start pulling out some clothes. A thought interrupts my packing. It's been three months. What if he doesn't care anymore? Or... found someone else? It would be humiliating.

I look down at the album crate. *That's it.* I'll tell him I'm there to return his albums. It'll be a perfect alibi for my surprise visit. I flip through them, taking out the ones I think are his. Todd Rundgren's face stares out from among the covers. It's probably the album we listened to the most. It's all I have—that... I look down at the macramé bracelet on my wrist... and this. I wipe the tears gathering in my eyes, then walk over and open my desk drawer. I take out the acceptance letter from the study abroad program and slide it into my purse. If Kris takes me back, I'll rip it into a million pieces. France will always be there. I'm not going to sway him, but if this works, we'll go together.

With Tang in one hand and a bag of albums in the other, I sprint down the attic stairs, feeling scared, nervous, anxious, hopeful, and happy, all at the same time. Kris's eyes will hold the answer to the question we've had from the beginning.

Chapter Fifty-Four
Bar Tender

Lena

The club is rocking when I walk in. I inhale like it's my last breath. Every screech from the band, the smoke, the beer, the laughing and talking—it can't drown out the urgency of my mission.

Spotting Kris behind the bar gives me a rush. A nervous giggle escapes me as I push through the crowd. I can't wait to see the look on his face. I squeeze along the side of the bar where he's standing and watch as he pours drinks and greets people. He directs his easy smile at a couple of women, but I ignore it as I edge up to the bar. When he stoops under the counter, I lean over the bar.

"Can a girl get a Harvey Wallbanger around here?"

His head jerks up. A blank look, then his eyes widen and his jaw drops.

"Lena! What the…? What are you doing here?"

He stretches across the bar and throws his arms around me in an awkward hug.

"Hold on. Wait," he says, then grabs another bartender's attention with shouts, points at me, then races around the bar and swallows me in a full-on hug.

Oh, God, I've missed this. Missed him. I squeeze back the tears. I've got to keep it together. Got to act cool. Can't give anything away until I know.

Kris takes my hand and leads me to a barstool where a guy is sitting with a mug of beer.

"Trade you a pitcher for that stool," Kris says.

The guy nods and jumps up.

Kris pats the seat and I hop on. He stands close and we stare at each other, his grin wide, mine tentative. The music is so loud, we lean in to hear each other speak.

"So... how are you?" Kris asks. His lips brush my ear.

"I'm good. Good."

He waves at his ear and yells, "I can barely hear you. It'll let up in about a half hour and I've got a break coming. We can talk then."

I nod and shoo him away. This is going better than I expected.

I watch him as he goes back to work. Between pouring drinks, he catches my eye. How in the world did I think the muddy water of the Seine could compete with his deep blue eyes? His hair is parted in the middle and pulled off his face into a ponytail. His denim shirt is unbuttoned at the neck and his sleeves are rolled up. I watch his arms and feel my blood warm. He points me out to his friends and introduces me as his "friend from Kent." My breath shallows as I listen to their conversations.

"Everybody's going to The Shack after closing time."

"Did you hear Smitty's back in town?"

"Did Laurie get ahold of you about the thing she's having next weekend?"

And on and on. They connect more to him than I do.

"Surprise!"

Hands grab my shoulders and I whirl around to see Jane.

"Oh, wow!" I jump up and hug her. Her long hair is piled on top of her head in a messy twist, strands hanging to her shoulders. She's wearing a lime green halter top and a jean mini-skirt. Large silver earrings dangle from her ears. She's so summer, not like the time she picked us up on the side of the road. Our last ride.

We stand and shout over the music into each other's ears. Yes, she's still in school. No, she's not singing tonight. Yes, her brother's club is doing well. She's helping him manage it and teaching music on the side. Kris comes up behind us, puts his arms around us, smiling his old smile. And suddenly the two of us are back on the road, free and open and sharing ourselves with strangers and each other. Jane has brought the old us back together.

She smiles at me and says, "Well, have fun, Lena. I'll see you later." Then she turns and says something into Kris's ear. He gives her a look I can't read. She eyes him for a moment before making her way to a back room.

We walk over to an empty table and sit down. Kris reaches across the table for my hands and we interlace our fingers. No Merlin ring.

I swallow hard. "Jane looks good."

"Huh? Oh, yeah." He scans the room.

"And this place is hoppin'. Is it always like this?"

"Mostly. It's kinda dead early in the week," he says, looking everywhere but at me.

"Sounds like you're here a lot."

"We switch off days and nights. Got full time, the minute I turned twenty-one."

I gulp. "Oh, yeah. Happy birthday."

"Thanks." He leans back in his chair as a tall, slender Asian girl comes up to the table. Her long black hair falls sleekly over her shoulders. Her almond-shaped eyes are shining.

"You left these the other night," she says, handing Kris a paper bag. "I found them down by the pond."

Kris looks inside the bag and breaks into a slow grin. "I wondered where these were. Thanks."

"Anytime," she says. With a Mona Lisa smile, she turns and walks away.

I look at Kris with a question mark on my face.

He crunches the bag and stuffs it under his chair. "My cut-offs."

Don't overreact, I tell myself. Don't jump to conclusions. I take a long deliberate breath. Slow steady exhale. I took him by surprise. We have to ease into each other again.

Kris slides his chair back. "I'll be off in an hour. Been here all day."

I nod and watch as he heads to the bar. I pick up my drink and crunch on an ice cube while my thoughts spin.

This might be harder than I thought.

Chapter Fifty-Five
The Dungeon

Kris

I say my goodbyes, and Lena and I leave the bar. She slips her arm under mine.

"I'm parked over there," she says, pointing to Ginny's Pinto.

The ten-minute ride to my apartment is filled with "How's it going?" "What's happening at Kent?" "Did you hear about the latest riot?"—aimless questions as if we were on our first date. Then things get uncomfortably quiet. Have we run out of things to say to each other? A few months ago, I wouldn't have believed we'd ever be uncomfortable with each other's company. But now, all I can think is, *Why is she here?*

I lead Lena down to my basement apartment, carrying my old nemesis Tang. I open the door and flip on the light. Babe is wagging her tail in greeting.

"Babe, meet Lena."

Lena sets down the paper bag she's holding and stoops to let Babe lick her hand. "She's so cute."

My eyes zero in on a flat, odd shaped piece of rubber on the floor. "Oh, no! She's done it again," I hold up the remnant of one of my sneakers. "Don't leave your shoes lying around." I conveniently forget to mention that Babe's favorite chew toy has been women's high heels.

I sweep my arm out over the living room. "Welcome to the Dungeon on West Third Avenue."

"Dungeon?" Lena says, taking a few steps back, fake horror on her face.

"It's underground. You know, like a dungeon." I walk her to the couch, hoping she doesn't ask for a tour. There's a possibility that my bedroom may have a stray article of female clothing left behind. A little smoke and good music should help this situation. I drop the needle on Crosby, Stills & Nash. That'll warm things up.

Lena opens a shopping bag filled with records. "You left these."

"Thanks."

I glance in the bag as I pull out my stash from the end table drawer. Lena watches me roll a joint. We move closer as we pass the reefer. We keep the conversation in the here and now. But something isn't clicking.

"Wine?" I ask.

On my way to the kitchen I peek into my bedroom... nothin'. Whew. I grab a bottle of Lambrusco and two wine glasses.

"The Botanist seems like a nice place," Lena says, taking a glass. "Friendly." Her voice is casual, but there's a familiar undertone. I choose to ignore it.

"Yeah. Good people."

The mood relaxes. I lie back against the couch and pull Lena close. I smell her hair. Mmm—attic nights. But something is still missing.

"Hey, where's the patchouli?"

"I've changed," Lena murmurs, "to musk."

I know how to fix this weird disjointed feeling. Taking Lena's hand, I lead her to the bedroom. This should have been the first stop. Must be losing my touch.

In the cool of the room, we pull each other's shirts off and kiss with sweet Lambrusco breath. Lena sways forward, and then tumbles backwards on the bed. In a frenzied second, we're naked under the covers, pushing, groping, urgent. Our tongues press together, muffled sounds escape our lips. We do all the things we used to do. But...

Afterward, I stare at the ceiling, fighting off feelings of edginess and desperation. Something isn't right. I roll over and reach for my cigs on the nightstand. Tomorrow will be better.

***

I awaken and look up through the open casement window. Morning sunlight sprinkles through the emerald tangle of tree branches in the yard, my new jungle. Bright green leaves flutter in a light breeze and I can smell the fresh cut grass above us. It's the start of a beautiful day. Lena touches my side. I turn toward her, but yesterday's uneasiness seeps into the space between us. I can feel her waiting. I run my hand down her back and try to pretend we're back at school, alone in the attic... but the weird sensation persists. I extend my arm over her body as I reach for my glasses on the nightstand. Things are different. We're in a basement, not the attic.

I glance away from Lena's bewildered look. She keeps her voice nonchalant as she slides out of bed. "Are there towels in the bathroom?"

"Yeah, there's a clean one in the cupboard."

She gives me a sideways glance as she gathers her clothes. Should I join her? Wild horses couldn't have stopped me before. Lena opens the bedroom door and Babe runs into the room. It's time to let Babe out and feed her. I hear Lena close the bathroom door. Oh, well, next time. I pull on my jeans and drag myself after Babe. Yeah, next time.

After my Babe duty is done, I sit on the couch, wondering what I can do to shake off the numbness. When I hear the blow dryer, I head to the kitchen and start making strawberry pancakes. When all else fails, cook.

"Ella's recipe?" Lena asks when she walks into the kitchen. Her hair cascades in damp curls around her shoulders. I remember when I first saw them that way in Cheet's kitchen after our first night together.

"No, it's a new one I picked up."

She peeks over my shoulder and slides her arm around my waist. "Yum."

I turn, lift her onto the kitchen counter, and step back to the stove. The sun streams in through the thicket of bushes planted around the casement window. It creates a green and gold aura around her. The image my mind held the past couple of months doesn't compare to how beautiful she is right now. My stomach twists. Why is she here? It's not just to drop off my albums. It's got to be to settle things before she leaves. She never liked going to bed angry. Even if it took all night, we made things right. I bet she just wants to ease her conscience.

Stopping mid-flip on a pancake, I turn to face Lena. All my feelings logjam in my throat. She's the only person in the world who ever understood me, but I don't know what to say to her. I go back to flipping pancakes.

We sit at the table and eat, lightly probing the past couple of months. It takes a bit, but I finally get to the point. "So, did you get into the program in California?"

Lena busies herself, smoothing out the creases in her napkin. "I'm still waiting," she says in a measured tone. "How about you? Going to State in the fall?"

"Probably. I need at least a Masters to do anything with psych. But you know me and studying." I give her a sly smile. She smiles back with a familiar flicker in her eyes, then quickly looks away. I fork some pancakes into my mouth and muffle out, "Nothing else really interests me."

The conversation trudges onward, circling around new bars popping up in Kent. Ginny's latest boyfriend. The peace vigils. Then we run out of things to say. I stare at her. My breath quickens and sweat beads on my forehead. I have to say something.

"Lena, I don't know what's wrong with me," I blurt out.

"What do you mean?"

Her expression is concerned, like I have some kind of terminal illness. I stand and walk to the window.

"When I try to hold you, it feels like my arms are chained to my side." Now it's out. I feel immediate relief. We can sort through it, like we used to do.

"Chained?" The color drains from her face. She slides her chair back from the table.

"Something's missing. I mean, it's got nothing to do with you."

She gets up. "But it's got everything to do with us." She turns and walks out of the room.

Us? *That's* what's missing. There *is* no us. Not anymore. "Lena." I follow her into the bedroom and watch her pack her bag. As she moves past me toward the front door, I catch her arm.

"Why did you come?" I ask.

Her eyes settle into a dull glaze. "To return your albums."

We both glance at the records on the floor. Todd Rundgren looks at us from the top of the pile.

"I'm sorry I came," she says, pulling away.

I can't think of anything to say to make this better. I grab an empty matchbook and scribble down my phone number. "If you ever need me, call." I unzip Tang's pocket and shove in the matchbook. The disbelief in her eyes says it all. How lame can I be?

She picks up Tang and opens the front door, then turns. Her face holds all the sad songs I've ever heard. The door quietly clicks shut. Should I run after her? Make her stop? Promise her I'll...

I stand frozen, staring at the door. She'll come back. We'll make things right. Outside, Ginny's car revs up. I close my eyes and listen to Lena drive away.

Chapter Fifty-Six
California, Here We Come

Lena

*J*ournal:

> *The Dungeon*
> *I enter the door beneath the ground*
> *We move through the attic remains*
> *Eyes searching through filtered messages*
> *My arms fumble for what we once held*
> *But yours are chained to your sides.*

After the longest week of my life, Ginny drives the Pinto, loaded with all our belongings, onto the highway heading southwest. When we pass through Columbus, I stare at the exit ramp to Third Avenue and replay those last moments for the zillionth time. Damn him! How could he pretend the whole weekend? No. *He wasn't pretending.* He tried. I felt it in the twisting, pounding, wrenching love we made. We were both in denial. I swallow hard and wring my hands in my lap. Breathe. Let him be who he is. Let me be who I'm meant to be.

Ginny slides a Beach Boys tape into the dashboard tape deck. She rolls down her window and turns up the volume. Happy, carefree songs of summer mix with the warm air and whirl around us. She belts out, "Everybody's going surfing. Surfing U.S.A."

I halfheartedly join in. She's up for an adventure and I don't want to bring her down with my rehashing. It's too late for that anyway. The letter is signed and on its way to California. And so are we.

The highway stretches through the fields of Indiana, green and lush with crops. It's so different from the frigid, barren landscape of my last time here. We pass the billboard announcing Camper Country. I picture me and Kris standing below it with our thumbs out—before we were picked up by the school bus with Deadhead Ken. Memories swirl. I tried telling Ginny about our adventure, but she only picked up on the bad vibes. Only Kris could have understood. I run through the memories that only Kris and I share, stop on one and turn to Ginny.

"We're not going through Chicago, are we?"

"Nope."

"Good."

I roll open my window and tilt my face into the bright glare of the sun. Breathing in the sweet smell of the planted fields. The warm breeze sweeps through my hair. I open my eyes and take in the here and now. In Missouri, the Travelodge's sleepwalking bear beckons us and we stop for the night. The next morning, we gobble down bagels and coffee, and point the Pinto toward the thunderous skies of Kansas. A summer storm opens the heavens. I think I see funnel clouds. *It's Kansas, right?* I point out the eerie tails streaming above us and beg Ginny to pull over.

Ginny laughs and says she's not going to lose time because I've got *Wizard of Oz* phobia.

We're in Kansas, I argue, and if she won't pull over, I'm going to jump out of the car. She grumpily agrees to pull over at the next ditch. But it's so flat there *are* no ditches. So I sit, frantically scanning the sky while she laughs, points at the clouds, and says, "Look! That one could be an elephant swinging his trunk. And over there you can see a monkey hanging by its tail—not a flying one."

Kris would pull over. I picture myself in his arms counting the seconds between the lightning and thunder. He would hold me until the storm was gone or until I fell asleep counting.

But Kris isn't here.

And then out of nowhere—rising up to heaven with splendor and force—the Rockies. We wind our way up the mountains and drive around thickly wooded back roads looking for a place to camp. A clearing next to a rushing river is perfect. I inhale the fresh pine scent, the cool clear mountain air, and I sit down against a tree trunk to savor the tranquil forest sounds. I wouldn't be surprised to see Buddha sitting beside me. While I meditate, Ginny explores and brings back a group of longhaired guys who've been fishing. They offer to share their fish if we cook them. Ginny takes them up on it. I envy the way she goes with the flow. I hate that I can't loosen up on demand.

The guys bring a hibachi, and Ginny cleans and cooks the fish while I try to be creative with potatoes and canned vegetables. After dinner, we sit around the campfire smoking a joint and playing euchre. One of the guys, Rick, strums his guitar and we sing *Take Me Home Country Roads*. Rick suggests skinny-dipping. Everyone strips down and wades into the stream. Everyone but me.

It's dark except for the moonlight, and everyone's just splashing around. All the nerves in my body are begging me to get in the water. Ginny is calling me. The guys are teasing me. What's the big deal? I'm never going to see these guys again.

Another river flows into view—Kris and I rollicking like children, at Mud Jam. Damn. Will déjà vu ever end? I need a new visual. So—I throw off my clothes and run into the river. Cheers all around. I sit low in the water, letting my arms float to the surface. As the ripples lap at my shoulders, I lean back. Through the aspen leaves, the moonlight flickers. I'm free. And freezing! I follow Ginny as she runs butt-naked to the car, grabs our towels, and tosses me one. I dress behind the open car door.

We all huddle around the campfire for a while, then roll out our sleeping bags under Van Gogh's *Starry Night*. I nestle in the bag, staring upward at the light spread across the sky. Like a highway to heaven, filled with awareness and unlimited possibilities.

Like a... 'Path of Souls.'

A wound breaks open, hurt seeps out. I twist and turn in my sleeping bag. Like a snow angel... in a straitjacket.

The sun rises. We say goodbye to the guys and drive onward. I'm subdued as we pass through canyons with alien-shaped rocks poking into the sky. As we speed along the drifting dunes of the Mojave, my thoughts travel over the miles of mountains and ocean—what's out there? Something inside of me awakens.

Chapter Fifty-Seven
Hitting the Road

Kris

The last few months have been like living on Twinkies. The cheap buzz that burns out way too fast. Its crash leaves me empty and shaky. After work and on my days off, my apartment turns into party central. I have more money, more friends, and more time than common sense. Tending bar at The Botanist, everybody wants to be my friend, have my back, meet my connections, and hang around the girls that hang around me. The endless party with abundant refreshments is a world away from the attic and Lena. She never called me after her surprise visit. Why would she? Her life's playing out the way she wanted it to. As for me, I stuff my feelings deep and live on the surface.

I don't date women—it's just their place or mine. Any night at the bar, it doesn't take a genius to figure out who's game. They glance over their shoulders throughout the night, or linger at the bar, or separate from their friends to wait for me. They buy their own drinks, tip me well, and all I have to do is smile and say, "Why not?"

Every night it's someone different, but by August, I've fallen into a routine with three women. Rum Runner is Monday and Thursday. Tequila Sunrise is Tuesday and Wednesday. Sloe Gin Fizz on the rocks is Saturday.

I can only keep up this juggling act for so long. My balls finally collide when all three show up on a wild Friday night. Like a tin duck in a shooting gallery, I run up and down the long bar trying to placate each of them. By the end of the night, they're onto each other and... me. Then comes the pushing, shoving, curses, and tears.

After closing, Ray is not amused and Jane shakes her head. "Why don't you use your energy more constructively?" she asks. "Like take a class or play a sport?"

"Some would consider what I do a sport."

She rolls her eyes. "You training for the Olympics?"

The cycle continues. Women come and go. I try drowning the 'what was' in warm bodies and make believe I'm looking for what I want to forget.

Tonight's buzz is equal parts pot, booze, and someone ready and willing. I wonder why? Is it me, the sex, or the game? We're all players in the same scene. Tonight, Connie—Bonnie, whatever her name is—she's a laugher. The snorty kind. Everything I say is hilarious. At first, I thought I was pretty witty, but when she lost it over me giving her a lime instead of a lemon with her shot of Cuervo, that's when I realized it was her, not me. I'm not sure how long I can tune out the laugh, but with that body I'm willing to give it the old college try.

Last call for alcohol and the bar lights go up. Our doorman hollers out, "If you ain't got it, you ain't gonna get it. Time to drink up. You don't have to go home, but you can't stay here." In the incandescent truth of those last fifteen minutes, shaky deals are slapped together with a six-pack and four words: "Your place or mine?"

When I come out from the back room, tonight's entertainment is giggling and swiveling on her bar stool. Her raven hair is short and curls around her pixie face. Large dark eyes are lined in black. She has a small, upturned nose and cupid-bow lips. Betty Boop cute.

"So," I ask, "your place or mine?"

"Do you have any tequila?" The lime rind hangs out of her mouth.

"Sure do."

She slides her petite butt off the stool. She puts one hand on my arm to steady herself and grabs her purse with the other. I turn out the lights, set the alarm, and we walk out the back door into the parking lot.

She tugs on my sleeve, "Your place?"

"Yeah. Where are you parked?"

She points and says, "I think I'm over there."

"I'm driving."

"Oh, where are you parked?"

"I don't have a car. I'm driving yours," I say.

"You lose your license or something?"

"No. I walk. My apartment's not that far."

Ten minutes and fifty radio station changes later, I lead my date down the steps to my apartment. Babe can hardly contain herself. She's so happy to see me and what's-her-face, she's wearing a doggy smile.

I'm embarrassed that my living room's a mess. Earlier in the day, I had rummaged through a box of crap from Kent, looking for a pipe. My ready supply of pipes and papers had been disappearing over the past few parties. I had picked through T-shirts, albums, Frisbees, and textbooks, when I saw it. The photograph of me and Lena sitting on Aunt Ella's basket swing, with Lena on my lap, her head against my neck. The soupy smiles on our faces had reminded me of what we were doing, minutes before Aunt Ella walked in and snapped the picture. It made me catch my breath. I could almost smell Lena's hair. Feel the softness of her skin. I had flipped the picture face down onto the table. That was then, this is now. Unfortunately, I didn't put the shit away before I left and it's all over the floor and table. I turn the lamps down low to cover up my past life. I put some Stones on the stereo, pour a couple of shot glasses of tequila and grab two bottles of beer from the fridge. I sit down next to my new-found friend and Babe tries to squiggle in between us. On cue, what's-her-name does that laugh.

"I'm sorry, Bonnie. Babe can't get enough of me," I say, pulling Babe up onto my lap.

"Bonnie? My name's Brenda."

"Bonnie sounds kind of like Brenda when the band's playing."

"Bonnie? That's not even close to Brenda, Well, they both start with 'B'." She giggles.

I lift my shot glass. "Bottoms up, Brenda!" We shoot the shots.

She reaches over to cuddle Babe, slurring, "I got you, Babe! I got you, Babe! Ha, ha! I love that song."

Babe backs up suspiciously.

I stand up. "I'll get you a piece of cheese and Babe will be your best friend."

I go into the kitchen and listen to, "Baby looove, oooh Baby love, I need you, oh how I need you." Snort, snort.

"It's Babe, not baby," I call out, annoyed that she's killing my mood and the music.

When I come back with the treat, Brenda is on the floor with her shirt off, flailing it around, trying to entice Babe into a game of tug-of-war. Normally, I would be thinking *jackpot*. A fleeting memory of my last strip tease on Green Lake makes me smile for a second, but this is just plain sloppy. Then the shirt flinging knocks her beer off the table, spilling brew all over my Kent stuff. Not funny. Not sexy.

"Oopsie! Sorry." She slaps her hand over her mouth.

I jump up to get a towel, thinking I'm gonna need a couple more shots of tequila to make it through this night. When I come back I find topless Brenda, mopping up the end table with her shirt. She holds out a piece of paper and lets Babe lick it dry.

"See? Baby loves me and my beer," she says with a smile.

"What is that?"

She scoots across the floor and holds the soggy paper under the lamp. "Ha, ha, snort, ha, ha. It's a two-headed blob. I think one of the heads is yours." Snort.

"What? Give me that!" I snatch the photo from her. It's the one of Lena and me at Aunt Ella's. The only thing I can make out is our heads, the rest of the picture is a smear. "Put on your shirt."

"Why? My shirt has beer on it. Do you have one I can borrow?"

"You're going home."

"What? I thought we were having fun." Her face droops into a baby-face pout.

I shake my head. "Nope to the fun. Nope to my shirt. I'm staying and you're going."

Her eyes narrow. "You're an asshole." She pushes Babe away and fights her way into the wet shirt. "I should've never picked you up."

"Watch your step and drive carefully." I close the door behind her and wait for the tire screech.

I sit on the couch with Babe's head in my lap and look at what's left of the picture, faces from another time. I can still make out Lena wearing my blue flannel shirt, the one we took turns wearing on the road.

I look around the Dungeon. I've got to get out of this place—this life. I down a shot of Cuervo, then grab the phone.

Jane answers in a muffled, middle-of-the-night voice. "Hello?"

"Hey, it's me," I say. I go on and on about the only exercise I get anymore is beer bottle curls and love push-ups. I'm tired of waking up next to someone and neither us of cares that we don't know the other's name. I dump it all out, then hang up and stretch out on the couch.

Twenty minutes later, Jane walks in. She looks around the room, sits down next to me, puts her hand on my shoulder, and looks me in the eye.

"Oh, Kris. What are you doing to yourself?"

I stare back at her. "You like me, don't you? I mean for real?"

"I like the real you."

"Which one is that?"

Jane leans over me and holds my head in her hands.

"The real one. Not the one behind the bar."

I close my eyes and pull her on top of me. She feels so good. Not just some body, but someone I can hold onto. A real someone with a name I know.

***

Babe wakes me in the morning with her usual morning licks. I hear movement in the kitchen. Smell coffee. I squirm. How do I play this? I stare up at the ceiling, trying to gather my thoughts on friends and lovers. It's happened before. But her being my friend and my boss makes the situation trickier. I'll follow her lead. Jane's sitting at the table with two steaming mugs and a bag that I recognize from the corner bakery.

"Good morning," I say as I make myself busy, letting Babe out into the yard, putting dog food and water into her bowls. Then I sit down at the table and put on my 'everything's cool' grin.

"Good morning." She pulls a doughnut out of the bag and hands it to me.

I take a deep gulp of coffee and shuffle around trying to come up with something meaningful, other than 'How wasted was I last night?'

Jane holds up her hand. "I know what you're thinking. No need to explain. We both know what last night was about."

I take a deep breath. "We're okay, then?"

"I'm okay. You aren't."

I stare into my cup and the words flop out. "I need a change."

"So you're quitting."

It's a statement, not a question. I nod. "I've got to do something different."

"Like get your shit together?"

"Yeah."

Jane sighs. "Go on, then. Take all the time you need. Jimmy's been asking for extra hours."

"Are you sure? I hate bailing on friends."

"That's what friends are for," she says, then smiles and adds, "among other things."

I feel buoyant. Hopeful.

"So what are you going to do?" Jane asks.

"Think I'll give the road a second chance."

"What about Babe?"

"She's coming with."

"Hitchhiking?"

"Why not? I've picked up lots of people thumbing with their dogs." I pat Babe on the head, rub behind her ears. The last time I left my dog behind, it didn't turn out well. I'm not letting that happen again.

She points to something shiny on the floor next to the recliner. "Hey, what's that?" She walks over and picks it up. "Pretty cool," she says, holding Merlin in her open palm. "Looks like real silver."

It must've fallen out of the Kent box when what's her name knocked over the beer. I take the ring from Jane and put it on my finger. "Yeah. It's real."

Chapter Fifty-Eight
Disillusion Delusion

Lena

*J*ournal:

When I was with him, I thought of all the things I could do without him. Now that I'm without him, I can't do a thing.

Picking oranges off backyard trees and lying out on the beach gets old after a while. My friends welcome me back and return to their lives. Ginny heads to San Francisco, searching for hers. I lie on my bed and stare up at the sparkly popcorn ceiling wondering what the hell I'm doing. I test myself—try to feel the shape of Kris's snuggles, try to taste his kiss. I fail. It's all fading away.

The study-abroad class begins. Three nights a week of international culture and politics. Lots of thought-provoking discussions, lots of interesting books to read and papers to write. Thirty-five hopeful students vying for twenty-five open slots. Those with the highest scores will be divided among six countries and leave in September. I won't know if I made the cut until late August.

Although I have a financial aid package, there are extra costs of living abroad, and neither parent will contribute. Without a degree, and no office experience, I find out I don't even qualify as a check filer for a bank. Discouraged, I get a job at a donut shop, working the dawn shift.

Then I meet Jeffrey, who's in some kind of public relations. He comes in every day and orders a banana muffin and black coffee. Tall, dark and mustached with intense black eyes, he drives a convertible sports car. At the end of a week, he asks for my phone number.

Jeffrey turns out to be the perfect gentleman. My father likes his "reasonable head," my girlfriends drool over his good looks and bulging wallet. His quick banter matches mine, quirk for quirk. I'm not in love, but I'm in a helluva lotta like.

Sexy sundresses oust the bellbottoms. He lavishes all his attention on me. I haven't heard from the green-eyed monster and it feels wonderful. Normal. He wants to make love, but this time I'm following my "must be in love and ready to commit" plan. He waits patiently. I think I'm almost there. Halfway through July, he slips a gold bangle on my wrist. I unclasp the macramé beaded bracelet and press it into the crease of my journal. This is starting to feel real.

***

"**P**ull over, pull over." I bounce on the front seat as Jeffrey drives us down the Pacific Coast Highway. He parks his Austin Healy and I dance my way toward the surf. No matter that we're dressed for a fancy dinner party with his beautiful friends that he wants me to meet—the ocean is calling me.

"C'mon," I say, slipping off my sandals and tugging him to the shoreline. He rolls up his pants and allows himself to be pulled barefooted and knee-deep into the surf. We stand in the waves, arms around each other, kissing.

"I'm in love with a gypsy," he says.

I look into his deep, dark eyes, trying to feel something. Not yet. But I don't pull away.

The dinner party is held in a house of marble pillars and crystal chandeliers. It's open on all sides, inviting in the salt air and sounds of the pounding surf. Waiters bring hors d'oeuvres I've never tasted before. We make small talk, sip strong drinks, and smoke hashish from silver pipes. It's all so new and exciting, and everyone knows Jeffrey. He puts me on display, introducing me to everyone as Gypsy. The looks on their faces show I'm not his usual date. "A diamond in the rough," I hear one of them say. "Potential," another whispers. I don't know if that's a compliment.

The night moves on. Groups gather in rooms around white powder in silver bowls. Cocaine? Heroin? I pass on the offer to join in. Jeffrey steers me to the dance floor in front of a band playing funky music. This is so not me, I think as I bounce around to the music. Projectors begin showing X-rated films on the surrounding walls. I'm uneasy. Jeffrey leads me down a winding staircase to a patio with plush deck chairs and a marble bar. A pool-sized hot tub pumps steam into the salt air. The beautiful people glide down the stairs and start peeling off their designer clothes. They slide into the burbling water like mermaids. Jeffrey is shedding his neat white slacks and perfectly tailored shirt. I look out onto the shoreline where the surf shimmers.

"C'mon, Lena," Jeffrey says, holding his hand out, standing naked and waist deep in the bubbling water. "We can do whatever you want. Promise."

I stand freeze-frame still and look at the breasts and butts and penises glistening under the moonlight. The beautiful people are poking and tickling themselves into a frenzy. I look into the night sky. A movie camera is pointing down from the balcony.

My heart pounds. I don't want this. I turn and stumble down the stone steps to the beach. I feel all the beautiful eyes watching me. It looks like Jeffrey's rough diamond is really a piece of coal, after all.

I stand in the ocean letting my thoughts roll back and forth like the surf. Oh, God, where am I? What am I? Jeffrey's gold bangle feels cold and heavy. I throw it into the waves. Jeffrey shows up and we walk to his car. His tone is cold and calculating as he tries to explain himself. How much money I could make—we could make. He begins to lose his composure.

"What the fuck is this gypsy free spirit crap? You're just an uptight tease."

"I'm just being myself. It's not my fault if you got the wrong impression."

I ignore his excuses and accusations and insults. It doesn't matter. It's all bullshit.

***

The summer drags on. Every day is the same: up at 4:00 a.m. and frying dough by five. By 6:00 a.m. the intersection out front is choked with traffic, and by seven, the heat waves mix with the grease in the air around me. I catch glimpses out the front window as I carry the donuts to the counter. I know mountains surround me and an ocean is just beyond the canyon, but I can't see them through the haze. I can't feel them in my soul. I try to visualize them, but it just makes me dizzy. I can't breathe. I can't think. I need some space, some ocean air.

I leave work an hour early, pleading sick. Well, it's the truth. I'm sick of this whole scene. I need some trees… real ones, with lush green leaves that spread out in umbrella canopies like the ones over Willow Street. Not these pencil sticks stuck in cement boxes along the sidewalk. I point my VW Bug toward Topanga Canyon and the scent of dust and eucalyptus trees. Then beyond, the salt air of the Pacific.

The freeway to the canyon road is bumper-to-bumper traffic, even though it's in the middle of a Tuesday afternoon. Stopping at the light on the exit ramp, I gasp. It's Kris, standing with his thumb out. Long brown hair down his back. Skinny in his T-shirt and jeans. Kris!

"I'm picking him up," I say aloud. I pull over and call out those memorable words. "Where you headed?"

"To the beach."

"Hop in."

He climbs in the passenger side and extends his hand. "Grant."

His eyes are as blue as Kris's, his smile as sweet. He pulls out a joint. "Mind?"

"Not at all. I could use a toke or two."

We puff our way through the where're you froms, and where you beens. Grant is twenty-four, an electrician, but hasn't had a real job in a couple of years. He works under the table to stay on food stamps. Likes his freedom. Something in his attitude sounds more scheming than free-spirited. But who am I to judge? I'm living with my grandparents.

It's mid-afternoon and the heat simmers in the hills. The conversation slows as I navigate the twists and turns of the canyon road. The pot blurs our thoughts and words. Then the blue waters of the Pacific shimmer into view.

"What beach do you want to go to?" I ask.

"It doesn't matter," Grant says.

"Coral Cove?"

"That's cool."

Coral Cove is off the beaten path. Its rocky shoreline and riptide keep away surfers, swimmers, and kids playing ball. I like to read there, sitting against the rocks, sheltered from intrusion. When I reach Coral Cove, I pull over onto the berm and park.

"Do you mind if I hang out with you?" Grant asks.

"Not at all." *In fact, I'd love it.*

I open the trunk and pull out my ever-ready beach bag, packed with a towel, cotton Mexican blanket, book, and Frisbee. We walk along the beach. Grant picks up shells and hands them to me. He skips rocks across the tiny waves that foam at our feet. I find a craggy boulder to lean against and spread out my blanket. I give Grant my towel.

We sit and stare at the waves. I pull out my novel, Hesse's *Steppenwolf.*

"What's that about?" Grant asks.

"Oh, a guy who's sick of being bourgeois. His spiritual side fights against his animalistic side."

"Bourgeois?"

"You know, upper class. Privileged."

"Oh." Grant stares out at the sea. "Hey, are you thirsty?"

"I have some Seven-Up in the car, but it's probably boiling."

"No, I mean like wine."

"There's a market a little ways down the road."

"I'll go," he says getting up.

As Grant walks away, I stretch out on my blanket. LA weighs me down. What the hell am I going to do if I don't go to France? I can finish my degree, but then what?

The heat and the lingering effect of the pot hinder my attempts to decipher anything, including Hesse. Grant's return is a welcome interruption. He passes me an open bottle of Strawberry Hill. I take a few gulps. It tastes more bitter than usual. Probably the heat.

I take a few more gulps and by the end of the bottle, Grant is morphing into Kris. I wobble my way down to the shoreline. The breeze from the breakers fills my lungs. The seagulls *ke-ow* in my ears. I'm free! I'm where I'm meant to be! I can do anything—except stand up. Everything is spinning. I crawl back to my blanket. Grant is sitting on it. His smile is watery, not Kris's. He grabs my hand.

"We'd better go," I say. "I don't want to drive through the canyon in the dark. And you need to drive."

"I forgot my driver's license."

"What?" No one goes anywhere in LA without a driver's license.

"Just give me the keys," Grant says.

I can barely keep my eyes focused on his strange grin, let alone canyon curves. We get up and Grant starts gathering my stuff. We stumble up the rocks to the car.

I give Grant the keys and get in the passenger side. He starts up the Bug and we chug onto the highway. He turns onto the old canyon road. A mist is rolling in.

"Take the freeway home," I say.

"No, this is shorter."

I can barely see the edge of the road, but it doesn't matter—I'll be home soon. Grant stops at a crossroad and makes a right turn.

"Wait, this isn't..." I can't make out the sign. Nothing but fog.

"It's a shortcut."

We drive slowly, and I hang my head out the window hoping the haze outside will clear the haze inside my head.

Grant pulls the car off the side of the road and stops.

"What's wrong?" I ask.

"I can't see any more."

"Go back."

"I can't."

"I'll drive." I'm starting to feel antsy.

"You're still drunk. C'mon, let's take a walk."

I think maybe the walk will help, as we get out of the car and head along a dirt path. I can see the mountain silhouettes poking up over the fog line in the twilight.

Grant puts his arm around me and I lean into him.

"Grant, I have to go home. Are you sure you can't see to drive?"

"I can't get pulled over. I don't have a license."

"Why not?"

"They took it from me."

"Who?"

"The guys at the pen."

"What's a pen?"

"You know, prison."

He pulls me to him and kisses me hard and deep, plunging his tongue down my throat. Startled, I pull back, but he pins my arms to my sides and pushes against me. He's hurting me.

"Stop it!" I twist and turn but can't get out of his grip. A muffled scream escapes my lips.

"C'mon, girl, relax." His mouth is gnawing every inch of my face, his body thrusting, trying to wrestle me down.

The haze blasts away from my head. My heart is a jackhammer against my ribs. We're on the ground, the rocks and weeds clawing my back, Grant mauling my body, yanking my clothes. My brain screaming. *Think! Think! Focus on thinking your way out of this!*

They say don't fight. It only excites them. Try to reason with him. He doesn't want to go back to the pen, does he? I just have to mention it. No, he'll think I'm threatening him. It'll make him angry. Just go along.

"Grant, wait. Wait." I force myself to stroke his back. Nuzzle his chin. "I want it, too." The words gag me, but I force them out. "Let's get comfortable."

He hesitates, then moves off me. I have to make this good. I lean over and give him a deep kiss. Run my fingers down his thigh. "Let's get a blanket."

We walk back to the car. I put my arm around his waist, stroke his side, slip my hand into his butt pocket. Oh God, oh God. Help me do this.

He puts the keys in the trunk latch and it pops open. In one fell swoop, I can grab the keys. Buzzing in my brain. *Do it. Do it now.* But no, I freeze. I just can't. If I screw up, this will go bad for me. I have to think my way out. I get the blanket and lean over to give him a hungry I-can't-wait kiss.

He's all over me, falling for it. But how do I get in the car? I've got to stop this without making him angry.

I spread the blanket out near the car and we sit, then lie down. Oh God. I might have to go through with this. It might be my only way out. I feel sick to my stomach.

That's it.

We're making out heavy. I force my fingers to fumble with the button on his jeans. I've got to be convincing. Our clothes are almost off. Then I turn sideways and stick my finger down my throat, jerking my head next to his. A stream of strawberry puke spurts out.

"Fuck!" he yells, jumping up. "Shit!"

More is coming and I let it go—all over me and the blanket. All over where he was. Chunks of lunchtime burrito soaked in gooey strawberry bile stream out.

He's bent over, gagging, wiping his face and neck with his shirt. The putrid stench penetrates the canyon air.

"What the hell's wrong with you?" Grant's body lurches with an involuntary heave. "Jesus Christ!"

I fake giant sobs. "I'm sorry. It's the wine. I'm so sorry." I blow vomit from my nose into my shirt.

"Let's get the hell out of here," he says. "I've got to get this shit off of me."

Have I gone too far? Get back to lovey-dovey. I walk over to him and put my arms around him.

"Let me drive... babe... I don't want you sent back to... the pen."

He stiff arms me and pushes the keys at me. I get in the driver's seat and tears of relief burn the insides of my eyes. But I'm not safe yet.

"I'll make it up to you," I say. "Please, Grant. Call me next week? I'll make it up to you."

I beg, promise, and cajole until we get to the exit where I picked him up. The exit where this bad dream began. He gets out.

I get some paper out of my purse and write down a fake number. "Call me," I plead.

He snatches it out of my hand. "You owe me big time."

I smile sweetly and force my gaze to linger on him, then pull away slowly, every nerve in my body a razor.

As soon as I merge onto the freeway, I press down on the accelerator and turn on the radio full blast. Everything pours out. Oh, sweet Jesus. Thank you. Oh, my God. *What ifs* rock around my brain, scream through the traces of strawberry puke in my mouth. My hands clench the wheel until they throb. I focus my eyes on the freeway's straight and narrow lanes. I concentrate on staying between the road lane reflectors, they'll bring me home. I can't talk about this at home where I might be overheard, but I've got to tell someone. A mile from the house, I pull into a gas station with a phone booth. I put a dime in the slot and dial Ginny's number. When she answers, I tell her the story in broken sobs.

"You picked up a hitchhiker? What were you thinking?" she yells into the phone.

"He looked so normal." *He looked like Kris.*

"You're taking a chance picking up a guy by yourself."

"I just wanted to help him out. He looked desperate." This is a lie—I was the one who was desperate.

"Yeah, he was desperate—to get laid. You're lucky you walked away from it."

"I know."

"You could've been hacked up and thrown into the canyon!"

"Don't say those things!" My hand is sweaty, gripping the phone.

"Well, someone has to! I'm your best friend. I care about you. And I'm begging you—stop living in a dream world, Lena."

She's right, but I can't talk about it anymore. I want… I want someone to hold me. I end the call and dig out the matchbook from my purse. I dial Kris's number. *Please be there. I need... I need...*

"The number you are dialing has been disconnected, please check—"

I slam the phone down. I'm on my own. Totally alone.

But I did it, I didn't freeze.

When I get home, I go in the back door and my grandfather calls out from living room.

"Soma guy name Peter, call you from a school. He giva me his number. Said you agoin' to France."

Chapter Fifty-Nine
End of the Road

Kris

Sunset colors the September sky. The earthy scent of the upper Midwest swirls around as I reattach the last shutter to the bunkhouse. Babe sits contentedly watching me. She hasn't been any trouble. There was no guesswork about what she needed on the road: a plastic jug for water, a bag of dog food in my pack and an occasional belly rub. Leaving Columbus was a snap. Amazing how a dog and I landed on Aunt Ella's doorstep in just three long rides and...

I put down the screwdriver and review my handiwork. Not bad. Aunt Ella said the cabin could use some fixing up when I called her a few weeks ago and gave her the abbreviated version of my life. It's been therapeutic tinkering around the place. Mostly grunt work. Sanding, painting, trimming, and hauling.

I run water out of the hose for a drink, straighten, and wipe my mouth. I hear tires crunch on the gravel behind me, and I turn around to see Aunt Ella's Jeep approach. She's been coming up on Saturdays to check things out and give me a little cash for the work. Being a Tuesday, this is an unexpected visit.

I walk her around the cabin to show her my work, then we sit at the picnic table and I crack open two cold beers. Babe lies at our feet, lifting her head to search out the source of the occasional hoots and howls of the local wildlife.

I offer Aunt Ella a cigarette and she takes it, complaining it's part of a corporate conspiracy to get us all hooked. She starts telling me about the demonstrations taking place at the university. I let her ramble on, wondering why she's here.

She pauses, ready for my comments, my contribution. I shake another smoke from my pack.

Ella looks at me closely. "Are you a conscientious objector?"

"Nope."

She sighs, disappointed.

I could give the explanation I gave Lena after the ride with the Congressman, but I don't feel like going into it. I bring out a couple more beers and turn on the porch light as dusk approaches. Aunt Ella takes a joint out of her purse. Now I get it. She just needed some company. We smoke in the semi-darkness while she tells me about what's happening at the art gallery. She goes on about the expanding psychology department. We talk 'til the dark covers us.

Aunt Ella stands as if she's ready to leave. "It's too late and I'm too buzzed to drive home. I think I'll stay here the night."

I give her the back bedroom and sprawl out on the living room couch. The open window curtains sway in the cool lake air. Through the window I can see the stars twinkle and shoot from one end of the galaxy to the other. I pull on a T-shirt and stuff my feet into my moccasins. I step out on the porch and Babe tags along. The cloudless night is thick with stars. I start picking out the constellations I know and making up some new ones I don't. The possibilities are endless. I trace some lines between stars to reveal a snowman. The thought of snow transports me back in time. Lena and I staring into the vastness, our breath frosted, our frozen lips thawed by kisses. I scan the stars. There it is—our snow angel.

A dull emptiness settles deep in my gut and works its way into a heavy sigh. I hurl a stick as far as I can throw and hear a distant splash in the lake. Why did I let her go? Why did she come to Columbus? To be forgiven for Reggie?

No, we settled all that, when I left Kent. It had to be something else.

I stare into the infinite black between the stars, hearing her say, *"If you don't know, I'm not going to tell you."*

Was it to be friends? I know only too well her opinion on friends being lovers. Half-formed thoughts streak through my brain. She was more than friendly that weekend. So that must mean she didn't want to be "just friends." Why didn't she say it? My breath slows down as it becomes clear. She wanted *me* to say it. That I wanted to be more than friends. And what did I say? Nothing. I cringe. *'It feels like my arms are chained to my side.'* But what did she expect? She chose California over me.

I open my arms wide and breathe in the thick lake air. Merlin's wand waves over my brain. *'The magic is not in what you see, but in why you see it.'*

I stare deep into space. A few stars start to align. I follow the dim swirl of the Milky Way. *Path of Souls. Connect the dots.* A shooting star separates from the glow, arcing over me as it streaks into the infinite blackness.

I got the road back, I'll get Lena back, too. I'll hitch to LA. and say everything I should've said in Columbus. I'll tell her I love her. Here, there, wherever. It doesn't matter. It never did. I'll make the call tomorrow. I drift asleep with a lightness I haven't felt in months.

The next morning the smell of coffee wafts from the kitchen. I feed Babe, then shower and dress. Aunt Ella has a steaming mug waiting for me. I sip the mild Swedish coffee and ponder if I should tell Aunt Ella what I'm going to say to Lena. No, Lena should be the first to know. I'm anxious to make the call, but I don't want to wake her grandparents. Inside, I'm all smiles. I can't wait to talk to her and tell her all the things I should've said before we slipped away from each other. I look at the clock above the sink, take a deep breath, and put my mug on the counter. It's time.

"Aunt Ella, I gotta make a call. I'd kinda like to do it in private."

Aunt Ella's brow wrinkles as she looks at the phone on the wall and back to me. She walks into the living room.

I take out my wallet and unfold the tiny, smudged slip of paper Lena gave me before we started hitching. She wasn't speaking to her dad, so I was to call her grandparents only in a "dire emergency or as a last resort." Well, this was both of those things. I dial the number to Joe Borelli.

"Allo? Allo?" A male voice with a heavy Italian accent answers the phone.

"Hi, is Lena there?"

"No, Ima sorry. Whosa this?"

"Kris. Kris Anderson, a friend of Lena's."

"You justa missed her. She went to France lasta night."

A bucket of ice falls over me. "France?"

"Yeah, the France. With thata... Peter. His name. Peter. Maybe they be there now."

"Oh, I see. Uh, Okay. Well, when you hear from her, will you tell her Kris called?"

"Okay, but maybe no soon. Too much money. I tella them they crazy, everything good here in America. Why they wanna go so far?"

I slump against the wooden wall of the kitchen. "Don't know... Well... thanks anyway."

I mechanically hang up the receiver and stare at the phone. France... Last night. *Peter?*

I pick myself off the wall, and push my way through the screen door and sit down on the porch step. I stare into the surrounding pines and out to the blue of the lake. France and Peter, Peter and France, and Peter. *Who the fuck's Peter?*

Taking a deep breath, I slowly twist the silver ring on my finger. No amount of wishful thoughts is gonna change the fact that she's left. Taken the magic with her. I'm back where I started.

Aunt Ella comes out and sits on the porch step beside me. She heard enough of one side of the conversation to figure out what's happened.

"You know, Aunt Ella," I say, grabbing a handful of black earth, "I've had people on the road tell me life's just made out of dirt. I used to think they didn't have much going on. But now it seems my life is nothin' but a dirt road to nowhere."

Aunt Ella clears her throat. "I don't believe that," she says. "Life is full of detours and sometimes the only way to get to the best places, like home, is by traveling those dirt roads. Remember all roots start in dirt."

I let the handful of earth crumble through my fingers and fall back to where it came from. I brush my hands off on my jeans, take off my Merlin ring and flip it to Aunt Ella. "Keep this for my sisters, just in case one of them is lucky enough to take the right detour."

She puts the ring back in my hand. "*You* better keep the ring." Her forehead creases. "Kris, I have to tell you something. It's why I drove out here. I should've told you last night, but the weed and the beer... well, I was looking for any excuse to procrastinate. I thought this morning might be the right time. But now it's such a mess and I—"

"Tell me what?"

"Your dad called yesterday. You need to call him."

"About what?"

"You got a notice in the mail. From the draft board."

Part IV: Now, and Then Again

Chapter Sixty
Age Ed.

Lena

I mingle through the Kent Hotel bar, squinting at nametags, greeting old friends and dorm-mates. A woman I half remember is introducing everyone to her famous baseball-player husband. My old roommate Lyla, who collected road-kill on the weekends, just retired from a career in marine biology on the west coast and now volunteers saving the whales. Bullhorn Bob, the guy who used to lead all the anti-war rallies, is going on and on about his taxes and our liberal government. Apparently, someone switched sides. Ned, who tagged along to Mud Jam, has spent years as a freelance photographer for Rolling Stone.

I scan the "regrets, missing and memorial" boards standing near the entrance to the banquet room. Mike has a string of addresses around Europe and can't be located. According to the memorial page, Cheet was killed in a skiing accident in his forties. Sad, but no surprise.

I find my photo nametag on the reception table. A smiling, youthful face, filled with hope, and overwhelming, wavy black hair. I pin it on, and then shuffle through nametags with pictures of long hair and beards until Kris's thoughtful blue eyes gaze up at me through wire rims. What sights have they seen through the lens of time? At any minute, I'll be introducing him to the sixty-year-old version of me. I've got to find a restroom for a touch-up.

I look in the bathroom mirror, noticing the lines around my eyes and mouth. Running my fingers through my salt and pepper curls. I smile, remembering how I fought them all those years. Pressing them out on an ironing board, using blow dryers that sounded like jet engines and chemical straighteners that smelled like pesticides.

I let go of all that when I hit fifty. Stepping over to the full-length mirror, I turn from side to side. The figure staring back wears jeans—not belled at the knee and frayed at the bottom—but tailored and… stretch. A knit sweater set takes the place of the tie-dyed peasant blouse. My heart drops. Where did that free-spirited girl go?

A glint of light catches the silver peace signs dangling from my ears. At least I've held onto those. Those and—I pull a small vial of patchouli oil from my purse that I bought online for this occasion. I dab a drop on each wrist and sniff. It brings me back. Back to that girl. I smile at my reflection in the mirror. I'm ready.

I push through the door and walk out into the bustling reception area. A tall, thin woman I vaguely recognize passes by me. She has short and spiky silver hair and is wearing a tie-dyed shirt and bell bottoms. How fun that she went all out. I wish I had. She stops and sniffs the air.

"Lena?" she says with a thick drawl. She grabs my arm. "I knew it was you!"

"Oh, my God—Anne?"

She's one of my dorm mates from freshman year. We hug and walk over to the bar where we are greeted by Trish. In no time at all it feels like we're back in our dorm chatting on our bunks—but this time it's over Cosmopolitans instead of bottles of Rolling Rock. Trish brings us up to date on her recent struggle with cancer. The treatments, the fundraising walks, the expense.

Anne, still single, complains about the endless hours she puts in as a resort recreation planner for health spas across the Gulf Coast.

"You always were good at recreation planning. Remember all that recreation that went on in our dorm room?" I giggle, remembering my nights on the couch in the lobby.

"Argh." Anne lowers her head. "Let me apologize for all that. Guess I really took women's lib and free love to heart."

"Don't apologize," I say. "Those were the times. Everyone was doing it. We were just lucky to do it between the Pill and AIDs."

"You'd better believe it. The world's changed so much. I run a search on every guy I meet on those online dating sites. Thank God for the internet," Anne says. "But I do miss the spontaneity."

I flick my eyes over to the doorway watching. And waiting. Then my stomach flutters. That might be him. I squint as he walks to the front desk. A little beer gut, a lot less hair, but… I dig my glasses out of my purse. *It's him.* I glance around. He's alone.

Breaking away from the girls, I walk over and stand quietly behind him as he checks in. Another place and time, backpacks, not suitcases propped against another front desk. Does he remember? I peer around his shoulder and smile inside as he signs in. Did he keep 'our secret'?

Now he scribbles a confident signature, one that has documented his journey through decades of a life I had no part in. He turns around.

"Lena!"

His voice is the same. It settles inside me.

"Hi, Kris."

We hug. I linger and let it wash over me. Then I pull back. Something's missing. I give him an exaggerated once-over. "No wire rims?"

"Lasik."

"I almost didn't recognize you," I say.

"I guess the short gray hair jolted your memory." He sniffs the air and wrinkles his nose.

"I wore it just for you," I say, laughing. "I don't smell tobacco."

"Quit years ago." He points to my shaggy curls. "I see you finally gave in."

I run my hand over my "gypsy" hairstyle. He once called it a "fancy frame."

We make our way to the bar. He orders a beer. I shake my head no when he offers to buy me a drink and I point at my half-full Cosmo. We move to a high cocktail table and get acquainted with our grown-up selves.

Kris glances around. "Did your husband come?"

"No. He's a firm believer that reunions are for those who were there. In other words, boooring."

Kris's wife, a veterinarian, couldn't make it due to an animal adoption fundraiser she had organized.

"You married a vet? I should've seen that coming!" I say.

Kris smiles. "Not so fast, Sherlock. Diane's a farm vet—horses, cows, chickens, goats. However, we're on the board of a local rescue agency, so we foster. Which has led to our own personal menagerie: two dogs, three cats, one rabbit, and a miniature pot-bellied pig."

"So, you live in the country?"

"Semi-rural. Just outside Minneapolis. Great place to raise kids. We've got four, all grown and settled nearby. And you?"

"Empty nesters, too, but our kids are city slickers."

There's an awkward pause. I clear my throat. "Did you ever do anything in psych?"

"Sort of," Kris says. "I took some courses in comparative psychology and long story short, I became an animal behaviorist. I own a dog training business called Puppy Love. How about you? You said you're a travel writer?"

I nod, still not believing how adult we've become, with careers and kids. Two mature, responsible adults transported straight out of the belly of the 1970's. How strange life is.

"I'm strictly freelance now," I say. "Mainly boring stuff like restaurant and hotel reviews."

"But you got to see the world, like you always wanted?"

I smile. "I filled up my share of passports. But we don't travel as much these days."

We both sip our drinks and scan the room.

"Hey," Kris says. "I know what your next travel story should be." He sings, *"It took us two days to hitchhike from... Calumet."*

Clapping my hands, I lean back in the chair. "I love that song. Every time I hear it on the oldies station, I think of our trip."

"Me, too. No one hitchhikes anymore. I'm surprised you haven't written about it."

"Um, well... Minnesota seems like a dream to me now." There's a lull. I look into my drink.

"Have you—"

"Did you—"

Nervous laughter escapes us both.

"Did you ever get that beer in Costa Rica?" Kris asks.

I smile and sigh. "No, but I still have the coin."

"I wonder if that dentist ever got his friend out of jail."

"Hopefully he did," I say. The thought of fleeting time sinks into me. "He's probably retired by now."

"Hey, how's Ginny? Did you guys stay in touch?"

"Absolutely. She's on a Mediterranean cruise or she would've loved to have come." I chuckle. "You'll never believe this story. After we drove out to California, she moved to San Francisco and got a job as a waitress at a seafood restaurant. One of the waiters had the hots for her and they started dating. Turns out he was a geology student working on his Masters degree. He went out to Wyoming to map water tables or something, and convinced Ginny to go with him. They shacked up in the middle of nowhere without electricity or running water."

"You're kidding!" Kris slaps the table. "Makeup-and-curlers Ginny?"

I nod. "She lived in that cabin for a year with a wood stove and an outhouse."

We both laugh, picturing Ginny putting on her makeup by lantern, hauling water from a well to make her gourmet macaroni and cheese dinners.

I lift my hands in the air. "But it paid off in the end. Steve found silver. And lots of it. Now she's primping in a mansion with five bathrooms. I see her about once a year," I say. "When we reminisce about our Kent State years, she says she wishes she'd had all the fun I accuse her of having. Maybe we can all get together some time and you can back me up on some of my memories."

"Great idea. I'd like Diane to know our old gang."

"Uh, that'd be nice," I feel a momentary pang of possessiveness. I brush it away and ask, "Did you know about Cheet?"

"Yeah," he winces. "I got back in touch with Cheet after... when he came back to Columbus. His parents called me when it happened. They were devastated. You remember his brother was killed in the war? Can't imagine losing both my sons."

I nod. "Tragic."

I notice the woman and her baseball player husband opposite our table are making their way toward us. She's wearing a tight, low-cut dress, designed to show off her well-maintained body.

"Kris? Kris! Is that you?"

"Eve?" Kris jumps up, walks around the table, and gives her a bear hug.

"It's so good to see you," Eve says. "This is my husband Roger Bostock. You might remember him, he played for your Minnesota Twins. And belted a couple home runs in the '87 World Series."

"Yes, I do. Thanks for that." Kris shakes Roger's hand.

"Roger, Kris helped me with my geometry and I got him through Shakespeare," Eve says. She turns to Kris. "I wasn't a half bad tutor, was I, Kris?"

"Uh, no, not at all. I passed." Kris shifts to one foot, tilts his head with that same 'who me?' expression on his face as when he spent a little too much time with my old roommates before coming to bed.

"And you were the expert on shapes," Eve says, eyeing Kris. "And angles."

No mistaking the wink-wink in her voice. Kris half turns, his face a rosy blush. He points at me, "Remember Lena? She was in our Shakespeare class."

"Uh, sure," Eve says. "How long have you two been married?"

"We're not." I say. "Married. I mean, to each other."

"Well, it's so refreshing to see ex-lovers can still be friends."

The old friends and lovers thing, only this time in reverse. Does he remember?

Kris squares his shoulders. "Friends? Yes. We're just catching up."

"Ohhh," Eve says, picking up her and Roger's drinks. "Don't let us interrupt. We'll chat at lunch."

Kris waves goodbye. We watch Roger follow Eve across the room.

"What was that all about?" I say, wondering when all that tutoring took place.

"No idea," he says, tugging at his shirt collar.

I finish my drink and push the glass away. "This is my first time back here. Have you been back since—"

"No. Nothing really brings me down this way."

"What about your folks?" I ask.

"They're living it up in a retirement community in Florida."

Lunch is announced. At a table in the banquet room, we find Trish and her husband Eric, still together since the first day of freshman year. There's a slight shuffle as I try to take a seat not too close, but not too far from Kris. Eve and her husband grab the chairs on Kris's right. I settle in across the table, between Lyla and Anne.

I want to hear Kris's every word. But how do you fill in the gap of decades in a few hours?

Chapter Sixty-One
Same Difference

Kris

Some things never change. I find myself having to sit next to, who else, but 'Lude Dick. Why couldn't it have been Lena? I watch her across the table playing musical chairs with her old roommates. I swear if Dick slurs his words or falls out of his chair…

'Lude Dick has a huge grin on his face and starts to lean toward me. I brace myself to catch him. But it's all hugs. I guess my old habits are hard to break.

"How are you, buddy?" I right myself back in my seat and notice his nametag reads Richard not Dick.

"Great. No, better than great, fantastic! I owe you a shitload of apologies, dude. At least that's what they say in my AA meetings."

"Forget it, you owe me nothing," I say with a sense of relief.

Over salad, people talk about grandchildren, retirement, and body parts that don't work like they used to. But Dick pours out his gut-wrenching struggles with addiction, and the final straw of losing his wife and kids. He's been clean for thirty years now and is happily remarried. I pat him on the back, but I'm a little embarrassed because I'm paying more attention to Lena chatting across the table. She's wearing the same bright smile she used to greet me with in the attic.

After my second beer and Dick's third Diet Coke, we start cracking everyone up with re-enactments of the dorm antics. Over the laughter and people cringing, I find myself still staring at Lena. What's wrong with me? It's not like she's going to disappear. I shouldn't have left my damn sunglasses in the car.

When the servers clear our table, Dick stands up with his glass. "I wish to apologize to any women here that I might have been obnoxious to at any of our parties," he says, grinning. "To those who weren't offended by my advances, you shall remain nameless. I'd like to say I had the most amazing time."

Over laughter and applause, he sits down and clinks his glass to my beer bottle.

"I never could remember a name in the morning and I got smacked more than once for guessing," he whispers. "Then there were those who played hard to get and gave me fake names. Right, Kris?"

"Like Juliet?" I say, remembering the party where 'Lude draped himself all over Lena. I look over and see Lena eyeing me. I turn back to Dick. "Remember our rule, 'no name, fair game'?"

Dick looks puzzled, and says, "Maybe it'll come back to me." Then he gazes around the table and asks rather loudly, "Speaking of famous love affairs, where's Sophie?"

I shrug. "Couldn't find her. I called her sister. She told me Sophie's a social worker in Rhode Island and said she'd give her the message about the reunion. I never heard back."

My peripheral vision catches Lena's face showing a slight flicker of 'the look.' I never told her about Sophie. Although we talked about everything under the sun, for some strange reason, we never talked about past relationships. Sophie was the first one who made me aware that something inside of me was lost. It was Lena, though, who made me want to find it.

"Hey," I say, my mind churning, searching for a new topic. "Remember the Dunbar dorm duck races? And our RA... What was his name?"

"Peeping Tom," Richard says. "He saw everything."

"Right! Man, was he pissed when I dropped my bong in front of his door."

My story gets a good laugh all around, and I'm relieved to be talking about something other than old girlfriends.

"Still the die-hard Vikings' fan?" someone shouts to me.

"Is there any other kind?" I shoot back.

"Anyone march on Washington lately?"

Lena raises her hand. "When we invaded Iraq. I saw the Vietnam Vets Against the War booth. I stopped by and told them how I marched with a group of them at Kent State. We wondered why we were still protesting the same old stuff."

There are some solemn nods.

Bullhorn Bob, a table over, throws out a snide remark about liberals. I give him a dark look as the hair on my neck bristles. Now where did that come from? She's not my girlfriend anymore. I hear some rumblings. Time to detour the discussion. I compose myself, grab my beer, and stand.

"Let's toast to five-fingered bags, the smell of patchouli, and hitchhiking down the road."

"Aye, aye!" echoes around the room.

I glance Lena's way. Her eyes meet mine and sparkle. The same sparkle I saw when I watched her stick out her thumb for the first time. A long buried pang nudges me.

Lunch moves on with additional toasts to great music, tie-dyed bed sheets, and never trusting anyone over thirty. I grip my bottle and raise it higher. "Here's to peace and love and—

Lena jumps up waving her glass in the air. "And a time to wander."

I swallow the last of my beer and pound the bottle on the table. I wondered how I'd feel when I saw her again. Nostalgic? Sentimental? All those things that we did. *Does she remember?* I thought it'd be so easy to meet someone like her. Ha! It took me seven years to meet Diane. I feel a nagging sense of unfinished business. *Let it go, and just be cool.* The last thing I want to do is freak her out—make her think I'm carrying a torch or something. Still… *does she remember?*

We get our jackets from the coatroom for the campus walk. About twenty of us follow a student guide out of the main entrance. Lyla stays behind, engaged in a heated discussion on climate change with asshole Bullhorn Bob. Eve and her husband go off to find a TV showing the World Series. Others head out to the shops or stay and watch college football on the hotel bar's big screen TV. I walk ahead with a group of guys including Ned, Dick and Eric. Lena strolls behind with Anne and Trish.

Our guide, Tyler, is a communication major with short blond hair and thick black glasses. He leads our group downtown. The area has changed dramatically from our time there. Gone are the headshops and most of the divey bars. Now sports bars and dance clubs line the streets along with chic boutiques and trendy restaurants. Everything is clean. But I miss the old hole-in-the-wall diners and bars with their uneven floors and peeling paint… the funkiness.

Passing a vacant corner lot, I feel disorientated and slowly make a 360-degree scan. The Robin Hood bar. Gone! Lena spins around and looks at me, tilting her head with a sad smile. Tyler says it was torn down a few years ago with plans for a chain restaurant in the works. Something inside me dies a little.

Lena approaches me and says in a low voice, "Some of the best and worst things happened to me in that old bar. I'm not sure I like this campus tour. I want to remember everything just as it was."

"Me, too. Remember Claudette?"

"Your poster girlfriend. How could I forget?"

"Hey, hey, be nice. You were the first girl Claudette ever approved of."

We step through the front campus arch and walk along the loop until we reach the commons. Tyler points out the markers the University has installed commemorating the tragic May 4th shootings. They show the movements of the students and guards that fateful day. Jay, in our group, admits to being one of the rock throwers from back then. He takes over for Tyler in describing what happened.

As I read and listen, it feels like I'm re-watching a movie I know ends badly. I want to turn it off. I look up and see Lena watching me. That weekend, that ended with hatred and death, was the beginning of our time together. We drift back from the rest of the group.

Around us, buildings old and new slip in and out of view. But it's the same solid ground under our feet. I angle my head and look toward Lena. Nostalgia mixes with something else. Something warm and comfortable. A black squirrel scampers through the leaves in front of us. I point to it.

"I forgot all about those critters," Lena says. "In fact, I've forgotten a lot of things. Probably couldn't write our hitchhiking story even if I wanted to."

"I'd be happy to help you fill in the blanks," I say, with a grin. Now that's an intriguing thought.

Her eyes rise, then glance away.

"Did you ever tell your parents about it?" I ask.

"No, I never did." She smiles. "Dad passed years ago. And my mom has Alzheimer's. She wouldn't begin to know what I was talking about."

"Sorry. That's tough."

We pass the Fine Arts building. Newly completed in our day, it was a state-of-the-art structure made from light-yielding panels designed by artists. "It's funny how your perception of time shrinks. What seems like just a few years ago was really forty." Now the panels look as frail and worn as are, most likely, the former artists.

We approach the Victory Bell and Lena gives it a ring. The sound clangs out memories of being called to action. We were going to change the world. Right. As if reading my thoughts, Lena says, "I guess it's time to hand over the world to the next generation." She turns and holds out her hand, as if she's addressing that generation. "I'm sorry. See what *you* can do with it." She looks up the hill and nods toward our group. "We should catch up to them, I guess."

I reach out my hand to help her up a sharp incline. I'm taken aback that it feels so natural. We stumble against each other, slipping on the leaves, muddy from a recent rain.

I let go of her hand as we reach the top. I remember when we climbed that hill holding onto one another because we wanted to, not because we had to. We join the group in front of the May 4th Visitors Center and walk through an emotional exhibit of the events that took place on this spot forty years ago. We walk down the other side of Taylor Hill and come to the parking lot where the four students were shot and killed. Now, the places where the students fell, are marked by small memorial light posts. As Tyler presents a biography on each of the students, Lena and I slowly move away from the group. We remember.

Passing my old dorm, Lena says, "See any flames?"

"Just an old one standing next to me."

She laughs. "We're not so old. I bet you can still hitchhike with the best of them."

I wave my thumb in front of her. "But can you still stick out your leg so we can get a ride?"

She does a couple of Broadway kicks, then bends down and rolls up the cuff of her jeans. Above her ankle, a tattoo of a quilled pen marks the spot of the snake bite.

I laugh, then shake my head, "What? No viper?" I put a hand on her shoulder. "We need to make one more stop."

She takes a deep breath. "Should we?"

I grin. She hasn't changed one bit. "Relax," I say. "What kind of trouble can a couple of sixty-year-olds get into?"

Chapter Sixty-Two
Peace

Lena

I try to act breezy and nonchalant as we walk toward the house on Willow Street, but there's got to be some protocol about revisiting the most sensitive scene of the crime with the guilty parties.

"Still have all those crazy rules?" Kris asks with a smile.

Can he still see through me after all these years? I sigh, remembering how uptight I had been about being free and easy. "I had more boundary lines than the Rand McNally road map."

He shakes his head. "And a lot of detours. But I think I convinced you that we were always on the right road."

"I've changed," I say. "More open to traveling the back roads."

"Yeah, I've taken a few myself."

A young woman walking a small white dog passes us, chatting on her phone. I want to shout, 'Look up! Look around! It'll be over before you know it.' I turn to Kris, "So tell me, how many chick-bait mutts did it take to finally get you down the aisle?"

He's slow to answer. "A few." His shoulder brushes mine. "Is my good buddy, the green-eyed monster still alive and kicking?"

I shake my head. "We called a truce years ago, thanks to a little therapy." I cringe remembering the scenes in the attic. "I had so many hang-ups. How did you ever put up with it?"

He kicks a buckeye down the sidewalk and shrugs. "I don't remember it being all that bad. Except maybe that one time when your hand slipped and almost caught me in the jaw."

"Slipped? I was going to clobber you! God, I was a mess. I was so insecure—and that horrible jealousy!"

"I knew that wasn't the real you and, in spite of it all, I always knew how our night would end."

I blush. Should I crawl under a sarcastic reply? No. His words run deeper than they sound. He deserves more than a quip. I stop walking and put my hand on his arm. "I never thanked you for just listening when I needed you to. I didn't realize what a rare quality that was until I got older. Hearing me out without judging."

He looks me in the eye. "It was something new to me, too. That someone could be so honest about embarrassing or hurtful moments. It made me feel closer to you, Lena. You were probably the first person I really connected to."

I feel a trickle of the old excitement gathering speed. "We did have some kind of special awareness of each other. As if… it was like…" I stop and change course. "There was just so much to talk about!"

"Sex, drugs, and rock and roll!"

"Civil rights! Women's lib! Hey, whatever became of Ella?" I ask. "She's crossed my mind from time to time."

"She passed away in her sleep a few years ago. Totally with-it 'til the end. The kids loved her. She always brought them special gifts from her travels."

"I remember that cool silver ring she gave you." I glance at his ring finger and see his gold band.

"Yeah, good ol' Merlin." Kris clears his throat. "He never really came through for me though."

I fend off the urge to ask if he still has the ring. Why should it matter? Not everyone is a sentimental hoarder like me. Instead I ask, "Do you still visit the cabin?

Has it changed?" My heart softens at the visual I've kept through the years. The cottage on the frozen lake surrounded by snowy woods. Snowflakes on the window pane... naked in the firelight... his arms around me—

"Diane and I go there with the kids a lot. I love that it's been part of their childhood, like it was mine. They've heard the dairy stories so many times, they know them all by heart."

I feel deflated. Why? Those stories are his to share. Especially with his family.

As we walk through thin slats of the late afternoon sunlight, I remember the first time I walked across campus to my first college class. Nervous anticipation. Afterward, exhilaration. So many things to discover.

We reach the corner of Midway and Main, cross the street and turn left. Old fast food chains have been replaced by new fast food chains. We turn right onto Willow. Giant trees of red and gold make an archway over the street. Do they remember us? Remember the first time we walked and talked and kissed under them? We arrive at the house. Still the same rickety three-story, only with a fresh coat of paint for the new school year. Someone's old floppy couch sits on the front porch. It doesn't look like anyone is home. My eyes drift upward toward the attic. I glance sideways and see Kris looking up too.

"Funny how a chance meeting led me to my home away from home," he says.

We walk around the side of the house, tromping through the overgrown weeds. Leaves crunch under our feet. We lean against the rusted metal fire escape, the one Ginny's boyfriends used to climb when the front door was locked. I look up into the sky as geese fly overhead in a V-formation. Their honking breaks the stillness of the evening.

Kris takes a joint from his jacket pocket. "For old times' sake?"

I nod.

He lights up, takes a toke, and hands it to me.

I inhale the sweet herbal smoke. The years flip backwards, like a video on rewind.

As if reading my mind, he asks, "Whatever happened to us, anyway?"

There it is. I hesitate…

He turns and reads my eyes. "Lena, it's me."

My breath catches his three words. They go right to my heart. "Well… California kind of threw a wrench into things."

"We both knew that was your plan from the beginning."

I take a deep breath. "And there was Reggie."

Kris flicks the ash into the grass and looks far off into the distance. "I made peace with Cheet that summer." He turns and puts his hand on my shoulder. "We were all just victims of bad timing and unforeseen circumstances. I hope you knew that, too."

"I did… eventually." I turn and stare at the ground. *It's now or never.*

"Well… and then… that… that weekend in Columbus."

Kris turns his head away and rubs the back of his neck. "I don't know what the hell was wrong with me that weekend. I must've gone over it a million times. I remember it being surreal, like I was on the outside looking in and I couldn't control anything that was happening."

I hand the joint back. He takes a draw. I keep my tone nonchalant. "Awkward and sad is how I remember it. I got the feeling you'd moved on. Had a girlfriend."

He leans back against the fire escape railing. "I did have a girlfriend. Her name was Lena."

I run my fingers through my hair, tugging on the ends. *Here it goes.* "I thought you felt sorry for me because

I came thinking things would be the same and you already had someone else."

"There was no one else." He shifts from one foot to the other. "That Saturday morning I made pancakes. You were so beautiful with the sun streaming in behind you. But I couldn't shake off this sensation that something was wrong, out of sync. I wanted to talk to you about it so badly, but I couldn't find the right words."

"I remember that morning," I say. "Things seemed to be getting back to normal. I thought, 'This is it. He's going to say don't go to California, stay here, with me.' And I would've said, 'Okay.'"

"You would've *what*?" His voice is a freight train, barreling through the still night.

"I wanted to stay. That's why I came that weekend." My words tumble over each other. "But I needed to know you still wanted me. I needed you to tell me. Only instead you said—" I look down, feeling his stare. My throat tightens. I force a slow, measured tone. "You said you were having a hard time touching me. Like your arms were chained to your sides." The memory that I had buried inside me now rattled. I feel the old anguish rise. Chains.

He looks down and shakes his head. "Lena, so many feelings were inside me. Anger, hurt, love. I couldn't tell them apart."

I look up. "Well, after you said that, I knew it was over. And obviously you felt the same way, because I never heard from you again. You never called."

He grabs my arm. His voice intensifies. "I did call. But you'd already left for France. Didn't your grandfather tell you?"

I bite my lower lip, feel my brow wrinkle. "No. No, he didn't." Time unwinds in front of me into a slow murkiness.

Kris's face tightens and he swallows hard. "And, when I got out of 'Nam, I called again."

"'Nam?" My jaw drops and I step back. "Oh God, Kris!" Questions burst like fireworks in my head. "What... did anything... happen...?"

"No. I did what I had to do and got the hell out."

There's more behind his words. I look at him with questions in my eyes, but he stares straight ahead. Keeping thoughts, that before we would have shared, to himself.

"Anyway," Kris interrupts my thoughts, "your grandfather said you were still in France. I thought you had something going on. With some guy named Peter."

"Peter?" I tilt my head. "No, he was the director of the program. I turn to meet his eyes. "After the initial thrill, France was pretty much like you said. Remember? You said 'People are people. They just live their lives out in different colors.'"

Day has dropped into night. Someone in the house turns on the back-porch light. The garish yellow glare coaxes us into the shadows of the frame.

"I can't believe you left California," Kris says. "What did it take?"

"A job offer with a travel magazine. I couldn't refuse. Now, I've lived in New York longer than I lived in California."

"And I've lived in Minnesota longer than I lived in Ohio."

Miles and years race between us, dragging with them all the words said and unsaid. Seems like another lifetime.

Strains of music float from a downstairs room. Songs of peace and love? War and revolution? A wave of emotion breaks over me. This is not something imagined or lost. It was us, Kris and me, as real as now. *This lifetime.*

Our eyes catch and hold... I feel his slow, steady gaze sink into me.

"A part of who I am is because of you," he says. "I've always hoped to tell you that."

I see it. We've always been connected in a small but important way. In a surge of familiar intimacy, I reach out and put my arm through his. Not trying to relive what we had or alter the future, but to be in the moment, a part of what I had learned from him.

A window rattles open and we look up. A small light in the attic turns on. Behind the sheer curtain, the shadows of two people move across the room. We exchange a certain smile. Kris drops the roach to the ground, tamping it into the dirt. Into the ashes of joints tossed off the fire escape for the past forty years. Everything becoming a part of everything else. I get a warm feeling from that thought. He reaches up and picks a leaf off a branch overhead. It glows golden under the porch light. He tosses it into the air and Ella's words float into the space between us: "First times... some you want to remember, some won't let you forget."

The End

About Chera Thompson

Chera Thompson attended Kent State and has a BS/Journalism from Ohio University and an MS/Adult Education from Buffalo State College. She held careers in travel and teaching. Her fiction has been published in the *Los Angeles Review* and was selected as a finalist in the *Glimmer Train* Short Fiction Contest. Other publication credits include *Let's Have Fun Vol. 2, Queen City Flash, and Have a NYC 3*. Most recently her non-fiction pieces were published in Pamela Des Barres's *Let It Bleed: How to Write a Rockin' Memoir*. She lives with her husband on a bluff overlooking Lake Erie and enjoys traveling and collecting beach glass.

Social Media

Website: www.cherathompson.com

Facebook:
https://www.facebook.com/author.cherathompson/

Twitter: https://twitter.com/cherathompson

About NF Johnson

NF Johnson attended college and worked for Kent State and The Ohio State University. His preferred mode of transportation in the late '60's to mid '70's was using his thumb. He hitchhiked over 15,000 miles crisscrossing the Midwest. His work has been published in *Flash Fiction Press*. A Time to Wander is his first novel. He now resides in Dublin, Ohio with his wife and two dogs. He's a regular tailgater at OSU games and a loyal Minnesota Vikings fan. He enjoys cooking for extended family and friends.

Social Media

Facebook:
https://www.facebook.com/author.NF Johnson/

Twitter: https://twitter.com/NealFJohnson1

Acknowledgements:

Many thanks to our numerous readers who patiently plowed through the early drafts and countless revisions over the past years. Giving us valuable insight and endless support were: Michaela Apruzzese, Christine Armesto, Mary Faith Bonney, Diana Hight, Royce Hill, Michael Marrone, George Morse, Kirby Nielsen, Mary Ostrowski, Terez Peipins, Lou Rera, Becky Russell, Susan Solomon, and Eileen Werbitsky.

Sunflowers from Chera to Gloria Kennedy, Gail Zink and angel, Pat Schauer, my original bell-bottom blue jean buddies. Thank you for helping me get the feeling back by retracing our mental and physical footsteps at Kent State on numerous occasions.

Peace sign flashes to all our Kent Friends past and present, roommates in Prentice and Dunbar, housemates and couch surfers in the White house and the Brown house.

Hippie handshakes to thumbing aficionados Gary Bradshaw and Kathy Webb, who added their stories to ours to make this romp even more exciting than memory serves.

We are deeply indebted to the strong editing skills of Linda Gorelova, Lynne Herold, Longview Bill, Dasha Marshall, Julianna Ricci, and Tim Vargo. Special recognition to Thomas Grace for his experienced eye on the May 4th chapter and to Dan Bolick for sharing his personal experience at Kent Friends reunions.

Major appreciation to the members of Book Buffs, the Columbus Creative Co-operative and Just Buffalo Writer's Critique Group, for providing a platform to discuss the first draft of our novel and for the questions, suggestions and constructive criticism they offered.

Sincere gratitude to Just Buffalo Writer's Critique group moderator, Gary Earl Ross, who patiently but persistently guided us out of our comfort zone and encouraged us to not hold back.

Whispered thanks to members of the Sleep Lab and EEG. Shhh- you know who you are.

Kudos to photographer, Ned Miller for his attention to detail with the artifact photos. And to Jim Kelly for his impromptu cover design.

The Above and Beyond Award goes to our spouses, Ed and Lynne, for being supportive and good sports, on the long and winding writing road. We owe you that beer on a Caribbean beach! Also, a wink to the Thompson kids, Lauren and Evan and the Johnson kids, Neal and Grace, for being open to and maybe a little intrigued by what their parents might have been like in their youth.

And last but not least, heart hugs to Kris and Lena, who let us dip our toes into being nineteen again.

Made in the USA
Columbia, SC
12 August 2019